Gk RC

James Phelan is the bestselling and  KT-142-877

discover libraries

This book should be returned on or before the due date.

JAN 6/19		
B1 11/19		
03/08/20		
2/9/20		
14. NOV 20.		
29 DEC 23		
17/1/24		

To renew or order library books please telephone 01522 782010
or visit https://lincolnshire.spydus.co.uk
You will require a Personal Identification Number.
Ask any member of staff for this.

The above does not apply to Reader's Group Collection Stock.

05253927

BY JAMES PHELAN

The Lachlan Fox books
Fox Hunt
Patriot Act
Blood Oil
Liquid Gold
Red Ice

The Jed Walker books
The Spy
The Hunted
Kill Switch
Dark Heart
The Agency

The Alone series
Chasers
Survivor
Quarantine

James
Phelan

Liquid
Gold

CONSTABLE

CONSTABLE

First published in Australia and New Zealand in 2009 by Hachette Australia,
an imprint of Hachette Australia Pty Limited.

First published in eBook in Great Britain in 2018 by Constable

This paperback edition published in Great Britain in 2019 by Constable

13 5 7 9 10 8 6 4 2

A CIP catalogue record for this book
is available from the British Library.

ISBN: 978-1-47212-932-1

Typeset in Simoncini Garamond by Bookhouse, Sydney
Printed and bound in Great Britain by CPI Group (UK), Croydon CR0 4YY

Papers used by Constable are from well-managed forests
and other responsible sources.

Constable
An imprint of
Little, Brown Book Group
Carmelite House
50 Victoria Embankment
London EC4Y 0DZ

An Hachette UK Company
www.hachette.co.uk

www.littlebrown.co.uk

New York Gazette

HOSTILITIES MOUNT BETWEEN INDIA AND PAKISTAN

The UN Security Council is considering sending a peacekeeping force to the mountainous India–Pakistan border in an attempt to stave off escalating tensions between the two countries. The decades-old trouble in this region over the disputed area of Kashmir has a new angle, as both nations lay claim to the natural water resource beneath Siachen Glacier. Artillery exchanges at the Glacier have stepped up dramatically, with two hundred military personnel on each side killed in the past week alone. Both India and Pakistan have nuclear capabilities and both countries have stated they will use whatever force and weapons necessary to protect the resources they consider their own.

A recent feature article in *Vanity Fair* magazine by investigative reporter Lachlan Fox brought the issue of fresh-water scarcity to worldwide media attention. Fox's article identi-fied Russian businessman Roman Babich as being behind plans to build and operate one of the world's largest hydro-engineering projects, in northern Pakistan. While Babich and his Umbra Corporation claim the proposed water extraction plant will 'boost the Pakistani economy and lift the standard of living significantly', Fox's article revealed the cost this project will have for neighboring India, where the underground water table is already lowering at an alarming rate, and millions are suffering through a crushing drought that is fast on its way to becoming a humanitarian disaster.

It hasn't taken long for the sparks of war to ignite as these two countries flex their muscle and claim sole right to a resource both need and refuse to share. The UN Security Council will vote early next week on whether or not to act. ■

Prologue

BELLAGIO, LAKE COMO, ITALY

He rested the espresso cup on its saucer and looked out over the multimillion-dollar view. He faced a large window that formed the northern wall of the café; the long wooden table, like the building, had seen better days, but it would serve its purpose. The overcast day gave him a good reflected view of the movement behind him.

He looked around, casually surveying the scene, his senses on high alert. As he turned back to the view he caught his reflection in the window: he was already getting used to his short dark hair, parted without being neat. His deep tan could be from any country around the Mediterranean. His clothes were casual, Milan-fashion smart, too slick for him to be important, too creased to be average: muted tones, no stark blacks and no bright colours. He could be part of the new Lake Como crowd, or he could be part of the establishment. He could be any well-to-do Italian or western European. He could be a simple guy enjoying a coffee at his local café. He could be a nightclub owner. He could be a killer. He could be anyone.

His eyes fell on the fresco of Mary to his left. He looked at her, unflinching, as his hands moved quickly under the table, positioning the C4 explosive device – no bigger than three cigarette packets end-to-end – in the recess where the table met the wall. The explosive packed enough punch to take down the front section of the old brick building – anyone within twenty metres would be vaporised. He sat back and took one last look at the view before casually tossing a five euro note on the table.

He put on his sunglasses as he exited, the door's brass bell jingling in his wake. His eyes were immediately drawn to a passing woman and he turned to watch her walk, with that certain sway of the hips that the women in this part of the world knew how to do so well. She looked over her shoulder, clocked him, smiled: *Thank you for noticing.*

He paused amid the busy winter morning, technicolour all around him. Locals finishing their morning espresso and pastry, tourists parading flesh in an attempt to keep up with the effortlessly stylish locals. He strolled down the main street and melted into the crowd. He had time to kill.

PART ONE

1

NEW YORK CITY

The anchor of NBC's *Dateline* leaned towards the camera.

'The UN has called this the decade of Water for Life,' he said. 'This is fitting when we consider that countries like the United States use up to four hundred litres of fresh water per person, per day, compared to some of the most populous regions of the world where people have to get by on less than twenty litres per day. Lack of access to fresh water, and compromised sanitation of existing supplies, results in millions of *preventable* deaths every year. This is a big issue, but it's not a new one, and it doesn't look like it's going away anytime soon. Our guest tonight is an investigative reporter with news agency GSR, Lachlan Fox, whose recent articles have focused world attention on this increasing global problem. Lachlan is here with me in the studio in New York. Lachlan, welcome.'

'Thank you, Matt.'

'Our guest on yesterday's program was Roman Babich, the resources tycoon listed by *Forbes* 2009 as Russia's second-richest man. His company, Umbra Corp, has significant business interests in oil, natural gas, metals and the automotive and television industries – and is also one of the world's biggest suppliers of fresh water, servicing water to some 900 million people in four continents, including the United States. Mr Babich joined us via satellite from our London studio to explain his company's activities in his newest water venture, in northern Pakistan. Lachlan,' said the anchor, turning to Fox, 'you have written a lot about this issue. What's your take on the consequences of this new endeavour?'

Fox straightened in his chair and took a deep breath. 'Water is not just a political issue or a money-making venture,' he said. 'It is the key to life. Pakistan shares a ground water resource with India, and this new water plant will significantly impact how much water can flow into each country.'

'Via rivers and irrigation canals?'

'And the underground water table. Mr Babich has said that this project will be a boon for Pakistan, but the flipside to that is the impact it will have on India. India's drought is dire, and their underground water table is already disappearing faster than it can be replenished. I don't believe the full consequences of this project have been adequately thought through. Over a billion people rely on an agricultural area affected by this project, and as water grows even more scarce, so too do the livelihoods of those billion people. I fear that with the broader issue of fresh-water scarcity, one day we are going to wake up and it will be too late. But the point here is, it's not too late *yet* for this region.'

'So do you see this as Pakistan having the potential to take *unlimited* water from this shared resource?'

'They are already – before this plant has even gone online – extracting water at a quicker rate than it's being replenished,' Fox said. 'The UN is working on a treaty that would facilitate all countries having appropriate access to the water from natural sources—'

'But it's not in place yet?'

'No. What we have to realise, even here in America, is that underground water is not a limitless tap. The central issue here is responsibility.'

'Since your first story was published,' said the anchor, checking his notes, 'we have seen mass rallies and protests in India against the project. Let's take a look at some footage.'

The monitors in the studio showed the streets of Punjab: residents protesting, rioting and looting; locals demanding access to fresh water and calling for retaliation against Pakistan.

Fox took a sip of water and watched the monitor. An image of windswept plains of dust gave way to one of thousands of farmers walking in protest to Delhi, reminiscent of the land reform marches of 2007.

'This is shaping up to be a bigger security issue for these two countries than the 2008 Mumbai terrorist attacks,' the *Dateline* anchor said. 'India and Pakistan have long jostled and postured about their nuclear capabilities – is this new crisis inflaming an already volatile situation?'

'Absolutely, Matt,' said Fox. 'India and Pakistan have fought over Kashmir for more than fifty years, and the location of this water plant has only added to the issues in the region.'

'No other newspapers or networks were covering this, but following your articles it is now headlining news everywhere viewers turn.'

'Well, we are living in a time when knowing the world is not a trivial luxury – it's of vital urgency,' said Fox.

The anchor turned a page in his notes. 'Roman Babich made mention of his water project helping to keep Pakistan together. What do you think he meant by that?'

'It's a fragile state, it could collapse any day. Due to our military presence in Afghanistan, Taliban numbers in Pakistan are up, many areas are lawless at best, and the political situation is tenuous—'

'And with that in mind, did you consider how your stories might impact the region? I mean, the UN Security Council is now considering sending in peacekeepers . . .' The anchor ran through a list of statistics about the growing death toll from the long fought-over region of the Siachen Glacier.

Fox nodded, listened. He had heard these stats and clichés so many times since his first article appeared in *Vanity Fair* and the shit storm between India and Pakistan made it to the front pages of newspapers round the world.

'Listen, Matt,' Fox said. 'I spent over five weeks investigating and writing that first piece, and more time since for the articles that followed. I wrote it for the same reason I signed on to be an investigative reporter in the first place: I want the world to know the truth – we need and deserve to know it. We need to take risks and report on issues and events that matter.'

Sitting under the *Dateline* studio lights was like sitting in a sauna fully dressed, and Fox felt sweat beading across his forehead and dripping under his arms. He imagined he looked like Nixon in the debate with Kennedy, when the poor old SOB was practically melting. After seven years in the Australian Navy's Special Forces and then the last two years on the road as an investigative journalist, Fox was used to tight situations, but he wasn't used to wearing a suit – or make-up. He drank more water as the anchor spoke:

'Do you think your article could lead to a war between two nuclear powers?'

'Matt, India has been a nuclear power since '74, Pakistan since '98 and, not to sound blasé, nuclear war has been a risk ever since.'

'But clearly it was your—'

'I didn't chase this story to create a diplomatic stand-off; I chased it because we need to know what is really happening and have public debate about the consequences.'

'Every commentator says your articles, Lachlan, kicked off two countries on a path to one irrepressible place: all-out war between two—'

'The bottom line is,' interrupted Fox, irritated now, 'that the issue of fresh-water scarcity is a global one, a fundamental one. This story would have broken one way or another. Yeah, sure, what we're seeing in Pakistan – what Roman Babich and Umbra Corp are doing – could well be the beginning of a whole new reason for warfare in the twenty-first century. I've been trying to talk to Mr Babich for weeks now and he has refused to sit down with me. But this story isn't going away, and I'm going to keep asking questions.

'Make no mistake,' Fox said, 'water, like air, is a necessity of human life. It's liquid gold.'

2

MOSCOW, RUSSIA

'It certainly is . . .' Roman Babich murmured as he leaned back in his Aeron office chair, then flicked off the television after the Lachlan Fox interview ended. He had just witnessed what he had hoped to dissuade with his appearance on the program, part of a campaign to appear more often in the Western media since his new London-based PR team handled Umbra Corp's expansion into Western Europe and the Americas. He had even flown to London for the studio interview before returning to Moscow to do some real work.

He needed, apparently, to make himself more visible, more accessible; to project an image of himself and Umbra Corp as a pillar of stability in a shaky global marketplace. He had poured significant cash into advertising, buying time with networks and wire execs, in order to shape Umbra Corp into another Coca Cola or Apple or Sony or Exxon and to present himself as a figure of old-school industrialist who understood new-tech wonders and had resource control bigger than most countries. *The New York Times* once put him at the top of a list of 'What's wrong with corporate Russia', but now *Time* magazine had called him 'Russia's Rockefeller'. It was a start.

Becoming the recognisable face of the company, in a decidedly new-Russia way, took money and patience: he had ample of the former, less so of the latter. His PR people were focusing on glamour, strength and stability – he now had manicures, dyed his hair to cover the grey and was considering a facelift. Fox News recently described him as 'more Berlusconi than Yeltsin', which made him laugh. He wondered if he should get hair plugs too. His wife wouldn't notice or care, but his mistress in St Petersburg would love it, and his PR people would approve. All this and he had just turned fifty-nine.

Babich opened a folder on his desk. The *Dateline* interview with Fox hadn't gone as he had hoped. He scanned the contents of the folder a second time, more carefully, considering yet again a way of doing business that he had hoped was no longer necessary, but one that he revisited because it worked so well; a smooth, dependable way to rid himself of an annoyance, be it legal, commercial or even personal. It was affordable and decisive. Fuck *Dateline*.

Fox's reportage from the Kashmir region had singled out Babich and Umbra Corp as the cause of the area's water woes. Babich couldn't allow this: in the last year alone, that division of Umbra Corp brought in 1.2 billion euros – profit – from Colombia to Colorado, Western Africa to Wyoming. This new water plant in Pakistan – he wasn't interested in the decades-old border scuffles over Kashmir or where the water actually originated – would contribute 200 million per year, rising at least five per cent every year for the next fifty years. The World Bank had even footed some of Pakistan's capital investment through a no-interest loan – why didn't *Dateline* make more of that?

The total cost of the project was around US$20 billion; all done from his end without external financial support, which meant he had been forced to cut every cost he could, including labour. Local men had been contracted to work on the drilling and concreting equipment under his own workforce's supervision; men he didn't know but who journalists like Fox could get to.

Truth be told, he had halved the bill another way, a very fortuitous way, through the aid of another government backer; but that would never come out. This water project would reap billions of euros for Umbra Corp, annually and in perpetuity. The project had already added almost 4 per cent to the share price of the parent company, not to mention the 2 per cent spike after Lachlan Fox's articles first appeared across Western news agencies – all that press had helped put Babich and his company more decidedly on the map.

There was a sharp knock and his executive secretary entered, followed by two division heads. He motioned for them to sit in the armchairs by the fireplace; they would not begin the meeting without his GM, who handled everything in a management committee of CFOs and division heads – a system Babich had modelled on the workings of the old Politburo. Putin was right about that at least – he, too, missed some of the old ways of running things.

Babich tapped the folder as he watched his computer screen update the company's stock price: it had risen another 0.5 per cent since the *Dateline* episode screened. Babich owned a controlling stake in Umbra Corp, and Fox's reportage equalled money in his pocket.

But Fox was heading back to snoop around further. If he got hold of the right people he might just find the source of the other income stream to this water project; cold, hard cash delivered via their diplomatic transport services – the *only* way to courier, he often joked – to Italy. That further income would equal more power and, most importantly, the beginning of a business relationship that would bear much fruit for as long as he wished to harvest it. He had worked hard to cultivate that relationship – many years' worth of luxury gifts and wining and dining – and he could not let Lachlan Fox jeopardise it. Not after all this work, not now.

His GM entered and took a seat with the others. Babich motioned he would be over in a moment.

He knew Fox would not leave this alone, not until he was waist-deep in affairs that didn't concern him; there was no telling what Fox might uncover, despite all their precautions. He well knew what the reporter had managed to do in Nigeria just a few months ago, how a plan years in the making had come undone so quickly, so resolutely, all in the name of chasing his story. And what a story this would be. But enough was enough; no more investigating, no more articles.

Babich picked up his desk phone and asked for a connection via his encrypted line, to be transmitted via his own satellite network, the principal function of which was to transmit data for his telecommunications and cable-television network that delivered content to television screens around the globe. Now it would carry a very different message, a final address regarding Lachlan Fox of New York City, and any other loose ends.

3

NEW YORK CITY

Fox executed a flip turn at the end of the lap and kicked hard off the wall, swimming underwater for ten metres before breaking the surface with a steady, practised freestyle.

This wasn't a political thing, like the Bush-bashing of old that got reporters into hot water. Then, it was speaking and writing the truth in an age of disdain for evidence – Americans will believe in angels, ghosts and the Immaculate Conception, but tell them their President lied about the Iraq war and that's just *way* too much for many of them. Fox had expected trouble last week when he appeared on *The O'Reilly Factor* – he knew it when the host introduced the 'Personal Story' segment with: '*My next guest used to kill people for a living. Now he writes news stories that get people killed.*'

He gritted as the pain in his shoulder flared, but didn't ease off the pace.

Much of the commentary had been the same: looking past the Pakistan–Umbra story to probe him personally, dig into his past, create issues from nothing. The death of a soldier under his command, his service in Iraq and Afghanistan, his discharge from the Australian Navy – all old news rehashed. That he had been the central reporter of stories covering a bloody coup d'état in France, the death of a Kremlin-friendly head of Chechnya, the recent upheaval in Nigeria and terrorist attacks in America – they had likened him to the grim reaper, even cartooned it thus in *USA Today* with the tag-line: '*Can the world afford another two more years of this man's reporting?*'

Did he draw death into his world? Was he so conditioned to war and conflict that he somehow attracted it? Could he be making his situation worse by seeking out stories no other reporters would touch?

He swam over the black tiles that marked the end of the lane, did another flip turn, and pushed off from the wall.

The truth at what cost? War over water? All those lives lost through armed conflict rather than thirst and starvation? Harry Truman once said that when Kansas and Colorado have a quarrel over water in the Arkansas River they don't call out the National Guard in each state and go to war over it. They bring a case before the Supreme Court of the United States and abide by the decision. There isn't a reason in the world why it can't be done internationally. And the key to access is control – who has their hand on the tap. Much of the media were trying to control him, offering opinions, not suggesting solutions. What was it *The Post* had said of him? – he was a 'diligently lazy writer'. Fuck *The Post*.

He neared the end of his last lap, rolled onto his back and drifted toward the deep end, floating, looking up at the ceiling. There was only one other swimmer at this late hour.

The lighting was dark in the boutique hotel's pool; just a few minutes' walk from his apartment, it was a nice, quiet place to chill. Fox listened to the rhythmic sounds of the other swimmer, floating there until the person finished and left.

Silence. Looking up at the dark ceiling, he could be floating anywhere: Christmas Island, the Caribbean, a nice warm lake or river. Being in water was the only time he ever really felt free, but tonight the chaos ringing in his ears had followed him in here, intruding into this sanctuary. He let it wash over him, finally drifting underwater where he held his breath and waited for the noise to quieten.

4

NORTHERN AREAS, PAKISTAN

He drove alone, which was not something he would normally do through this lawless area, especially after dark. Pakistani militants and radical militia groups frequently attacked by night, ambushing convoys and what little infrastructure was here – and when things were fixed and new supplies arrived they came back to loot again.

The town was empty. He approached the small shack that he rented from its owner for a mere five hundred rupees per month – about ten dollars US – and used to store the sacks of spices and rice that he regularly delivered to this area. These made up half of what was stored in the twenty-metre square building; the other half was made up of basic, bulky medical supplies, general tools and drums of fuel. Nothing was of much value; the only security was the local Pakistani Army patrol, but he paid them well and he hadn't had any problems in the eight years he had been coming through here.

There were no lights, no electricity at all in this remote, high-altitude town.

By the light of a thin torch beam he lifted the rock under the potted mulberry tree and retrieved the key he had hidden there last week. He entered the storehouse and flashed the light around the dark interior, unsure of what he would find in the shadows.

Everything was as he had left it. Almost.

On top of a sack of rice three down, in a corner, he saw what he'd come for – a brown paper-wrapped package the size of a house brick. He felt sweat tracing a line down his stomach as he let the torch beam settle on it for a few long minutes. He stooped, looking at the package from different vantage points.

If they had no use for him, if this was the end of his work . . . but it wasn't, was it? They needed him until everything was settled, they'd told him that. But could he take the risk of trusting these people? He set the torch down on a drum of diesel so the light shone on the package, and reached for a broom – he held it out, his arm extended to push the broom handle as far as it could go. He involuntarily held his breath.

He knocked the package onto the hard floor. It landed with a light thud and bounced slightly. Nothing happened. It wasn't a bomb. He tried to breathe normally as he picked it up – it felt right. He tore the corner off in a hurry.

Cash; enough to make a real difference. So they did still need him, after all. He tucked it under his arm, took his torch, shut and locked the door, got into his Land Rover and headed back home towards India, the pitch black of winter in Kashmir only pierced by his vehicle's headlights.

5

NEW YORK CITY

It was summer in Fox's dream, the bright summer just past, a lifetime ago. The best, the worst. It had everything and left him with nothing more than scars and memories and a set-up for worse times ahead.

He watched himself from a distance. He was different then, a little heavier, a little younger, perhaps a little naïve.

A medley of scenes intercut in the way of dreams and bad memories, and try as he might he was stuck there, a spectator to things he mostly regretted. There was a woman, his age. She was an idealised version of a lover, if he could create such a thing. Kate Matthews. She pervaded every scene: a blur in a palatial room; a central figure of desire in a train cabin; a naked body on top of him. It played over and over in his vision. A fight. A train ride. Making love. Dead bodies. She'd been betrayed, used. Blood. Her tears fell into his eyes.

Fox knew it wasn't the right chronology but he was powerless to shape how it played. A funeral – that look from her parents that told him he had failed to keep her safe, to get her back. A close-up of her face as she gazed down on him, her sweaty body, her dark hair and those fathomless brown eyes – there was no telling how deep they went and how far they peered into him. Her smile. Kate.

Through these flashbacks and memories of things said and moments shared, he knew he'd failed. The chase, the boats, the rain that night, the crash, the fight with the French agent that almost killed him, *should* have killed him . . . but she saved him and, instead, she died. *She* died.

But she was there in his dream, not gone, there to talk to and there to listen. He wanted to stay and talk with her forever.

I've seen things you wouldn't believe, he said to her. He knew he would not remember what he said, how this dream played out. It would be like hitting reset until he saw her next, in another dream, or in death. All those moments lost in time like tears in the rain—

Fox woke in a sweat, his heart beating wildly. That much was always the same.

He looked up at the ceiling and took a deep breath. The room was dark but for the faintest glow of street lamps through the curtains. He could hear the occasional street noise outside. He turned to his bedside clock: it was just after 5 a.m. It was cold and his chest felt heavy as he got out of bed and went to the bathroom.

In the dim pre-dawn light he could just see his reflection in the mirror as he washed his face with warm water. His blue eyes seemed black and the scars on his body looked translucent in this light. It was quiet in here, just the trickle of water down the basin. His body shook. It was still too early to run.

In a city full of life and distraction, there was nothing that kept Kate from his mind's eye. No matter how quickly he moved or how far he travelled or how hard he worked, she was there. And the face that looked back at him wore the many faces of the departed.

6

PRAGUE, CZECH REPUBLIC

As Vladimir Kolesnik danced to Jay Z the blonde licked sweat off his stomach and the redhead ran her hands down his back and removed his T-shirt. Everyone in the club was under thirty except for a few older guys lingering around the edges of the dance floor, watching the young and beautiful shake their thing.

None had his physique. There was plenty of female flesh on show, all that youthful skin and sexual hunger for fame and fortune. The feeling took him back ten years to his university days when he was a future leader with pedigree to burn, when he was a ranking member of the Kremlin-backed Nashi youth organisation. Sex parties then – and now – were common practice, part of a deliberately targeted state program to lift Russia's flagging birth rate. He had done his bit in the organisation but he had never bought into that side of it – he had learned a lot in those three years, at school and in Nashi, and he applied the best of it now, away from home, in ways he felt would best serve *him*.

Everything he did here in Prague was for himself, not for anyone else, although there were still favours to be called in. *Occasionally* called in, and usually outsourced for a small fee. He respected those he owed, and was respected in kind for it

– being good for a favour, that was important in his world. It was vital for survival.

Kolesnik picked up the blonde and she wrapped her legs around his waist. He pulled her in and kissed her and she passed a pill into his mouth. He swallowed it and tasted her wet mouth before turning his head as the curvy little thing with the short, bright red bobbed wig pressed a Heineken to his lips and tucked his T-shirt into his trouser pocket. He drank, then pulled her in and they kissed as the blonde clung tightly and ground herself against him, licking his neck.

In his line of vision between the two women, over the heads of the thronging crowd, his bodyguard held a cell phone up, its screen and keys illuminated with an incoming call. Kolesnik acknowledged and moved the blonde off him to the floor where she danced as she had been classically trained since a child, before someone with money had taken a fancy to her and taught her things that only the richest men could afford to appreciate. What she gave up to achieve material wealth was her choice; he understood this simple belief system and respected it for what it was.

As he walked across the dance floor he felt the drugs kick in, his second trip in a few hours: the tingling down the spine, the lucid rush and feeling of indestructibility before the sweat came, that cold prickling across his shoulders and down his back and arms. He felt lighter as he moved towards his bodyguard and took the phone, such a tactile, shiny thing in his hand, a featherweight in his fingertips.

He checked the incoming number as he took his black North Face jacket from his bodyguard and slid it on, the material hugging his sweaty body, his muscles pumped from the past few hours of dancing and drinking. He aimed for the lean, ripped body of a surfer, not thick in the shoulders and neck like his security guys, or like he had been at twenty. His physique allowed him to blend in. He could be any millionaire's son, but he wasn't – he was the owner of this club, and two others like it, one in St Petersburg, and one in Baku.

There was a lot to love about this club. It was so cheap to fit out – an old warehouse, boarded-up windows, painted black, a couple of bars and bathrooms. The only significant cost was the Bose sound system and crystal chandeliers over the bar. Through the alcohol income – twice the price for the men than for the women – and the commission from the drug sales, a fat profit rolled in every night of the week. With a little capital and the right staff to oversee things, there was serious money to be made, and it couldn't be easier or more enjoyable: the leased private jet, the Ferretti yacht in production in Italy. He was considering a Greek island – a friend of his had just bought a half-acre rock for two million euros; pocket change for such an extravagance.

The phone continued to ring as he walked out the front doors into the breaking dawn, the noise and power of the club now shut behind him. Women loitered outside, either coming or going; a few Benzes and Beemers lined up in wait to take some of them off for jobs. The music rang in his ears, the deep vibrations loud enough to be felt out here. Street sweepers and snowploughs worked a few blocks down, so he rounded a corner for privacy as he answered his cell.

'*Da?*'

'I want you to go ahead with the plan.'

Kolesnik's eyes scanned the street as he walked, still moving to the beats he had absorbed over the past few hours. He pulled his jacket collar up against the cold and zipped it up to his throat. 'Okay,' he said, turning a corner and heading towards home, now with more purpose. 'Which targets?'

'All of them.'

He smiled. This was a serious favour being called in – taken off his tab. He still owed so much, but this would go a long way . . .

'When?'

'Yesterday.'

'That will—'

'Yest' chelóvek, yest' probléma. Net chelovéka, net problémy.'

End of conversation.

Kolesnik checked over his shoulder and waved to his man-mountain of a security guy, some fifty paces behind; he was part of the club's security staff, there to keep the more entrepreneurial of the aspiring young women from him and the Brits out entirely, as well as to keep him out of trouble. Kolesnik's first couple of months here had been rocky: two young women and their boyfriends had disappeared after they'd tried to outsmart him, tried to take advantage and blackmail him. More of an inconvenience than a worry, but he had a new life here to protect. A life like this was easy in Russia too, as long as you had the start-up capital, but it was dangerous, no matter who your father was. Trust, even among family, was a luxury in a power structure that valued wealth and power above all else – it was like living with a wild beast. Russia was a bear with claws, more so now than at any time in Kolesnik's life. But here, in this town, *he* was the bear.

Yes, there were others more entrenched, better connected, wealthier and showier by far, but he didn't make waves and for that he was respected here. A respect for success was one of the few things he admired about the Western world: you kept what you made, and there was a killing to be made if you were smart enough. This was one of the many contradictions of his Russia, one of the reasons he found it so easy to walk away, to fit in here like it was the home he had always known. But he never forgot where he came from, or how he came to be in this fortunate position.

Kolesnik walked down the cobblestone street, wishing now that he hadn't taken the extra pill, but moved with it and looked forward to a cool shower. Perhaps he would get a girl to come by for a few hours to help work it off.

But before anything else, he needed to get some people working for him immediately. He would call in status reports, confirm target locations, give directives, and the ball would be rolling. He walked faster. His head was spinning. This was the good life. He threw his hands up to the sky. Welcome to the good life.

7

NEW YORK CITY

The early morning was quiet enough for him to hear an aircraft suck low through the sky somewhere overhead. Snow crunched underfoot as Lachlan Fox ran through the cold winter of Manhattan, monochromatic in the pre-dawn street-lamp lighting, all white and grey and black in the frozen shadows. Steam rose from the subway vents, road crews cleared the streets and rats scampered from men in boots hauling black and green bags for mid-week garbage day.

Dressed in a hoodie and training pants, Fox dodged early risers and shift workers and garbage bags piled on the sidewalk, heading down Bowery towards Broome Street. He had felt at home in this area of SoHo and Nolita more quickly than anywhere he had lived outside of Melbourne. Wedged between apartments, businesses, cafés and shops, this area was, for Fox, the real essence of New York: a vast melting pot of the best and worst, past and present and a glimpse of what the future might be. Whatever it was around here, it was moneyed, although like the nearby areas of Little Italy and the East Village, it had its share of struggling artists and services employees sharing the worst apartments on the cheaper streets, and aspirational types living big, hoping for a Park view someday but never moving beyond that dream.

In less than a year in this neighbourhood Fox had noticed things shifting, as they had done for many years, only the tenants came and went faster than ever before: what was once a baker became a butcher, then a tanner, then derelict, then a storehouse and then a café or bar or restaurant selling bottled water for $10 and organic, carbon-neutral meals. Like the property prices, nothing sold here seemed rooted in real-world economics.

Fox slowed to a jog by his local newsstand, took a paper from the vendor who was setting up, and waved thanks and moved off.

The bleary-eyed old vet jotted down the purchase in his accounts book and then yelled at Fox, 'I see the world didn't end yesterday!'

Fox turned around and jogged on the spot.

'This situation,' the guy held up the *New York Times* and tapped the front page, which shouted a headline including the words 'UN', 'India' and 'Pakistan'. 'This water thing? It ain't over.'

Fox smiled and tucked the paper under his arm as he moved to stay warm and keep his rhythm. 'Are you sure?'

'It's never over.'

Fox gave a little salute to the fellow ex-military man before heading off.

The sounds of a big city rising filled Fox's ears and the faint glow of dawn broke as he rounded the corner into Broome Street and slowed to a walk. When he reached his apartment building he stretched out against the front wall, his protesting muscles an aching reminder of all the damage his body had withstood throughout most of his adult life. His breath fogged under the street light as he checked the reflection in a window – the car that had followed him on his run had pulled to a stop across the street. In the sedan sat two men about Fox's age, both of average height, weight and dress-sense. Cops? More likely Feds. He turned to clock them, and one of them waved; they looked settled, it was just another day out of the office. Fox recognised something in the face of the man who waved but couldn't place him. He didn't recognise either of the younger guys who had jogged at a discreet distance behind him; they had stopped down the street and were moving on the spot to keep warm, one watching him, the other scanning the street.

Fox looked back at the Fed car, that familiar face . . . He turned back to the joggers: both had bumbags just the right size to conceal a quick-release firearm.

Suddenly a car rounded the corner at speed and came to an abrupt stop in front of him. A door opened.

8

PRAGUE, CZECH REPUBLIC

Kolesnik rolled from his bed and unrolled a wad of cash. He counted out double what the girls charged for their time and paid them while motioning for them to leave. They were pretty things, earning a good living while their looks held.

KanYe West played on repeat on Kolesnik's iPod, loud and clear over the Bang & Olufsen speakers set into the ceiling. He was coming down already. The highs were getting shorter and less intense with every swallow and snort despite having access to the best of everything; there was something nice about the occasional cheap mix of an ecstasy pill over pure MDMA.

He stood under a cool shower drinking a sports drink until he felt sober enough to pack what he needed and organise his movements. Barefoot in a robe, he moved to the kitchen and put croissants under the grill before popping another drink from the glass-fronted bar fridges under the marble bench. He had come to Prague two years ago to lead an uncomplicated life – all play and no hard work – and it was now home, and his work was all play. Still, sometimes he got to play in a very different league – hell, in a different ball game altogether.

He opened the front door and retrieved the morning paper and small glass bottle of milk that was beaded with sweat. The electrics in this building were wired like a space station: the LED strip lighting that illuminated the floor in the hallway leading to the elevator changed ambience to suit the time of day. In place of a doorman in the marbled foyer was an electronic keypad that facilitated entry into the seventeenth century building. Kolesnik's apartment was late Baroque style: fifteen foot ceilings, open fireplaces, a grand bedroom and a series of living rooms, not ten minutes' walk over the Vltava from his club.

This was an old-money and emerging-yuppie district, the medieval centre of the city, a UNESCO World Heritage site full of theatres, cafés, galleries and museums, boutiques that sold antique furs, and artisan milliners and jewellers who sold to tourists and the local elite. It was quiet through the day here in this corner, except for those who had no need to work but a great need to fill their days accumulating and being seen.

Kolesnik's apartment was a corner suite on the fourth floor. There were linden trees outside his main windows, all green leaves in summer and stark empty branches in the cold months. He checked his Omega: it was just before noon. He saturated his croissants with butter and jam, made a decaf and carried his breakfast to the study, where he sat behind a double-screened PC and flicked it from sleep.

Secure communications were vital for any intelligence officer, and he'd not only received good training from Russia's intelligence agency, the GRU, he kept his trade-craft current by being informed. Last year, an al-Qaeda bomb maker had been caught out in Beirut after communicating via a generic email account, where he'd save his draft emails and the receiver would log in using the same details and read the message without it ever being sent across servers. Last month, by blocking text messaging services sent via suspect websites, French DGSE agents foiled jihadists from blowing up iconic landmarks in Paris. Kolesnik had long been wary of the internet as the silver bullet that would keep communications untraceable. In this business he had to stay a step ahead of his adversaries, and in the case of the US intel community, two steps, if he could help it.

His fingers tapped on the desk to a constant beat as he logged on to an online gaming website, triple-checking the list of names he had saved a week ago as a calendar event. It was one of a few such online dead-drop sites, places where seemingly benign information could be traded among business associates in the vast, open expanse of the internet. It looked like any other piece of information – a list of names, nothing more – but it was the context that made it explosive, something that police and intelligence agencies would be interested in. Not to mention those on the list – they would be very interested.

Six names and one GPS location.

A death list.

The location was a speck in Kashmir – a shanty town, a mix of ancient and temporary structures on a long-abandoned trade route in northern Pakistan. Population unconfirmed, but from reports of the project he figured it to be about six hundred men, some with families there as well.

Kolesnik had built his reputation on the quality of his work, and he knew that outsourcing was a gamble – ultimately, he was responsible for this mission, so all work must be completed to his standard.

He scrolled through the World of Warcraft site, the world's largest online game. He had several methods of relaying information to his contractors, but this was currently his preferred option, a means of breaking the information up to as many locations as possible. With over fifteen million subscribers involved in this online role-playing game – all sending and receiving messages similar to the real-life instructions transmitted by Kolesnik – WoW was the perfect place to get lost, away from the prying eyes of the American and European security agencies. Better than meeting some guys in an out-of-the-way crowded bar in Mexico City.

It took just a few minutes to get his avatar to a mailbox, where he typed in three separate pieces of mail and sent each to the appropriate contact, who would check their Alliance avatar's mail within twenty-four hours.

They did actually play the game, occasionally, to ensure their avatars – mid-level humans – were nothing more nor less than millions of others being played from homes and offices around the world at any given moment. Another value of this game was the type and speed of communication it allowed. One of his guild players replied instantly. Kolesnik typed a reply, gibberish at first glance until applied to a simple side-stepped cipher, which contained information imbedded in the calendar note.

The wheels were in motion; it was no longer just him working on the list. He had the last-known locations of the six targets, all of whom had been tracked by local assets since he had received Babich's first message.

Kolesnik had a particular contractor in mind to take care of the shanty town in Kashmir. As he chomped down on a croissant he sent a spam email to what was seemingly the MySpace page of a twenty-two-year-old middle-class Pakistani girl, complete with real-life 'friends' added from the local area and abroad. The profile was, in fact, the online contact point for a former

Pakistani Intelligence officer who now coordinated a terror-support cell out of northwestern Pakistan that specialised in attacks across the Indian border.

The US-based target would be the difficult one – or rather, the expensive one. But Babich wanted this done ASAP, and he knew the cost as well as he knew Kolesnik – better than anyone. Everything Kolesnik had here in Prague, in Baku, in St Petersburg, was due to Babich, and he dirtied his hands for him whenever the need arose.

As a former paratrooper and GRU officer, Kolesnik knew loyalty and appreciated what Babich, much more than merely his General, would continue to do for him. He was a friend – family – in the highest of places, and it was Kolesnik's job, as part of a collection of many such men, to fix his boss's problems. From his first hit job for Babich in Moscow five years ago – an arrogant journalist he'd shot in the face in the lift of her apartment building – Kolesnik had known that his life, and Babich's, were inextricably aligned forever.

He logged off and went to his bedroom to pack. He threw a light summer shirt, T-shirts, a jacket, walking boots and laptop, with spare batteries, into a carry-on rucksack.

He moved aside some hanging shirts and pressed his thumb to the biometric lock of the bar-fridge-sized safe, then spoke the password. He flicked through a pile of passports on the top shelf and selected a cold one: Polish, with the full diplomatic cover of a senior embassy official, visas and stamps running up until a year ago which said he'd been stationed in the embassy in Prague. Inside were the corresponding Amex and MasterCard, along with an international driver's licence. He took a few thousand in US dollars and euros.

Kolesnik paused to look at the two 9 mm firearms, a Glock pistol and an MP5K. Under his cover identity in Prague, a name now so familiar, so comfortable, he was licensed to keep both weapons in his home under safe lock, although a police search would find any one of his seven passports cause for arrest. He was not concerned by this, though – his eight years working for Russian Intelligence in Prague did offer some level of diplomatic protection. Babich had set it up via his old KGB colleagues. Like many intelligence officers, Kolesnik had had other employers over the years; free market all the way.

He pulled on jeans, a shirt, boots and a leather jacket, and tossed his carry-on bag over his shoulder. Babich's voice still rang in his ear, the familiar tone he had known all his life. *Yest' chelóvek, yest' probléma. Net chelovéka, net problem* . . . Who had first said that? He wasn't sure, but he knew that Stalin was said to be fond of it.

Yest' chelóvek, yest' probléma. Net chelovéka, net problémy: If there is a person, there is a problem. If there is no person, then there is no problem.

Time to make these problems disappear.

9

NEW YORK CITY

'They're with us,' said a recognisable voice, dropping the 'r', all Boston minor chords. Fox watched the figure emerge from the car that had just pulled to a quick stop – another familiar face, a friendly face.

FBI Special Agent Andrew Hutchinson walked over from his car, overcoat hanging loose off his Average Joe frame. Hutchinson was about six feet to Fox's six-two, was neater looking and on par for tiredness, but the lawman had the puffiness and build of a desk man.

The two shook hands.

'Thought you'd had enough of New York,' Fox said.

'Visiting from DC,' Hutchinson replied. 'Can we go inside?'

Fox knew that Hutchinson, with all his guys about, had good reason to want to head indoors, so he led the way into the building and up the stairs. Inside the apartment Fox dropped his newspaper on the kitchen table and flicked on the espresso machine.

'You go clean up, I'll make the coffee,' Hutchinson said, taking off his overcoat. He held up a paper bag from Dunkin' Donuts. 'The cornerstone of any nutritional breakfast.'

After a quick shower Fox returned in jeans and T-shirt and switched on the Sony LCD on the wall at the end of the kitchen before taking the coffee and doughnut offered by Hutchinson.

'More technology on that thing than the space shuttle,' Hutchinson grumbled about the Gaggia as he added sugar to his cappuccino. 'Not to mention that thing,' he added, motioning to Fox's shiny new BMW K1200R motorbike.

'I'm hoping to find time soon to ride across the country,' Fox said, looking at the hardly-broken-in naked bike. 'Start here in Manhattan, head south, then chase the sunset across to TJ, follow the coast north, maybe even up through to Anchorage, then back east, all the way to Maine and then back down.'

'You had me at Tijuana and then lost me somewhere around Washington State and the border,' Hutchinson said. 'It's cold enough here.'

'I thought you Bostonians didn't feel the cold.'

'It's a different kind of cold.'

'I was there a few weeks back,' Fox said through a mouthful of doughnut. 'Drove up, should have ridden. Learned that the first parking space you see will be the last parking space you see.'

Hutchinson laughed, wiped his hands on his trousers and looked around. The floorplan of Fox's apartment was all polished boards covered with Persian rugs, blasted brick and white plaster walls, pressed metal ceilings; the open-plan living space was sparsely furnished but for gym equipment up one end and a leather couch at the other. Hutchinson sat at the island bench and Fox on a corner of the couch as BBC News showed images of the burgeoning crisis in India, protesters rioting in the streets.

Fox watched Hutchinson's face as he stirred his coffee.

Hutchinson was a special agent with the FBI's counter-intelligence branch. They had met about a year ago and come into contact a few times since, more often than not related to Fox's investigative reporting into Umbra, and had a healthy respect for each other.

Fox checked his Bell & Ross watch. 'Andy, you know what time it is?'

'I heard you were an early riser.'

'What's with all the boys out there?'

'I'll get to that in a sec,' Hutchinson said. 'So, how are you doing, Lachlan?'

'I'm doing great,' Fox replied. It had been two months since they'd spoken at any length, about seven or so months since they'd met in person. A lifetime ago. 'You?'

'All right. I got a nice promo, effectively heading my own mobile field office now.'

'So it's Special Agent in Charge Hutchinson now?'

'Yep.'

'Seems you've got half your boys outside my door.' Fox looked to the ajar front door, noticed another Fed hovering outside: jacket ready-open, showing the added bulk of a heavy gauge Kevlar vest, carrying the fire if he needed to respond. 'Is all that for my benefit or yours?'

'Yeah . . .' replied Hutchinson. 'As I said, I'll get to that.'

Fox let it go, for now.

'Anyway, here I am, one coffee and doughnut in already,' Hutchinson said, 'and you look like you've just done a few miles round the park.'

'Ten, around Roosevelt, but who's counting? Refill?'

'Yeah, thanks,' Hutchinson said. 'How's the body holding up?'

'Not like it used to. I've got pain in places I didn't know I had muscles.' Fox worked the Gaggia, grinding beans and flushing out the system before packing in a few shots of fine Arabica coffee. 'That said, I've discovered that a few weekly sessions of pilates is damn easier than hours of free weights . . . Is that Capel in the car out front?'

'One and the same; he's been out there since the early hours.'

Fox shot him a quick, questioning look. Last year, Special Agent Capel had watched over him for a few days when rogue French agents had been actively pursuing Fox around Manhattan – he'd done a good job, which is more than Fox could say of himself. But Hutchinson hadn't known about Kate's involvement then, none of them did, until it was too late.

'He said he missed babysitting your sorry ass,' Hutchinson said, shuffling on his stool. 'How are you doing otherwise?'

Fox smiled. He knew this was probably, at least in part, a recruiting op for Hutchinson. He had tried twice before, in similar circumstances, to no avail. After Kate's death, going after the group behind it in any way other than through his reportage was too much too soon. Last year, following the death of his friend and colleague Michael Rollins, who'd infiltrated Umbra's shadowy dealings in Nigeria, he wasn't physically up to the task. Now . . . now Fox wanted more than the law could provide. He would be honest with the guy, again; he had no reason not to be, and his instincts told him it would be a two-way street. Fox passed over a second cappuccino and watched the federal agent spoon in a couple of sugars and mix them roughly with the spoon.

'Insomnia,' Fox said, sipping black coffee. 'I'm restless, worn out, fed up, frustrated – how else can I put it? I'm fast becoming a sad, angry, lonely old man. I'm thirty-two and . . . I think I'm almost done with this work. Maybe I'll go into academia for a bit, do a bit of post-grad study, Yale maybe.'

'Yeah, I get it . . . kind of,' said Hutchinson, smiling.

Fox laughed. 'Look, jokes aside, I want to do some different stuff away from GSR someday, but all's good, I'm not going anywhere.'

'You are teaching a class at Columbia though?'

Fox nodded.

'Anyway,' Hutchinson said, something else in his eyes, something like uneasiness, 'are you taking something for that, the sleeplessness?'

'Not really,' Fox said, reading Hutchinson's face, the look that asked if he was taking drugs, legal or otherwise. 'No, nothing at all.'

'Fair enough. Are you seeing someone for it?'

'Nah,' Fox said, looking absently towards the television that showed Pakistani protesters burning an American flag. 'Been through all that, and now I've just been taking it easy – even having a fun time in the press lately.'

'Yeah, I saw you on *Dateline* yesterday.'

'I'm in the eye of a big fat story,' Fox said, 'and shows like *Dateline* seem more interested in the ramifications than the underlying cause.'

'I know what that's like – being questioned for raw results and nothing more,' Hutchinson said, his Adam's apple moving as he swallowed. 'Anyway, we've got a lot of good shrinks here in Manhattan that we use, if you ever need to talk to someone. They're used to dealing with the kind of trauma you've been through.'

'Getting grilled on national TV?'

'Your Nigerian thing, dumbass,' Hutchinson said. 'That and . . . losing Kate.'

'Look, I got it,' Fox said with a tight smile to force away the memories. 'I needed a rest, which I've had. I needed to cut back on stress, which I've done. I'm not driving a desk at GSR a hundred hours a week any more.'

'You went to India for work. I read the water piece you did for *Vanity Fair* that started all this scrutiny.'

'I've been there a few times recently,' Fox said, sipping his coffee as he sat on the stool opposite Hutchinson and looked him right in the eye. 'So, come on, why are you here, Andrew? Or are federal agents now making house calls to journalists to discuss articles they've written? Or are you just a fan? And what's with all the bullet-stoppers out there?'

'Lach,' Hutchinson said, his voice serious. He took a breath. 'There's someone out there who wants you dead.'

'Mate,' Fox said, half smiling, 'I've been shot at more times than you've been to the doughnut shop. Seriously – you know how many threats we get at work? Unless you're talking Ozymandias or Dr Manhattan, I think I've got good offence and defence and have run this play hundreds of times.'

Hutchinson took an envelope from inside his overcoat and put it on the table. Fox tilted his head to the side.

'So what's this, another job offer? How many times do I have to turn you down . . .'

Hutchinson watched Fox closely as he pulled out some printed pages: email and cell-phone transcripts, screen printouts from an online gaming website. He flipped through the pages, reading as quickly as comprehension permitted. He stopped and looked at Hutchinson.

'Lachlan, this ain't bush league. This here threat against you and the others; it's the real deal.'

Fox looked back to the printouts. 'Al Gammaldi?'

'We've got guys on him too,' Hutchinson said, tapping his watch without checking it. 'They're taking him into GSR right now.'

'This—'

'It's a freelance hit list. It's been authenticated separately through a couple of our intel agencies. The intercepts came in overnight—'

'After my *Dateline* thing yesterday.'

'Yeah, we got it about six hours ago. It may be up to twelve hours old.'

'What . . . Where'd this originate?'

'We're working on that, believe me. You'll get details when I do – right now, I've got a mosaic of scraps of intel that have just been verified.'

'But how credible is credible? I mean, I've had death threats—' Fox cut himself off, caught up. '*Verified?*'

Hutchinson looked at his coffee as he replied, 'Ambreen Butt is dead.'

'No . . .' Fox said, gutted. Ambreen was the fixer he'd used in Pakistan's northern areas, the woman who had shown them around, acted as a translator of Pushtu and Urdu, made them welcome in every house and situation they had encountered in the ten days he and Al Gammaldi had spent in the area.

'Shot point blank in her apartment in Islamabad; professional. Took out her husband, too, four hours ago.'

Fox had a thousand-mile stare, boring right through the paper in his hands. 'What are you doing about the others?' he ground out, gripping the list of names in his hand: *Lachlan Fox, Alister Gammaldi, Omar Hasif, Sardar Yusufzai, Ambreen Butt, Art Kneeshaw.*

'Hasif is in Libya and we're looking for him. Sardar Yusufzai – engineer on the water project, yeah?'

Fox nodded.

'He's somewhere in Pakistan – last seen in Karachi – and we're fighting through all kinds of bullshit to get the ISI to help find him. The Libyans are fucking organised next to those guys.'

Fox knew that the Pakistani Inter-Services Intelligence, ISI, was going through its own troubles at the moment after the fallout of the 2008 Mumbai terrorist attacks and subsequent Taliban battles, not to mention the shift in their scope since Pervez Musharraf left office.

'This Art Kneeshaw, who's he?' Fox asked.

Hutchinson shook his head. 'I was hoping you could tell me. We've got nothing.'

'Never heard of him.'

'Is there something else to this story that you haven't reported?'

Fox shook his head and kicked into gear, scrolling through his iPhone contacts, then calling the head of GSR security.

'Rick, I just got info on Ambreen – there's a hit out for—'

Hutchinson watched Fox as he listened, his face tense. Richard Sefreid, a former US Army officer, was an adept leader when it came to his present job description, protecting GSR personnel. His nine-member outfit was constantly crisscrossing the globe pulling security duty for the investigative reporters, often also supervising outsourced security contractors. Hutchinson waited while Fox heard something he clearly didn't like.

'All right, I'll work it out now, thanks,' Fox said, about to hang up, his face flushed with anger. 'What? No, I'm all good, got the Feds here now. See you at the office.' Fox ended the call and shook his head.

'What did Richard say?'

'I've got another fixer, Govind, in India – not on this list. Shot dead an hour ago in a home invasion.'

Hutchinson's thumbs worked overtime at his BlackBerry's keyboard.

'Can you bring Hasif into the US to protect him?' asked Fox.

'Yes,' Hutchinson said, still typing. 'Temporary visas are being sorted today. This Hasif, he's an engineer too? What did he do for you?'

'He's good people, gave me a lot of background technical info,' Fox said. 'He oversaw the piping and pumping installations at the water plant. The whole project was divided into teams; he only knew of the plant and its immediate outflows but he cooperated fully.'

Hutchinson stopped typing and looked at Fox. 'He proved significant water theft from the Indian side of things?'

'He's – that's still the trillion-dollar legal question.'

Hutchinson nodded, slowly. He had almost given up believing that someone with Babich's power and influence – not to mention his contacts in the intel world, both in Russia and abroad – could be stopped. But just maybe . . . he clicked a few more keys on his BlackBerry then looked back to Fox.

'I'm waiting on confirmation that the embassy in Tripoli picked up Hasif and his family,' Hutchinson said. 'It's a long list – we've got everyone from the deputy mission chief down out looking for him, checking in with all known family and friends.'

'He's a family man,' Fox said. 'Find his family, you'll find him.'

10

TRIPOLI, LIBYA

'This is the life . . . This is what home really feels like.'

Omar Hasif flexed his heavily cracked hands and squinted through his glasses against the bright sunlight as he watched his young son, Wasim, playing with a friend in the neighbour's front yard.

The tree-lined street was clean and tidy, and many of the houses had well-kept plants in their front yards. There was plenty of green, thanks to Hasif's engineering work. Meters were non-existent here; water was an infinite resource provided by the state. It bubbled up from deep in the ground hundreds of kilometres away and was treated and supplied safe for household consumption.

Hasif's work was important, and it paid for his comfortable life, although being good at his job kept him in demand, on the road with his family, regularly having to settle into different large-scale engineering projects around the world: Iran, Pakistan, India, Malaysia, Malta. One month consulting on a new dam, the next a desalination plant. He earned good money but had nowhere to settle down and spend it. He was even going to Israel next month, a two-week trip without his family, and that water company had paid half his fee upfront – it was now parked here out the front of his sister's house in the form of a new Audi SUV, big and shiny and destined to be garaged here in his old home town for the short times he was here. The irony in this was not lost on him. He would settle down soon enough, not so much early retirement as a downsizing to appreciate the good life.

'Omar, come in and keep me company,' his brother-in-law, Broseph, said, his head jutting out the flyscreen front door. 'The women, they are driving me nuts.'

'Come out here and sit,' Hasif said, gesturing to a set of chairs at a table on the lush green lawn. The join lines were still visible on the roll-out turf.

'I am in the outdoors too much,' Broseph replied. 'Besides, the football is showing, come see it with me. I have ice-cold beer in the fridge in the TV room.'

'Beer?'

'Non-alcoholic – it's good, brother.'

Hasif nodded and looked over to his son. 'Wasim, not too long, hey?' he said and then smiled as his son ignored him, too busy playing and making shooting noises. 'Wasim, lunch soon, okay?'

Wasim half-turned towards his father and nodded while continuing his plastic toy-soldier game. Both kids were a little on the heavy side; too much junk food and not enough exercise, not like in his day. He had provided a better life for the next generation, but they were always hungry for more and bigger and better – Hasif wondered when that cycle would end as he walked into his sister's house.

He could hear his wife and his sister's high-pitched laughter from the kitchen as they rolled spiced rice into dolmades and prepared flat breads and dips. It smelled of his childhood, long summer days when his mother would spend half her waking days in the kitchen for their family. His aunt was often there, too, and he loved her cooking. He missed this country. He should tell his wife more often how happy she made him. He should get a job here in Tripoli – his old engineering school at Al Fatah University sent him an invitation to join their teaching ranks each year, and each year he politely refused and instead gave a donation – and slow down, in a home full of good food and family. On weekends he would sit on the couch like his brother-in-law, not having to take the family to the major shopping centre in whatever new city they were in that week. To have a house like this, a street like this, food like this, routine like this. The beauty of conforming to the old ways.

Hasif poked his head into the kitchen and watched his wife wrapping spiced rice in vine leaves; some rice had stuck to her pregnant belly. She was seven months along now, and as she looked up at him and smiled she wiped her sleeve across her forehead to remove sweat. Her eyes were alive: perfect almonds framed with thick black eyeliner. She was as beautiful now as when they'd met as teenagers. He snuck in behind the other woman and pinched a dolmade, then left the room as his sister flung a kitchen towel in his direction. He didn't mind that they joked and laughed and called him fat because he knew that when he settled somewhere soon, and stopped chasing the big pay days, he would have his wife cook like this every day. He'd stop eating so much McDonald's, and their friends would speak Arabic instead of a foreign tongue.

11

NEW YORK CITY

Fox's iPhone rang – it was Alister Gammaldi, his best mate since high school. They had joined the Australian Navy together as eighteen-year-old officer cadets and had been by each other's side ever since, through too many crises to count. Gammaldi was now a pilot with GSR and had accompanied Fox to some of the world's most volatile places.

'Mate—'

'Lach, I've got Feds here—'

'I know,' Fox said. 'Pack for India and meet me at GSR.'

'We're still going to India?' Gammaldi seemed surprised. 'Not sure if you heard me right. There's FBI dudes here saying that my life – our lives – are in danger.'

'Al – just pack, I'll meet you at the office to talk. Organise a flight to India as soon as you can.'

'All right,' Gammaldi said. 'Lach, what's this about?'

'We've got too close – there's a price on our heads.'

'Really?' Gammaldi asked, more impressed than worried. 'How much?'

'Figure of speech, Al. Who knows? But this is real,' Fox said. 'They took out Ambreen and her husband last night, and Govind just now – all shot.'

'Jesus,' Gammaldi said. 'And we're wanted, hey? I'd feel like Ned Kelly, but Ambreen and Govind—'

'I'll meet you at work in thirty.' Fox ended the call and took in Hutchinson's expression. 'I'm not going to wait this out; I have to finish this story.'

'I know.'

'They intimidate and scare journalists all the time and it's not happening this time.'

'I agree,' Hutchinson repeated. 'It'll be harder for us to protect you over there, though.'

'I can look after myself,' Fox said. 'And you know Al . . . Hell, drop him in the middle of the ocean and he'll reorganise the food chain.'

'Yeah, I thought as much,' Hutchinson said. 'Listen, I've got my own ideas, but who do you think this is?'

'I'd put money on Umbra, but they're too smart and cashed up to leave a trail like this,' Fox said.

'We're working on that angle, tilting the earth, believe me. More often than not it's the simple mistakes that lead to the big results – this may just be Babich's. You know we've been trying for years to get this guy, Lach.'

'I made waves for them . . . Hell, they've probably got all sorts of Pakistani nationalist nuts for hire lining up to take us out.'

Hutchinson stood and slipped on his overcoat. 'We'll pick up Hasif. I'm meeting with State later today to fast-track an emergency asylum request for permanent residency and FBI protection. But I'll need to hear it from you before they hear it in Hasif's debrief: what are you working on that's not here, that hasn't been in the press? What's this really about?'

'Water.'

'Water?'

'It's that simple.'

'I thought this could have been about Rollins and Mendes,' Hutchinson said quietly. His words hung in the air for almost a minute of silence between them; for both men, the memories were too fresh. Michael Rollins had been an experienced GSR reporter who'd got too close to a story last year in Nigeria and paid the ultimate price. A story that led to Umbra. Rollins was a good man, ultimately, and like too many good men in his profession, he'd got in too deep. So deep it became difficult to tell friends from enemies, and he was never able to clear things up sufficiently for those he left behind . . . And neither was Steve Mendes, an ex-CIA agent who'd proved to be in on the ground during Umbra's founding, although his departure was no loss.

'You know this water project goes back to Umbra, and you pissed them off a few months ago.'

'Yeah, that's just it,' Fox said, leaning on the side of the kitchen table opposite the Fed. 'I want answers. I need them. You were right about that months ago. Rollins, Umbra . . . This is big . . . This water issue is scratching the surface of what Babich and his companies do, all headed by these ex-KGB/FSB types. Strip mining for gold in Borneo; Arctic exploration for gas and oil; an alternative gas pipeline around the Ukraine, another that snakes through South Ossetia – they're into everything, and everything they touch makes them billions and turns the local area to shit – no rules, no governance, a corporation gone mad.' Fox sighed. He took a final sip of coffee before rinsing the mug hard under the tap.

'You turned me down a couple of months ago,' Hutchinson said quietly.

'Before then, too.'

'You could have been a part of this, I mean really . . . A part of our investigation.'

'I wasn't ready for something like this a couple of months ago,' Fox said. 'You knew that.'

'Yeah, I knew it,' Hutchinson said and buttoned up his overcoat. He flicked though the *Times*, seeing but taking nothing in. 'Can't turn the country down three times.'

'Who's rule?'

'Mine,' Hutchinson replied. 'We had a good opportunity at that time, is all. You could have gone into Umbra from the inside, like Rollins.'

'Opportunities come up all the time.'

Hutchinson looked up at him quickly, expectantly.

'I've been working on this on my own for a bit, nibbling around the edges,' Fox said. 'This is the break, Andy. They've been forced to act and this will be their undoing. I've got under Babich's skin, and as long as I keep at him, he'll be worried, he'll make mistakes.'

'Yeah?'

'Let's do this,' Fox said. 'Let's bring this bastard down, him and all his—'

Hutchinson held up a hand.

'This isn't something for your own—'

'Two dead,' Fox said, tapping the transcript on the table between them, 'and a guy who's going to be seeking asylum because he's connected directly with Umbra. What he knows, and what they believe he may have told us, is damaging enough to kill everyone on this list. It's a start. You asked me if there is something we haven't reported. There is, and it's not because I'm holding back, it's because I haven't put it all together yet. I need to talk to these guys again, I need to dig some more, to see what I missed. I need to draw Babich out, try to get to the real Russian power players.'

'And you really believe you can unravel this, expose this project in Kashmir – through their water company?'

Fox nodded. 'It might be enough to force him to the table – put pressure on him, get him to talk.'

'You know how many safeguards Babich will have in place?'

'I reckon he's pretty near the head of the organisation,' Fox said. 'The days of these ex-spooks scratching each other's backs and making each other rich, beyond ordinary law – it's over. I can feel it, we'll get the proof.'

'Proof.' Hutchinson's eyes searched Fox's face. 'Europol and Interpol have been chipping away at Babich's business dealings for more than a decade. He's got a wall of lawyers and limited-liability companies, not to mention all his subsidiaries.'

'Show me a billionaire who's not a crook.'

'Fox, my team investigating US connections to Umbra has grown steadily in size since your Patriot Act thing.' Hutchinson didn't need to remind Fox about the story he'd been working on that had resulted in uncovering the fact that Kate was being worked by an undercover French agent intent on hacking into government files. The FBI may have got their man but Fox had lost it all. 'We know Umbra funds thugs and wars and finances politics and all the usual mafia-type shit, not to mention our suspicions about them being responsible for the deaths of over two hundred intelligence assets since the end of the Cold War – but we've had nothing to get us in the door—'

Hutchinson's BlackBerry vibrated and he checked the screen. 'I've got to leave for Washington,' he said, pocketing the phone. 'Keep that,' he said, motioning to the paperwork he had brought, 'and call me on my cell when you're at work, before you head off.'

Hutchinson and Fox walked to the door and shook hands.

'Stick with my guys, do what they say,' said Hutchinson.

Fox nodded.

'Keep your head, Lach, for all our sakes. I believe you can do this, I think it's the beginning of the end of these Umbra guys, too, but you have to take this threat seriously, don't take any—'

'I'll be right. You just hold up your end when we get more dirt on this son of a bitch.'

Hutchinson smiled. 'Don't worry, I've got good cops and prosecutors all around the world waiting in line to take a shot at Babich.' Hutchinson watched Fox's face as he moved out the doorway.

Then he turned back. 'Lach?' he said. 'Don't trust anyone out there.'

'Does that include you, Andy?'

Hutchinson gave him a hurt look.

'Don't worry, mate, it's my nature,' Fox said with a smile. 'I believe little of what I hear, and only half of what I see.'

Hutchinson smiled and departed. Fox closed his apartment door and went to pack. He didn't have much time and one thing was for certain: this was going to be a tough match.

12

TRIPOLI, LIBYA

'This game—'

'It's not a game.'

'Oh, yes. This *match* is from last night?' Hasif asked as he and Broseph sat in leather recliners and sipped German beer.

'Yes – and don't tell me who won,' his brother-in-law said, jumping in his chair as his team's striker missed a header right in front of the goal.

'You're sure?' Hasif joked. 'I heard the result on the radio coming over here . . .'

Broseph gave him a look that he usually reserved for his underlings in the customs bureau.

'Okay,' Hasif said over the top of his drink. 'But if you get bored by half-time, I can tell you.'

They laughed and drank and talked about Gaddafi and sport and stock prices.

'I might get a new car like you then, hey?' joked Broseph.

'We have not bought it yet – we are testing it over the weekend, but my wife seems in love with it, so I'm sure I will sign the papers on Monday,' said Hasif. 'I just hope that she does not crash it while I'm away.'

'That would be expensive,' Broseph said. 'If she does, say

that I was driving – as a government employee I get good cover, much better than any woman.'

'You remind me that this country still has far to travel in some areas,' Hasif said and drained the last of his beer; the lager wasn't entirely non-alcoholic – it was 0.1 per cent. His wife entered the room and passed them each a dolmade.

'Don't tell your wife,' she whispered to Broseph and he laughed while he ate. Hasif patted his lap and when his wife sat down he cradled her in his arms.

'We need goat's curd, lemons, and ice-cream for the kids,' she said. 'Shall I drive to the shops?'

'No, I'll do it,' Hasif said, making to get up.

'You're my guests, I will go,' Broseph said as he stood.

'Here.' Hasif fished around in his trouser pocket and pulled out the Audi key and tossed it to him. 'Just don't get me a speeding fine.'

They could see him through the lace curtains as he walked down the front stairs and through the garden to the kerb-side SUV. Hasif muted the television's half-time commentary.

'Have I told you how much I love you?' Hasif asked, nestling his face in the nape of his wife's neck.

'Not today,' she replied, and lifted her chin to let him kiss her neck. She smelled of jasmine oil and her short dark hair of cooking spices. He kissed along her jawline and nibbled on her ear—

The front windows of the house blew inwards at them with devastating ferocity. Hasif leaned to cover his wife and spun the chair so that their backs faced the blast. A thunderclap and orange flash filled the street, followed by a whoosh and a sucking noise – then he couldn't hear anything but the ringing in his ears. He looked into the frightened face of his wife and held her head. She looked down at him with a little blood on her cheek and nodded she was okay.

'Wasim,' she said faintly.

He got out from under her and ran through the open doorway and down the front steps, holding his arms up to stop the intense heat from scorching his face.

Where the Audi had stood a massive fire raged. The timber garden fence was in a million pieces. Car alarms sounded along the street as Hasif's hearing slowly came back. He heard a cry to his right and he ran toward it.

His son lay on his back, blown into the bushes, the neighbour's brick fence blocking the worst of the blast. Wasim looked up into his father's eyes: he looked okay but blood poured from one of his ears and his clothes smouldered in places. The neighbour's child was nowhere to be seen. Hasif picked up his young son and walked to the neighbour's large circular fountain in the middle of their paved driveway. He climbed in; the water was knee-deep and the mosaic tiles were a brilliant blue. He held his shaking son in the water and repeated that it would be all right, that everything would be all right. As he washed his face he heard screaming and crying all around him.

13

NEW YORK CITY

Fox swung his backpack over his shoulder, scanned his apartment and then pulled the door shut as his phone rang. He saw the caller ID and considered bumping it, but pressed answer.

'Hey, Jane,' Fox said as he followed the hulk of an FBI agent downstairs.

'Hey, you,' she replied. 'We're meeting for breakfast, yeah?'

'Jane, I'm sorry, something's come up,' Fox said, following the Fed out the front door to the waiting FBI sedan. 'I'm headed to the airport—'

He looked to his right and saw Jane standing at his buzzer. She looked quizzically at him and then at the Fed who had stepped between them.

'It's cool,' Fox said to the man, then walked over to Jane and kissed her cheek.

'What's going on?' asked Jane, looking over his shoulder at the agents: one stood scanning the street; one was in the double-parked car with an NYPD sedan pulled up behind it – Fox had never seen cops more alert, and he couldn't help but tense up. He had played down the idea of a threat with Hutchinson, but he knew the reality: if they wanted to find him, they would.

'Look – we're going to swing by GSR,' he said. 'Do you want to ride with me?'

She searched his eyes, saw the uncertainty he tried too hard to mask. 'Sure.'

The Fed stood guard as they climbed into the back seat, then closed the door and moved quickly to the front passenger seat. The cars rolled on, the NYPD sedan taking the lead.

'Lachlan—'

'It's something I'm working on. There's been a threat against Al and me and some sources I used.'

Jane's face showed it all: anguish, concern, regret. She knew the score – she was a journalist, too, but of the feature-writer *New Yorker* breed. Since the Conde Nast redundancies she had been freelancing, even writing a column for GSR's online magazine, applying her sprawling style to observations about being a thirty-something-single-mum-divorcee in America today; observations that generated more blog comments than any other column on the site.

'Is this about the Kashmir water story?'

'Yeah, partly,' Fox said. 'Look, Al and I are headed back to India today to follow up more leads. It could be big – bigger than I've already reported. There's got to be more . . . I might be gone for a bit.'

He looked forward as the NYPD car whooped its siren short and loud to get a few cabs out of the way.

'How long?'

'However long it takes,' Fox said, turning back to Jane. 'Depends what we find, how far it goes.'

'But this threat—'

'I'll tell you more when I know more,' he said, squeezing her hand. 'Sorry, all I know is that our names came up in a thing and these guys are going to look out for us.'

'Who are they?' She motioned to the guys in the front.

'FBI.'

Her alabaster-pale face went a little whiter, highlighting the stark contrast to her dark hair, which was cut into a fringed bob with the barest hint of red highlights – all part of her cleansing move after being made redundant. Jane was pretty in a PBS kind of way – pretty for a smart writer. Fox missed her long hair, missed her moods that so easily turned to laughter even when she was under deadline pressure. They'd had a few months of laughter and comfort, but now – now she had time to burn and things had changed. It wasn't the carefree relationship they'd initiated. Far from it, he guessed.

'Will these Feds take care of you and Al wherever you travel?'

'We'll be fine,' Fox said, smiled. 'Al can look after me.'

The look in her eyes told him she wasn't sold, and he smiled in a way that used to make her laugh. Nothing.

'I'm feeling the way you should, Lachlan.'

'How's that?'

'Someone has threatened to kill you, the FBI are your bodyguards – and you're *smiling*?'

'It's my default position.'

She searched his face.

'Look, Jane,' he said. 'I've been through this kind of thing before.'

'So, you're invincible?'

'No. Lucky, I guess.'

'Lucky? On what planet is being on some kind of hit list a lucky thing?'

'At least *someone* wants me,' he replied.

She turned away and watched wet snow fall on her window, spoke softly: 'You know?'

'I guessed,' Fox said, looking out his window.

'Why didn't you say anything?'

Fox spoke quietly to the glass: 'He who knows how to speak, knows also when.'

'We – we have a daughter, he and I,' Jane said, facing Fox. 'I – we – owe it to her to try again. Can you understand that?'

Fox nodded.

'But what?' she asked.

'I seem to recall you wanted your ex-husband on a hit list.'

'I wanted him hurt, not dead.'

'Maybe I can hang out with him,' Fox said. 'He might get caught in the crossfire.' He turned to her, held her gaze, saw the tears damming in her eyes. 'Jane, I'm joking.'

'I don't know how you can joke about this. They might kill you!'

He turned back to look out his window. New York traffic, perpetual magic hour. Park Avenue at 7.30 in the morning was not quite gridlock, but almost. Horns, cabs, vans and town cars were all settling into the commute and no one was happy about it—

Suddenly there was a bang on the back of the car and in the same second the agent in the passenger seat was up with a Sig pointed at the threat—

A courier on a bike flashed by the side windows, didn't bother stopping or waving.

'Jesus,' exhaled the agent, turning back around, looking at the driver.

Jane's hand had dug hard into Fox's knee at the sudden noise and the appearance of the gun. Fox glanced at the passers-by behind Jane's head; he knew any one of them could pull a nine mil and start blasting . . . He pushed the thought from his mind, looked at Jane, held her hand.

'Look, I agree you need to do this, for Gabriella,' he said. 'She's that something special you two will always share, your whole lives. And who's to say it won't work out for you this time around? It's all right, I'm cool with it. And if you need a friend, I'll be here.'

The NYPD sedan bleeped its siren and blasted a hole through some stationary traffic across 34th. Jane jumped at the sound and squeezed Fox's hand, then let go quickly; it wasn't meant to be like that anymore.

'He wants to make it work,' she said, then paused. 'People change.'

'That much?' Fox searched her expression – she had never been so unreadable.

'And you *don't* believe in forgiveness, redemption?'

'I want to, believe me.' Fox almost laughed. 'I've wanted that so badly in so many ways. I don't know what to believe any more; I'm close, but I haven't quite figured it out.'

'How can *you* say that?'

'I believe in the truth.'

'And you search so hard for it that it keeps you imprisoned. Can't you see that? This obsession of yours – look what it's doing. People want you dead!'

Fox stared at her. He understood it easily enough, wouldn't question her motivation further. She knew what he did in the line of work and how so much of what he'd seen haunted him at every turn. His eyes showed the slight edge of a smile that came with awareness: 'You know who I am.'

'But I need more,' she said. 'I need someone who's here, with me. You're so *closed*, you won't let me in. I don't need that, and I don't want it. It wears me out.'

He faced her. 'And if I could be who you wanted?'

Her tears fell.

Fox's gut twisted. He looked away. He just couldn't seem to make it work with women. Before Jane was Kate. It had rained the night she died, and it was grey for a long time afterwards. Months of befriending bartenders and drug dealers ended with the presence of Jane Clay. She had helped pull him through all that, and now here they were, with nothing left to say.

Jane looked out her window, talked to the glass again. 'You've worn me out,' she whispered.

'You saved me,' he whispered into her ear.

She faced him. Her eyes searched his.

'We found each other at the right time,' Fox said. 'We gave and we took, and it's meant to be like this. It's okay.'

The agent in the passenger seat cleared his throat: 'Ah – we're here, Mr Fox.'

Fox looked across to Jane, apologetically. 'Jane, I've got to get to work.'

She bit her bottom lip, something resolved. Sleeved her tears away. 'Right.'

'Ah, Mr Fox?' said the same agent, looking straight ahead. 'We have to get you moving.'

Fox nodded as another Fed sedan pulled up in front of their car: Gammaldi and his protection detail.

Jane leaned over to Fox and kissed his cheek; he held a hand to the side of her face. She left before she regretted it all.

•

Alister Gammaldi stood on the grey granite plaza of the Seagram Building at 375 Park Avenue flanked by three FBI agents. He watched Jane climb into a cab and take off, then motioned for them to get going.

'What's with—'

'Al, I don't think we'll be seeing much of Jane anymore.'

They were shepherded towards their building by six Feds and two cops, the group weaving around pedestrian traffic like a Porsche turbo on the autobahn.

'I never really got Jane,' Gammaldi said.

Fox looked at his friend, and Gammaldi looked back sheepishly.

'Too complicated?'

'Too . . . New Jersey.'

Fox smiled and shook his head as they walked into the Seagram, the top five floors of which housed GSR. The cops remained by the doors, the Feds followed close by, and a couple of GSR security staff, Eyal Geiger and Rob Goldsmith, waited in the lobby, their faces more serious than usual.

'Too New Jersey?' Fox asked Gammaldi as they waited in the lift lobby. 'What does that even mean?'

'Stuffed if I know,' Gammaldi said. 'Let's just go with "too complicated".'

Fox laughed.

'Let's make this quick,' Gammaldi said as they walked into the lift foyer and pressed the call button.

'Why? Do you have to be someplace else?' Fox asked as they entered the lift and pressed 37.

'I've got to eat some real American food before we fly to India.'

14

FBI, QUANTICO, VIRGINIA

When he joined the FBI after 9/11, he was a poster boy for recruitment. When he joined the ranks of their elite Hostage Rescue Team and participated in a high-profile mission, *USA Today* described him as an Olympic athlete who killed for a living. He liked to think his job was about saving lives, but the press weren't that far wrong.

Special Agent Jake Duhamel nodded to the man on his left and they charged through the door with well-practised skill, their vision sharp down the sights of their silenced H&K UMP submachine guns, firing .45 ACP rounds at hostile targets and changing clips so fast they'd put a Ferrari pit crew to shame. The .45 round was about one thing: stopping power, and these men liked knowing that one shot would do the job.

Just over three minutes later the two men exited the rear of the building and the exercise was over. Anything under four minutes, with all hostiles down and friendlies unharmed, was a perfect score; five minutes was par for members of the FBI's Enhanced SWAT Teams. Hogan's Alley was the name of the mocked-up training town at Quantico where the FBI's special agents could hone their trade, their 'Practical Applications'.

Often actors or training agents would play the roles of hostages, bystanders, criminals and terrorists, and usually paintball guns were used to simulate live-fire weapons.

Quantico was also home to several divisions of active and support units of the FBI. For Jake Duhamel and his Hostage Rescue Team – HRT being the pointy-end element of the Tactical Support Branch of the FBI's Critical Incident Response Group – it was home sweet home, a place from where they rapid-deployed to any emergency situation with one goal in mind: to save lives. The mocked-up buildings were constantly being shot to shit and then rebuilt, only to be shot up again as agents practised live-fire forced entries until, like Duhamel and his team, it was second nature. HRT didn't do things by halves – their dedicated live-fire urban combat section, sandbagged off to prevent stray rounds escaping, kept several local carpenters in jobs.

Jake Duhamel removed his clear goggles and cleared his two firearms: the H&K UMP45 that succeeded the venerable MP5, with slower fire rate but lighter and carrying much more punch of the .45 over the 9 mm, and his H&K .45 UCP pistol. Like all elite units, members of the HRT knew the practicality of keeping their firearms in interchangeable calibres.

As Duhamel and Brick walked with their cleared weapons back to the support building, one of the HRT's matt-black Bell choppers buzzed overhead.

'They paged you?' Brick asked his team leader. 'We're going out?'

'Nup, I reckon it's a maintenance flight.' Duhamel shrugged – their team wasn't on active use, but any deployment of the 'go team' would be communicated to them ASAP. They took the path double-time and entered their support building. Through the windows they saw that the chopper had landed, and they watched two suits disembark.

Duhamel handed his firearms to his team's most junior agent, whose duty it was to quartermaster the team's gear and weaponry, and went over to the Special Agent in Charge, who was watching the new arrivals approach. Brick soon followed, munching on a power bar.

'What's with the suits, boss?'

'Just ferried them in from Dulles,' he said. 'Cops. One from Italy, one from Russia. Can't tell which is which from here.'

Duhamel looked to Brick and then back to his SAC. 'And?'

'And Jake my boy, you're taking them through their paces until fourteen hundred this afternoon. Full tactical rundown of a high-risk arrest.'

'What?' Duhamel was pissed off. 'Who the fuck are they?'

'Interpol, Europol, take your pick. They're lawmen.'

'Define lawmen.'

The SAC raised an eyebrow.

'That's—' Duhamel took a sharp breath. 'I'm not babysitting some amateur mo's through live fire – they'll probably shoot me trying to load their hammers.'

The SAC cracked a smile and slapped a hand on Duhamel's shoulder. 'This comes from up high, you and Brick requested specifically. No details yet but these guys need to be ready for a live situation; something big's in the works. We don't know who the target is or where they'll need to go get him, but you'll put these guys through their paces and then fall in back here for a briefing by fourteen-thirty.' He moved to leave.

'Boss? What's this about?'

'If I knew more, I'd tell you more,' he replied. 'And if you knew more, you'd probably not want to turn up for the meeting. But you will, since I asked you to so nice.'

As the SAC left the building, Brick flipped him the double bird, short and sharp, there and gone again.

'I hear you, Bricko,' Duhamel said, looking over to his junior agent. Brick had heard most of the conversation and barely needed the nod Duhamel gave him to head off to organise additional training firearms from the armoury.

'Fucking suits.'

15

NEW YORK CITY

While Fox headed up to see the GSR director, Gammaldi checked his cubbyhole office, down the hall from Fox's, and packed a few final items into his backpack: Kevlar vest, hand-held GPS, satellite phone, a couple of good maps of the areas they were headed to.

Tucked into a room on the eastern side of the building, on the same floor as the research and editorial teams, was the GSR flight office. As Gammaldi approached he saw that the admin assistant was talking on a phone that had a couple of lines blinking. She was like many of the junior assistants here: twenty-something, well educated, hungry for a career in the media.

Gammaldi smiled as he squeezed past her and leaned over the vacant self-booking desk. Tapping away at the keyboard, he checked the booking schedule of GSR aircraft: the Gulfstream 650 was available, so he typed in the times and locations he would need. The staff here or at their terminal at JFK would then make arrangements for landing clearances, refuelling, and customs for all crew and passengers.

Gammaldi never ceased to be amazed by the resources at GSR's disposal. For a pilot, GSR was a sweet gig with good pay, use of all GSR's leased aircraft – a few intercontinental jets and a couple of choppers – and he had quickly grown to love New York. The admin girl was still on the phone; she smiled at him and motioned that she wouldn't be long. Gammaldi was a favourite with the office girls; the class clown who hammed it up, but also with the seniority within the company – both as a pilot and as Fox's 'wing-man' when they had to chase a story – to get away with pranks. Today, however, there was no joking. He waited for her to finish her call, demolishing the sweets she kept in a bowl on her desk until she moved them out of his reach.

She finally hung up and turned to him, ignoring her phone, which continued to buzz quietly with incoming calls. Gammaldi pointed to the projection on the wall that showed the shared flight schedule.

'The other 650 hasn't landed?'

She shook her head and checked her computer. 'They were delayed a couple of hours while refuelling at Heathrow,' she said as she typed, bringing up details. 'ETA touchdown at JFK . . . momentarily, but there's a delay pattern in the air, maybe up to an hour. Do you want me to contact them?'

Gammaldi checked his watch. 'Nah, it's good, thanks.'

•

'A Libyan engineer? What information has he got that's worth killing for?'

'He worked on the project in northern Pakistan, part of this underground water network . . . What he's got is what I've got to find out – this must be bigger than what I've already reported, bigger than we thought.'

'No story is big enough to die for,' said the GSR chief of staff, Faith Williams. She was dressed in her usual fashion-runway-meets-corporate wear, stunning and perfectly put together: crisp white Donna Karan shirt, navy pinstripe Ralph Lauren pencil skirt, and Jimmy Choos in a red that rivalled her flame-coloured hair, which was pulled back into a tight ponytail. 'I want you to stay here under FBI protection until this blows over.'

'Faith—'

'You should be protected, hidden—'

'I'm not going to be bubble-wrapped—'

'Lachlan, I won't have you – or any other staff member of mine, for that matter – killed chasing a story. Period.' She paused. 'Dr Wallace, back me up here.'

The room was pin-drop silent. Tasman Wallace was a fatherly figure to GSR staff, particularly so to this young Australian employee who'd risen to bureau chief in record time. Sure, he knew that Fox had a knack for getting himself entangled in hot spots around the globe, but the stories were syndicated as a result of his tenacity and were something that reminded the fifty-six-year-old director of his own time as a young reporter, long before the empire of GSR grew to be what it was today. He smiled and leaned back in his Humanscale chair.

'Lachlan, can't you delegate this one from here? Use our local contacts in the region? The Feds can protect you here, it's the safest place.'

Fox looked from the director to the chief of staff and back again. 'Tas, what are you saying?'

The older man held up his hand. This kind of story, Fox knew, was the kind of thing that drove Wallace, was the reason he set up GSR in the first place. He wasn't one to look the other way, nor to be told to leave something alone.

'I'm not going to stop you,' he said. 'It's your call, Lach, but I'm with Faith on this – only because I don't want to lose you. If we have to we can get the story some other way.'

'Some other way? Tas . . .' Fox looked at the man, spoke softly. 'This is my story. I've got to do it, I've got to see where it goes. This is going to be something, *really* something. For the first time I know what it feels like to pull together a big story that's world-changing.'

'Is this is an ego thing?' Faith asked. Fox looked at her with disbelief, and after a moment she blushed – she knew him, probably better than anyone in the company except for Gammaldi.

'No,' Fox said calmly. 'It isn't about me or my reports; it's about Babich and Umbra Corp trying to cover up their shady operations. They want to silence me because I'm getting close to some other side to the water business. Something bigger than Pakistan being able to get a stranglehold on the water situation in Kashmir. But I won't know what that something is until I go back and start asking more questions.'

'As far as I can see, this boils down to one country stealing another's water,' Faith said. 'It doesn't explain the threat against you and Al, the deaths of—'

'Yes, but it's the scale of this thing that puts it into—'

'But why, if this is already out there in the public domain through your investigations,' Faith interrupted, 'would Umbra want you and those connected to the water project dead? What will that achieve?'

'That's what I was wondering,' Wallace said. 'Is it a reprisal for shining a light into this dark corner? If anything, such actions would legitimise your accusations of wrongdoing.'

'Maybe two reasons,' Fox said. 'First, killing reporters in Russia is commonplace, so maybe it's just Babich's natural reflex. And second, the reason it's done isn't simply for retribution. It's to silence them, to stop them digging any further.'

The intercom buzzed on Wallace's desk. He pressed a button and the voice of his executive secretary, Emily, resounded in the room.

'Mr Wallace, Alister Gammaldi just phoned to let Lachlan know their plane is being readied, and they need to leave in fifteen minutes.'

'Thank you, Emily,' said Wallace and pressed the same button to end the call. He leaned forward and looked directly at Fox.

'Lachlan, you don't have to go out there.'

'I know, Tas, I know,' Fox replied. 'But there's more to this than we've uncovered, and when I get back there I *know* I can get to the bottom of it. Whatever it is, it's damning – damning enough to kill a lot of people for; damning enough to put an end to Babich for good.'

'FBI agent Hutchinson is behind you on this?' Faith asked. 'He can protect you?'

'Let's call him,' Fox said. 'Hear it from him, then I go.'

16

PAKISTAN

Kolesnik knew that helicopters were often tempting targets in these lawless regions, which is why he was driving between objectives. His chartered flight had landed earlier today in Muzaffarabad, Azad Kashmir, northern Pakistan, and from there he had hired a vehicle. It was slower, but safer this way. He had dropped off the cash payment to the agreed location, from where the cell would collect it and set to work on eliminating the GPS target while he took care of the surgical tasks. He had included the sum he instructed them to deliver to the aid building yesterday, with a small bonus, as promised, for their effort. He doubted very briefly that the money got through to the aid worker – but of course it would have. If there was something he knew about these people, it was that they were men of honour. They operated by a code not dissimilar to his own.

Ambreen Butt and Sardar Yusufzai had been soft targets; Yusufzai's body was likely to go unfound for some time. Govind been harder to track down, but that was done now, too. He'd had to change his clothes after that one, stuffed his old set into a garbage furnace on the side of the road. He tapped the steering wheel to the thumping beat that played through the Nissan

Patrol's sound system. Now he would cross back over the border, into India, and fix the engineer, Kneeshaw. He had hidden his pistol under the air-filter housing as a precaution, although he doubted the border guys would inspect his vehicle.

Kolesnik tore through the desert, the middle of fucking nowhere. The part of the border he wanted to cross was still an hour's drive away. He slowed only for the checkpoints, where underpaid soldiers sat and smoked and occasionally stopped him for a small bribe.

Muse's *Take a Bow* skipped a beat as he hit a big pothole, so he dialled down his speed to 120 km/h. Ahead, a low wall ringed a couple of farms, and a few signs advertised the wares for sale in the small speck of a town. He slowed, falling in behind a truck as the road narrowed, and then pulled into what appeared to be the dusty main street – not much more than a gas station, a few goat pens, a baker and general store, some kind of smoke house and a few date groves that were little more than stalactite holders in the cold.

Kolesnik paid the guy at the gas station US$10 to top up his SUV's tanks with diesel, and, with his backpack slung over his shoulder, went to take a piss in the abysmal lean-to toilet next to the concrete block hut. Walking back to the car, he didn't like the look the guy gave him, but he brushed it off and tore out of town. He left the road and headed up to a ridge that had good sight-lines and access; he let the car idle and left the heater on as he plugged his laptop and satellite dish into the Nissan's twin 12-volt outlets and logged onto the WoW site.

The web connection was slow but serviceable, and a mail symbol soon popped up on his screen. He ran his avatar to the mailbox: three new messages.

The first was from his Pakistani cell, known as Darkforcer: *'Location will be taken care of within 24 hours . . .'*

'Report when it's done,' he typed, knowing that gamers around the world sent messages just like these in this environment, with very different consequences.

He clicked to open his next message, from Shadowserpent: *'Done.'*

Simple, efficient work by the former Spetsnaz paratrooper who'd made a name for himself as a highly paid Special Forces consultant to several caucus armies before vanishing into obscurity somewhere in Greece. Omar Hasif was no more. Kolesnik knew he could rely on a compatriot.

The third message took a while to open, and he popped a Dr Pepper while he waited, absently tapping to the beat on the dashboard. Two large, overflowing Pakistani Army trucks rumbled along the road below him, headed towards the little town.

The final message popped up, from Darkshadow: *'Targets leaving location, destination unknown, will update ASAP. May need to outsource.'*

Kolesnik grimaced. He would have enjoyed killing Fox and Gammaldi himself. Whatever, the job would get done. He shut down and packed away his laptop, then put the car into gear and sped off.

17

NEW YORK CITY

'And you haven't been able to contact Omar Hasif?' Tas Wallace asked.

'No, nothing,' Fox said. The director of GSR always seemed to age a little when news like this came to him – his Scottish skin went a little paler, his white hair a little whiter – and Fox was conscious that he was the only bureau chief of GSR who continually had to break information like this to the boss.

'And Agent Hutchinson,' Wallace said into his speakerphone, 'you're saying you can't find Omar Hasif right now either?'

'That's right,' Hutchinson said from onboard the C38, a government-owned Gulfstream G100 that belonged to the Department of Homeland Security fleet. 'We've got the State Department tracking him down; his last known location is with his family.'

'When was that?'

'In country two days ago, from Pakistan.'

'Do you need more eyes looking for him?' Faith Williams asked. As Wallace's chief of staff she had thousands of names she could call on, scattered around the globe. 'I can get a contract security team in the field.'

'We'll find him; we've got local support assisting us.'

Fox wondered how good that support would be in Libya. He leaned forward and spoke into the phone. 'Might not hurt to have some extra eyes.'

'It won't matter,' Hutchinson replied, 'we'll turn him up ASAP.'

'Then what?' asked Wallace.

'We can only help him if he wants our help,' Hutchinson said. 'This imminent threat is cause for granting asylum, so it's there if he wants it.'

'What if he's heard about the hit?' Fox said. 'Maybe he's gone underground.'

'Then there ain't much we can do.'

'That's a good point, though,' Faith said. 'Maybe he can hide himself and his family better than you can hide him?'

'Ms Williams,' Hutchinson said, 'we're pretty good at hiding people.'

'What kind of support can you give our guys?' Wallace asked.

'The State Department has passports made up for Fox and Gammaldi reflecting official diplomatic cover,' Hutchinson said. 'That will give them the highest access to embassies that can be afforded to State Department employees. They'll be covered under the reciprocal diplomatic-immunity laws, and we can legally go in and provide protection to them akin to what our high-level diplomatic protectees get in places like Iraq.'

'So they'll have armed protection?'

'Yes. FBI agents are being readied, and we're working on providing on-the-ground assets in India ready to greet them on the tarmac and transport them. But make no mistake – and I'm sorry to be so blunt, Lachlan – you don't have many friends in the region since your stories have syndicated.'

'Yeah . . .' Fox said.

'What about contingencies?' Faith asked. 'What if the threat changes when they're in the field?'

'As we speak I have a team of agents readying to deploy,' Hutchinson said. 'They're heavy hitters. If things get heated, they'll exfil Lach and Al to the nearest friendly location for air evac.'

'Agent Hutchinson,' Faith said. 'Do you think they should stay here in New York?'

'Sure, maybe,' Hutchinson said. 'They can lie low. We can hide them – hell, we can give them new IDs if it comes to that. But I know Fox isn't for that – it's a lifelong thing, hiding like that.'

'It's fine, Andy, we're finishing this story,' Fox said. 'We're not going to let—'

'What's that?' Wallace interrupted, pointing to one of the flat-panel televisions: breaking news running on the BBC World News channel.

'A bomb blast in Libya . . .' Faith said.

They watched the screen.

'I've got another call coming in,' Hutchinson said. 'Hang on the line.'

Scenes of panic filled the screen in all-too-familiar images of smoke fumes and the burning wreckage of a car. A suburban street. Wallace, Faith and Fox watched in silence, their thoughts all beginning to head in the same direction—

Hutchinson came back on the line.

'It's our man – he's okay.'

'Hasif?' Fox asked.

'Yep, he's at our embassy in Tripoli right now, and he's asking for asylum,' he replied. 'His family, too; his wife and kid, and his sister; we should be able to take them in, too. He headed there right after the attack, didn't even wait for the cops to show at the scene. His brother-in-law was killed – a car bomb, in Hasif's car. It should have been him.'

Fox looked at Wallace and Faith but spoke to Hutchinson. 'I need to talk to him before I head back to Kashmir. I've got to find out what else he knows.'

'All right,' Hutchinson said. 'They're headed Stateside via a military base in Spain, where they'll get another medical. Debrief him there, then let me know where the story takes you.'

Fox looked at his boss. The older man nodded. Faith looked reluctant.

'We'll leave for Spain within the hour,' Fox said. 'Call me back with details.'

'Will do.'

'And Andy?' Fox said, leaning close to the phone. 'What if we let it get out that it wasn't his brother-in-law killed in the blast?' Fox said. 'We let everyone think it was Hasif. These guys will think they got their man – it'll take the heat off.'

Silence from the other end.

'Andy?'

'That's good,' Hutchinson said. 'I'm about to land in DC. I'll work on that from my end.'

18

THE WHITE HOUSE, WASHINGTON DC

Bill McCorkell walked up the stairs from the Situation Room, said goodbye to the National Security Advisor and walked through to the foyer and along the expansive Cross Hall. He could tell that the new guy, who had taken over from McCorkell just a month ago, had pulled an all-nighter. A former four-star Marine General, he was right for the job; a good, strong military choice for a young President whose insight and intelligence outweighed what shortfalls he might be perceived as having on the national security front. Not that any person in this building wouldn't bleed on the flag to keep the stripes red.

McCorkell didn't miss his former job, nor did he miss working in this building – although he had hardly gone far; just across the street. He didn't miss the National Security Council meetings and all that preparation and wrangling, didn't miss riding in the Bubble – that ever present inner sanctum of Presidential senior staff – at all hours, being in the eye of the storm . . . didn't miss much of anything. He'd done his time, far more than most, and at fifty-four he was easing himself out of this life. Academic and thinktank offers were piling up in his office back home, a space already knee-deep with requests for him to serve on boards and write books: it was all a promise of an easy time and easy money, but he didn't want either, not yet. While he still had good advice to give the President of the United States, he would stick around. Working on the golf handicap would have to wait a little longer.

As he walked out of the White House McCorkell passed the President's body-man and offered a closed-fist high-five greeting. The 6"2' former wide receiver and college basketball star was also a Poli-Sci graduate from Duke who had secured an aide's job in Obama's Senate office and been with him ever since. Valet, confidant, PA, butler, work-out partner and general buddy to POTUS, this twenty-something year old reset the bar of exceptional service; he had a 24/7 work ethic beyond most others in the House.

'Hey L-Train,' McCorkell said to him, 'how's it treating you?'

'Good, B McC, this is the good life,' he replied with a grin, already heading back to the President, from whom he was usually no more than a few paces. 'You ready for that rematch?'

'I think my basketball glory days came to an end after that one and only comeback.'

'Too bad, old man, you had some skills.'

McCorkell smiled as he passed security at the Western exit. It was invigorating to see so much enthusiasm among the executive staff. Sure, it was still honeymoon days for the Obama Administration, but there was a gloss here that wasn't going to tarnish in a hurry, credit crisis be damned.

McCorkell's new office was in the Eisenhower Executive Offices Building next door to the White House. He walked across West Executive Avenue, holding his jacket collar up against the cold, and into the huge nineteenth century granite building – an imposing presence compared with the understated tack-on structure that was the West Wing of the White House. The EEOB housed the bulk of the offices of the Executive Branch staff, and there was a constant stream of junior staff assistants shuttling back and forth to the White House – not a sought-after duty on a cold February day.

The title on his door gave away very little about who McCorkell was, beyond 'Special Assistant to the President'. Dozens of staff in this building and the West Wing of the White House had such a title, and their roles were as varied as Special Assistant to the President for Legislative Affairs; for Speechwriting; for Domestic Policy. McCorkell's field of expertise was national security in all its guises, and he had agreed to stay on into this next administration on a year-by-year contract. Technically it was a couple of rungs below his previous post as Assistant to the President, but this was a Presidency that looked for all the world to be a shift in historical significance beyond the ordinary; and no Presidency was ordinary by any means.

This morning's brief was something he had worked for months on – an update on the peace in Georgia following the flare-up during the 2008 Olympics. Sarkozy had brokered peace in the spotlight while McCorkell organised a serious US military presence in the region, a presence serious enough to back the Frenchman's words. McCorkell knew from decades of experience that when the bad guys received intel that the United States were prepared to intervene with armour, air power and a wall of steel on the sea, they usually relented. And Russia was no different; the flames from the Kremlin were dampened.

As he took the stairs to his second-floor office he was saluted by a guy coming down the stairs, unlit cigar in the corner of his mouth.

'Hey Tony,' McCorkell said, shaking hands with the National Intelligence Agency man.

'Hey Bill. Thought you'd be out on the driving range.'

'Can't get rid of me that easily,' McCorkell replied.

'Yeah, you know this place, once they get you . . .'

'They don't like to let you go . . .' McCorkell conceded with a smile. 'What you up to?'

'Just briefed the VP on South Ossetia,' Tony Niemann said quietly. Until recently, he had been a deputy director at the CIA; now he was the White House National Intelligence Agency liaison, where he oversaw and coordinated all intelligence agencies that fell under that jurisdiction. 'A bunch of stuff has come up, some arms and personnel deals that may cause more heat with Georgia, and our NATO exercises are pissing off the Russians.'

'Funny that.'

'Yeah. We've got a State Department and EU delegation meeting on the ground in Gori today.'

'Oh yeah?' McCorkell said, the two moving close to the wall to let people pass on the busy staircase. He gestured upstairs in the vague direction of his office: 'Walk and talk?'

'Yeah, then I gotta get to a thing,' Niemann replied, following McCorkell up the stairs. 'I read your brief on DoD working on putting UN boots in there instead of NATO.'

'UN, EU – or more specifically cutting back US numbers – moving us back to our pre-war levels of training support.'

'Which the VP has been championing,' Niemann said, still in hushed tones. 'The situation's a real cluster fuck: all the usual Russian military and political bullshit, and now we've got evidence of a bunch of private outfits giving militants a helping hand.'

'Russian?'

'Mainly,' Niemann replied. 'This is becoming a private war as much as a political and military one. There's gas and oil pipelines involved, so we're talking some big commercial players who are keen on protecting their assets, like Umbra Corp's contractors, who are mainly—'

'Ex-Russian Special Forces guys from Chechnya. I'm up with it,' McCorkell said, scratching around the back of his collar as they paused at the first floor landing. 'Wanna grab a coffee, chew it over for a bit?'

'I'm good. I've got to get to that thing,' Niemann said, looked around.

'Anything I can help out on, you just need to say hey, okay? Remember, you can't win them all. I won't be walking the halls around here forever, you know . . .'

'Yeah, thanks, we got it,' Tony said and checked his watch as two Army officers passed them on the stairs with a nod. 'Although . . . Yeah, how about that coffee? Something else has popped up that would be good to run by you.'

'Sure,' McCorkell said, and led the way to his office as his cell phone rang.

19

JFK AIRPORT, NEW YORK

'Okay, thanks,' Fox said and ended the call. He turned to Gammaldi.

'Bill McCorkell sends his love.' Fox tucked his iPhone away and not for the first time found himself thankful that they had a friend with so much clout in the White House. Almost like a brother to Tas Wallace, McCorkell had been instrumental in several big GSR investigations and it was a relationship that had literally saved many lives in recent years. Not that any of the finer details would make the press.

'Nice, what a lovely guy,' Gammaldi replied. 'You surprised he's still working in the executive branch?'

'Nah,' Fox said, holding onto the oh-shit handle as he rode in the back seat of the fast-moving SUV. Gammaldi sat next to him, two GSR security guys up front. 'Bill's worked for a few admins now, couldn't imagine he'd sit out on this one.'

Eyal Geiger pulled hard into JFK's Hangar 12, the tyres of the Mercedes 320 BlueTEC squealing on the painted concrete floor. The whole fleet of GSR vehicles had switched to BlueTECs for the grunt work, their new-technology diesel engines even cleaner than petrol–electric hybrids. Sure, there was cleaner tech available like hydrogen-cell fleet vehicles that emitted nothing but H_2O, but outside LA there were too few filling stations. All emissions for the entire GSR fleet of vehicles – plus all the air miles travelled via the leased jets and the thousands of commercial seats they used each year – were offset by the hundreds of acres of woods on Tas Wallace's Connecticut farm, plus a large parcel of former mining land the company had bought in Canada and was reforesting.

'He'll work on getting us clearance to land at the US military airport in Spain,' Fox said. Gammaldi looked at him with a raised eyebrow as they got out of the car. 'What? McCorkell will get it done – he's still got pull.'

Fox and Gammaldi walked towards their G650, backpacks over their shoulders, followed by Geiger and Goldsmith. As another Gulfstream pulled into the hangar Fox saw Gammaldi's face light up.

'What's with you?' Fox asked him as the security men loaded the bags.

Before Gammaldi could answer, the door to the newly arrived jet opened and a few GSR staff poured out, led by security operator Emma Gibbs. She and Gammaldi came together slowly and hugged, then kissed.

'You guys are sick,' Fox said as he walked past them and shook hands with a few reporters returning from their tour in the Middle East. GSR was good at rotating their overseas bureaus and on-the-ground hot-spot teams, constantly streaming back and forth from Afghanistan and Iraq and Gaza for the most part, relieving stressed personnel while maintaining good on-the-ground and company-wide knowledge. And as other news agencies tightened their belts GSR picked up more and

more outsourced work, advancing the company's good name
and facilitating a broader public awareness, thanks in no small
part to Fox's endeavours. Not quite two years in the job and it
felt like many a lifetime.

'Where are you boys heading?' Emma asked, taking her bags
from the ground crew.

'Spain,' Fox said.

'Then India,' Gammaldi added. 'Back within a week.'

Emma's gaze fell over their shoulders, and Fox turned to see
Geiger and Goldsmith loading their weapons cases and several
bags of US military field rations onto the G650. She looked at
Gammaldi, who flushed a little, and then she looked at Fox,
questioning.

'I'll leave you two to catch up,' Fox said, beetling off to help
finish loading their aircraft.

•

Emma Gibbs was a security member with GSR, a specialist
sniper to whom Al had been engaged for the past few months.
She didn't take well to the news of the death threat.

'It'll be a quick trip,' Gammaldi said, looking into her eyes.
She was strong and didn't need consoling, but that was double-
edged: she knew the risks – too well.

'You don't need to go,' Gibbs said. 'You're a pilot, not a
reporter.'

'Lach needs me.'

She didn't say, 'And what about me?' She didn't need to.

'I won't be long,' Gammaldi said, taking her hand and
brushing a wisp of her shoulder-length mousy hair behind
her ear.

'It's not that . . .' she said.

'Just don't go spending *all* our savings on the wedding,' Gammaldi said with a big grin, but she wasn't buying into it. 'Seriously, two hundred people max.'

'It's not that either . . .'

'I won't come back with black eyes or broken bones, I promise. Eyal and Rob'll be with us the whole time,' Gammaldi said. 'What? What's wrong?'

She looked up at him, her eyes no longer showing concern. She took his hand.

'What?'

She smiled a little.

'What?' he asked, confused. 'You're killing me . . .'

•

Fox buckled into the copilot seat and Gammaldi was ready at the controls. They'd said their goodbyes, and Gammaldi had hurried around the outside of the G650 doing his preflight, checking visually for any wear or tear on the tyres, joins, seams and flaps – these new aircraft used metal bonding instead of rivets, more aerodynamic and carefree – and fluid leaks. The G650 taxied out of the hangar, as smooth a ride as their SUV, and headed towards runway 4R-22L to await take-off. Gammaldi adjusted and quadruple-checked flight instruments as he went. He was grinning from ear to ear. Fox looked at him sideways.

'What the hell's up with you?'

A smiled played at Gammaldi's lips as he toggled the interior lighting on and off.

'You're creeping me out with this chipper mood,' Fox said, looking out the windows at the JetBlue, Qantas and United aircraft that were coming in to land in tandem on the parallel runways; at this organised chaos of an airport sometimes the aircraft seemed so close you could reach out the window and touch them.

'Fine, suit yourself,' Fox said, adjusting his seatbelt. They sat in silence for a few minutes as they waited in line for their turn on the smaller of JFK's runways.

'So,' Gammaldi said, looked at Fox deadpan. 'What MREs were packed?'

'How the hell do I know?' Fox answered, adjusting his headset. Meal, Ready to Eat was the ration pack of today's US military force, from whom GSR logistics purchased supplies for their remote-post staff – plastic bricks stuffed with twenty-four hours' worth of food that a soldier – or in GSR's case, a hungry reporter, photographer, fixer, diver or security contractor – would need. MREs ranged from edible to non-edible, with not much in between save for the improvements Tabasco sauce could make. A two-word review would read: 'calories, portable'.

'This army travels on his stomach,' Gammaldi said, patting his gut. He was several inches shorter than Fox and never seemed to stop eating, energy that was usually burned lifting heavy weights. To boot, he had recently shaved his black hair down to his skull – he could pass as a silverback, Fox thought.

'Al, you're going to have to travel around everywhere on your stomach if you don't pick up the cardio.'

'Ah, the wise, lean Fox slays me again.'

'Well,' Fox said, 'if you're so concerned about us lugging in MREs, you could have checked it out instead of playing tonsil catch-up with your lady.'

'Yeah, well, at least I have—'

He stopped himself and Fox punched him in the arm.

'Okay, I deserved that . . . almost,' Gammaldi said. 'Anyway, corned beef, hash, biscuits and paté – that's the bomb of MREs.'

'Dude, corned beef and hash is the devil's own vomit in a foil bag, and the paté is like cat food,' Fox said, laughing. 'Your guts are made of rope.'

'So, what, you're all Chicken Tetrazzini?'

'Actually, I think they stopped making them.'

'Oh, what a pity,' Gammaldi said, adjusting his head gear.

'Well, at least I didn't cry about it like you did when the Jambalaya went out.'

'It was an emotional day,' Gammaldi said, flicking on the seatbelt light in the rear of the aircraft for the two security men. 'Anyway, so long as they gave us some with those jalapeño cheese spread things, I'll be happy.'

'Yeah, well, the greatest thing about MREs is still the lemon pound cake,' Fox said, taking a drink of water from a bottle. 'No contest, nothing comes close.'

'Freak,' Gammaldi said and nudged the aircraft forward as another took off; they were now next in line. He took a HOOAH! chocolate bar from a bag by his side and barely got the package off before chomping on it. He looked across at Fox with more than the usual amount of mischief in his eyes.

'What?' said Fox.

'What yourself,' replied Gammaldi, smiling.

'Come on, spill: what are you so damn happy about?'

Gammaldi demolished the last of his bar, adjusted his seatbelt and earphones and looked out the front window.

'Nothing my best man needs to know right now.'

'What the hell does that mean?'

Fox squinted at his mate, who looked back at him, amused, so Fox squinted harder and Gammaldi laughed.

'You look like Brad Pitt in *Burn After Reading*,' Gammaldi said. 'You know, that scene where he's in the car with John Malkovich trying to sell him back his secret spy shit.'

They were both laughing as the call came in with their take-off clearance. Al replied and started the final turn to approach the runway, where he moved into take-off, gunning the twin Rolls Royce BR725 engines as the aircraft turned on a dime and took off into the headwind within seconds.

'I *am* going to get to the bottom of whatever is going on with you by the end of this trip,' Fox said as they began banking hard to starboard, the thrust of 17 000 pounds-force per engine forcing him back into his seat.

'Mate, knock yourself out.'

20

KOCHI, INDIA

Kolesnik walked up the single flight of stairs and followed the numbers down the hallway. The apartment complex was nineties style: low-rise, middle-class, harbour-fronted. The only aspect that reflected the country he was in was the smell of Indian cooking; otherwise, he could be anywhere in the world. The hallway was empty as he inserted a lock-pick in the single tumbler; he was inside Art Kneeshaw's apartment as quickly as if he had used a key.

In a single, swift motion he took his pistol from his jacket pocket: the Glock 26 fitted neatly into his hand, a little front-heavy with a Gemtech suppressor screwed in. He clicked the door closed gently behind him and walked softly, his rubber-soled boots silent as he scanned the dark room.

Silence. No one home. He tucked the pistol into the back of his belt.

He worked quickly, going through Kneeshaw's things, aided only by a pen light. He quickly noticed a pattern of gaps: between the luggage on the top shelf of the wardrobe, between the uniformly spaced hanging clothes. Kneeshaw had left in a hurry. Kolesnik closed the wardrobe and walked through to the study, where he spent fifteen minutes checking for documents on the water project, unrolling blueprints and then stuffing them back in their box. Nothing. He opened the curtains in the lounge room to let some rays through the windows. The place was clean. There was nothing on the water project, nothing at all.

Kolesnik inspected the closed-in balcony; it was glazed like a greenhouse with a dining table and bench seat covered with tomato and cucumber plants, dozens of them. There were tomatoes of so many colours – blacks, vivid greens, striped, orange, bright yellow, crimson – that Kolesnik had never seen in such fruit. He poked his finger into the soil of a potted plant – it was dry, but not bone-dry; it had been watered this week. He picked off a large black tomato and sniffed it – it smelled ripe. He bit into it as he would an apple – it was juicy and sweet. He ate it as he poked around the apartment. In the kitchen he opened the fridge – the power was still on, and nothing was rotten. He took a bottle of grape juice and sat on the couch.

As he drank he noticed marks on the walls, from where frames had once hung. Now, thought Kolesnik, why would Kneeshaw take his . . . The frames were in the bin, all emptied. He was travelling light. He wasn't coming back—

Kolesnik heard a key in the door and slipped through to the study. He grabbed the box of blueprints and returned to the lounge room a few seconds later, his aimed gun concealed behind the box.

The man – Indian, mid-forties – looked as surprised as shit, wide-eyed. He clearly wasn't expecting company.

'Art left some things of mine here,' Kolesnik said casually, with a smile. 'Asked me to pick them up.'

'Oh,' the guy said, looking a little more relaxed. 'He didn't tell me – you need a hand?'

'No,' Kolesnik said, tucking the pistol into the belt at the small of his back, under his jacket, as he walked towards the door. 'Oh,' he added, turning back, 'did he leave a forwarding address with you? I only have his cell number.'

'No,' the guy said, shaking his head. 'He left a note under my door last night saying he wouldn't be back.' He looked around the room, perhaps calculating how much all this stuff would be worth.

Kolesnik nodded thanks and walked out, dumping the box of plans as soon as he made it outside. He headed for his car.

21

EEOB, WASHINGTON DC

McCorkell was making his sojourn back from a West Wing meeting when his cell phone chimed with a local page. His secretary, Anne. All White House and senior executive cell phones had this local paging function, delivered via an encrypted internal wireless network.

'Yes?'

'Good morning, Bill, you have Special Agent—'

McCorkell walked into his office foyer and she stopped talking into the phone. McCorkell saw a guy sitting in wait there.

'This is Special Agent Andrew Hutchinson of the FBI.'

McCorkell nodded his thanks, and Anne handed him his messages and mail before leaving to make tea.

'Mr McCorkell,' Hutchinson said, standing and offering his hand.

'Call me Bill,' replied McCorkell with a firm handshake. 'Come on through.'

McCorkell motioned Hutchinson to a chair while he flicked though his mail and added it to the overnight pile already on his desk.

'How do I know your name?'

'We spoke late last year about the Umbra connection to—'

'Michael Rollins,' McCorkell finished.

'Yes. Nigeria. And Steve Mendes, former CIA shooter turned Umbra employee.'

'I remember,' McCorkell nodded, taking off his jacket and hanging it over the back of his chair. He cleared some room from his pile of notes on the Russia–Georgia situation and then sat down. 'I've got an eleven o'clock – most people make appointments around here.'

'I know, I rang on the way in from the airport. You've got a few minutes,' Hutchinson said.

'I'm ribbing you. I did my time in the Bureau, spent most of it overseas,' McCorkell said with a smile as he fingered his tie and collar button loose. 'This is about Fox?'

Hutchinson nodded. McCorkell's secretary came in with his tea – Irish Breakfast in a pot, his old rowing mug on the small tray – and a coffee for Hutchinson.

'Thanks,' McCorkell said, pouring tea and milk.

'Bill, DoD just rang. GSR Gulfstream has permission to land at Morón Air Base in Spain.'

'Thanks, I'll let them know,' McCorkell said, tapping an email into his computer.

She nodded and left, closing the door behind her.

'So, where are you at with the Bureau – National Security Branch?'

Hutchinson nodded, took a sip of his coffee.

'Counter-espionage, CT—'

'Ops Two?'

'Yes.'

'TFOS?'

Operations II included three sections: Weapons of Mass Destruction and Domestic Terrorism; Communications Exploitation Section; and Terrorist Financing Operations Section – TFOS – the latter of which, McCorkell knew, had been putting huge resources into the Magellan fuck-ups that had led to Umbra and its unique strength. Magellan was a CIA-instigated NATO operation; they'd managed to pick up a lot of Russian spooks who found themselves unemployed after the USSR collapsed, but many slipped through and went on to the more lucrative work of applying their skills to crime, Umbra being the most organised of these alumni.

'I'm mainly responsible for finding links between terrorist and national security dangers abroad and finding threats from within here at home,' Hutchinson said. 'It's a bit of an open slate. Right now, all focus is on Umbra.'

'So *you're* running that unit?'

'Yes.'

It was McCorkell's turn to nod. He knew about this man, knew about his mission. He had pushed to help get it established after a few serious flaws in the intel community were raised after 9/11. Hutchinson was part internal affairs cop to the nation's intelligence agencies, while working across every national security department and overseas ally to shake up entrenched networks of crooked spooks. McCorkell knew that Hutchinson's outfit, formed in relative secrecy after the 9/11 commission's findings, did much more than appease those on the Hill who were calling for carte blanche reform of the intel community – these guys got results, big-scale, measurable ones. They were part of the new model of what could be achieved in twenty-first century intelligence.

'Bill,' Hutchinson said over the steam of his coffee, 'I met with Lachlan Fox this morning.'

'About his water story?'

'Roundabout.'

'Tas Wallace is an old friend of mine,' said McCorkell. 'I'm in the loop on your recruitment efforts to get Fox to pick up on some of Michael Rollins' investigative work.'

'We don't have to worry about any of that now.'

'Oh?'

'Umbra – they're coming after him.'

'How?'

'International hit list, looks like they're freelancing it. Six targets: one down already, an attempt on another one failed, and another one not on our list got hit,' Hutchinson said. 'We intercepted the intel overnight.'

'Jesus . . .' McCorkell put down his tea and looked absently towards the world map that was framed on the wall to his right. 'You think this goes back to Roman Babich?'

'Fox has made a lot of waves for him and his company, and at the very least it's pissed off his friends.'

'But you've got nothing to pin on him.'

Hutchinson shook his head: 'You know the score.'

'What's Fox hoping to find?'

'Hopefully not too much trouble. He's going back, right now, to file more story, see what he missed the first time around.'

'He's like that,' McCorkell said. 'What are you doing?'

Hutchinson sat forward in his chair. 'We know Babich has good access inside the CIA,' Hutchinson said. 'I'm meeting with them straight after this. This is a once in a lifetime chance to draw them out—'

'And use that leverage to get something concrete on Babich?'

'It's the best shot we've ever had. Forget his wealth and companies, he's got people everywhere. He's an ex-spook who knows the score and how to play. We've got courts in several countries willing to try him – we just need to keep probing, keep bugging him, force him into further action, into making mistakes that are big enough to catch him out.'

'And Fox is your man?'

'Could be.'

'And what do you want from me?'

22

GORI, GEORGIA (EASTERN EUROPE)

Petro Sirko's cell phone beeped a designated tone: a new text message from Roman Babich. The contents of the SMS were disappointing – a job in Spain; two targets. Disappointing that it was work again, disappointing that he was being used as a back-up option, disappointing that until last night Babich had not contacted him for, what, more than six months? But interesting that he had already been booked for the Spain job by another source; that meant two separate pay cheques. Time would be an issue; it would be very tight getting to Spain and setting up, but then he would charge accordingly.

Sirko wore a Georgian police uniform and was sweating despite the cold. He dried his hands on the uniform and put the phone back in his pocket. In the other pocket rested a little plastic box. He ran a hand through his thinning brown hair and kept walking towards the square in the centre of town.

Having two sets of orders at once was not new to him – it had happened in Chechnya all the time – but it was odd that Babich and Kolesnik wanted the same targets eliminated. Sirko smiled. Kolesnik. The prodigal son. Babich's hatchet man. His brother-in-arms and his competitor must really be in a jam.

He walked across the cobbled square past a beautiful young woman being filmed by a young guy. She had long dark tresses and the kind of big brown eyes, pouty lips and porcelain skin that got most men into trouble – but not him. He preferred looking at the guy taking the video – her brother perhaps. Young, lean, just a hint of facial hair. Sirko watched him as he guided his sister, filming away in front of the statue of Stalin. Probably after some kind of artistic juxtaposition: beauty and the beast, gorgeous purity versus ugly monster. He had met such monsters.

As he'd left his hotel he'd heard about the confirmation of his Omar Hasif hit in Tripoli. He had planted a brick of C4 on the vehicle when it was still at the dealership, timed it to go off the tenth time the ignition was started. He couldn't wait around for the ID afterwards – he'd had to hightail it to Georgia for this job – but *Fox News* had named the deceased, God bless them. He believed that results spoke for themselves, and unlike Kolesnik, he preferred work that went boom.

Even though this job in Georgia was last minute, he'd managed to plant the bomb in plenty of time – no need to worry about the counter-sniper protection the Americans insisted on when they transported senior politicians. He was just here to positively ID the entry of the targets, which he had just done using the intel supplied by the Washington contact, and detonate the device.

Two successes in twenty-four hours, and another one around the corner. Soon, it would be time to create a successful mission of his own. No outsourcing, no instructions, no payment. His job. His target.

Sirko's phone beeped with another message: his jet aircraft was waiting for take-off on the tarmac. He walked faster towards the motorbike he had parked around the corner. He would be in the air in five minutes.

Sirko smiled. He had been surprised by the message last night: Babich had gone through a repass recently, putting this kind of activity on the backburner, relying more on his divisional heads to control his business interests, using silver instead of lead. This situation must be really out of hand to be bringing back these old ways with such urgency – Sirko knew this was his opportunity.

He had helped set up Babich's security in Lake Como – he knew Babich's movements, the frequency channels the security guys used to communicate, the features of the safehouse and the location of the fall-back cash stash. It made him sick with envy to see those untold millions of dollars and euros and pounds. Here he was, doing contract jobs, private security on the side, mainly for wealthy Russians like Babich who were happy to take their cash and get out of Russia, set up new lives filled with soccer clubs and Ferraris and young girls. All that bullshit, the easy, painless lives of the rich, while he worked and worked and made do, but only just. Even Kolesnik took a cut from the jobs he outsourced to Sirko . . . Kolesnik, once a friend, a brother. But one day soon Sirko would get a break.

Still, he was here and had a job to complete. The delegation of Americans had arrived in their typically high-visibility convoy; representatives from the EU were in rental and embassy cars. He was almost five hundred metres away when he hit the button in the radio-controlled detonator.

After the deafening blast, glass, dust and debris drifted out in a sandstorm-like cloud from the Town Hall. He turned to see the statue of Stalin shrouded; pity he hadn't thought to take that out as well. People close by lay still in the street; the brother helped his sister to her feet, both unharmed. As people began to run and scream and a siren started somewhere, he turned and headed west, following the sun to his next location.

23

NEBRASKA AVENUE COMPLEX, WASHINGTON DC

It wasn't the last place on earth he wanted to be, but he really didn't have time for the cab commute, particularly in lunch time traffic. Hutchinson was meeting the CIA men on neutral ground – the headquarters of the Department of Homeland Security.

They finally arrived, and he walked through the lobby, took the stairs and was puffing by the time he reached the third floor of the former naval facility. The hallways were busy; each one of the two dozen temporarily leased DC sites were overcrowded and disjointed, and it was clear that the staff were itching to relocate to their new headquarters: a sprawling campus out at St Elizabeths Hospital, Anacostia.

Hutchinson would have preferred to have his whole team in on the briefing, a show of force that the Bureau was serious about breaking the back of this counter-espionage case. Since last year's terrorist attacks at the Louisiana Offshore Oil Port and the White House, Hutchinson's staff had gone from twelve to thirty-two – some ex-CIA agents had been involved, and some current members may be compromised. His Originals – as he liked to think of the first Special Agents who'd come on board – were all seasoned Bureau vets who'd worked mob cases. For over a year now they had compiled intel on Umbra that was up 3000 per cent on what the FBI and CIA had gathered over the past decade and a half. Their investigation was codenamed UMBRA after the founding of the corporation had revealed that most of its senior staff were ex-KGB and FSB officers of interest to international agencies. The US and UK joint taskforce at the time had labelled the group thus and it had stuck.

Michael Rollins, an investigative journalist for GSR who'd managed to infiltrate Umbra by working undercover, had been working a major investigative story from the inside while posing as one of them. So convincing had he been, he'd flagged security and had been taken by a CIA rendition team to Afghanistan. While the erroneous nature of his rendition was being worked out by GSR, he'd been busted out of prison by the very group of men who he sought to take down: Umbra. It was a pity he hadn't lived long enough to finish his investigation, but what little he did leave behind was something to add to the case, at least. And that was just the half of it.

Hutchinson walked into a glass-walled meeting room purpose-built in the centre of a large open-plan room; the meeting room was soundproofed with anti-eavesdropping technology. The senior CIA agent who ran the desk on Umbra, Ryan Kavanaugh, and his deputy, James Riley, were both talking rapid-fire on landline phones. McCorkell shut the door behind him, took a seat at the conference table and poured a coffee.

Riley was regarded as a real up and comer in the Agency and had a reputation as a hothead with a good analytical pedigree. He was dressed in a stockbroker shirt and suit reminiscent of Gordon Gekko, complete with short, dark hair neatly parted in a Mark Wahlberg hip kind of way. Like Kavanaugh, he was some kind of cyber geek.

Red-haired Kavanaugh dressed more like Hutchinson, complete with crumpled dress shirt, collar undone and tie loosened from the neck by a finger or two. He'd started out as a Manhattan lawyer and then entered government service for patriotic reasons. He'd since been around the block at the Agency, including hands-on door-kicking work in the War on Terror, but word was he'd lifted his foot off the gas of his stellar career trajectory when he turned down a couple of station-chief posts.

Riley and Kavanaugh reported to the Director of the National Clandestine Service. The NCS was the new-look Directorate of Operations; they were the agents on the ground, the field spooks, those at embassies around the world under official diplomatic cover. Those guys and girls with Non Official Covers, usually posing as journalists, members of non-governmental organisations or business executives, were very small in number, less than ten per cent of the Agency's twenty-five thousand workforce of human intelligence officers. There were two training grounds for these agents: The Farm on the York River in Virginia, and The Point in North Carolina. The Farm grew 'em, the Point sharpened 'em. Hutchinson had trained at both, a rarity for a Bureau man, necessitated by his specialist skill in knowing America's spooks better than anyone. He'd met Kavanaugh at The Farm, back when they were both fresh business-school grad students, although Hutchinson already had three years at the Bureau under his belt.

Riley hung up his phone, didn't bother extending a hand. 'Andy, how you doing?' he said.

'Been better,' Hutchinson replied.

'How's the Hanssen case going for you guys?'

'Great, thanks for asking,' he replied with a mock smile, sipped his coffee. The phone next to Riley rang again. He picked it up, spoke, listened intently. Hutchinson checked his cell phone – no signal; this room was a virtual vault for anything transmitted, nothing in and nothing out.

Robert Philip Hanssen, a veteran FBI counter-intelligence agent, was arrested by the FBI in 2001 and charged with espionage. Hanssen was caught clandestinely placing a package containing highly classified information at a pre-arranged dead-drop site for pick-up by his Russian handlers. Hutchinson had watched the arrest from afar, his anger too palpable to be in the immediate vicinity of a guy who had undermined so much of his work. Traitors like Hanssen were what kept Hutchinson going forward, and it kept Agency men around him on guard; maybe they were thinking what he did at times: Why did it take so long for the FBI to catch a mole who had operated with impunity within its ranks for so long?

'Tip of the iceberg, that traitor,' Riley said with a big shit-eating grin. 'A betrayal by a man sworn to protect our nation's security . . . Man, that must be a killer.'

Hutchinson forced himself to smile at the barb. He could have retorted with the arrest of CIA agent Harold Nicholson, a former station chief, the highest-ranking CIA official ever to be charged with espionage; he had been caught selling information to Russian intelligence . . . but Hutchinson wasn't much liked in the CIA, and he needed to get on with these men here today.

'Shit, is Rare Breed ever going to get off the phone?' Hutchinson asked. Kavanaugh signalled that he was winding up the call. 'I've got a tight schedule. We don't try and run down Uncle Sam's clock like you boys.'

'Yeah,' Riley said, 'plenty of counter-espionage work you got to get back to doing, I'm sure. Forget looking after the country, you just concentrate on making life harder for your own.'

'What, you don't think we're doing this good work to free up the agencies for national defence work?' Hutchinson said with a smile of his own and checked his watch in a way that got the message to Kavanaugh, who finally hung up the phone. 'Anyway, this is a policing matter.'

'Yeah, well, justice delayed . . .' Riley said. He flicked a switch on the table and the glass walls of the room went opaque – they couldn't see out, no one could see in. On a projector running from his laptop he brought up a file sheet of the Umbra case, complete with a photo of Babich as the head of a family tree – side bars ran to Russian politicians and several other oligarchs. Babich was connected; on the surface it looked legit.

Hutchinson pulled out the file on Fox he had brought, passed it over the table and watched as Riley skimmed it.

'This is the guy on the hit list?' Riley asked.

'Yep.'

'And he's en route to Spain right now?'

Hutchinson held back on looking surprised.

'Oh, I'm sorry, haven't we been introduced?' Riley said. 'We're with the CIA.'

'Andy, you know we're all over this Umbra stuff . . . you looking at this?' Kavanaugh asked, pointing with a laser pointer at Umbra's company listings on the screen.

'Yeah, I'm looking,' Hutchinson said, scanning the branches that led off to the company's water, gas and oil, arms, telco and media divisions. 'Good job, looks pretty, but you got anything new in there?'

'It's a work in progress,' Kavanaugh replied. He put the pointer down. 'So, where'd you get the intel for this hit list?'

'I'll have details sent through to your office,' Hutchinson replied, knowing that no real detail on the sources would make it to Kavanaugh's desk.

'And they already took out some targets?'

'Yep.'

'You know who's hunting?'

'Not yet.'

'Any chance we can sit back and see who comes for him, this Fox guy?'

Hutchinson cringed. 'I've got him working on this,' he said. 'Fox has been digging at Babich, as deep into Umbra's dirty deeds as any assets we or our allies have.'

'Big call.'

'He's got skills that'll be useful.'

'And you're trusting him,' Riley said with a sideways look at his colleague. 'Just like that, you bring him into the fold? He's going to do what we couldn't do in all these years?'

'Sorry about that, didn't realise the Agency wanted Umbra picked apart,' Hutchinson said, saving his most condescending tone for: 'Shit, if that was your goal all along, why aren't you doing it already?'

Riley's neck flushed with anger.

'The Umbra list,' Hutchinson said, pointing to the 'family' tree. 'You got anyone in there you wanna tell me about? Any assets that can help us?'

'Maybe. Maybe not,' Riley said. He leaned forward, spoke right at Hutchinson. 'Maybe go fuck yourselves.'

'I'll be sure to pass that on to my director.'

'If he can get his dick out of the ass of your Exec AD of the National Security Branch.'

'Nice picture, thanks.'

'Babich – his money's in a lot of dark holes,' Kavanaugh said. Riley laughed. 'He's got guys in his private security division paying for weapons that could be used against the US, certainly in situations that pose a clear and present danger against NATO and our allies.'

'He's in it up to his neck,' Riley said. 'Look at South Ossetia, Georgia, Russia's own caucuses, Chechnya and such. No qualms about arming others too – Poland, the Ukraine. He's not letting his lieutenants run shit for him without knowing about it. He arms militias and extremists and he kicks up trouble – that sort of instability affects his energy side of things, his gas pipelines and such, driving prices up – and Umbra has always made big profits out of conflicts, in every area that they operate in.'

'Some deals we know are on the down-low from a Russian press POV – usually Babich is a media whore; selling military gear to the Ukrainians certainly isn't something he lets out to become public knowledge.' Kavanaugh said. 'The Russian politicos know he's doing it, and he's put a lot of them in power, so they're not going to give up their meal ticket.'

'He must have pissed off someone in there, surely,' Hutchinson said. 'Someone who gives a shit about what he's doing?'

'No one who'll stick their neck out for you. Babich has made the right men rich, you know the drill. Conflict, like South Ossetia and that pipeline, means big money; disaster and destruction mean dollars or euros or gold, whatever the fuck he trades in.'

'What about water?'

'He pulls the strings of the Russian water minister,' Riley said. 'The guy used to be his VP for Russian press affairs, so he's sewn that up. Provides water for most of the big Russian cities, building desalination plants in the Persian Gulf and Africa, making his empire bigger, but there's a few other biggies in Russia who've got their fingers in the energy industry too, bigger players.'

'He tried to buy into the Nigerian coup last year,' Kavanaugh said. 'Would have seen him becoming a serious player in world crude but that fell through. I think he sees water as being less of a hot topic, less risk all round, less complicated, so he's all in.'

'He set up an ex-FSB guy as a pro-Russia President of Chechnya two years ago,' Riley added. 'That didn't work out so well either; so, he gambles big and it doesn't always pay, but he's good enough to appear cleaner than most.'

'Yeah, well, anyway, an FYI?' Hutchinson said. 'Fox will end up making contact with these guys, try to press Babich to the table.'

'What's he want from us, a medal?'

'I just want you in the loop – we're acting on this: Europol, Interpol. It's coming to a head. We're bringing him in.'

The Agency men exchanged looks.

'You sure you want some soft-hearted Aussie reporter going after this?' Riley asked. 'These are dangerous people.'

'He's got skills.'

'Yeah, ex Australian Navy,' Riley said, reading over the file. 'A bunch of real tough nuts I'm sure. Fuckin' Navy queers.'

'Riley has an interesting personality,' Kavanaugh said. 'Forgive him.'

'It's a Boston thing,' Hutchinson said. 'I'm well used to it.'

'Roxbury?'

'South End.'

'Yeah, well, your man Lachlan Fox,' Kavanaugh said. 'If these cats want him dead it's just a matter of time.'

'Short money's on a car bomb,' said Riley. 'Me, I'd put a bill against a close-in pistol shot, point blank, dead of night.'

Hutchinson shook his head.

'Anyhow,' Riley went on, 'I'm sure he'll start a nuclear fuckin' war between Pakistan and India in the meantime, do the Russians' work for them. So fuckin' smart he gets himself killed as collateral.'

'What's this?' Kavanaugh said, tapping at a note in Fox's file. It was a Bureau numbered code.

'I can't talk about that,' Hutchinson said. The two agents looked at him hard. 'Really, I can't.'

24

FBI, QUANTICO, VIRGINIA

Duhamel gave them nicknames – Ivan and Luigi. They took it in their stride, happy to be part of the club. Nothing like a bit of sweat and shooting to bind men. One of the Hostage Rescue Team's specialties was high-risk arrests – and with the nationalities of these two agents, it was a no-brainer as to where they'd be involved. But there were still variables, plenty of them, and these two guys seemed to know only as much as he did – or they were holding back. Duhamel was going to put them through a two-hour physical training session this afternoon, so that might loosen their tongues. But first, some fireworks.

Ivan and Luigi turned out to be pretty decent, not your usual suits. They had spent the morning with Duhamel and Brick putting rounds down a range – and proved to be well above-par shooters, both with pistols and subs, which was all that would be required of them according to the brief. Both Duhamel and Brick felt confident that in a tight situation, both these ring-ins could be depended upon – and coming from HRT members, that was really saying something.

Duhamel took them on a final assault to get them mission-ready. They rode in a golf cart to the joint-DoD MOUT– Military Operations in Urban Terrain – range: mock office complex, houses and shops made from rendered brick and concrete to resemble a Middle Eastern environment. The Israeli team had just cleared out, showing off their new assault rifles, which the Bureau was considering. Brick fielded a new awesome member of the HRT's assault arsenal – a Gatecrasher.

'Okay, the bad guys have booby-trapped all the doors and windows,' Duhamel said. They were hunkered down behind the corner of a building to the rear of their target. 'So we're going to cut our own way into the building.'

'Think of this,' Brick said as he rapped his knuckles against the hard plastic sheet that was the Gatecrasher, 'as a kind of portable door.'

'We enter here,' Duhamel said, drew on the ground with a stick of chalk with quick motions. 'I'm through first, then Brick, then you two, and we never stop moving.'

'Don't shoot me in the back,' Brick said to the two guys. They nodded, half smiles. 'Seriously now: don't shoot me.'

'Scenario is there's two hostages and the bad guys have issued an ultimatum and we have no choice but to go in,' Duhamel said, drawing on the plan with a few cross marks. 'We clear in here, you hang back here, and Brick and I move upstairs. Only come in further if we call you in. Got it?'

'*Sì*,' Luigi said. 'Got it.'

Duhamel looked to them, then Brick. 'You guys think it's a good plan?'

Ivan looked at the little diagram, then peeked around the corner at the target building.

'No,' he said. 'By the time you go upstairs, hostages might be – taken out? Dead, I mean.'

Duhamel smiled. Brick patted the Russian on the back.

'Good work, Ivan,' Brick said. 'That's why we've got two of these.'

He pulled another Gatecrasher from behind the other. The size and thickness of a battleship door, these black plastic 'portable doors' weighed just a few kilograms each when filled with water and could blast through almost two feet of brick or solid concrete, using water to direct a small amount of explosive to make a powerful cutting tool: you filled it up, put detonation cord or C4 or any plastique around the edge and . . . kaboom. On the water-protected side there was no blast back, meaning you can stand in close. Good for forced entry when door-breaching isn't an option, perfect for urban combat mouse-holing – creating small passages between adjoining rooms or buildings by manually tunnelling through walls when you need to avoid open streets and sniper fire.

'Ivan and I will take downstairs, Brick and Luigi will enter the building next door, hugging the wall in from the east, and blast a hole through the neighbour's wall on the first floor,' Duhamel said, replacing his earlier chalk marks with new ones. 'Call it in when you have the Gatecrasher set up, then we enter at the same time, wrap it up in the target house within a few seconds. Clear?'

The two newbies nodded.

'Remember, there are live people in there, so go easy where you point your blanks, just in case,' Brick said.

They ran in their two teams to converge on the target house, keeping out of sight-lines of the windows, then signalled readiness.

Brick ranged the wall with a depth reader, making sure they weren't cutting into a cross wall behind. Thickness: twelve inches of concrete blocks; the three layers of detonation cord in the Gatecrasher would be more than enough. A thermal reading picked out the bodies in there – two figures, far wall to the front of the building, almost fifteen metres to their right.

'Ready,' Brick called.

'Call it on three,' Duhamel replied over their mics.

Three seconds later the two teams went through neat man-sized holes cut through the wall – straight in, bad guys disoriented, pop pop.

'Clear upstairs.'

'Clear down.'

Brick and Ivan were moving downstairs, the two 'hostages' between them. Job done, fist pumps. Ready as they'll be in a day's training.

25

NEBRASKA AVENUE COMPLEX, WASHINGTON DC

'This is coded like a witness protection file,' Kavanaugh said.

Hutchinson shrugged.

'It is,' Riley said.

'Who?'

'No one.'

'We need to know.'

'You really don't.'

'Andy, this is my op,' Kavanaugh said. 'I've got reach on this, direct from the Director of National Intelligence. You want me to go there? Maybe get you off this?'

'Sure, tell him to go suck a bag of dicks while you're at it.' Hutchinson was resolute. 'Your team has a leak – we've had too many coincidences over the years.'

'It could have been someone in Justice, anyone with high clearance.'

'It could be your team,' Riley added.

'Yeah, it could be,' Hutchinson said. 'It could be me, could be you. All the more reason to use Fox.'

'I don't like it. You'd trust him over some of our guys?'

'It's my case. And yeah, I trust him as much as anyone. He's the real deal. Old school.' Kavanaugh looked at the files on the table in front of him.

'Fox was in the military for how long?'

'Seven years, give or take. Australian Navy. Served in Special Forces alongside our guys in 'Stan and Iraq. He can take care of himself.'

'Look, Andy, we've got to produce some results. CIA wants blood as much as everyone else. I've got to go back to the Director with something—'

'I'll give you something. Buy me a week, we'll close the net on these guys. I just need you to keep the rest of the Agency out of the loop until we do, just in case.'

'You're that close?'

'With Lachlan Fox onside, yeah, we're that close.'

'And what makes you so sure he'll want to help you out?' Kavanaugh closed the file. 'He bugged out of the Navy and has moved around a fair bit these past two years. Doesn't seem like a stayer to me.'

'He was discharged from the Navy after following his gut on a good op that went bad. The guy's got good instincts, good morals. Like I said—'

'Yeah, I heard you before,' Kavanaugh said. 'I just don't think it'll be that easy getting him onside. He's got nothing to gain from this.'

'Let me worry about that,' Hutchinson said. Kavanaugh watched him drain his coffee and toss the paper cup in the trash can.

'You seem pretty sure.'

'Just you work on getting your assets off this, or at least

keep them in the dark long enough for me to make a play,' Hutchinson said.

'All right,' Kavanaugh conceded. 'I'll work my stuff. But I want to know how you're so sure about Fox – how you're going to get him to go point for us on this.'

'Because for him, this has been building. They've pushed him and he won't be forced into hiding – I mean, killing his contacts, then coming after him? For him, this is personal.'

'And you think you can pin this hit on Babich?'

'If I can, that'd be great,' Hutchinson said. 'Read the file on him. NSA has picked up enough chatter of him and his subordinates to know what he's up to.'

'Good luck using NSA transcripts in an international court.'

'Any court. Good luck with that.'

'If we get him linked directly to this,' Hutchinson said, 'we can take him down for this and everything else out there. Bribery, money laundering, evading taxes, illegal arms deals, the actions of his private security contractors . . .'

The agents shared a look. 'Look, Andy . . . We don't want him taken down. Not like that,' said Kavanaugh.

Hutchinson half expected this. His face was unreadable. 'What's he to you?'

'Important.'

'I need more.'

'That's what you got.'

Hutchinson waited.

'He's not an asset, we're not in any contact with him, if that's what you want to know,' said Riley. 'Babich is at the head of something that is bigger than one man. While he's there at the helm, we can watch him, track him, predict him.'

'So it's better the devil you know.' Hutchinson was disgusted.

'We know his armaments company sells twenty thousand firearms in this country every year,' said Kavanaugh.

'And we know his water company supplies fifteen per cent of Western Europe's water. A quarter of their natural gas,' said Riley.

'And if we find that he's linked to these murders?' Hutchinson asked, well sick of the two-hander going on. 'If we find that he's got a bigger motive in the water project in Pakistan than making a dime?'

'Andrew, what else do you want from us?' Kavanaugh said. 'Hmm?'

'I've got Lachlan Fox out there chasing this. Just making it clear I don't want you to get in our way.'

'Using reporters to do your pointy-end work,' Riley said. 'Softer over at the Bureau than we thought.'

'If things go sour, we'll have a team on standby to quick evac and exfil if necessary.' Hutchinson left it at that; Kavanaugh didn't need to know he had Duhamel training; he'd assume DoD or State Department, maybe both.

'Okay,' Kavanaugh said.

'If we hear anything, we'll give you a heads-up.'

'Same goes.'

Hutchinson stood to leave. 'James, you ever wanna try some real work, send me your resumé,' Hutchinson said. 'Get a job where you actually catch the bad guys.'

'I trust too many people to be a Fed.'

'I'll be the judge of that. You boys are like Robert Redford from *Three Days of the Condor*, reading spy thrillers and entering the plots into your computers to look for threats. Like I said: you should come over and do some real work.'

'Yeah? Why don't you send us *your* resumé?' Riley countered. 'I'll read it while I'm taking a shit.'

'You ever taken a shit and it felt like you'd had a good night's rest?' Hutchinson said. 'That's what your resumé would do.'

'Fuck you.' Handshake.

'Always a pleasure.' Meeting over.

The Agency men took the lift down to the basement car park while Hutchinson headed for the helipad on the roof. Hutchinson signalled to the pilot to get the rotors started up, then placed a call.

'Lach, Hutchinson. Go ahead and debrief Hasif, then get back in the air. By the time I arrive we'll be ready to take him in – my team's getting ready to be with you on the ground in India.'

26

SEVILLE, SPAIN

Gammaldi touched down smartly on San Pablo Airport, putting the engines into reverse thrusters, barely a hum inside the cockpit of the luxury corporate jet as it taxied towards the cluster of small private aircraft.

'Nice landing,' Fox said. 'How's she compare to the G5?'

'Electric dynamite, my man. Fly-by-wire works well, and the fully trimmable horizontal stabilisers are a nice touch.'

Fox rolled his eyes, sorry he asked.

'Mind you, that was the first time I've flown the 650 without a copilot,' Gammaldi said. 'And my first landing outside the sim.'

'Now you tell me,' Fox said. 'Anyway, I took the controls for a bit.'

'Yeah, and your fifteen minutes of flying fame was the easy bit,' Gammaldi said. 'And as for you, you're what we in the avionics business call dead shit – oh no, wait, dead *weight*. That's it, dead weight.'

'Yeah, landing's the bitch, I got that,' Fox said, taking his backpack from behind the seat and heading out. 'If I'm dead weight, what are you, heavy weight?'

'Oh, Lach, you slay me,' Gammaldi said. 'And for the record, the heaviest thing I've ever lifted is your unconscious ass.'

'I don't know if I want you near my unconscious ass,' Fox said. He tried to think of a time in the field when Gammaldi had needed to carry him out of trouble. 'Hey, when was that?'

'My twenty-first?' Gammaldi said. 'One minute you were holding up one end of the bar, the next you were talking to a plant.'

'Must have been my hippie phase.' Fox vaguely remembered a pub crawl that culminated at their cricket club.

'It's bloody hot here; it's meant to be winter,' was the first thing that came out of Gammaldi's mouth as they walked out of the air-conditioned cabin and down the stairs of the GSR Gulfstream 650.

'It's about twenty degrees Celsius, Al,' Fox said. 'It's just your extra layer of insulation that's keeping you warm.'

'The dead weight's saying *I'm* fat?' Gammaldi said to no one in particular as he went to talk to the ground crew about refuelling.

Geiger showed the four passports to a customs official while Goldsmith unloaded the bags. Spain was one of many places where the GSR security team was licensed to carry concealed firearms and Goldsmith unlocked the hard case and locked and loaded a couple of H&K .45 pistols and a Kriss MK9 submachine gun.

He also took out a duffle bag containing four bullet-proof vests. The Dragon Skin body armour was the most advanced personal ballistics protection system in the world, made from ceramic and titanium composite disks that overlapped and interlinked, meaning a bullet hit would be dispersed over a large area rather than wanting to punch straight through like it would with other body armours; this reduced the serious injuries or death associated with high-powered shots hitting body armour – and was something Fox tried not to think about.

A hire-car driver arrived with a black Lexus LX570, the luxury version of the Toyota Land Cruiser, all paperwork already handled from New York. He handed the keys to Goldsmith.

'No, you *can't* hang on to them!' Fox heard Geiger say to the customs guy, waving his permits in his face, loud and forceful enough to put the guy off.

In a quiet corner Fox watched his team doing their thing and checked in with Faith Williams at GSR.

'Yeah, we're fine here,' Fox said into his iPhone. 'Customs is getting sorted and the hire car just pulled up.'

'Good,' Faith said. 'Omar Hasif and his family have just touched down at the air base, which is—'

'Yeah, I got it,' Fox said. 'About fifty clicks southeast from here.'

'State Department are doing the processing work there, and the Hasifs are getting a proper medical check-up from the base hospital. They might even stay there overnight,' Faith said. 'His son has some ear issues, which they are attending to before the transatlantic flight.'

'Yeah, I hope the little guy's all right,' Fox said, watching the others load into the Lexus.

'And I'm sorry there's still no welcoming party there, no Feds on hand yet,' Faith continued. 'I'm told they should be ready to field by the time you get to India; worst case, you may have some local guys the State Department occasionally outsources to.'

'We'll be fine,' Fox said, walking over to the car. 'I'm surprised

McCorkell couldn't get us clearance to land at the Air Force base here, though.'

'Yeah, his message to us didn't go into it,' Faith said, 'but the Spanish parliament have been fussing about unmarked aircraft that are registered in the US – they want to try to stop covert rendition flights passing through their territory.'

'Fair enough,' Fox said. 'Anyway, I'll check in with you when we get back.'

'Fine,' she said. 'Just . . . watch out, okay?'

'Yeah, I'll be fine, thanks, Faith,' Fox replied and ended the call. He took the offered Kevlar from Gammaldi and strapped it on over his T-shirt; all men were now wearing the bulletproof vests. He tossed his sports jacket into the back seat of the Lexus and climbed in next to Gammaldi. The two security men up front gave the thumbs-up and they roared off.

'What was with the customs guy?' Fox asked Geiger.

'He wanted to hang on to the firearms,' Geiger said. 'Fortunately my dad taught me never to let people just take things from me.'

'It's your Israeli blood,' Goldsmith said.

'You know it,' replied Geiger, punching fists.

'Drive as fast as you can, Roberto,' Fox said. 'I wanna get in and out of this place ASAP.'

27

MOSCOW, RUSSIA

Babich sat a table in Sudar Restaurant with his colleagues from Gazprom and Itera; it was the kind of hard-drinking, self-congratulatory lunch he wanted to get away from as soon as possible. Located near the center of Moscow, by the Triumphal Arch and Poklonnoya Mountain, Sudar was decorated in the style of an antiquated Russian mansion: dark wooden furniture, snow-white tablecloths, silk lampshades and walls adorned with ancient portraits and paintings. His party had the VIP room to themselves, and a small army of aides and assistants remained outside the doors manning cell phones.

The fish soup with sturgeon, pike perch and salmon, with ravioli, pirozhki and vareniki was followed by a shared sturgeon stuffed with mushrooms and baked with truffle and wild berry sauce. The wine cart comprised of French, Italian and Spanish wines and various cognacs, liqueurs and nastoykas. Babich nursed a first-class beer made in the restaurant's brewery and browsed the cigar menu, tuning out to the boasting of the Gazprom chairman.

'This business in Ossetia isn't good for me,' one of the men said.

Babich smiled. He thought of Sirko. The boy never made mistakes – what he had done for him in Gori was perfect. He'd left no trace, even used American-made C4 and detonators. Babich checked his watch – it would be tight, but Sirko would manage to take care of Fox in Spain. If there was anyone in the world who could do such a job at a moment's notice, it was dear little Sirko. He had always been like that.

Kolesnik would be busy enough too. Babich took a cigar from the silver tray, sniffed it and nodded to the waiter, who cut it for him. Young Kolesnik was quick, but he was not as methodical as Sirko. There was room for both kinds of men in life, and he used each to their full advantage. Neither was a suitable successor for his role though, which was a pity.

Babich's PR woman entered as he lit his cigar, and whispered in his ear: 'Press are outside. You need to wear this tie when you speak to them.' She handed him a necktie. He had learned not to argue such points; he took it, pulled off his current one, tied off the knot. The other men didn't even notice.

'Remember,' she said, 'three questions only, and I will pick out the reporters I have screened . . .'

He tightened his tie and tuned out again, watching the men at the table without hearing their words. He had known them for most of his life; they represented true power. He was proud of his place in the new Russia, proud to be a part of the leadership, proud of what he had done for his people, despite the sameness of it all, the predictable nature of his compatriots.

'They will follow us out to the technical school that you're opening . . .' his PR woman interrupted his thoughts.

He nodded. She answered her BlackBerry – it seemed either

on constant vibrate on her hip or sandwiched between her hand and her ear – and signalled that it was time to go.

Babich said his goodbyes and left the room, smiling at the unease he left behind; the men still talked about the trouble in the caucus oblasts. There was a time, before they each had so much money on the line, when they'd talk about women and sport and the problems with the West. How life changes.

Outside it was overcast but bright: cameras flashed, accompanied by the sound of a multitude of shutter clicks.

28

OUTSKIRTS OF SEVILLE, SPAIN

The Lexus was quiet and smooth as it weaved through the traffic. Geiger navigated from the front passenger seat while Goldsmith drove. Fox's iPhone rang: Andrew Hutchinson.

'Lach, where are you at?'

'Just passed through Alcalá de-something,' Fox said, 'about forty clicks northwest of the US air base—'

'Wait – are you in a car?'

'Yeah,' Fox said, looking out the window as the outskirts of the small Seville satellite town flashed by. 'Couldn't get clearance to land—'

'The hell you couldn't!' Hutchinson said. His tone made Fox's heart beat a little faster. 'Who told you that?'

Fox looked to Gammaldi, who returned a look that said *what's up?*

'We had a message come through from McCorkell,' Fox said. 'Are you—'

'Lachlan, wherever you are right now, get off the road and head for safety. What car are you in?'

'Hire car—'

'Get out!' Hutchinson ordered. 'Get out of that car!'

'Andy – it's forty clicks, we'll be at the air base in twenty minutes, tops,' Fox said. 'What's—'

'Lach – I was there in the room!' Hutchinson said, and Fox felt heat rise up the back of his neck and flush his face, and then sweat. 'I was in the room when McCorkell got the message that you were cleared for landing at Morón – and he sent you the message at that moment! Get out of the car and stay off the road!'

Fox's mind was racing. He leaned forward and put a hand on Goldsmith's shoulder: 'Pull over now!'

The SUV shuddered under the ABS and the tyres came to a screeching halt on the shoulder of the road.

'Stay on this line,' Hutchinson shouted as Fox shoved Gammaldi's backpack at him and grabbed his own, almost dropping the iPhone. 'I'll get someone to come to your location.'

'Out of the car!' Fox yelled to the three men, who did it without hesitation, clambering out of the car and following his lead as he ran down the road towards an off-ramp.

They were barely fifty metres away when the Lexus exploded into a huge fireball. A bright orange flash blinded Fox's eyes and the concussion seemed to suck the air out of his lungs as he was blown hard against the crash barrier.

29

VIRGINIA

Hutchinson's hands shook. He sat in the rear passenger section of the FBI helicopter, almost at Quantico. He had placed a frantic call to his FBI liaison at the air base in Spain; no news. Fox's line was dead, but they were getting a GPS read on the last location. A special ops helicopter, on standby for security of this mission, was in Spanish airspace . . .

He had been in McCorkell's office when clearance to land had come in. That McCorkell – or his secretary – hadn't passed that information on to Fox . . . In fact, Fox had said McCorkell had specifically *not* cleared them to land at the Air Force base . . . Fuck! He'd been sure the mole was CIA. For the intelligence analyst, little, if anything, could be taken for granted – a lesson he had just relearned.

But Bill McCorkell?

Hutchinson had been an investigator long enough to know that looking him up would not be easy. He had guys who could track McCorkell's communications – as he'd done to get the threat list against Fox in the first place – but he'd need damning evidence. Problem was, his guys had got their hands on that first intel via a wide net, not by pinpoint targeting of a suspect.

McCorkell had worked in the Bureau, the Justice Department, the UN, and top global security thinktanks prior to his role in the Executive Branch of three administrations – including as National Security Advisor to the last President. That kind of pedigree led to all kinds of difficulties – not the least of which was that the guy had security clearance second below God.

But could he be *the* guy?

As his own chopper started its descent through the foggy FBI base Hutchinson willed his phone to ring and watched the seconds tick by, waiting for news that Fox was okay.

30

OUTSKIRTS OF SEVILLE, SPAIN

Dark smoke was thick in the air around the four men on the ground. Tiny bits of metal and glass and ash rained down as Fox forced his eyes open. He looked up and rolled to his left – out of the path of a wheel that bounced by his head as if in slow motion. He shook himself back to his senses and brushed grit from his eyes.

Geiger was up on one knee in firing position, looking down the sights of his Kriss Mk9 .45 calibre submachine gun, scanning side to side to the rear of their position. Goldsmith was just a few beats behind him as he drew his pistol, unsteady on his feet, scanning the other direction for threats. Civilians ran from cars, a truck's load caught fire—

'Let's move!' Fox yelled. He squinted against the sunlight as Gammaldi helped him to his feet and they hunted around for their backpacks. A secondary explosion sounded.

'You all right?' Gammaldi yelled into his ear.

'Yeah,' Fox yelled back, moving with Gammaldi. Gammaldi's jacket had been blown off in the blast but his bulletproof vest was still strapped tightly over his blackened T-shirt. 'Come on, into a vehicle!'

As they moved, they stayed low, alert, scanning around. Most vehicles had stopped and some were still screeching to a stop; a truck had jack-knifed and lost half its load of water-cooler refills; a ten-car pile-up in the opposite direction shut down the oncoming traffic lanes. People were out of their cars and on the road, some hysterical, some numb; a few were on cell phones, calling authorities and news services. Fox and his men passed two guys filming the scene on their phones, shouting to each other, *'Basque separatists!'* Fox didn't hesitate as he ran for their vehicle, a late-nineties SEAT hatchback done up like a rally car.

'Someone's watching us, Al,' Fox said, climbing into the back seat and shuffling across for Gammaldi. Geiger backed himself into the front passenger seat, slammed the door and pointed his weapon out the open window, continuing to scan the scene for threats as Goldsmith roared the car's engine.

'Rob, get us off this road!' shouted Fox.

'Onto it!'

Goldsmith manoeuvred around the immediate traffic jam, revving the gas pedal hard against the clutch. The front tyres spun. Once they reached a clear stretch of road the hatchback hit a loud eighty kilometres per hour in second gear.

'Push it, Rob!'

'It's to the floor!' he said as he dumped into third – the car was skidding on its bald tyres, entering the curve of the A92. A massive series of high-rise apartment blocks loomed to their immediate right.

'Chopper, inbound, northwest!' Gammaldi yelled over the sound of the add-on GPS system in tinny Spanish – *'usted se apresura, usted se apresura, compruebe la velocidad!'*

'They could be friend—'

The back window shattered. Geiger turned his head sharply away and brought his hands up to cover his face.

Goldsmith slumped over the wheel, his foot a dead weight on the accelerator, making the car hammer even harder down the motorway, bumping erratically between cars as it careened its way forward.

'Sniper!' Fox yelled, frantically looking behind to try to identify the shooter's location. The helicopter was too far out; the gunman had to be closer.

Their vehicle bounced off a Range Rover, then drifted left and ground along the concrete barrier that separated them from the oncoming lanes, sparks from the protesting metal firing into the open side windows.

Geiger was sitting still, in shock, painted with gore. He started shaking, useless for a few beats.

'Eyal!' Fox yelled. 'Take the wheel!'

The ex-Marine snapped around and pulled the wheel back towards him to get the car off the barrier, the engine still redlining.

Fox leaned forward and pulled Goldsmith towards the backrest. He reached to check Goldsmith's neck for a pulse but soon pulled away his blood-soaked hand when he saw up close that Goldsmith's head was parted like the Red Sea. He looked at Gammaldi, who had seen it, too—

Thump!

A dull thud announced another sniper bullet hitting the car, this time aimed at the engine block—

Thump!

Another shot punched a hole in the bonnet. Steam hissed out instantly as the radiator took the hit, green coolant spraying up onto the windshield.

'Eyal – hold the wheel steady!' Fox ordered, then grabbed Gammaldi's hand and put it onto Goldsmith's lifeless shoulder. 'Al, as soon as I'm out, pull him back here!'

Before Gammaldi could question the plan, Fox was out his side window and immediately pulled himself in close to the car as a speed-limit sign flashed by his back. He climbed through the driver's window feet first while Gammaldi man-handled the body of their comrade into the back seat, seeming not to struggle under the weight.

Fox, now in the driver's seat, gunned the accelerator and pressed the clutch in and out of third gear—

Thump!

Another shot hit the bonnet like a sledgehammer; the sound of grinding and scraping under the road was piercing as something was blasted free of the engine and hung below—

Thump!

'Shit!' Fox swerved the car as the round passed through the roof of the car and lodged in the headrest a couple of centimetres from the back of his head.

'*Dé vuelta a la derecha seiscientos metros*—' Fox ripped the sat nav from the dash and threw it out his window.

'Shooter's somewhere in the apartments!' Geiger yelled. The three men stayed low as Fox kept his foot flat on the gas and swerved erratically, hitting fourth gear as he tore around the motorway's bend.

'Chopper's coming in hot!' Gammaldi yelled. 'It's military!'

The Black Hawk hovered above, keeping pace with the hatchback while pivoting around, its side doors open. In the small window behind the copilot a helmeted gunner sat behind a Dillon M134 Minigun. As Fox continued to floor the car, the gunner opened up with laser-like tracer rounds of super machine-gun fire.

31

FBI, QUANTICO, VIRGINIA

As he walked the hall of the office of the HRT Hutchinson could hear the staccato of the nearby firing range and felt like he was in the daze of a dream.

Bill McCorkell. What motivation could he possibly have? Hutchinson walked to the kitchen and poured himself a coffee, absently adding a couple of sugars. There was a leak in CIA, he *knew* that . . . he thought he knew that. What if the leak was higher up? McCorkell had access to everything they were working on – could it be that simple?

But surely McCorkell would know that Hutchinson would figure it out – he was in the fucking room when McCorkell got that landing clearance! No, it couldn't be him. Hutchinson walked back towards the office.

'Hey, Andrew, come sing happy birthday,' a junior agent said.

'What?'

'There's cake. It's Michelle and Natasha's birthday, a double celebration.'

Hutchinson shook his head and continued to the office. He stopped at the door and looked back up the hall at the departing figure. *A double celebration.* Could McCorkell's action have been a double blind? Apart from Kavanaugh and Riley, McCorkell *was* the only person outside Hutchinson's team who knew that Babich was the target of this operation. Maybe McCorkell just put that information out there – maybe there was no clearance to land at the air base – to make it obvious that it wasn't from him. Jesus . . .

Hutchinson didn't have to collate information for a grand jury – and anyway he doubted he could actually find anything on McCorkell that would prove wrongdoing – but he *could* get a National Security Letter organised quickly; the administrative subpoena required no probable cause or judicial oversight, and would get him access to everything he wanted.

He dialled a number on his BlackBerry.

'I need you to get full info on Bill McCorkell at the White House,' Hutchinson said.

'He's in the EEOB these days, yeah?'

'Yep,' Hutchinson replied. 'I need all his communications, and those of his secretary, checked and triple-checked; transcripts of all calls, emails, faxes in and out of every device and mode he's got. Give the NSLs to the Deputy Director to sign off.'

'Got it. You want surveillance on him?'

'No, just the comms for now, thanks.'

He hung up. Still no call from Fox.

Suddenly the gunfire grew louder as the outer door opened. Two FBI HRT members approached him.

32

SPAIN

Brass shell casings rattled off the roof of the hatchback, the machine-gun fire sounding like a tear in the sky above them. It was over almost as soon as it began – a few seconds of firing, hundreds of rounds.

In one of the apartment towers to their right, the entire wall surrounding a window on the tenth floor was a shot-out hole, the Minigun taking to the reinforced concrete like a can opener. Ragged debris crumbled down to earth. The sniper, if he had been up there, was long gone.

Fox hit the brakes and the SEAT came to a loud stop at the top of the off-ramp that headed towards the A360 highway, which led directly to Morón Air Base, still some thirty-eight clicks off. He got out of the car, the little hatchback smoking and rattling under the bonnet despite the engine being cut, and looked back down the road – no vehicles were coming through from where their Lexus had exploded. He waved to the chopper, which came in and hovered ground-close some thirty metres ahead of them. *UNITED STATES ARMY* was stencilled on the tail section; the gunner waved them in.

The others piled out of the car and headed for the chopper,

Geiger carrying Goldsmith over his shoulder. Fox and Gammaldi helped him pass the body up to the chopper's Crew Chief and then the three of them climbed aboard. The Black Hawk pulled up off the highway and dipped its nose slightly as it rushed towards home.

Fox watched Geiger: the GSR security man sat in the fold-down seat opposite, looking down at Rob Goldsmith, his colleague, his friend. Geiger suddenly leaned out the open side of the chopper and vomited.

'You got a bag for our guy?' Fox asked the US Army Crew Chief who'd manned the Minigun. The senior NCO nodded and pulled a body bag from a webbing pocket that lined a wall of the Black Hawk. As he and Fox bagged Goldsmith, Fox noticed the soldier's patch bore 160th SOAR, airlift specialists to US Special Operations Command forces. They hauled the body against the closed starboard side door of the cargo cabin and strapped it to the deck.

Fox turned and saw Gammaldi standing by Geiger, holding the man steady as they watched the Spanish countryside flash by below. The aircrew let them be, and they rode in silence during the five-minute flight. Fox knew that Goldsmith would not be the last man to fall.

33

EEOB, WASHINGTON DC

'Yeah, right,' McCorkell said to himself. He scrolled down through the Intellipedia site on his PC screen. Russia simply searching ships for arms cargo? Who would seriously fall for that? No mistake, they were enforcing a blockade. He knew they still had around 10 000 troops across Georgia's frontiers – 6000 on land in South Ossetia and 4000 by the sea at Abkhazia – and he wasn't at all happy about their warships being deployed off Georgia's Black Sea coast, at arms length from the US ships there.

He sipped his water and studied the image of the *USS San Antonio*, on station in the Black Sea for Georgian operations. She provided a defence bubble against enemy aircraft and incoming missiles. He'd watched her sail out of Little Creek, Virginia, on her maiden voyage, with 400 personnel and ferrying 800 battle troops into that area, part of what was soon to be an EU-led peacekeeping operation. A Russian sub was shadowing the *San Antonio* but as it now stood, the only threat to the US warship would be from small watercraft laden with explosives and piloted by Russian-friendly Ossetian militias. That was the kind of asymmetric warfare his military were still learning to deal with.

Russian tactics in the 2008 war in the region . . . Yeah, that was something that they could deal with. Russian jets bombed a military airfield close to the Georgian capital, Tbilisi, taking out not only the factory producing Sukhoi Su25 fighter jets for the Georgian Air Force, but the US-run command post as well. Now, Patriot missile batteries encircled Georgia's capital. Two British C130s flying in supplies for the Office of the UN High Commissioner for Refugees mission were also damaged, and two UNHCR people were wounded on the ground, pushing back the humanitarian effort and investigation into genocide – both actions it was conducting cross-borders. Now, UNHCR were being guarded by US and EU infantry and armour. Actions and consequences, and as seasoned as he was, McCorkell was still as capable of being surprised as anyone.

'Bring back the fucking cold war . . .'

He was overseeing President Obama's national security team's options for a proportional response should Russia move into Georgian territory again. McCorkell wondered, not for the first time, what kind of action this POTUS would choose. While his team was working overtime to draw up first-strike targets, he could not imagine any of them being acted upon. The world was growing smaller every day – America's friends and enemies watched the intricacies of their 'proportional' responses live on television and planned their future actions accordingly. A disproportionate response was never seriously considered, but it was something that was always in the back of McCorkell's mind as a nice alternative to show an aggressor that his country, and her allies and their citizens, were not to be messed with. You blow up our ship? No, we won't hit your munitions camp in response; we'll take out every target on the board.

He clicked out of the site, glancing at the LCD television.

A CNN headline reported on the Ukraine's President, threatening to block the return of Russian warships to their Black Sea base at Sevastopol, saying he did not want to be 'drawn into a military conflict'.

'Mr McCorkell, NSC's Kashmir-group meeting is next door in fifteen,' a military aide said from the open doorway.

'Thanks,' he replied, making his final notes.

The phone on the desk rang. 'Yeah?'

'Pakistan's moving a tank division north,' the Deputy NSA for Asia said. 'Do we tell India?'

'They'll already know it,' McCorkell said. 'Any new movement by them?'

'You know they moved some Agni-III intermediate-range ballistic missiles?' he said.

'Nukes; yeah, I caught that one. What've we got in the area?'

'Not enough. See you next door in a sec.'

'Yep,' McCorkell said and hung up.

Two nuclear states at it again . . . McCorkell knew it would take the smallest mistake to escalate the situation and throw the region into nuclear—

More news flashed on the television screen: amateur footage of an attack in Spain, Lachlan Fox's face. McCorkell grabbed the remote and turned up the volume. It looked like an urban war zone in Baghdad, not Seville: footage of burning vehicles, the façade of an apartment block in ruins . . .

34

SPAIN

In the high-rise apartment, Sirko opened an eye and saw darkness, then patches of hazy light. His ears rang as if he'd been in a bell tower when mass was called. He couldn't lift his head, couldn't move.

A memory flashed, from his childhood years he had spent at the Hypatian Monastery, a beautiful looking place on the bank of the Kostroma River – each day in winter he was allowed to ring the afternoon bells, a series of different-sized bells with ropes hanging down just within his reach. One day he fell to the cobbled ground and couldn't move: both legs were broken and his neck was fractured. He was confined to bed for months, where he'd lived a nightmare, over and over. Ten years later he returned there and, in a first for him outside a war zone, he'd killed a man. Not so much in cold blood as in blinding hot retribution, for him and for so many young boys, past and present.

He blinked his eyes rapidly to flush out the soot. He tried to yawn to change the pressure in his ears but the ringing wouldn't let up. His flexed his fingers in his gloves and felt a surge of adrenalin – he *could* get up, he *must* get up. Sirko forced himself up off the floor of the hallway and coughed out a thick stream of dusty mucus—

Someone was running down the hallway towards him. He pulled a Glock and popped the figure twice in the middle of their bulk – they fell down and stayed down.

Sirko steadied himself against the wall and looked around through burning eyes. Above where he'd lain, the bullets from the helicopter's machine gun had punched through the concrete blocks; they had even torn up and pockmarked the wall through to the neighbouring apartment.

He went back into 'his' studio apartment – its true owner's body stuffed into the wardrobe earlier today – and looked out the new opening in the wall where he had perched for the assassination. The entire wall of the living room was now a ragged, open space, the void the size of a Volkswagen where a concrete wall and window had been just seconds ago. The contents of the open-plan studio apartment were now fine fragments of foam and feathers and material that filled the air like smoke.

As Sirko took a step towards the gaping hole, the glass and metal light fitting fell from the ceiling and smashed, its bare electrical cord sparking against the roof. The purpose-built briefcase that housed his sniper rifle was by his feet, shattered by the machine-gun rounds.

Sirko kicked some debris around, looking for his rifle: for this job he'd brought a VSS, *Vintovka Snayperskaya Spetsialnaya*, or 'special sniper rifle', a suppressed weapon developed in the late eighties for Soviet Special Forces, with which he'd had so much success in Chechnya. It wasn't his favourite rifle, but it was perfect for covert medium-range hits against armoured targets. It was now buried in this rubble somewhere, and he didn't bother digging around to retrieve it. He turned and walked out into the hallway, moved towards the stairs. Thinking . . .

A US military helicopter with a Minigun blasting away at him . . . now, that was *news*. They came in hard, prepared for him, which meant they were there as protection for his targets. Or to draw him out. Sirko knew about *Kylmä-Kalle*, the tactic employed by the Finns against the Soviets when the Red Army invaded Finland early into WWII: they would set out a mannequin dressed as an officer sloppily covering himself, and when a Soviet sniper was unable to resist such a target and took a shot, showing his position, the Finns would take him out with a heavy-calibre Norsupyssy or Boys anti-tank rifle. A tiny nation had repelled a giant. He had been set up.

But how did they see him, covered behind curtains in an open window? The VSS had virtually no muzzle flash, and he couldn't conceive that the suppressed shots had been heard onboard the chopper or car . . . But what was the chopper doing there, right at that time? This was supposed to be a soft target – all targets were, unless stated otherwise, that's how Umbra always operated him. The targets had fled the car before it properly came into his kill zone, forcing him to detonate the car bomb early. He had been forced to switch to the rifle . . .

This hit was set up for failure, and given who'd first asked him to handle this job, it was not difficult to finger the blame.

Kolesnik. The golden boy. He'd always treated Sirko like dispensable shit, giving him the tough jobs while he himself . . . He knew all about Kolesnik's life: painless, carefree. No living in Greece working a construction job in between to afford food; no anxiety waiting for the phone to ring for a real job; no burning hatred. That fucker has nightclubs, money to burn, an apartment in Prague. Sirko had cased it once, while Kolesnik was out of the country. Helped himself to the contents of the refrigerator. Laid in his bed. Tried on his jackets. Took a dump in his toilet, didn't flush. Maybe one day he would go back there, wait for Kolesnik to come home bent out of his mind on ecstasy or whatever he did . . .

Yes, it was time.

Justice served cold, kind of like how that Godfather guy spoke about revenge. Yeah, he would finish this job, and then pay his respects to that ungrateful killer.

35

MOSCOW, RUSSIA

Babich was mobbed by grateful teachers and parents and students as he left the school. He turned to wave one last time as his publicist whispered to him. Still smiling, he nodded and climbed into his car. The door closed behind him and the driver drove off; the television screen showed breaking news, coming in from Spain.

A woman reported live from the scene, cars on fire on a highway behind her, cutting to amateur footage . . . *A high-speed chase and terrorist attack has occurred in Spain, outside Seville* read the ticker . . . the amateur video showed a US military helicopter picking up three figures; they were carrying a body.

Babich smiled—

Then he saw the familiar face: Lachlan Fox, unmistakably him, getting into the helicopter, still alive.

His phone rang. Kolesnik.

'What was that?' Babich asked.

'He failed,' Kolesnik's voice replied, after a slight delay. 'Petro—'

'This was meant to be surgical.'

'It was not me, it was—'

'Don't blame others, this was *your* job,' Babich said. He was surprised that Kolesnik had also used Sirko; he had placed his own order as a back-up. He needed Fox removed more so than the others involved.

'I – I had to go wide on this.'

Babich smiled. Both these young men were sons to him. 'I understand,' Babich said. 'But nothing more like this, okay?'

'Yes,' Kolesnik said. 'Should I do something about Petro?'

'What do you mean?'

'Well, with this failure—'

'He's very useful to me.'

'He's a hack.'

'Yet you called him in to help you, as you have so often since you were little boys.'

'If he's ever in my sights—'

Babich coughed, angry and disappointed, perhaps even mildly amused.

'I mean—'

'Don't start something you can't finish,' Babich said, watching New Moscow traffic out his window. 'He's been doing this since you were a schoolboy.'

He thought of the two when they were young boys. Sirko was a three-year-old orphan he had supported before he and his wife had their own child, taking him from the monastery for the summer months. The boy became the older brother young Kolesnik never had, a real achiever in comparison. They saw each other a few times a year at holidays, continually measuring and comparing themselves in every capacity. They were always cordial, had always treated him like family.

'I need him, like I need you,' Babich said. 'You both have your place.'

Silence on the phone; Babich could almost hear the young man thinking.

'If he can't get this job done—'

'*He* has never failed me,' Babich said. 'He will finish what he started. And maybe, just maybe you will finally learn to trust in another fully. After all, he's family.'

36

MORÓN AIR BASE, SPAIN

The Black Hawk thundered onto the tarmac where it was met by a ground crew and a US Air Force medical team waiting by a base ambulance.

Fox and Gammaldi helped remove Goldsmith's body from the chopper. The blood on Fox's hands was sticky like honey, thick in some places and drying and caking in others. There was splatter on his T-shirt, and Gammaldi had specks of blood and collateral gore all over his face. Geiger sat on the open back of the ambulance while a graze was patched up and a cut along his cheek temporarily sutured, his eyes vacant, revisiting and absorbing what had just happened. The ambulance took him away for further treatment.

Fox approached the Black Hawk Crew Chief, who had started to clean out his aircraft, and asked: 'How'd you pick out the shooter?'

The Chief pointed to a kit on the rear of the undercarriage where it started to rise towards the tail. The add-on resembled a short metal broomstick with a series of smaller antennae spiking out of it – seven small microphones, arranged like the spine of a sea urchin.

'Boomerang shooter detection system. It's anti-sniper tech: can pinpoint a shot before you even see muzzle flash . . . Tuned up good, it's the best way I know to get a quick target acquisition, like about too late for y'all down there.'

Fox nodded. He'd seen a similar system fitted to Humvees in Afghanistan.

'Thanks for getting us out,' Fox said, shaking the man's hand. Gammaldi showed the same gratitude to the pilots.

'I'm sorry about your man,' the Crew Chief said. 'We never like putting a guy on a cooling board. We'll see he gets Stateside ASAP.'

'Thanks, Chief,' Fox said. 'Where's our—'

'Hangar's over yonder,' he said, pointing to a half-open metal hangar with the tail of a Gulfstream visible inside and a couple of State Department Chevy Suburbans parked out front, guarded by an entire platoon of Air Force Security Force airmen, distinctive in their dark blue berets. A row of smaller hangars lined a second runway, stretching out at least half a kilometre. Further out were massive hangars: Fox could see a B2 Stealth Bomber inside one, a couple of tanker craft in another, and a few C17s parked in a neat row. The smaller hangars were originally built for fighter-jet aircraft, but now they were full of Gulfstreams and the like: transport planes, maybe for VIP military brass – more likely for rendition transport crisscrossing the globe posing as legitimate flights at legitimate civilian airports. A squadron of F16s was parked on an open lot.

'Thanks,' Fox said, making to move off with Gammaldi.

The base protection force company commander pulled over in a Humvee with a guy in a suit.

'Get in,' the Air Force Captain said. 'I'll take you to my office and get you cleaned up. I've got someone waiting to talk to you.'

37

FBI, QUANTICO, VIRGINIA

Duhamel and Brick didn't look comfortable sitting in an office.

Hutchinson had spelled out their main brief – picking up a High Value Target for prosecution, one Roman Babich.

He was a hard target, with a personal protection detail that would stop at nothing to protect their guy. Ivan and Luigi were on hand as it involved a Russian national likely to be on Italian soil at the time of the arrest. And after that, whatever was required – Hutchinson knew that since 9/11 guys like Duhamel and Brick had been an integral part of protecting the country from both domestic and international terrorist threats – they were front-line agents, the ones who got things done, and would continue to, either within HRT or his own team.

'You're coming up on your time here,' Hutchinson said. 'At best, you'll be going back into Operations sooner rather than later. Or what, you think you're going to hang around here and be trainers? Takin' fat SOBs like myself through their annual sidearm proficiency tests? Sounds great.'

Brick looked to Duhamel, his mind ticking over.

'What does your unit do, exactly?'

Hutchinson smiled. He wasn't going to fuck these guys around. 'CT and CI,' he replied. Counter Terrorism and Counter Intelligence.

'So it's a part of ITOS One or Two?'

He smiled again. Hutchinson had been around long enough to know how to recruit; his area of the Bureau was chronically short-staffed of mid-senior level agents. Too many of them headed into other areas of crime fighting where they had more gratification of regular outcomes, or left the FBI altogether. He had enough to worry about without recruitment, but his post and the personnel short-fall situation allowed him to borrow staff from within. Where better than HRT?

'Look, guys, you won't find my unit on any organisational chart,' Hutchinson said. 'We were formed out of an Executive Order. We look for what slips through the cracks. We operate independently of any other agency, while having full access to any information and assets that may aid us. This is the Dream Team, and I'm offering you a walk-in role, no strings.'

Hutchinson knew they understood what he meant. Since the post-9/11 restructure, the Bureau's two International Terrorism Operations Sections contained members of the CIA, as well as other federal agencies, civilian and military, in a spirit of inter-agency cooperation. Among other things, the President's Executive Order of 30 July 2008 called for better-organised intelligence agency action regarding foreign threats against the United States and its interests – this gave Hutchinson's team direct Presidential mandated power, meaning he could call on support from all appropriate US agencies.

'This is an opportunity to continue to do what you do best, for as long as you like,' Hutchinson said. 'You'll retain your current pay levels, and while you'll likely spend more time with your safeties on, there will be overseas trips.'

'We travel a bit as it is,' said Duhamel.

'Yes, you just got back from Iraq, and you were in 'Stan last year,' Hutchinson said. That earned him a look – his clearance was as good as it got. 'And I know about the good work you did in Florida a few months back. Brick, how's the neck?'

'I've had worse injuries shaving,' the big man said, scratching the star-shaped pink scar on the side of his neck, courtesy of a pistol round. 'Just so we're clear, you're running the Bureau's covert action and sensitive intelligence operations?'

'Look,' Hutchinson said, sipping his coffee. 'That's pretty much it. You'll be on my team. You'll be in the loop on everything. You'll still get to do all the HRT training you want, as well as the cross-training programs you've been doing with DELTA and overseas military outfits – SAS and the like – although I'd rather you steered clear of SEAL door-kickers, for obvious reasons.'

That got a laugh from both men, having heard versions of horror stories of simple operations gone wrong when overzealous Navy SEAL boys were attached.

'Come on, guys, I'm not here to piss in your pockets and I'm not here with my hat in my hand saying that you're my only hope. You say no right now, there are six other guys I'm going to talk to.' Hutchinson drained his cup, well knowing that these boys were not just the most suitable but also his best chance: the three teams of HRT operated on sixty-day cycles, and Duhamel and Brick were currently on Training. The team on Operations were on a ready state of alert to respond, and the other was on Support, assisting the Ops team in maintaining readiness. For all his clout, he'd have to wait for the next cycle to pluck good operators from another team – time he didn't have. 'I know your team cycles onto duty in a couple of weeks; we'll have to give them time to shift others into your place. Reality is, I need some guys to run today, right now. If you say yes to this,' Hutchinson said, 'you'll be in the air momentarily.'

'Will the arrest go down in Italy or Russia?'

'Not certain yet. Could be either, could be a few trips over the next few weeks. First up, though, it's India. High threat protective duty on a reporter we've got there.'

Hutchinson saw that this got their attention. HRT was a good gig, especially once you got into its rhythm and it got into your blood. But these guys trained for days that likely never came, and here he was, saying they could really put their skills to use, on a world scene . . . It was a proposition with cherries on top.

'Intel good, prepped?'

'It will be.'

'Short lead time?'

'I wouldn't give the go-ahead if you weren't ready,' he said. 'Anyway, you guys are the kings of rapid response.'

He paused.

'You've been training for this,' Hutchinson said, standing up and sliding his jacket back on. 'You've played with the best, you've become the best, now it's time to take on the best.'

38

MORÓN AIR BASE, SPAIN

The hangar was guarded by a heavily armed squad of US Air Force Security Forces. Lachlan Fox, freshly showered, dressed in borrowed military-issue camouflage pants and a white T-shirt, entered the hangar and saw Omar Hasif sitting at a trestle table opposite a mid-forties State Department man and the local FBI legal attaché. Hasif's family was nowhere to be seen.

Every now and then aircraft would take off or land, the military air base as busy as any mid-sized commercial airport. There was some serious heavy lifting going on at this major staging point between the United States and the Middle East; being inside the sheet metal hangar was like being in an echo chamber.

'Omar,' Fox said. The Libyan got up from the table and the two men embraced briefly.

'I just heard you were attacked,' Hasif said, his open face showing craggy lines that were hastened by years of working and living in the elements.

'Yeah, we're okay,' Fox said, taking a seat at the table next to Hasif. 'How about your family – how's your son?'

'The children are with a base teacher, they are happy – and

my boy will be fine, thank you.' His expression darkened and he looked down at his hands. 'My sister – she's sedated. Lachlan, I want you to bring these men to justice. Whoever they are. Anything I can do . . .'

Fox looked at the State and Fed guys opposite. They nodded, eager to participate, the FBI Legat particularly angsty. Nothing galvanised an honest lawman like seeing kids hurt.

'I will, Omar, know that,' Fox said. He took his Moleskine notebook from his backpack – both were looking a little worse for wear – and opened it at his research notes. He looked at the papers on the table, a stack of completed immigration forms for the family members. 'I'm headed to India now. Can you show me where this place is – the main building camp for the water project?'

Hasif took his briefcase from next to his chair and placed it on the table between them. Fox popped it open. A Dell laptop, manila folders, a couple of maps. Hasif had signed a non-disclosure agreement with Umbra Corp about details like this, but that was all out the window now.

'These are all my engineering documents, everything I have on the project,' he said. 'There are schematics that show the main pumping station, and where the underground water system diverts. That's as far as my work went.'

'I know that, but there's more, Omar. There's got to be. How did—'

'Lachlan,' Hasif said. 'I've been over everything a hundred times – dredging history like this never helps. Before this, I worked on the Libyan water project. *That* got me noticed by Umbra Corp. When my country discovered oil in the desert in the fifties they also discovered a massive aquifer underneath much of Libya and northern Africa – the Nubian Sandstone Aquifer System. The water in this aquifer predates the last ice age and the Sahara desert itself. There's enough water to turn Libya into an oasis for centuries, but it's by no means infinite.'

'So it doesn't get recharged,' Fox asked. 'It's what they call fossil water?'

'That's right. The aquifer in Kashmir is even bigger, and it gets significant recharge from the Himalayan run-off and the rain belt. This is a resource that will transform the region forever – no more desert, no more disease, no more drought. Poverty there will eventually cease.'

'For Libya, and now for Pakistan,' Fox said. 'Maybe not for their neighbours, who lose out as the shared groundwater table drops.'

Hasif nodded.

'But there's more,' Fox said. 'There's something else we haven't uncovered. They want to silence us all – what haven't we revealed? The relay station? The final destination in Pakistan of the water?'

Hasif shrugged. 'The project's construction was divided into three separate phases. First phase was the pipeline network, completed over many years. My phase started in 2006 – the pumping stations that relay the water. The third phase is the existing pipeline that then linked up southern and western areas – that, I had no input on, only on the volumes of water getting through to there.'

Fox flicked through some of Hasif's files. Brown & Root and Price Brothers were responsible for the original design, and the primary contractor for all phases was an Umbra Corp subsidiary.

'Art Kneeshaw built a pipeline for oil, under the main highway running north–south. But oil has never flowed through it. For years many have wondered why the old government would have built that kind of pipe there.'

'And?'

'It's been converted to a water pipe. It may never have been designed for oil for all I know,' Hasif said. 'They built it across a span of hundreds of kilometres but they ran out of money, and then the Kargil War hit near the region where they needed to build the relay station. It's been shelved ever since.'

'So, really, you were finishing this project?'

'In a sense, yes,' Hasif said. 'But to be much bigger and more efficient than the original plans would have been. My system is self-powered by the water – the hydro power, you see?'

Fox nodded.

'And you were paid by Vritra Utilities?' the State guy asked, reading over the documents on the table. 'A company based in Italy?'

'Yes,' Hasif said. 'That's what they are called at the site – I am not sure where the company is registered. I did work for them there in Pakistan, also a desalination plant in Malta, and I consulted on a Caspian gas pipeline through Georgia.'

'They're one of the biggest utility companies in the world,' Fox said, opening a map of Pakistan, India and the disputed area in Kashmir. He spread it out on the table.

'And a subsidiary of Umbra Corp?' State asked.

Fox and Hasif nodded.

'Most of the water heads south, to Karachi, but far too much – ten times more than the city needs,' said Hasif.

'To safeguard against the future?' Fox closely watched Hasif's reactions.

'Perhaps. Another team, Sardar's team, handled that third phase. He had already been doing gas pipeline work there for years.'

'Sardar Yusufzai,' the FBI man said, making notes. 'He was killed yesterday.'

'Yes. His team headed from the west, laying underground pipe that can carry the water southwest.'

'So, what – Pakistan's going to irrigate the western part of their country?'

Hasif looked into the middle distance. He seemed to be thinking about his answer. Fox wondered if he knew more than he was letting on.

'That's about two-thirds of their country's mass out there,' he replied. 'All arid, for now.'

'I'd reported that pipes head to the Peshawar region?' Fox asked, looking at the map.

Hasif seemed unsure whether to go on. His brother-in-law, his son, his wife – Fox could sense he was weighing up how far Umbra could reach.

'Omar?' Fox prodded, hoping that Hasif took comfort in the resolute looks the three men at the table gave him.

'They dump into another aquifer that naturally drains into Pakistan's side,' he said finally. He leaned forward and penned a line along the map as he spoke: 'The main pipeline heads southwest; it runs for over 250 kilometres along a mountain road – here – where it splits – here – most draining into the water plant at the Tarbela Reservoir.'

'And that feeds Islamabad?'

'Yes, and Rawalpindi, they're the big cities there, but it's also a hub in Pakistan's major water network. Tarbela presently irrigates tens of thousands of acres of land via canals, pipelines and dams – soon it will be ten, twenty times that. It also feeds tributaries, and they're using the natural river system to transport much more water south, to their main areas of life and infrastructure.'

Fox looked up from his notes and passed his notebook to Hasif. 'What's the location of that terminal – the pumping station?'

Hasif checked through his own notes and wrote in an exact GPS coordinate.

39

NORTHERN AREAS, PAKISTAN

It was a speck on a map, a GPS coordinate transmitted via the mail system in an online computer game.

They were known as the avatar *Darkforcer*, one of the most proficient killers World of Warcraft had ever seen. In the real world, especially in this part of the world, they were feared even more, and the fear was palpable.

The four SUVs rumbled into the shanty town under full cloud cover; a mist had settled over the land and the snow was falling hard. All the inhabitants, most of them temporary, were indoors.

The men disappeared into the town. It was dark and cold. One stayed in the street near the vehicles, thermal-vision on. They all had silenced submachine guns. They were all well-trained, hardened operators.

The signage of the town read Vritra Utilities. Earth-moving equipment sat bare. They had nothing against the people here. It wasn't personal; the job was straightforward and the pay was good. As the armed men worked their way through the town, the sound of suppressed gunfire was like a crowd clapping.

House by house, room by room, shell casings hit the floor.

A few people managed to run into the street, where they were picked off, one by one, with deadly accuracy.

Within fifteen minutes the kill team emerged into the street. Two operatives placed timed incendiary charges around the temporary and permanent structures. Another tipped a drum of poison into the water supply. Clean-up and containment. They then packed back into the cars and headed east.

As their vehicles left the scene, the dust and debris and ash fell with the snow; fires burned hot enough to melt metal. A green flag burned free and floated through the air – it flapped, then lay dead, still on the ground. The town became a distant, silent glow in their rearview mirrors.

40

MORÓN AIR BASE, SPAIN

'Mr Hasif, do you have any idea why someone would want you dead?' The FBI Legat looked as if he felt stupid voicing the question, but it had to be asked.

'No,' Hasif said. 'I've done hundreds of these kinds of projects, and a few of this kind of scale. I mean, from what I read in the papers, this has become such a big political issue – this is tapping water in a disputed area of land, and we're talking a lot of water . . .'

'Do you know where we can find Art Kneeshaw?' Fox asked.

'No, I never met him, although I asked them repeatedly to consult him, or at least his project specs. They gave me nothing. He knew what he was doing, though; it was a good set-up.'

'Do you know anything else about him?' Fox asked. 'How he got involved in the original project?'

'He worked in the area – retired there afterwards, I think. He's an expert in engineering pipelines. He knew exactly where to place the main plant, which I built according to the sparse details given to me when I signed on, and the feeder lines.'

'We're working on finding him,' State said, taking notes of his own. 'Did you work with anyone else on this?'

'A local engineer and construction firm; its workers were stationed and recruited from the closest town, here,' Hasif said, tapping the map. 'That's at the location I just gave you. It's a very remote site; the roads in and out are barely navigable during winter.'

'And the workers are mainly locals?'

'Mainly, and they were good – they'd just come off building a treatment plant nearby, but . . . You could get better information from Umbra,' Hasif said. 'Why aren't they giving you all this information instead of me?'

'We'll be speaking with them,' State said. He looked at Fox, and wondered how much the government guy knew about all this. Probably just another asylum case for him to process.

'You really think Umbra might be behind this?' Hasif asked.

'From their standpoint,' the Fed spoke, 'they know we can't prove anything illegal, so they're unlikely to go out of their way to cooperate. We'll keep at this, don't worry about that.'

'Russians . . .' Hasif said. 'I've never had problems with anyone else in all my years working around the world. In hindsight, maybe their secrecy all the way through this caused these problems, but – what, it could be an Indian group out to get me. It could be anyone who sees this work I've done here, in this disputed area, as a threat.' Hasif circled the GPS spot on the map in the disputed Kashmir region – on Pakistan's side of a dotted line – and traced a road southwest.

'The project is now fully online?' Fox asked.

'We ran tests, it's operational,' he replied. 'As to whether they're running it and at what capacity, I have no idea; you'd need to see it for yourself. But it's big – the dual pipeline, which is diverted here—' he tapped the circled point on the map – 'was big enough to carry water on a scale I've never worked on. Are they splitting the diversion further? You'd need to speak to Art Kneeshaw about that. They never allowed me to see the earlier documents in full, and the Pakistani government has no official record of them – I tried to find out, checked everywhere. The capacity is huge, though. I mean, we wondered why on earth they'd need pipes of such magnitude. Who knows, that much water could be used for anything – it's nation-building quantities.'

'Thanks,' Fox said. 'I know you're scared.'

'Not for myself. But my family . . . How do I protect them?'

'They'll be safe,' the Fed said.

'We'll take you into the US,' State said. 'We'll discuss the details on the flight, but we've granted temporary residence to your family with the view to upgrading that to permanent status ASAP.'

'You'll be guarded by federal agents,' the Fed said. 'For now, the people who did this believe you died in the explosion, and as long as they continue to believe that, the heat is off you. Mr Hasif, make no mistake, we'll protect you and your family.'

Fox put a hand on Hasif's shoulder.

'These guys here and a few Feds on the ground in DC are the only ones who know that it wasn't you who was killed in Libya. When these guys hide someone, they stay hidden.'

41

CIA HEADQUARTERS, LANGLEY, VIRGINIA

The CIA man heard about the attack in Spain, saw the footage: the hit on Fox failed. He felt some responsibility – he had been tasked with organising the Fox and Gammaldi hits here in the States, and he had passed on their location in Spain – but then, he wasn't going to take the heat for the work of amateurs.

Using an online game as a dead-drop site was a good system – he knew no one was really looking closely into that area yet. Like all communications, it left a trace in the servers, but it was not as easily intercepted as a dummy email account. It was an area he was constantly learning about, and he was in the business, surrounded by the best. It was an easy way to communicate, and fine for the short term. This business was all about survival, and survival meant keeping ahead of the pack and adapting before being outdated.

His computer was a standard CIA tool with software developed by the NSA to avoid detection – specifically for use by agents and staff abroad. As far as anyone knew, it could only be breached by its own engineers at the NSA, by some kind of quantum cryptography system they were still developing. It was good, and maybe the Brits would one day be able to access it, too, but not for a long time – this technology was being kept close, much like the F22 fighter jet. Being the greatest nation on earth had to have some benefits.

That Hutchinson was closing in on Babich was forcing his hand on a course of action he had hoped – for financial reasons – was still a way off. It was no loss, though, and he hoped to be able to do business with the next guy who came through and filled the leadership void in Umbra.

He checked his secure email. Still nothing from his FBI contact about that numbered file in Fox's jacket. The longer it took, the more convinced he was of its contents. His man would find it, though – he was SAC of a Field Office and owed him a lot; it was the kind of relationship he had built a career on, first as an agent in Europe and then driving a desk here at home.

Whatever was going to happen over the coming days, he was taking steps to ensure that when the music stopped, if Hutchinson managed to get his man, he wasn't going to be the one left without a seat.

PART TWO

42

GORI, GEORGIA (EASTERN EUROPE)

'Sir, this ain't Russia.'

'Yeah? Tell a Russian that. Or a Nicaraguan.'

'Huh?'

'Anyway, it says so on this NATO map: *"Russian-occupied South Ossetian territory since October 2008".*' The US Army Captain dropped into his Senior Sergeant's dialect: 'Anyway, Top, the hell you know, you ain't never been past the Rockies.'

'Hell, me never been yonder the Ozarks.'

They both laughed.

'What's your GPS say?' A smile from the Captain.

Checked. Double-checked. 'Smart-ass. Sir.'

'The maps are changing all the time – been more border moves around here than you've had pussy. Anyway, five hundred metres back that way and we're definitely in Georgia.'

'This is Georgia, too – occupied, yes, but it's still Georgia, my map and GPS say so.'

'And the Nicaraguans say otherwise, don't forget them. Let's just get out of Russian-occupied territory.'

'You're the boss, Captain, sir.'

Captain Garth Nix and Senior Sergeant Top of 10th Mountain's 1st Brigade Combat Team were part of the vanguard of what would soon be a blue-helmet peacekeeping force set up to monitor the fuzzy border between South Ossetia and Georgia. Until the full complement of troops deployed, however, their main objective was to train and arm Georgian forces.

Nix and Top weren't much interested in who started the 2008 war; who did what during the conflict; who killed how many civilians. But if Nix knew anything for certain, it was that the Russians were the undisputed heavyweight champs when it came to disinformation and denial, spinning a line to the world's media about how they were the innocent party in the whole mess. Their political lies knew no bounds, were told by men not so much because it was their job but because of an indoctrinated idea that no one deserved the truth, especially when it ran contrary to the national interest.

Light snow began to fall.

'Captain, we've got trouble, north zone,' Nix's Radio Telephone Operator said as they approached their waiting Humvees. The RTO spoke rapid-fire, filling in his CO as they piled into their vehicles and tore off towards trouble. Life in the Blue Zone.

43

SRINAGAR, INDIA

'The FBI guys will be here later today,' Fox said over his shoulder to Gammaldi.

They had been choppered back to San Pablo Airport, from where they'd taken their G650 jet nonstop to India, while Geiger had hitched a military flight back to the US with Goldsmith's body.

Fox and Gammaldi were met on the ground by a local reporter and sometime GSR contributor, Thomas Singh, who was escorting them to the Line of Control at the India–Pakistan border. Thomas's Land Cruiser was flanked in front and behind by private security contractor vehicles.

'Do you live here?' Fox asked Thomas. He fitted the ideal of the tall, handsome, strong, proud Indian.

'No,' Thomas said.

Fox waited for more, but instead the three men shared silence for the next few minutes.

'Amritsar?'

Thomas looked at Fox, then back to the road. 'Yes,' he said.

More silence followed.

'Any tigers around here?' Gammaldi asked from the back seat.

Thomas looked at him in the rearview mirror, his face cracking into a faint smile. 'None that I have seen,' Singh said. 'Once, they would have been plentiful.'

The outskirts of Srinagar bustled with colourful humanity. Vendors, rickshaws, cars, bikes, trucks and cell phones and desperation – the full kaleidoscope.

'All that was once plentiful is now trouble, poverty and despair.' Thomas showed little outward emotion as he spoke, but there was something moving in his pragmatic tone.

'I've often wondered,' said Fox, 'how a nation with the biggest middle class in the world – it's over 300 million, yeah? – can have such massive poverty. What, probably 800 million people living in desperate circumstances?'

Thomas looked at Fox. Nothing. Then a nod. 'We were in a dire situation in the sixties, but we overcame it due to the work of a great man,' Thomas said. 'Now we need another man like Borlaug, a warrior saint, but I do not see one coming over the horizon.'

They rode in silence for a while, Fox watching the world flash by.

'Srinagar is the capital of the Jammu and Kashmir state,' Thomas said, his tone friendlier, if a little forced. 'I rarely go there, maybe once a year. Too many tourists, although Amritsar has that too. Too many memories of a different, happier time and place here.'

Fox wondered what was being offered: personal reflections beyond the small talk?

'Amritsar,' Fox said. 'That's the cultural centre for your religion?'

Thomas looked at Fox, who felt he was being judged, deemed worthy or unworthy of further information. Fox sensed that, even though Thomas Singh was affiliated with GSR, he didn't quite know what to make of two out-of-town reporters who arrived at short notice and called for a high-security detail.

'Yes,' said Thomas, looking back at the road. 'Amritsar is home of the Harmandir Sahib – also known as the Golden Temple. It is the spiritual centre of Sikhism, a home for my brotherhood. One can still sense the wisdom of our gurus there – you should see it, feel it, if you have time.'

'I'd like that,' Fox said, watching the expansive outer suburbs go by. The convoy was constantly speeding up and slowing down, weaving in and out and around traffic of every kind.

'In about two hours we will meet my brother at the border,' Singh said. 'He runs an aid agency. As an Indian reporter, I am not permitted to cross the Line of Control.'

'Your brother,' Fox said. 'He works solely in the Pakistani-controlled area?'

Thomas was silent for a while. He gazed out his side window as if trying to find words to describe what it was his brother did. Finally: 'Mainly he helps women and children, on both sides, but he is one of a few small operators who do work that stretches across the border – the NGOs do not do much because it is a relatively lawless land over the LOC, and the Pakistani government does not have enough money to treat their sick, nor to educate their children, nor to protect their women from violence, let alone police their frontiers – but then, you men know that.'

Fox and Gammaldi nodded, each taking in the sights around them while listening to Thomas's words.

After ten minutes of silence, Thomas turned to Fox and said: 'Lachlan, you started this global story about our water crisis. Are you still working this story for that purpose?'

'What purpose is that, Thomas?'

'Look around you,' he said. 'All these dry fields – this is a *wet area* of India. It has the run-off from the mountains, the rain belt from the Himalayas – yet every year it gets drier. We got hand pumps – the water ran out. We got electric pumps – the water table kept falling. Now, it is out of reach to most farmers and communities; only the big industrial pumps can get down to the water. So, when I ask about your purpose, I ask because we are a people with little to no water, and what little we had is now being taken from us. It is theft of life.'

'I know,' Fox replied. 'I know about your suicide farmers. I know about the millions, the tens of millions you have in this country who are sick and starving for lack of water.'

'A number growing every day.'

'Yes,' said Fox. 'If it continues—'

'Hundreds of millions of my countrymen will die.'

Fox could see that Thomas's hands were tight on the wheel, and his jaw was clenched in rage.

'And when do we stand up and say, enough? When does my country, its leaders, Pakistan's leaders, the world – when do they realise it is enough? When it is too late? When our side of the Punjab is nothing more than blood and dust? When the Beas, Sutlej, Chenab, Ravi and Jhelum all go the way of the Sarasvati River – just a few lines of verse in our mythology? Do we take so much from them that those downstream miss out on the life that they provide?'

Exasperation was etched on his face; the face that had held friendliness and warmth now shone with contempt and outrage.

'This situation is not new, but this is a crisis of new proportions, biblical proportions if you will, and it must be stopped. This project is an obstacle that must be destroyed to liberate our rivers . . . and this story must get out, outside the borders of this country.'

'I know,' Fox said. 'I'm working on that, I really am.'

Silence fell. Nothing but the noise of the engine and the tyres on the road.

'This area coming up, famed for its wetlands by the lake,' Thomas said, 'even here it is desperate. The birds, the geese and ducks alone used to block out the sun during migration; now the bigger birds are few, yet still we get record numbers of the smaller creatures because it is one of the last lonely places of water left.'

Fox watched the marshlands flash by the window. A small shaft of sun broke through the cold and the water twinkled like gold. He wound down the window: there was a breeze, and it spoke many languages.

44

GORI, GEORGIA (EASTERN EUROPE)

Excited voices crackled over their tactical radios. Nix and Top pulled the Humvee up four clicks northeast of their command position. A squad of their soldiers hugged the dirt behind an earthen berm, a few hundred metres ahead of the nearest Georgian military forward observation post. The troops were hard to pick out against the snow.

All soldiers wore the latest Army combat uniform. The jacket used Velcro-backed attachments to secure items including name tapes, rank insignia, shoulder patches and unit tabs, as well as recognition devices such as the American flag patch and the infrared tab – the latter sewn to each shoulder to help identify friendly personnel when night-vision devices were employed. Still, when Nix's boys were this far outside the Blue Zone – the protected bubble around Gori and Tbilisi – no camouflage or Kevlar would do what they needed. To survive, they needed to stay smart, and rely on their training – and luck.

'Stevo, what have you boys been doing up here?' Top asked the buck sergeant of the squad, the team's sniper spotter.

'Heard gunfire, came to check it,' Sergeant Steve Kynoch replied. 'Contact must have clocked us; took from taking pot shots at the water tower over there to keeping us hunkered down.'

The sniper and spotter were on higher ground atop the berm, nestled among some shrubs. All faces looked to their commanding officer.

Nix knew that the last Russian military formations left this area in late August 2008, and that Georgian law enforcement units moved back into the nearby city of Gori shortly thereafter – and right now FBI agents from the Tbilisi office were crawling through the rubble of the Town Hall after the US–EU diplomatic delegation was blown up. Georgian authorities were in control of the city and its outskirts but the town was a mess: most of everything was stolen and if not it was pretty well wrecked. The mayor of Tbilisi was arranging the return of tens of thousands of refugees to Gori, but until the Blue Zone was plugged against threats like the one presenting itself, those days were still a way off. Nix and his team were part of the current security attachment, officially there to train the Georgian Army. The closest Russian checkpoint remaining in the vicinity of Gori was located about a click to the north of here. Whatever this trouble was, it was in no-man's-land.

'So what's the deal?' Nix said. No gunfire was sounding now, despite his guys feeling threatened enough to stay low. 'I heard there was trouble.'

Ping ping ping.

The rifle fire zapped off Nix's Humvee; the rear side window cracked but it held. He looked to his senior non-com, Top, who looked as pissed as Nix felt.

'I know, you really like Humvees,' Top said to his Captain.

'That was a brand new one, too,' Nix said. 'Fucking commie bastards.' He looked through field glasses to scan for the shooter.

'Are we shooting people or what?' the sniper asked without moving from his sighted weapon. Specialist Pete McAllister was new to the team; he was nicknamed Mac, although some senior guys called him Poor Choice Pete, after a disastrous night out on the town in China.

Ping ping ping.

'Are we shooting?' the Radio Telephone Operator asked.

'That's what I'm asking,' Mac said.

Ping ping ping.

'Well, what's the answer?'

All soldiers except Mac turned again to face Nix. He looked at his men, then towards the concealed gunman, then to his wrecked Humvee.

Ping ping ping-zap. The last shot was close.

'Top, what calibre's he shooting at us?'

'Five-five-six, sir,' Top replied, referring to the 5.56 mm-sized standard NATO assault rifle round.

'Correct, and that ain't Russian.'

'He could be using a captured Georgian M4 or Tavor 21; they lost quite a few in the conflict.'

Nix nodded. Great. He really didn't want to shoot Russian soldiers – well, he didn't want the consequences of shooting Russian soldiers.

'What uniform's he wearing?'

'Could be Russian, sir,' Kynoch replied.

'Could be Russian? Like, could be Georgian even?'

'Sir,' Kynoch said, 'we can only see his head. No helmet, no hat, nothing but hair.'

'That's all I need. Call the shot, sir,' the sniper said down his scope. He was lying prone, the most accurate field position for sniping: on his stomach with legs spread out, feet arched down and partly embedded in the ground, his rifle tight in his shoulder. As ready as he'd be.

A single shot rang out. The US soldiers kept low. Nix looked at the guy he most trusted in life, Top, who triple-checked his GPS against the latest NATO map that had the control areas clearly marked. He knew Top's advice would be to set a precedent and example for all concerned. There was no dispute that they were in friendly territory, only a question of how far this situation might escalate.

45

ON THE ROAD, NORTHERN INDIA

'What will it take to change the Kashmir problem?' Fox asked. 'I mean beyond this current situation, beyond this water dispute?'

Thomas Singh sighed. He had been talking about this and writing about this for years, but Fox knew that this local reporter's voice wasn't nearly loud enough to make the difference.

'We need more good people doing good things,' he said. 'We need politicians to lead. We need to educate our children and equip them to change things – India will soon have fifteen per cent of the world's teenage population. Fifteen per cent! Think what they could do! Soon we will overtake China. We are a people and a culture exploding onto the world stage, yet we cannot even provide adequate drinking water to half our population.'

Fox waited a bit before asking the question he knew did not have a simple answer: 'Can you have long-term peace with your neighbour?'

'We need peace and reconciliation with Pakistan; the future of the Kashmiri people depends upon the two nations coming to terms,' Thomas said. 'Will that happen soon? No. In my lifetime?

Maybe, maybe not. Maybe there needs to be an independent Kashmir, who knows? The kids there do not get the chance to grow because of violence or fear. We need politicians who know that they are judged on what they build, not what they destroy – and it has to be more than dams and pipelines. We need schools, we need . . . so much.

'There will never be a solution in Kashmir if there is no forgiveness. Like the Truth and Reconciliation process in South Africa, India and Pakistan must come to terms with each other, accept the current situation and move forward.' He looked out the windscreen, his gaze unflinching. 'It is time to bring peace back to Kashmir. It is time my country stood up and shouldered the responsibility of peace. It is past desperate here. We are a billion people who have sent a spacecraft to the moon but allow starvation and thirst.'

'You need help,' Fox said. 'People need to know about all this. Those outside your borders – your friends – need to help.'

'We need help from more than men,' Thomas replied. 'We need water.'

46

GORI, GEORGIA (EASTERN EUROPE)

'We're right on the buffer zone, yeah?'

Top nodded to his commander and said: 'That guy shouldn't be in there.'

'Shouldn't be shooting at us, that's what he shouldn't be doing,' Nix replied. He looked around them: there was nothing but a dirt road that snaked through the woods along the southern bank of the Greater Liakhvi River. Most of it had an earthen berm pushed up, like this one; perhaps originally as a precaution or perhaps simply from the road grading, but now there were also some sandbags and concrete rubble scattered along its top in an effort to create a safer zone for whoever had occupied this area as a shooting alley in the 2008 conflict. In the nearby town – Tskhinvali, as it was labelled on Nix's map, the capital of South Ossetia – civilians were still few on the ground, compared with a couple of thousand Russian troops. Nix hoped none of the latter was dumb enough to be using false-flag techniques by firing a non-standard weapon at US personnel – in no-man's-land, outside the Russian-controlled territory.

Ping ping ping.

'He's reloaded!' Mac said, the highly-tuned shooter no doubt feeling naked with nothing more than a low-calibre carbine in his hands.

'Yeah, we got that,' Top said and turned to Nix. 'Captain, we bugging out or taking care of this bad guy?'

'Double-check there's no friendlies over there,' Nix said to his RTO. The Georgian Armed Forces numbered around 45 000, with about a quarter trained in advanced techniques by US military instructors. Nix had fought beside some of these troops in Iraq – they were pretty good, and he was happy to be here returning the favour. He'd even been made an honorary member of the 13th 'Shavnabada' Light Infantry Battalion; they were his brothers-in-arms, and he wanted to avoid blue-on-blue engagement even more than killing a Russian soldier.

'We're in the peacekeeping zone,' Top said to his Captain. 'He's firing at us from no-man's-land.'

'The Georgians confirm they've got no one in that sector,' the RTO soldier said. 'And the Russians aren't supposed to be there.'

Nix's wheels were turning. His briefing was still ringing in his ears. Their rules of engagement stated they could return *hostile* fire. This guy could be a militant, a Russian-backed South Ossetian gun slinger. Could be a kid with a .22. Could be anyone.

Pang pang pang.

A louder report; a heavy calibre, semi-auto with a slow rate of fire. Definitely not a .22.

'He's got a buddy joining in,' the spotter said. 'Make it a 12.7 mil, DShK-type heavy machine gun—'

Phraaaaaaaaang!

The front half of the Humvee tore apart like confetti as the heavier rounds raked in at full auto. Seconds later a tracer round flashed between Nix and Top; they dropped to cover and the Humvee's roof peeled back as if a wrecking crane had taken to it.

'Want to call in CAS, Cap?' Top asked as Nix shook his head clear of debris. The RTO was ready to make the call with their coordinates to the Close Air Support command centre back near Tbilisi. There was no carrier group in the Black Sea yet – a standing treaty limited NATO tonnage – but that had become a top priority back in Belgium since the attack on the diplomatic delegation here in Gori had pissed off most of Europe.

'Where's it at?'

Top listened in to the RTO's spare headset and replied to his company commander: 'Georgian fixed wing, about twenty minutes out.'

Nix knew the lag – once a request for CAS was passed to a jet by an Airborne Warning and Control System aircraft, it took the Air Force about that long to calculate the desired mean point of impact, which was required to ensure the bomb hit its target. Back in Operation Anaconda, his division had learned the hard way how to make the best of their own tools.

Ping ping ping.

'How about the 120?' he asked.

As a Reconnaissance and Surveillance Target Acquisition company, whenever deployed in a hot zone they had the RSTA company's 120 mm mortar section set up ready to rock. Sure, there were also Georgian fixed-wing fighter bombers in the air above – the only NATO aircraft authorised for use in the area were Black Hawks for medevac – and he knew that a French artillery battalion was within firing range of the shooters, but none of that was attractive to Nix right now. The fire was ready, and rumour was there were further fixed-wing NATO aircraft and helicopter gunships ready to roll out of Turkey, but that wasn't an option here today . . . Nix's boys weren't here as part of a beauty contest – they were here as part of a broader mission to keep the peace since the bombing of the City Hall building, and make no mistake, these 10th Mountain boys were ready to be used.

'I can take the shot,' the sniper said again. He had an M4, the standard rifle of light infantry; a smaller, lighter version of the M16. The shooters were a good four-fifty, maybe five hundred metres away, across the Kura River.

'Hold it, Mac,' Nix said, weighing it up as a few more rounds zipped into his Humvee.

'I can see both targets,' Mac said. 'The heavy is an NSV or Kord type.'

If Mac had been armed with his US Army standard issue M110 sniper rifle – with an effective range of double this distance – Nix would have ordered the shot. It would have been designated by the spotter as a true target, and engaged. But Specialist McAllister had something unique in his corner, something that evened the odds, even at this distance – a full-colour embroidered yellow tab, with the words 'President's Hundred' centred in green letters. This badge was awarded by the National Rifle Association to the 100 top-scoring military and civilian shooters in the President's Pistol and President's Rifle Matches.

Besides, Nix knew that the Georgian Air Force was busy slamming insurgent gun-runners' SUVs and other targets along its border with Chechnya. CAS was still twenty minutes out! *And* Nix doubted their accuracy, especially when he and his men were in the danger-close area of the kill box. Sure, the Georgians had a few modern aircraft and US-made JDAM bombs, but they didn't have Americans in the cockpit, and God knew what kind of Chinese whispers would ensue as his CAS coordinates were transferred through the various people involved in making things go boom.

'Mac, where's your one-ten?'

'Camp, sir,' the sniper replied. 'Not pulling sniper duty here—'

'We were doing a PT drill,' Seargent Kynoch said, looking rightfully embarrassed. 'Another section had watch.'

'Doing a fucking PT drill out here?' Nix said to Top, who nodded and made a mental note to chew out some arses when they got back to camp.

'I can take them, sir,' Mac said, still looking down his M4. 'Call it any time.'

Ping ping ping.

Right into his Humvee again.

Top had a gleam in his eye, shrugged a *give the kid a shot* look to Nix. He couldn't help but smile back. Another couple of tracers from the enemy's heavy machine gun tore into a tree to their right, spitting wood bark and leaves in the air.

'Okay,' Captain Nix said, motioning to a Private manning the Squad Automatic Weapon. 'Lay a bit of cover fire. Mac, take the shot.'

The gunner opened up, the rounds flying down range at the enemy; tracers sweeping left to right along the target's roof-line. Then he disengaged.

Mac, his M4 resting on a sandbag atop the berm, was as still as a rock. He sighted down his standard Close Combat Optic.

Pop plink. Pop plink.

Two shots fired, not a second apart, probably between two heart beats.

Sniper and spotter remained prone.

All enemy fire ceased.

Kynoch called it: 'Both targets down. Mac got 'em.'

Over four hundred metres, two targets, two shots. On this speck on a map, the engagement ended. Captain Garth Nix knew, as did men who had long looked at maps of places just like this one, how easy it was for a war to begin. An imaginary line in the ground had just been crossed, and no one could take that action back.

47

LINE OF CONTROL, TWENTY KILOMETRES NORTH OF KARGIL, INDIA

Thomas's brother, Amar, looked older than Thomas but he was a few years younger. The pair said a quiet hello and Thomas stayed by his own car well inside the Indian side of the Line of Control. They were civil to each other but distant; Fox sensed some serious family history. He handed over an envelope, ten grand in US bills as a GSR donation to Amar's NGO. Fox looked at Thomas and saw disappointment outshining his innate pride.

'Thanks for bringing us out here,' Fox said to Thomas as the others packed into Amar's vehicles: an SUV, two small supply trucks and an ancient US Jeep carrying five Pakistani shooters, their protection. They were all parked in a five hundred metre buffer zone on this checkpoint of the LOC. Several other vehicles in various states of repair were here too, even an all-terrain bus with a few British tourists having a tea break.

'Headed back to Amritsar?' Fox asked as he retrieved his backpack from Thomas's SUV.

'I'll be in Kargil until tomorrow afternoon,' Thomas said, looked absently at the Pakistani military who would not allow him passage across the border.

'Thomas, I know you're sceptical of my work here, but I *will* get this done,' Fox said, offering the Sikh his hand. 'This is on the world stage, it's getting more attention every day.'

'Yes, I know,' Thomas said, shaking Fox's hand. 'It is just that I am sick of seeing these two countries going to war. Partition is still an open wound, and neither side of this border is willing to accept the ongoing consequences.'

Fox wandered over to the Indian posts and took a few photos of troops playing a glass bead game. Despite the recent political tensions between the two countries, the extreme cold at these high altitude locations meant the posts were manned by minimal troop levels. The Indian troops wore well-maintained snow-camouflage suits and had gas-bottle heating; the Pakistanis were in mismatched second-hand ski gear and relied on wood and coal fires.

'Maybe Obama will make a difference,' Thomas said. 'I have hope that he'll help make our farms flourish and clean waters flow.'

'To nourish starved bodies and feed hungry minds,' Fox said. 'I believe he's serious about using the US's power to help weaker countries, to do some real good.'

Thomas nodded, his eyes unreadable.

'I'm here to uncover the truth,' Fox said, motioning to the others that he was ready to get moving. 'If that effects change for the better, then great. If not . . . Well, history will judge which side you and I are on, but I assure you, it's the same side.'

Thomas extended a hand; Fox took it. He was Fox's size, and his grip was strong. '*Bole So Nihal, Sat Sri Akal.*'

Fox smiled. 'What does that mean?'

'It means, "He be blessed who says truth is God",' said Thomas. Then he turned and left.

Fox returned to the others. It was so cold here – less than 10 degrees Celsius – about the same as Srinagar but with higher winds, usual for this time of year and at this altitude. Clouds overhead, not a patch of sky, but no rain.

Fox and Gammaldi climbed into Amar's Land Rover, and the convoy set off, the shooters up front.

'It hasn't rained here since . . . I can't remember,' Amar Singh said. 'There are children in this town, some of them teenagers, who have either never seen rain, or only once or twice in their lives. Can you believe that?'

Sadly, Fox could. It was the same in some parts of Australia and probably plenty of other places.

They had a few stops ahead of them before they arrived at the place Fox wanted to be, and the first was in a nearby town, where Amar's people unloaded some of the supplies into a little house that served as a makeshift storage warehouse. As Fox walked towards the warehouse he watched Gammaldi take photos of these kind Samaritans doing the good that should have been done by governments.

Fox looked in the storehouse, stacked with sacks of rice and medical supplies, as well as some large drums of fuel for the vehicles. There was a little lean-to room open to the elements, and he watched as people came and went. He popped his head in. Shrine. Incense. Dust. The place was dark, cold, surprisingly large. Empty. His footsteps were as loud as hell as he walked on the rammed-earth floor.

'Come on, we're going,' Gammaldi called.

48

CIA HEADQUARTERS, LANGLEY, VIRGINIA

Being an American spy had its advantages. Having the resources of the CIA and the sixteen sister agencies of the intelligence community at your fingertips was just plain unfair to everyone on the other team.

The CIA insider had the data in from his FBI contact; the numbered file in Fox's jacket. Seems Fox had a relationship once, not so long ago . . .

Kate Matthews was put through the FBI's identity-making machine several months ago . . . She had been a CIA-run woman working as a lawyer in the Advocacy Center . . . Photo, bio, details of the case that led to her needing to be protected. He flicked through the pages, stopping when he reached the report from the night Fox last saw her. A French nuclear sub in New York Harbor – that detail certainly hadn't made it into the papers – Fox and Kate were whisked off Liberty Island by medevac, taken to hospital, where the FBI declared her DOA and put her into witness protection as they went about cleaning out the rotten CIA agents involved. Her family, and Fox, believe she died that night – the file even included photos of them all at her funeral.

The file confirmed that Kate Matthews now had a new identity, and more importantly, it listed her current home and work addresses in the Netherlands.

Leverage. This would solve problems for his other employer and he'd earn a nice bonus along the way. He looked at the photo of Kate: auburn hair, dark eyes, great figure . . . Man, he should be so lucky to have a piece of that.

Kate Matthews. Won't stay hidden for long.

49

NORTHERN AREAS, PAKISTAN

They rolled as a slow-moving convoy: the beaten-to-crap Jeep as lead, the SUV carrying Amar, Fox and Gammaldi, and the two small trucks behind.

Their second stop on the Pakistani side was not a town so much as a logistics hub, with a row of parked trucks selling everything from food to fuel to the border-crossers, mainly NGO and media staff.

Fox noticed a group of UNESCO International Hydrological Programme workers, getting nowhere with Pakistani red tape. Back on the Indian side there had been a growing gathering of press as well as these UN types, also getting nowhere. Fox knew that a few days ago a BBC crew tried to get into the town where he was headed today, but they had taken an inland route through an area designated as a no-go zone for civilians, and had been ejected from the country for violating national security. Fox kind of got that – it was a dangerous area, and tensions were high, with the occasional artillery shell exploding in the no-man's-land of desolate, rugged terrain between them and the Indian-controlled side. The world's media would remain hungry for stories from here for a while yet.

'Two or three more stops before we get to your site,' Amar said as they continued on.

'Thanks,' Fox said as he tapped away at his MacBook Pro, organising copy and pics to email later to GSR.

'At the next town, twenty kilometres northeast of here, I'll be stopping to see if they're okay; winter has been harsh this year,' Amar explained. 'Couple more stops as we head north, then to where you're after. I'll pick you up on my way back tomorrow.'

'Thanks, that will be great.' Amar had to do his own work, and Fox was grateful for the taxi ride and tour he was providing. 'When we get back to Srinagar, we're going to head to Kochi and try and meet with an engineer,' Fox said. 'If we can find him.'

Amar looked to him. 'He's – he's hard to find?'

'Yeah, almost impossible,' Fox said. 'But I think we're close – got a research team on it back home, and some local reporters back in India. He'll turn up.'

Amar nodded, looking ahead, his hands tense on the wheel as he drove along the corrugated road.

'This water project you are interested in – it will provide more water for this area,' Amar said. 'I see that as a good thing.'

'What about it taking water away from your own people?'

'These are all my people.'

Fox nodded. These people had been one nation not so long ago. 'I meant the many millions of Indians who will lose out.'

'It's delicate, but it has always been happening,' Amar said, 'and not just with Pakistan. In 1975, India constructed the Farakka Dam on the Ganges River, just before the Bangladeshi border. Bangladesh still argues that the dam diverts much-needed water from their people and has created a manmade disaster in a country already plagued by natural disasters. That sort of thing, like this new project, has happened before and will happen every day in a different part of the world. I deal, unfortunately, with the consequences.'

50

HIGH OVER THE MEDITERRANEAN

'You guys didn't support our coalition into Iraq, did you?' Brick asked Ivan.

'No,' Ivan replied. 'I heard Japan sent PlayStations though.'

They all laughed.

'How'd you get that scar?'

'This here?' Brick said, running his fingers along the big star-shaped welt, still shiny and pink, on the side of his neck.

'Luigi, I've heard him tell a woman it was from bow-hunting polar bears,' Duhamel said.

'Like that time you said you lost a toe when you summitted Kilimanjaro.'

'That was the true story.'

Brick leaned forward. 'He drove a hire car into the Potomac to practise escaping.'

Duhamel shook his head and rolled his eyes.

'Anyway, this scar?' Brick said, serious tone for a change. 'Terrorist, with a 9 mil.'

'Ouch.'

'He fared a whole lot worse,' Duhamel said.

The Italian guy nodded. Even the Russian seemed impressed.

Jake Duhamel and Brick sat opposite their two ring-ins. Hutchinson's Big Stick was a motley crew indeed. Each had his own history in law enforcement, each had his own memories of what made them angry, and each would get to direct that anger soon enough.

51

NORTHERN AREAS, PAKISTAN

Fox couldn't help being angry at what he saw in the townspeople's desperation. As they drove past makeshift buildings and burnt-out vehicles, Gammaldi occupied himself by leaning out the back window to take digital photos for GSR's website.

'Any significant aid getting out here?' Fox asked. 'Any major NGOs?'

'No, it's too lawless for food agencies. The US cut aid for primary education in northern Pakistan a while back. If they're lucky some kids go to madrasahs,' Amar said, then shook his head. 'Then when they finish they get AK47s and RPG launchers as graduation presents from the local militant groups, who are the primary employers for such young men.'

Fox understood. This was something he'd seen before, in Timor and Indonesia, Iraq and Afghanistan: families on the downside of disadvantage with no options but to deal with the consequences.

'This is a military transit town, mostly,' Amar said, looking around. This was Indian Kashmiri territory; after almost three hours of driving along bumpy, weaving roads through moonscape-like terrains, there was still no difference in how the people looked compared to those on the other side of the line on the map. 'There used to be a couple of Mujahideen camps nearby but after September 11 the US threatened to bomb this town, with many other targets, back to the stone age unless Pakistan joined them in their War on Terror.'

'And they joined and got lucky, hey?'

'Oh, they joined with Bush,' Amar said. 'They joined; the Mujahideen camps moved somewhere new; and the US and British military aid that came into this country funded a whole new kind of criminal.'

Amar pointed out the window as they passed a group of youths playing in the street with AK47s.

'Groups like that are so easily brainwashed,' Amar said. 'Money and religion are the forces at work out here, and it's intoxicating to these young men to the point that they venture across the LOC and kidnap or kill, just for fun, often even Muslims like themselves – all because of a line on a map that didn't exist fifty-odd years ago. The Taliban is like a malignant cancer around here.'

Amar reached behind the seat next to Gammaldi and took a couple of T-shirts from a box of supplies.

'Here, put these on, for safety,' he said, passing a T-shirt to each man. The logo of Amar's charity was printed on the front. Fox and Gammaldi slipped the T-shirts over their parkas, under which they each wore a Kevlar vest. 'They know to leave me and my people alone, but you both look American, and that's not a good thing around here when you're viewed down the sight of a rifle.'

As the convoy pulled up, a group of kids emerged from the squat mud-brick building that served as a school. They were dressed in woven wool clothes that had seen many children's frames, and their cheeks were ruddy and their noses ran. All ages shared the class, from post-toddlers to almost-teens. The men stepped from the cars and instantly the children rushed at them, yelling and calling in broken English to the new faces of Fox and Gammaldi:

'Take me to America!'

'Take me to Australia!'

A couple of young boys clung onto Gammaldi's legs, speaking excitedly in Urdu.

'Looks like I'll be taking home some extra baggage,' he said, doing a strong-man walk with the kids piling onto him.

As Amar and his people set to work, Fox reached into his backpack. He had brought a shopping bag full of indoor cricket balls and handed one to each kid. He wished he had thought to pack cases of books and pencils but was sure that Amar's team would take care of that.

A father approached and shooed away the kids, who ran off laughing and shouting. He accepted the food offered by Amar, and Fox saw in this man pride that had been shelved a long time ago. He invited Fox and Gammaldi to his home and made them tea, which they drank out in the street, watching, talking, Fox doing most of the listening.

'It must be nice to live there, yes? No . . . None of this . . .' He looked out past the children and the animals and the crumbling buildings as if imagining a fairytale. 'We live in a house that in the winter shelters our animals, too – who wants to live with animals?'

He spoke of his worries, and wondered aloud what it would be like to live like the two Australians: happy all the time, with easy access to food and shelter and power and water.

'It's . . . Yeah, we have all that.' Fox watched the kids play cricket: smiling, happy; the greatest day of their lives with those fifty-cent balls, scratching fun out of the cold dust, using a small potted tree just beginning to leaf as their wicket. 'And sometimes it's easier to pretend.'

The man nodded; maybe he got it. Amar was with his people, expediting the handouts to keep to his schedule.

Fox enjoyed Manhattan, living in a brilliant, vibrant city; he had meaningful, challenging work; he had good friends – but none of that blocked out the memories. The nightmares. The time he had failed Kate, had been too slow, too blind to the situation around him. Then came the rare moments of clarity – like now, here with these people, when he felt he could still offer something, still be of use.

A small boy came up – Fox had noticed he had been ostracised by the other children – and tried to speak, in quiet, deliberate, broken English. Fox handed him a few five-rupee coins. His face was scarred but his eyes were bright. An older child, perhaps the boy's brother, ran up and explained the scar – a burn – and the boy hid his face in his hands, embarrassed.

Fox removed his upper clothing and felt the cold air bristle against his goose-pimpled flesh. He showed the boy his scars – bullet entry and exit through his forearm, cut across his collarbone, angry pink pock marks from where three pistol rounds had managed to push through the back of his bulletproof vest a few months ago.

He bent down and guided the boy's hand away from his face – the scars weren't so bad, but it tore Fox up to see such damage on a kid.

'Listen,' Fox said to him. 'Life – life is how you wear your scars. Can you say that?'

The boy nodded.

Fox held out another coin, expectant.

'Life is how—' He looked at Fox.

Fox pointed to his own scars. '. . . how you wear your scars,' he offered.

The boy smiled a sweet smile. 'Life is how . . . you wear your scars.'

52

GORI, GEORGIA (EASTERN EUROPE)

'South Ossetia and Russia have many men over there, but no soldiers,' a Georgian officer was telling some American troops. Captain Garth Nix tried not to roll his eyes – it was just that kind of talk that led to more trouble, and underestimating the enemy wasn't something he practised.

Most of his men were helping with reconstruction work today, building semi-permanent housing for refugees on the sports oval of a former boarding school the UN peacekeepers had taken over as headquarters of the Blue Zone. He was overseeing the construction and awaiting the arrival of some embedded reporters who would spend time with the men on the ground, trying to get the 'real' story of what was happening here.

Mac wasn't here, though: he was off duty, confined to barracks pending an inquiry into the shooting. It turned out those two guys he'd taken out on Nix's order *were* Russian, and the Russians were shouting to anyone who would listen, claiming that six civilians had also been killed in the exchange – although, conveniently, they refused to allow the UN specialists to inspect the bodies. Nix knew it was all typical Russian bullshit, his guys had selectively sprayed the Squad Automatic Weapon in a controlled burst, and Mac shot off just the two rounds. They engaged a deadly threat in the buffer zone, which was specifically designated off-limits to all civvies and military personnel, precisely to avoid this kind of exchange.

Peace talks were going on somewhere: Sarkozy doing his thing again, Hillary Clinton too, and no doubt Putin puffing his chest out in reply. Mac was in barracks and Nix was on babysitting duty until his superior said otherwise. This wasn't soldiering.

53

NORTHERN AREAS, PAKISTAN

There were hardly any men left in the next speck of a town. The inhabitants – women and children, and a few old guys – lined up for handouts from Amar's NGO staff, some looking spooked as a convoy of Pakistani soldiers rumbled west. Fox leaned against Amar's SUV, and Gammaldi sat on the warm bonnet, eating an MRE.

'Wazzup?' Gammaldi said, licking his spoon clean.

'Was that lemon pound cake?' Fox asked.

'Might have been,' Gammaldi said. 'Ate it too fast to tell.'

'Anyway,' said Fox, going over some pages of his Moleskine notebook, 'they say most of the construction guys for the water project were recruited from here. They relocated to the construction place about fifty clicks northeast of here; shitty track, takes about an hour and a half by car.'

'Hmm,' Gammaldi said, wiping his mouth on the arm of his charity T-shirt. 'And we couldn't take a chopper in from Srinagar because . . . ?'

'Because everyone around here's got a gun or an RPG, and the only choppers in and out of this region are Indian military – prime targets for the aforementioned weapons.'

'Fair enough,' said Gammaldi as he slid off the bonnet of the car and cleared away his meal packaging.

Fox looked around and saw Amar heading their way. He was walking quickly, purposefully, and his people were hurriedly packing their supplies into their trucks.

'What is it?' Fox asked as Amar reached the car.

His face showed revulsion. He wouldn't meet their eyes with his. He climbed into the car without speaking.

Fox and Gammaldi exchanged a look.

'Amar,' Fox said, getting into the passenger seat. 'What is it?'

He started the engine, his hands tight on the wheel, his mouth a hard line on his face. People were still in the street, only now they were walking slowly, aimlessly. Fox watched a woman stop in the middle of the road and bring her hands to her head, tears running down her cheeks as her children clung to her.

Gammaldi climbed in and they drove off, heading the convoy, northeast. They rode in silence for the next hour and a half. Fox stared out the window, thought about the faces of those women in the town, thought about Kate.

•

'Where is everybody?' Gammaldi asked.

There was no noise but for the barking of a few wild dogs as the vehicles pulled up in a levelled-off gravel shoulder. They walked behind Amar, through a canyon of excavated earthworks to reveal the town stretched out before them. 'Have they already left—'

Gammaldi almost slipped when they rounded a corner into what used to be the main street of the town. Dozens of temporary structures had been burned to the ground. Some old mud and stone huts had survived the flames, but their roofs were smouldering. What Fox thought had been fog or cloud was smoke.

'Oh shit . . .' Gammaldi said, stepping over a bloodied bone on the ground.

Amar lurched forward and vomited on the road. He wiped his hand across his mouth angrily and spoke for the first time since leaving the last town. 'There have been bandit attacks,' he said. 'This is . . . this area . . .'

He couldn't go on. His NGO staff tentatively picked their way forward. Four of them were the protection, armed with old semi-automatic rifles; no match for whoever did this.

Fox entered a hut. It smelled of burned bodies and charred bones. He picked up a few brass shell casings, 9 mm. He walked out to the car, took his camera out of his backpack and snapped away at everything. He stopped counting after tallying thirty separate human remains. He found Gammaldi sitting on the ground by the car, the colour chased from his face.

'There's no one left alive,' he said. 'No one.'

Amar made his way back. His people climbed into their vehicles, ready to leave this place. 'We're heading back into India to properly report this,' he said, getting into the Land Rover. He sounded determined, as if he had found some measure of resolve out there in the cold streets. He had not radioed the information, but had placed several calls on his satellite phone as he had walked around.

Gammaldi pushed himself up off the ground and opened the back door of the SUV.

'Good to go?' asked Fox.

Gunfire sounded – semi-automatic rifle fire. In these kinds of mountains it could be around the corner, or it could be five kilometres away.

'Yep,' Gammaldi said, climbing in and closing his door. 'Let's get out of here.'

54

MOSCOW, RUSSIA

Babich's office was in a corner of the new Norman Foster-designed Russia Tower, a monolithic piece of modernity clad in glass and steel rising up over Moscow. He looked down at Red Square, distant and minuscule from 118 floors up. His office had special acoustic glass, and Umbra Corp's offices were swept for bugs each day by a roving team, as much to combat industrial espionage as to stop prying ears becoming too familiar with his business dealings.

'So Fox has strong feelings for this woman?' he asked Kolesnik.

'Yes, and he thinks she's dead. Seeing her alive will be—'

'And when will he be taken care of?'

'Soon, in Pakistan,' Kolesnik said with a big grin. Babich could see where some money had gone – his son's teeth were blindingly white and perfectly straight. American teeth.

'So we need this girl for what purpose?'

'Well . . . Insurance,' Kolesnik replied. 'I am going to see her tomorrow for myself, to get a feel for her, just in case.'

'Just in case? For insurance? I don't like the sound of this. You should be more confident – you should not need such back-up plans.'

'Father . . .' Kolesnik said. 'The place that Fox and his friend are going to find themselves in is in the middle of nowhere, and – well, they won't last long, I promise you. If the cold and hunger don't get them, the inmates or guards will. It's a matter of time, a very limited time.'

Babich knew the look in his son's eyes. He was enjoying this too much. It was a game for him, watching others suffer.

'I remember the day your grandfather went to war, to fight for Stalin,' Babich said to him. 'He took us to the zoo here in Moscow, and then we all said goodbye to him. We all cried that day, even him. He bought me ice-cream. It came in an aluminium cup. I still remember that ice-cream, as well as I remember how hungry we were for the next few years. Do you understand?'

Kolesnik looked at him blankly.

'Do not mess around with this any longer,' Babich said. 'Suffering can do no good, not even for your enemy. So far you have done a good job for me on this—'

'Petro failed us—'

Babich held up his hand, and his son knew to stop.

'This isn't a movie,' Babich said. 'This isn't that *Brother* gangster-movie shit that you love so much, that glorified hitman bullshit. If you'd fought in Chechnya like your brother did, you'd take no delight in what you do. You are an instrument to me, a well taken care of instrument, and I need you to be efficient, not emotional.'

Kolesnik's eyes did not leave his father's, and he nodded that he understood.

'You have a few last things to complete. Don't make any final mistakes,' Babich said. 'When you have Lachlan Fox and his partner in a place you can control, you must end it then, while it's easy.'

Babich leaned forward and signalled that their time was over. 'I will see you again when this is all done,' he said, patting his son's face. 'Your mother wants you over for dinner soon. I want to feel proud of you that night, pride like she feels – only mine must be earned.'

55

NORTHERN AREAS, PAKISTAN

Amar Singh stood on a ridge, talking quietly into his phone. He looked over at Fox and Gammaldi sitting in the car, then away. Fox did a double take and turned to Gammaldi in the back seat – something wasn't right.

'Was that Thomas?' Fox asked when Amar returned to the SUV.

Amar looked at him blankly: 'Oh, yes, he'll meet us at the border.'

'Your brother's a good man,' Fox said, watching as Amar climbed into the car. 'He took a while to warm to us, but he's genuine.'

Amar turned the ignition key and the diesel started up with a roar. He slammed his door shut and put his seatbelt on – he hadn't bothered with that before. Perhaps they were going off road, so Fox followed suit and motioned for Gammaldi to do the same. The two supply trucks and the protection vehicle had carried on, but they would catch up with them quickly enough in the Land Rover.

'All happy families resemble one another,' Amar said, pulling onto the tracks in the gravel road, 'but each unhappy family is unhappy in its own way.'

Fox took a second to recall, then smiled. '*Anna Karenina.*'

Amar nodded.

'Huh?' said Gammaldi.

'Tolstoy.'

Gammaldi shook his head, vacant.

'Don't worry about it, Al.'

Fox settled into the seat as they rumbled along the road, which, for the most part, consisted of no more than tyre tracks in the ground. The incinerated town of the Vritra Utilities employees disappeared behind them as clouds swept over the dim afternoon, running the road ahead out of view and forcing Amar to switch on the Land Rover's fog lights.

'We are taking an alternative route,' Amar said, turning south and hammering down a double-laned gravel track. 'Easier to navigate, quicker to the border – more direct.'

Fox didn't think much more of it as they wound around to the left and drove through a small creek bed, meeting up with another corrugated dirt road on the other side. He could no longer see much ahead through the fog, and he was glad Amar knew the way so well.

Something in his side mirror caught Fox's attention. He looked behind – past Gammaldi playing with his satellite phone – there was something . . . Gammaldi noticed the look and turned around, too.

Out of the rear window was the faint glow of headlights.

'Is that the convoy behind us?' Fox asked Amar.

Before he could answer, a vehicle's horn beeped and Amar stopped the car in the middle of the road.

Fox watched Amar. His face was pointed forward, avoiding eye contact, his hands tight on the wheel.

Suddenly there was a hard rap on the glass of Fox's window and he flinched. A Pakistani soldier.

He wound the window down and saw a few uniformed men surrounding the car.

'You will both come with me,' the soldier ordered, pointing to Fox and Gammaldi. His eighties-model M16 was held in a quick-action grip.

Fox looked across at Amar, who was still staring dead ahead into the few metres of glowing space that his headlights illuminated in the fog.

'Amar?'

Nothing.

'You will come with me *now!*' the soldier ordered, knocking the barrel of his assault rifle hard against the side of Fox's head.

Fox clenched his teeth through the pain, raised his hands and motioned that he was opening the door. As Gammaldi got out, Fox saw that he'd managed to press SEND on his phone.

56

WASHINGTON DC

'They sent a distress message?' Faith Williams said over the speakerphone.

'Yes. And we've confirmed the GPS location on Gammaldi's phone, but we can't raise them,' Hutchinson replied.

'Could it be an accident?'

'No way.'

'Maybe they stayed in the town they were going to investigate, and they're out of range.'

'We just had a DoD Predator fly over it – it's a ghost town,' Hutchinson said. 'Visibility wasn't good – clouded over and fogged in – but infrared picked up no life at all.'

'Jesus . . .' Tas Wallace said.

'The GPS location came up empty, but there's plenty of cloud cover; they might be close by,' Hutchinson said. 'My guys will be on the ground in India momentarily, and I've got the FBI field offices in Pakistan and India working with all local assets.'

'All right, keep me posted, and let me know if we can help,' Wallace said. Their connection went dead.

Hutchinson immediately placed another call. He had an American spy to catch.

57

JAIL, PAKISTAN

'You are American spies?'

Fox shook his head. After fifteen minutes of going around in the same circles, he was getting frustrated.

'Do we sound like Americans?'

'We're Aussies,' Gammaldi said. 'You know, cricket?'

'You have official American passports,' the Pakistani Army guy said. He was a senior officer of some sort, and this was either a very poor military base or some kind of prison. He had their brand new official US passports which were empty but for their stamps for Spain and India. 'These have US State Department credentials . . . and you wear American Army pants.'

Fox had forgotten about the pants, and briefly considered arguing the point that they were actually Air Force pants. He figured this guy got his line of questioning out of a book, or probably a bad movie. Fox and Gammaldi watched helplessly as he picked through the contents of their bags, now scattered over his desk. The room was smoky and smelled like dope. The guy's assistants, or whoever they were, were clearly pretty whacked. They may not drink booze around here, Fox thought, but they get their kicks in other ways.

'And here you have American military ration packs,' he said.

'You can buy those in any—'

He held up his hand – probably out of a movie, too – and Fox didn't push it.

'I'll look into all this, make some calls,' he said, leaning back in his chair. 'You will be guests here until I find out more. You *will* tell me more.' Then he waved them away.

They were led out through a small gated area into a large walled yard, an expanse of cold, hard gravel with a water trough in the middle.

'Clothes.'

'What?' Fox asked.

A guard tugged at his jacket.

'You're—' Fox stopped himself when he saw the rifle barrel aimed at his forehead. He and Gammaldi took off their jackets, belts and shoes as directed. They left their gear on the ground and were pushed along, Gammaldi's teeth chattering like morse code.

'Why not just let us go?' Gammaldi said to the armed guard walking beside him. The guard remained silent as he led them towards an ancient-looking squat building with a domed roof, and a heavy-gauge steel-plate door. The guard passed his cigarette to his colleague and slung his rifle over his shoulder as he unlocked the door.

'Maybe offer a trade, Al,' Fox said. 'His weight in fine, uncut Turkish hashish.'

Al laughed and wrapped his arms around himself for warmth. The guards opened the door and—

A smell hit them; a smell and a hum, coming from the darkness within.

'In,' the smoking guard said, motioning inside with his rifle. 'In!'

'After you, mate,' Fox said, nudging Gammaldi into the building. He stepped in behind him, followed by the guard. They walked down well-worn stone steps and came to a thick timber door. The guard turned a key in the lock and then slid a bolt across. The door opened and they were shoved inside, the door slamming behind them.

They stood on a small stone platform, dusty stairs leading down. The room had a vast domed roof with a single skylight. The hum, and the smell, emanated from the people corralled there. Men, as far as Fox could tell in the dim light; some young, most old, at least two hundred of them.

A heaving sea of humanity.

'I'm slipping!' Gammaldi said, grabbing Fox's arm. The landing they were on was worn with use, angled down towards the stairs—

Before they could stop themselves they were in the crowd, just another two added to the mass that moved around the room in a slow circle. It was so crowded, none of the men could stand still against the motion.

'This is just great,' Gammaldi said, pushing past a white-haired man to get back to Fox.

'Just stay close, Al,' Fox replied, moving sideways until they were shoulder to shoulder, getting into the rhythm of the place. 'We won't be here for long. Hutchinson. GSR. They'll find us.'

'How will *anyone* find us in here? Where the hell *are* we?'

'They'll—'

'Hey!' Gammaldi turned and pushed back at a couple of young guys who seemed intent on prying his jumper off him. They came straight back at him, the swell of the human tide behind them. One had something shiny in his hand—

Fox laid him out with an uppercut to the chin, and Gammaldi threw the other guy a few metres through the air ahead of their position.

The crowd moved on, no one perturbed; both young men vanished beneath two hundred pairs of feet.

Gammaldi nodded to Fox as they were forced along and fell into step. Each had mastered the escape and evasion survival techniques required in their former jobs in the Navy. Fox's experience included rigorous anti-interrogation techniques with the SAS – and he'd been through this kind of thing once before, and so had Gammaldi. He still had the dental work to prove it.

They kept close as they walked in rhythm to the room. The men around them looked like walking ghosts.

After a while Fox spoke loudly in his mate's ear: 'We'll be right, Al. Won't be long.'

58

LOUDOUN HEIGHTS, VIRGINIA

The CIA agent walked into his house, kissed his wife and checked on his kids – six and four, boy and girl, everything picture perfect in their catalogue-neat home. He'd had a vasectomy two years ago, so these two little sleeping angels were as good as it got. He picked up some toys in the hallway, and dropped them in the basket in the lounge room.

He poured a neat bourbon and took it with his warmed dinner into his study. His wife had Tivo'd *Idol* and was half a bottle of merlot and two packets of popcorn into the evening. He had work to do. He shut the noise out behind solid oak and sat at his desk. He started up his laptop and tasted the chicken – some kind of one-pot number: chicken thighs, rice, tinned tomatoes, onions, orange slices, wine, herbs. It was good. He typed in his password, a twelve-digit random combo.

The commute from Langley was short in miles but took far too long, especially in peak hour, which he usually circumvented by being busy enough to put in long hours and travel home at night. Their previous place, a rental, had been near the Springfield Interchange, where he and his fiancée had spent five years listening to the traffic of the Beltway converge with that of the I95, a mixing bowl of noise and pollution that was still a hum of anger in the back of his mind. She blamed her fertility problems on that place, and that had been the tipping point.

He had planned to have dinner with the family, a rare treat that tonight would have included a vomiting son and a daughter who refused to eat – fortunately, work was predictably demanding. There was a time, just a few years ago, when it wasn't even dinnertime for them yet; they'd be laughing and joking and talking and entertaining.

He switched on the Net through his regular connection. He never did sensitive work on a computer plugged into the mains – it could all be read. The only Agency work he did at home was reading over printouts, reports and briefs that he hadn't managed to fit into his working day. He was only a couple of rungs below Deputy Director, so he pretty much saw it all.

He logged on to World of Warcraft and saw the small envelope icon at the top right of the screen, attached to the mini-map. He took his avatar, *Darkshadow*, around the streets of Stormwind and headed for the nearest mailbox. As he navigated the streets, he thought back to today's conversation with Hutchinson. Fuckin' Bureau queer.

He ran his avatar up to a mailbox and right-clicked it. His inbox was brought up onscreen and he clicked on the latest mail icon – a message from *SwordsmanM*, his occasional pointy-end guy, an Agency asset who did black-bag work in the US. This man was a Marine once, but he had been a little too trigger-happy even for them, and after a mess in Iraq he'd been welcomed home to undertake simple but blunt work for the Agency. He'd been tasked with taking out Fox and Gammaldi in New York.

The subject line was: *F and G*. The message read: *Unable to engage target. Fed protection. Left from Kennedy. Advise.*

Little late, he typed in reply. *Already onto it. Stand down until further instruction.*

Each message was capped at 400 characters, so although they couldn't write an essay, it was good for, say, a brief list of targets. The downside of this type of communication, as with most dead-drop sites, was that it was seldom real-time; each receiver accessed the information in their own time, and none of the gamers in his guild was in the habit of being online at a specific time. It was slow, but it was relatively secure, and that was the most important thing.

He logged out, then remotely checked into the desk at Langley – the real-time tech team was there, responding to him via an Intellipedia link: the JFK flight plan for all GSR aircraft; visa documents logged for Lachlan Fox; and the scan of all communications regarding Fox showed he was in India. The latter revealed a relationship that for him was opportune – it would be informative, and his scapegoat. He had re-routed all communications to and from Bill McCorkell's computer and phone system so that there was full NSA Echelon intercept and remote ghosting of McCorkell's programs. He could now listen to, read, intercept and replace all McCorkell's communicated data. Technology operating outside the law was a handy thing.

59

THE WHITE HOUSE, WASHINGTON DC

Bill McCorkell walked into the Roosevelt Room more than an hour late for his meeting with the President's science advisors. There were two men there, each with laptops and slideshows ready and mountains of papers on the table. On the table sat several pots of coffee, long cold.

'Hey, Charlie, thanks for waiting,' McCorkell said to Dr Kaufman. As a science advisor to POTUS, he was a regular face in the House but not regular enough to get an office in the West Wing – he had a basement cubbyhole in the EEOB next door.

McCorkell knew that the pace of this meeting would be a little slower than his usual security briefings – four-star generals tended not to talk in scientific jargon or get too excited about pie charts – and he hoped to get through it as quickly as possible.

'I wanted you to hear as many opinions as possible,' Kaufman explained. 'You've probably met Dr Jonze?'

'I was here last year presenting the proposal to build the Antarctic cryobot—'

'To melt down into Lake Vostok,' McCorkell finished. 'How'd that turn out?'

'We're still working on next-stage funding,' he said, resigned. 'It's an important step if we are to test the technology to make a system to get into Europa.'

'But we're not here to talk about Jupiter's moons,' Kaufman said. 'Bill—'

'You've got five minutes,' McCorkell said, taking a seat.

Kaufman looked deflated, the Apple remote in his hand suddenly limp. 'I asked for half an hour . . .'

'Sorry, Charlie, we've got a couple of situations to deal with at the moment.'

'India.'

McCorkell looked at him.

'And Pakistan,' Jonze added. 'That's why we're here.'

He looked from Jonze to Kaufman, then said: 'All right, you've got my attention.'

'Okay,' Kaufman talked slowly. 'We're talking about Siachen Glacier, that's Siachen as in—'

'And like I said,' McCorkell said, 'I've got to get back to a thing, so can you, like, give me the *Reader's Digest* version?'

The two doctors traded looks.

'Five minutes?' said Jonze.

'That was half a minute ago,' McCorkell replied.

'Well, sir, if you listen very carefully,' Jonze said, 'I might be able to teach you how to spell it.'

'Ha!' McCorkell laughed. 'Way to break the ice.'

He picked up the phone and typed in an extension; told his secretary he would be a little longer than expected.

'Okay,' McCorkell said. 'What have you got?'

Kaufman brought up a map onscreen. 'The Siachen Glacier is located in the disputed Kashmir region and is claimed by both India and Pakistan,' he explained, clicking through slides. 'The glacier is the highest battleground on earth, where India and Pakistan have fought intermittently since . . . but you know all that.'

McCorkell nodded, leaned forward and watched the screen as the slides clicked through to the next relevant section.

'The glacier's melting waters are the main source of the Nubra River, which falls into the Shyok River,' Kaufman said. 'The Shyok in turn joins the Indus River, which is crucial to both India and Pakistan. And the real volume of water is where we don't see it – underground.'

'Which is what's being tapped into by Pakistan's new water project.'

'The roots of the conflict over Siachen lie in the non-demarcation of the ceasefire line on the map beyond a map coordinate known as . . .' Kaufman trailed off, noting the look McCorkell gave him. '. . . the Karachi Agreement, and the 1972 Simla Agreement presumed that it was not feasible for human habitation to survive north of NJ9842.'

'Which is incorrect,' Jonze added.

Kaufman continued, 'Prior to 1984 neither India nor Pakistan had any permanent presence in the area—'

'Guys, you've got to cut to the chase.'

'Okay, best case?' Kaufman said, 'We've got a hundred and twenty years.'

'Best case what?'

'I think we've got thirty, tops,' Kaufman countered.

'That's why you're stuck at Stanford.'

'Oh, and Yale's better?'

'Do I need to knock your heads together?' McCorkell asked.

Kaufman sat up a little straighter.

'If global warming continues at its present levels, there will be too little weight at the north and south poles,' Kaufman said. 'And the earth will shift on its axis and we'll enter a global cataclysm of weather patterns not seen on this planet since—'

'Oh come on, Chuck, is this your third-pole theory?' Jonze interrupted sharply.

'Third pole?' McCorkell asked, but neither seemed to notice him as they set on each other—

'That's all you got?'

'It's a long way—'

'Can't happen.'

'*Guys!*' McCorkell said. 'You've used up your five minutes. *What's the bottom line?*'

'Okay, Bill,' said Kaufman. 'You wanted a scientific opinion on this water issue in this region. Here's my read: there has been conflict over this region for decades. The reason is simple: water. Collectively it's the world's biggest fresh water source outside the north and south poles—'

'So you agree this is a third—'

'*And,*' Kaufman put his hand up to silence his colleague, 'if there is a severe conflict in that region – if the area itself is compromised by a large-scale attack, be it by India or Pakistan, be it large-scale conventional or nuclear, that's fresh water for over a billion people that dries up within weeks. Through evaporation, through massive disruption of water tables, through the devastation of a vast weight of frozen water – and it's something that won't be replaced, not in our lifetime, anyway.'

The science men were finally silent while McCorkell took this in.

'Bill, this area needs to be protected,' Kaufman said. 'The ramifications of it being jeopardised are beyond dire. You *must* secure lasting peace in the region.'

The phone rang; McCorkell took a moment to pick it up. His secretary spoke rapid-fire: 'Tas Wallace just left an urgent message. It's about Lachlan Fox.'

60

JAIL, PAKISTAN

'Remind me to punch Amar in the nose the next time I see him,' Gammaldi said.

'I'll do more than that,' Fox replied.

What had once been a brick factory was now a death pit. The prisoners were herded out twice a day for food scraps and a brief reprieve from the oppressive stench below, before being driven back inside to continue their human treadmill. The smell didn't improve on going back in; it hit like a hammer to the face and never went away.

During their first outdoor break Fox and Gammaldi had tried to communicate with a few of the inmates, but it was clear most were afraid of the guards and tried to steer clear of the new guys. One ancient man, who seemed to have been here so long he was beyond fear, told them quietly in broken English that more than half were political prisoners.

'Maybe political reasons, or because they are poor, maybe some steal something, maybe commit acts of unnatural lust . . .' He looked around and kept his voice low. 'Our own army put us in here – they are meant to protect us, but who protects us from them?'

As they'd moved through the night in a semi-asleep state, Fox had started to feel like everyone else looked. He didn't feel cold in the pit anymore – the heat of the constantly moving bodies around them lifted the ambient temperature a few degrees, and that was enough to make a difference. All through the long night Fox had counted his breaths as he shuffled along, zoned into a place of inner peace.

There were no quick or obvious ways to escape. Outside the pit was the walled gravel and dirt yard, about the size of a sports oval; beyond that, mountains rose to the north. The air was thin here – they weren't far from where they had been captured, which was a couple of hours south in the military trucks. Around the yard, the brick wall – an ancient-looking handmade mud, brick and stone construction – looked as wide at the base as it was tall. It was topped with rolls of new razor wire, and there was a single guard tower made from thin steel supports that looked like it was originally designed as a water tower. Two guys were up there, both with rifles. Escape was not an immediate option.

Fox rubbed his head from where the rifle had clocked him; he still had a ringing headache. The fresh air of this morning's outdoor break helped a little, but not enough.

'We're in the middle of nowhere,' Gammaldi said. 'Arse end of the world . . .'

'We'll be right, Al.'

'Yeah? You going to dig a tunnel out of here?'

'Maybe. We could do that and dump the dirt out of our trousers as we walk outside each day.'

Fox looked down at his mate, who was lying on the ground. He sat down next to him, feeling the relief in his legs that had been holding him up for twenty-four hours straight. Gammaldi gazed up at the sky. He smiled and blinked.

'There should be a law on how long they can make you stand when you're a prisoner.'

'There probably is,' Fox replied. 'Some kind of Geneva thing . . .'

'Reckon they're going to realise that we shouldn't be here any time soon?'

Fox squinted against the sun and watched as a tired fight ended as soon as it had started in the middle of the yard, near a rusty old hand water pump. The man who fell didn't get up. His attackers drank.

'I reckon someone will figure it out soon enough,' Fox said. He lay back and closed his eyes, and felt the dangerous need to sleep. 'Remember when you were locked up that time in Italy?'

'Hmph.'

'That big guy you told me about, what'd you call him?'

'A pirate,' Gammaldi said. 'He looked like a pirate.'

'At least there's none of them here.'

'Yeah . . .'

They lay in silence for ten minutes, the shaft of sunlight warm on their faces, and then the bell rang for them to move back towards the pit. Neither rushed.

'Remember that meal we had in Venice, when those girls came over?'

Fox smiled. 'Yeah, that was awesome – pasta?'

'And osso bucco. Let's not talk about food,' Gammaldi said as he sat up. 'Wonder how long it would take me to eat one of these skinnies.'

He helped Fox to his feet and they trudged over to the well and took a drink from a dusty old tin can. The water was briny, and they knew it would leave their lips chapped and caked in white salty powder.

The final bell pealed and they shuffled into line with the rest of the prisoners, their morning outing over. Gammaldi tripped over a divot and stumbled forward. Fox caught him before he fell and helped him shuffle towards the door.

'Top five basketball players . . .' Fox said, knowing that his best friend liked sports.

'Jordan. Just him, he'd beat the next four,' Gammaldi said. 'Also Bryant – he'd slay 'em, he's got something they ain't.'

'More air time?'

'Bigger stones.'

Fox smiled at his mate, who swayed in the bright sun.

'How about,' Fox said, 'top five Australian bands . . .'

Fox stopped walking. Guards were there, right next to him – four of them, wooden clubs in hands.

'You will come with us,' one said.

Fox took a step towards them, then Gammaldi took a couple, unsteadily, and muttered something at them. One of the guards unleashed a blow to the side of Gammaldi's chest, and he doubled over, out of breath, clutching his side in pain. As Fox went to him, the guard unleashed another blow at Gammaldi's back – Fox caught it mid-air. It felt as if it broke something in his hand but he held it, slowly lifted it up; he had easily twenty kilos and plenty of muscle over the Pakistani. Fox stood between the guard and his fallen mate, let go of the club, looked the guard in the eye. If it came to it, he could probably mess these four guys up as much as they could him; use the kind of final violence you didn't walk away from.

'We're coming,' Fox said.

The guy's angry eyes searched Fox's face – then he backed down, and motioned for the others to help get Gammaldi to his feet. They were herded into the command building through a steel door set in the old brick wall.

'So,' their familiar friend, the commandant, said. He was smoking, and a steaming cup of tea sat in front of him on his battered timber desk. The guards hung back by the door. Fox stayed standing, but Gammaldi was still catching his breath and was partly doubled over – tough as he was, he couldn't take much more of this.

'So . . .' he repeated. He had Fox's laptop out, and his iPhone's screen was glowing like it had just been used. 'Ready to tell me the truth? Hmm? You are American spies, yes?'

61

GEORGIA (EASTERN EUROPE)

'He's kinda gone into his shell,' Top said.

'What, you Dr Phil now?'

'Started off angry, now he's withdrawn,' Top said. 'About as much energy as a recruit after first-week training at Benning.'

Nix nodded – confinement would do that to a soldier, especially when he knew he hadn't done anything wrong. Pete McAllister would pull through, Nix was about to see to that – the Army needed good young men like him, even if politicians and the media thought otherwise. Only those who served knew what it was really like; he hadn't until he'd graduated West Point and had his first operational deployment to the Balkans.

'And he wants to know why we can't just blame the shooting on the White Tights,' said Top.

Nix laughed. It was a Russian urban myth that female sniper mercenaries participated in combat against Russian forces in various armed conflicts from the late eighties.

'At least he's still got his sense of humour,' Nix said. 'I'll go sort out Mac, get him moving in the right direction. Is that his M4?'

'Yep,' Top replied, handing it to Nix.

'Go give him his one-ten once I'm done talking to him,' Nix ordered. 'He needs to stay ready to get out there again ASAP.'

'Hooah.'

Nix walked down the hall to Mac's room. Mac was the only soldier ever, in his command, to be confined to barracks, not counting medical reasons. He rapped on the door and entered. Mac was lying on his bed, reading a paperback.

'Sir,' he said, not bothering to get up or turn his attention away from his book.

Nix sat on the wooden chair next to the trooper and handed him the M4. 'This is yours,' Nix said. 'I know what it's like when carrying a weapon has become second nature and it's not there.'

'Yeah,' Mac said, the M4 nestled by his side, a hand clasped around the forward grip. 'It's a piece of me now. You know, since I turned in my one-ten, I've been looking for it all the time.'

'I'm doing everything I can for you, Specialist,' Nix said. 'You should be back out in a day or two, all going well.'

Mac looked to Nix, put his book down and sat up on the bed.

'You shitting me, sir?'

'I wouldn't do that.'

'I heard I was going to be kicked out of the Army.'

'Who told you that?'

Mac looked at the door, didn't answer. Nix assumed it was one of his buddies who'd brought him his meals the past couple of days.

The Army had transformed the way it trained soldiers. Gone was a lot of the spit and polish that had been a staple of basic training for decades: marching, standing at attention, pressing uniforms. Instead, the focus had shifted to the skills that recruits needed to stay alive in places like Iraq and Afghanistan: how to spot a roadside bomb, how to defend a convoy against an ambush, how to save a wounded comrade. Mac was a product of this new era, and it made him itchy to be so cut off from all he'd been taught.

'Don't believe everything you hear, unless it comes from my or Top's mouth, understand?'

'Hooah, sir,' he replied. 'I thought maybe things might get, you know . . . things might be different . . . I mean, it's not like we got McCain as Commander-in-Chief. That would have been good for us, right?'

'It's hard to know, Mac,' Nix said. 'And with Bible Spice as VP, who knows what it would have been like. McCain'd feel our cause, no doubt, but we serve no matter who's sitting in the House. Like them or not, agree with them or not; they represent the people we protect.'

A nod.

'Your dad served, right?'

'Eighty-second Airborne. My uncle was in 'Nam, sixty-eight.'

'Third brigade?'

Mac nodded. Nix knew they'd seen some serious fighting, right at the start of the conflict to boot, before any of the serious horrors started circulating back home and into the minds of fresh soldiers.

'He was out fighting while Hillary was at Woodstock.'

'A "cultural and pharmaceutical event", McCain called it,' Mac said.

'And he was "tied up at the time" . . .'

'You know it, Captain,' he said, picking up a tennis ball he had been playing with earlier. 'They never got this kind of scrutiny back then, not for this.'

He launched the ball at the wall. Nix caught it mid-flight.

'Good men. Different times. So different.' Nix bounced the tennis ball off the wall and caught it. 'Look Mac, you've got a lot more soldiering to do, then I expect you to make Sergeant real quick so you can go back and be a drill sergeant and make sure our next boys are trained right, just like Top did. Hooah?'

'Hooah.'

Nix nodded. He was among the fraternity of Iraq veterans who worried about the kind of recruits the Army was now accepting: older guys, plenty without high-school diplomas, who had received waivers for crimes or medical conditions, or had scored lower on the military's aptitude test than was needed in the past. Times had changed, and he was left with some guys not up to the task. But this young man was none of that; he would be a top soldier in anyone's army, and to peg him back for doing his job – hell, for obeying orders – was not going to happen, not in Nix's Army, especially since he was making Major when they rotated back to Fort Drum in a couple of months.

'You've got some special skills, son, and I need them to stay sharp.'

'Thanks, Captain.'

'What have you been doing all this time, reading?'

Nix picked up the book – a well-thumbed copy of Sean Naylor's *Not a Good Day to Die*.

'I spent some time in that place myself,' Nix said, referring to the Shahi-Kot Valley in Afghanistan and the cluster fuck that was Operation Anaconda. 'It's good you're reading this; it should be required reading for all the brass.' Nix stood to leave.

'Hooah, sir.'

'Get your shit together, get your mind on the job, Mac. When I need you, I want you to do exactly what you did the other day. Every shot.'

'In the shadows, sir,' Mac said, referring to the recon unit's motto. 'One shot, one kill.'

'Our American heritage is greater than any one of us,' Nix said. 'It can express itself in very homely truths; in the end it can lift up our eyes beyond the glow in the sunset skies.'

'Where's that from sir?'

'Think it was some graffiti I read on on a toilet wall at Al Salem.' Nix smiled, thinking of the well-decorated bathroom wall at the Air Force Base in Kuwait, a major traffic point for US troops. 'It's from the early fifties, a Civil War historian called Bruce Catton – guy wrote some of the best books on that war. Read some of 'em after that book.'

62

JAIL, PAKISTAN

'Top five books of all time?'

Gammaldi shook his head.

'Okay. Albums, then.'

They had been shuffling around in the prison chamber for hours. It was sometime in the day; there was light coming through the opening in the roof. Their interrogation had lasted only ten minutes, passing much like the day's before, and the commandant had not bothered to spring them out for another session since – he evidently figured that he had time on his side.

'I'm sick of this Top Five game,' Gammaldi replied, clutching his ribs as he moved. Fox kept close; a hand on his mate's shoulder. 'Besides, yours would be all Radiohead albums.'

'All right. Five hottest chicks in Hollywood.'

Al looked at him, interested. 'All-time hottest,' he asked, 'or present day bombs?'

'All-time *and* present day,' Fox concurred.

'All-time . . . Sofia Loren.'

'Nice. Ingrid Bergman.'

'Who?'

'*Casablanca?*'

'Oh,' Gammaldi said. 'Really?'

'Damn straight. Who else?'

'Marilyn?'

'Nah . . . Grace Kelly.'

'Yeah.'

'And Elizabeth Taylor!'

'No way.'

'Back in the day, Al, when she was young, like *Cat on a Hot Tin Roof* young, she was premium.'

'I don't know . . .'

'Yeah, Al, you really don't,' Fox said, half-dragging him through a group that had stalled. 'Come on, who's hot these days?'

'Monica Bellucci.'

'Boom! You've just redeemed yourself . . . And Natalie Portman.'

'Maybe . . .'

'Fuck you, "maybe". Her, Bellucci, and Minka Kelly are my picks.'

'Scarlett Johansson. And Jessica Simpson.'

'There's a trend going on with your picks, Al. Badonkadonk much?'

'Huh?'

'You're so white, Al . . .' He could see his friend's spirit slowly lifting, but it was a fragile thing.

They laughed, and then fell silent for a while as they moved in time with the other detainees and listened to the ongoing murmur of hungry, tired men. They almost tripped over a body on the floor, but there was no way to stop to check for vitals as the momentum pushed them forward.

'Lach,' Gammaldi said, close to his ear, his voice weary. 'Has there been anyone you could have seen yourself with?'

'Kate.'

He nodded that he understood.

'Could be worse, Al.'

'How you figure that?'

'Well, let's see . . . Imagine it's Saturday and Barney's are having their once-a-year sale, or Ikea.'

Gammaldi gave a small smile. He and Fox bumped in close together, part of the unending tussle to keep together among the moving sea.

'It'd be as packed as this place, only it's women with prams, elbows everywhere, weapons of mass consumption. And there's only one route through the store, and you know that even if you get the chance to overtake a few of them, it'll take hours to get out of there . . .'

Half a laugh.

'. . . And that's not even counting the cost of your girlfriend's shopping . . .'

Gammaldi's laugh petered out to a cough and he clutched his side where his ribs were broken. 'Okay,' he said, wincing. 'It could be worse.'

Fox helped him forward, pushing back at a wall of bodies, light and skeletal to the touch.

'Emma – she's going to have a baby,' Gammaldi whispered.

'What?' Fox said, pulling his mate in closer. 'A baby?'

'Yeah.'

'Jesus . . .'

'Yeah.'

'I mean, that's great, good on you, Al. Shit – that's awesome, we've got to celebrate.' Fox looked around for a place to pull up against the wall for a few minutes, but they were near the centre of the room. The dim glow of the skylight meant they could at least see around them, the floor dusty under their socks, worn smooth by countless years of thousands of feet.

'Hey, my friend's going to be a dad!' Fox yelled into the room. 'Your finest bottle thanks, barkeep!'

'Couple of beers!'

'And some beers for my mate!'

'And bourbon!'

'You get that order?'

Faces around them lit up – a few cracked smiles, a few amused looks; some kind of stimulus against the mundane.

'I'm going to get us out of here, Al, no matter what. I'll figure it out in the yard,' Fox said, squeezing his mate in a friendly headlock. 'In the meantime, let's bring the house down!'

Gammaldi let out a scream, then a big 'Yee-ha!'

'Come on, you beauties!' Fox yelled. 'Let's celebrate. Raah!'

Fox leaned forward, pushing the men ahead of him, moving the room faster, the swirling hurricane picking up a few paces, the mass of weary men transformed into a swarm of energy.

63

INDIA

'Hutchinson's guys are in Pakistan,' Faith said.

'Have they got a location, or are they driving around aimlessly?' Wallace asked, concern all over him.

'They've met up with—'

'I mean, the Pakistanis don't exactly have the greatest record-keeping system in the world,' Wallace said. 'Nothing integrated, they'll be names handwritten into a ledger at some remote prison – if *that*.'

'They're working through all diplomatic channels, working military to military—'

'Damn it!' Wallace pounded his fist on the map of Pakistan on his desk.

Faith let him cool down in silence.

'They're going to try all the prisons in the region,' Faith said. 'And try the army unit in that area; they must have helped bring them in.'

Wallace's secretary put Bill McCorkell through on speakerphone. Faith stayed silent as Wallace explained the situation to McCorkell.

'They better be trying everything,' Wallace finished.

'We *will* try everything,' McCorkell said. 'We owe these men and it's payback time. Let me check in with Hutchinson.'

•

'I thought you were going to keep me in the loop on this,' McCorkell said.

The Bureau man paused on the line. 'It was just a time thing. I've got this, we'll find them,' Hutchinson said. 'GSR provided last-known details, we're working assets on the ground.'

'Well, I just checked in with Defence – they've got a squadron of Predators at Shamsi airfield—'

'Yeah, we've done a fly-over of their last known location,' Hutchinson replied. 'I've got a team on the ground there now, being met by a local military intel General who's taking this on as his pet project.'

'Sounds like a nice guy.'

'He's very pro-American, part of the new breed coming through who realise we're better to side with than the alternatives.'

'Does he know where Fox could be?'

'He's narrowed it down significantly,' Hutchinson replied. 'Couple of Army guys involved with the pick-up and transport of Fox and Gammaldi – they're loyal to their area commander, but they're currently in a nice little room as guests of the General. He'll get the locale.'

'Let's hope you're right,' McCorkell said. 'And let's hope that when we find them there's enough of them left to bring home.'

'There will be,' Hutchinson said. 'Besides, I'm close to finding someone else who may help us out.'

•

Hutchinson hung up his phone, stared at it for a while.

'We're here,' his driver said.

'Wait, I won't be long,' he said, leaving the junior agent behind as he entered the National Open Source Intelligence Centre.

Duhamel and his team were ripping it up across Pakistan. GPS coordinates of the last-known location had amounted to nothing – but they were working human intelligence assets, HUMINT, which looked like it would come through soon. Guys from the embassy in Islamabad were squeezing everything they could out of those who played in their sandbox. Duhamel was with the General, out on the road in a convoy hammering down the highway. They'd get results.

Hutchinson cleared through security and headed to where his subordinate team was set up, a group of government super geeks tracking open-source communications. They had cracked one of the World of Warcraft gamers, and he wanted to see and hear about it in person.

Then, and only then, would he spoon some information to McCorkell. He wasn't prepared to give him everything, but just enough . . .

•

Duhamel and his team were waved through the security gates behind the General's vehicle. The General had been talking himself up big-time, as if these guys could somehow prop him up like Musharraf. He was convinced the country needed men like him, big and good for America, their ally in the Muslim world. He hated the Taliban – half the northern country, half the big cities, were sympathisers, but he would educate these people, give them a better life so they wouldn't need to turn to these terrorists for cash and support. That was what the government was for. And his military was good at one thing – killing people, the same as any military. That's what he would do if he were President, he'd told them excitedly. Clearly he'd convinced himself, long ago, that he'd fix his nation's problems with brute force.

Duhamel looked out the window at the vast prison complex they were leaving behind them, no Fox or Gammaldi in sight. He wondered how anyone could live like this: in a country that went to war with its neighbour with disturbing regularity; in a country with a thirty-second nuclear warning – they wouldn't even have time to double-check if India launched their missiles; it was a yes-or-no, die-alone-or-die-with-them nuclear policy. Who would want to live with that kind of threat looming over them? It made the old days of the Cold War seem civilised.

64

JAIL, PAKISTAN

'What did these people do to deserve this life?'

'Huh?' Gammaldi said, waking up.

'Nothing, man, keep sleeping,' Fox replied. He gingerly rubbed his right hand, scared to flex it, all black and blue and swollen from catching the club yesterday.

'I thought you just said, "Always look on the bright side of life" . . .'

Fox laughed. 'Yeah, that might be a good idea.'

They were outside for their evening breather, and the moon was out amid clear skies. Gammaldi shifted slightly. Neither had slept during the night; most of the others in the yard were now sleeping in packs to keep warm, a well-practised routine.

'I needed that nap,' Gammaldi said. He'd laid flat on his back on the ground, and hadn't moved for half an hour.

'Cool, keep sleeping, man, I'll keep my eyes open,' Fox said. Greasy old spotlights stood at the corners of the yard, throwing enough light to cast shadows and little else.

'Nah, I'm good now.'

'Close your eyes,' Fox said. 'Like you did when you banged that ugly chick in high school, Judy Glipnick?'

'You thought Judy was ugly?'

'Is that even debatable?'

Gammaldi coughed.

'How're the ribs?'

'Fine if I don't move.'

'Yeah, well, we've got about ten more minutes,' Fox said.

'What, you keeping a watch hidden up your arse?'

The sounds of a vehicle convoy rang loud and clear in the crisp mountain air – someone was coming in hard and fast. The gate was out of sight, hidden behind the solid walls, but they could hear shouting in Urdu, then English.

'What was that?'

'Probably some fresh meat coming in.'

'We've got to get out of here.'

'Could be worse, you know.' Fox said.

'So you keep saying.' Gammaldi tilted his head and faced Fox. 'Okay, how do you figure that?'

'Could be in Bruges.'

Gammaldi smiled. Laughed. Then cringed. 'Fucking Bruges.'

Four guards emerged from the dark recessed door in the wall and headed over to their corner, wooden clubs out. Fox stood and took a few paces towards them, ready to tussle if it came to it.

'You will come with us,' one of the guards said.

Fox stared at him. The guard's three mates weren't taking an interest – it seemed they were there to keep watch on the other inmates as Fox and Gammaldi were rounded up.

'What for?'

'You will come, now,' he said. 'Your friend can get up. Come.'

He didn't look like he was there to round them up for a beating, but then he didn't look as if he was taking them in for a spa treatment, either. He waved his makeshift baton in the direction of the commandant's office.

Fox grabbed Gammaldi and helped him to his feet. Al was red in the face and at the point of tears with the pain of the effort. He walked next to Fox under his own power, though, gritting through the pain. The two men entered the commandant's office.

The prison commander was red-faced too, but for a different reason: blood ran from his battered eye and cut lip. A senior Pakistani Army officer – covered with brass and ribbons – stood over him.

Standing rod-straight nearby were two Americans.

'Special Agent Jake Duhamel; and this here is Brick,' Duhamel said, shaking Fox's good hand. 'Hutchinson sent us – we're taking you boys out of here.'

Fox nodded; he was too weary to really take it in but he felt a slight rush of adrenaline that came with freedom. Brick collected the backpacks of the two men from the commandant's desk, and Fox and Gammaldi let themselves be ushered out, Fox half-carrying Gammaldi, leaving the Pakistanis to sort each other out.

They walked out to the convoy – a big Chevy Suburban guarded by two other FBI-types, and four Pakistani military vehicles. All had their engines running, lights on, exhaust steaming in the air.

'He's got a couple of busted ribs,' Fox explained. 'Got some bandages?'

'You can walk okay, though?' Brick asked, evaluating Gammaldi.

'Yeah, it's bearable,' Gammaldi said. 'Need food, though.'

'Breathing all right?' Brick asked, opening the Chevy's tailgate and reaching for a medical kit. He passed over a few aspirin, which Gammaldi chomped down.

'Yeah,' Gammaldi said, spying something in the back seat of the Suburban. 'Is that Gatorade?'

'Yeah,' Brick said, taking a couple of bottles from the stack of drinks. Gammaldi took both.

'Lach will want some too,' he said, already halfway through his first bottle.

They piled into the vehicle, Fox and Duhamel last in.

'Where are we headed?' Fox asked as Duhamel closed his door.

'Amritsar,' he replied. 'We've got a flight ready, can take you back Stateside.'

'We've got a company jet back in—'

'Make some calls on the way,' Duhamel said, passing over a satellite phone. 'Get another pilot in to fly it out – we're staying with you, and we've got a Justice Department bird and flight crew in Amritsar.'

'Can we bump the flight to the morning?' Fox asked. 'Recoup in a hotel overnight, make a few final calls while we're here?'

Duhamel didn't look convinced, but then Fox saw him glance at Gammaldi, who had closed his eyes and was trying not to move the top half of his body.

'Yeah, okay. I'll call in to Hutchinson and sort it out.'

65

GORI, GEORGIA (EASTERN EUROPE)

'She sure is sweet,' Top said as they watched a Georgian girl, maybe twenty, with long dark tresses, big brown eyes and pale skin, walk past them, guided through the busy room full of uniforms by a female US soldier.

'She could be your daughter,' Nix said, helping himself to a cup of hot coffee from the mess table. He made one for Top too, adding plenty of sugar.

Most of his men were still working construction outside on the abandoned school's oval, but the area inside had been set up to record human rights abuse by soldiers on both sides of the war, and it doubled as a press room. Technically, all US personnel had first been deployed as a training force for Georgian troops, but then their mission changed to include the protection of senior diplomatic staff after the Gori Town Hall bombing. Today, the NATO Personal Protection Specialists were arriving, high-risk protectees travelling with serious steel, which was welcome news for Nix's outfit.

The school, now swarming with US military and UN personnel as well as reporters, was cordoned off outside by Spanish armoured vehicles. Most of the building's windows were boarded up because they'd been shelled and bombed out by Russian artillery and air strikes, and the danger was still apparent – just yesterday a soldier almost blew himself to Mars after taking a piss on top of an unexploded cluster bomb in the overgrown and weed-infested perimeter. When the Russians went through in late 2008 they stripped the place of anything of value or use – clothes, bedding, food; they even pulled out the copper piping and wiring to re-sell. They certainly were thorough – it was like locusts had swept through a wheat field.

'The Colonel's moving real quick on Mac's clearance,' Nix said as he handed over Top's coffee. 'A few things to fill out and sign off.'

'I'm right tired of paperwork,' Top said.

The two men looked out the window at the sports field, at the big heated tents housing media and UN personnel.

'See those birds?' Top asked, pointing to a flock flying in formation over the yard. 'Just like they fly at home. Everywhere's the same these days.'

Nix clapped him on the back.

'Come on, we've got to go pick up our embedded reporter for the week,' Nix said. 'I got the Colonel to assign her specially, after you couldn't get it organised right.'

'I told you before,' Top said, following his CO. 'I only done what you told me.'

Through the hall they entered the gymnasium. The room was the size of eight basketball courts and hummed with activity. The immediate vicinity had been taken over by security contractors protection for the building of an upgraded local runway and police station, as well as a semi-permanent US base about a hundred clicks east. This building was to be converted to a military police academy run by trainers of the EU's new fandangled European Gendarmerie Force – ostensibly part of the long-term payback that came with Georgia being an active member of the Coalition of the Willing. It would mean that pointy-end specialists like Nix's squad could bug out, and none too soon.

'Listen to this guy talking up the six-eight round,' Top said out the corner of his mouth. They paused by a group of moneyed-up gunslingers.

'Six-eight round is the future,' said the guy, who sat on a table in front of a bunch of Nix's 10th Mountain boys. 'Stopping power of an AK; velocity of the five-six. Enough weight behind this baby that a single shot will force the target down.'

He had a Barrett M468 assault rifle across his chest, with a big chunky suppressor screwed onto the barrel. The guy's right hand never left the buttstock; he probably didn't even have the safety on.

'Six-eight can shoot through car windscreens, the works, and still pack a lethal punch. It's all about kinetic energy. When I hit a terrorist, I want him to stay down – learned that the hard way.'

Top turned to Nix, spoke under his breath: 'Terrorist my ass.'

'You want to neutralise a threat with a minimal amount of shots, and 556 struggles to do this – I've seen guys shot and then turn around and start shooting back at us. It's not like the movies. AK rounds fall out of the sky after about four hundred yards, but the six-eight, man, it's the only assault rifle round big enough to stop a bad guy and accurate enough to ensure a kill with just one shot.'

'One shot my ass,' Top said, this time loud enough to be heard.

He and Nix left the conversation and joined a group of Army media liaison troops who were in the process of allocating the embedded reporters, who were starting to stream in.

'Ah, if it isn't the popular bunch,' the Colonel said to Nix and Top. 'We've got every news agency begging to field with you guys.'

'What can I say, Colonel?' Nix said. 'We're good at what we do.'

The Colonel grunted. He looked down his list and then up to the crowd of journalists in the adjoining room, most of whom were interviewing local civilians.

'There's your reporter,' the Colonel said, pointing to a middle-aged woman sitting at a plastic table conducting an interview. 'With GSR, as requested. Make sure you bring her back in one piece. There's some Ruskies out there deliberately targeting reporters near the South Ossetian line.'

'Hooah.'

'Yeah, we got it, sir,' Nix said, signing the form. 'What's with all the air traffic coming in tonight?'

'EU Battlegroup pouring in; French Force Headquarters assume operational command in a week, got some Irish outfit of bomb-disposal experts among them.'

'I thought the European Council were dragging their feet?'

'Sounds like you've been reading too many newspapers,' the Colonel replied. 'Russia was firm they didn't want a NATO force here; we're bad enough. Go get your reporter, lie low for a few days. I just got some more heat from up high about your sniper kills. I really don't want to hear any more.'

'Thanks, sir,' Top said to the Colonel, saluting as he went through.

'You believe that gun for hire?' Top asked.

'About the six-eight round?'

'Yeah.'

'I like the sound of it,' Nix admitted.

'I am all for lethality,' Top said, nodding. 'Diameter, weight, kinetic energy – I was starting to get turned on.'

Nix was laughing as he extended his hand to meet the reporter. As she shook it he saw the person sitting opposite her: the young Georgian girl Top had admired earlier. His mood sank as he saw the look on the young woman's face.

66

ON THE ROAD, PAKISTAN

Fox took a deep breath of the fresh air streaming in the open window. The fields of dirt were endless, and rocks and mountains rose up as bare, jagged totems of loneliness. A single gravel road wound its way north and south. Remnants of a few mud-brick or stone buildings sat about a click north. It was the middle of nowhere. Perfect killing fields. Fox thought about the inmates back at the walled prison compound. Sure, some of them were likely to be criminals, had likely done something worthy of incarceration, but still . . . The landscape flashed by. Birds were the only life he saw, far off specks riding the thermal flows off the mountains, soaring and floating in their own space – even animals were smart enough to keep away from this place.

Fox had called Faith at GSR, Gammaldi had called Emma. The driver and Duhamel were up front in the Surburban; Fox, Gammaldi and Brick were in the middle row, and two others – introduced by Duhamel only as Ivan and Luigi – were up back. The guys in the rear had the back window popped open and M4 assault rifles ready to rock.

Gammaldi's shirt was off. Brick cut four long strips of two-inch adhesive tape, each long enough to stretch from Gammaldi's

sternum around to his spine, to go directly over each fractured rib.

'I was our HRT team's deputy medic,' Brick said. 'Done this
plenty of times. Hold still.'

'Oh man . . .' Gammaldi cringed in pain as Brick applied
the tape.

'Strappings should lessen the pain,' Brick said, placing a
few additional pieces of tape on either side of the broken ribs,
running parallel to one another. 'It restricts movement of the
area, which, believe me, is a good thing.'

Gammaldi nodded. Fox smiled at his mate's appearance.

'How's it feel?' Brick said. 'Too tight?'

'No, it's not that,' he replied, 'I'm just so fucking hungry!'

They all laughed, and Gammaldi started coughing, tensing
up with the pain of it.

'If you feel like coughing, good,' Brick said. 'Do it frequently.
It's going to hurt like a bitch, but it'll prevent anything pooling
in your lungs, which might cause pneumonia.'

'Great . . .'

67

GORI, GEORGIA (EASTERN EUROPE)

'I met Lachlan Fox about six months back,' Nix said to the GSR reporter. 'He's a good man.'

'Yes, the best,' said Sara, a reporter from Russia who usually freelanced for the radio station, Echo of Moscow. 'He's helped out many of my friends in getting good journalism work outside Russia. Fox is probably the bravest reporter I've met, as smart as anyone out there and always wanting to know more.'

'Fools rush in where angels fear to tread,' Nix said with a small smile. 'A little learning is a dangerous thing.'

She looked at him, impressed.

'What, you thought us soldiers were all dumb, stupid animals to be used as pawns for foreign policy?'

She smiled.

'I'm sorry,' Nix said, squatting down next to the two women at the table. 'You two were talking when I came over here . . .'

Sara nodded and motioned to the young woman. 'This is Anna. She has something to tell you. Go ahead, tell them what you just told me.'

'My brother,' said Anna. 'He saw the men who shot at your people.'

Nix glanced at Top; the Sergeant looked as if a breeze could blow him over.

'Where is your brother?' Nix asked.

'He won't talk to you. He doesn't trust you, and my mother – she fears reprisals. If she knew I was here . . .'Anna looked desperately from Nix to Sara, and back again.

'And where is your mother?'

'Our home is over the river.'

'In South Ossetia?' Top asked.

Anna nodded.

Nix put a hand on the edge of the card table, spoke softly: 'You're sure he saw them?'

'Yes.'

'Would he give you a description?'

'My brother – he has a photo . . . a film.'

'A photo?'

'Video, I meant video,' she said. 'He was taking a video of me to send for audition. He heard shooting and went out and filmed them – it's at home. He is – he's not like me, he thinks Russia will be better for our people. He's too young to remember what they were like.'

'Could you get me that video?'

Anna shook her head. 'They check me, us, at checkpoints – they'll take it from me, they take everything that might have value . . . and I don't want to go back there and then here again so soon.'

Nix instinctively looked over at the Colonel who'd assigned him this reporter, but the senior officer was busy with a group of UN and French brass. He turned his attention back to the girl.

'Anna, you're an actress?'

'Yes,' Anna said, smiling a little. 'I am trying to be.' Her face hardened and she looked into Nix's eyes. 'They . . . they took my friend, the Russians, they took her on the first day. She's my age, and we don't know where she is. I don't want them to get away with that, or this.'

Nix nodded. This video would clear his squadron, clear Mac, show the Russian spin for what it was. It might even be the turning point in getting this shit-cold caucus off the ground once and for all.

'Tell me,' he said to Anna. 'If we go with you – in total secrecy, so no one will see us – could you get us this video?'

68

AIRPORT SCHIPHOL, AMSTERDAM, THE NETHERLANDS

Kolesnik switched on his cell phone as he walked into the passenger terminal, and listened to his message.

The voice of an agent from the FIA, Pakistan's Federal Investigation Agency; a middleman who was proving very useful. Not only had he introduced Kolesnik to the terror cell he had recently utilised, but he had kept tabs on all his targets in the country and organised for Fox and Gammaldi to be locked up.

'Just this moment your two guests were released following high-level intervention . . .'

Kolesnik stopped walking and clenched his phone tighter to his ear.

'. . . I am sorry, this happened without my prior knowledge. They are to stay overnight in Amritsar, and I have intercepted a call that they are to be at the Harmandir Sahib – the Golden Temple – at nine a.m. tomorrow. They will be meeting your Indian Samaritan there.'

Okay, there *was* a silver lining. The 'Samaritan', Amar Singh, had been useful, but his usefulness had come to an end –

Kolesnik could now tie up two loose ends for good. He would take care of Singh, *and* finish off Fox and Gammaldi, as Sirko should have done in Spain . . .

Kolesnik quickened his pace and flashed through EU customs with his diplomatic passport. This trip started out as an insurance policy, had turned into a necessity on hearing of Fox's release, and now was again a useful back-up. Either way, he was here, and he was being thorough, and of that his father would surely approve.

He climbed into a cab and told the driver the address for his hotel. First, he had to get his Pakistani friends into gear again. Then, he had a date with a beautiful woman.

69

AMRITSAR, INDIA

Four hours later at the five-star Raj Intercontinental Hotel, Fox was cleaned up and sitting back in a plush dressing gown, while Gammaldi lay on a bed, halfway through a sixer of Heineken.

The concierge desk had sent up three shopping bags of new clothes to their room – their own gear was long-past wearable, ransacked and soiled.

'Oh man, best – beer I've – ever – had!' Gammaldi said through a series of hiccups. He took a handful of fries from Fox's room service plate and stuffed them all down. 'Oh my God, these chips . . .'

'You're not my bitch – buy your own damn fries.'

Gammaldi grunted. 'Sarah Shahi.'

'What?'

'Sarah Shahi,' Gammaldi said. 'She's on my list. Preity Zinta, too.'

'Are you still going on about that?'

He burped in reply.

'Dude, I have to use your laptop,' Fox said. 'Mine was all fucked up by those—'

'Bloody Pakistani prison assholes,' finished Gammaldi. 'The password's Franklin.' Another hiccup.

Fox typed it into Gammaldi's MacBook. He used the room's wireless connection to log on to the GSR website, and started writing copy for his next syndicated story on the water crisis.

'Why Franklin?' Fox asked as his fingers blurred over the illuminated keyboard.

'Motherfucker was awesome,' Gammaldi said with another hiccup, before popping open another Heineken. 'This one night, when he was kicking in his crib with his bastard son, Bennie Franklin is like, "*Bastard son, there's rain and lightning outside – let's go fly a kite. With a key on it.*" And then, "*Oh yeah, by the way, YOU'RE flying the kite!*" And his son's like, "*What?!*" But Ben Franklin's like, "*You have no mum, and you're going to become a loyalist governor one day to spite me, I can feel it – just do it*"—'

Gammaldi hiccupped, hung over the side of his bed for a few suspicious seconds, then turned back and winced from his rib pain. '"*William,*" he went on. "*It'll be like rubbing your feet on carpet and then touching metal – when the lightning hits the kite, touch the key, and tell me what happens.*"'

Fox shook his head and logged into his email. 'Al,' he said, reading about the escalations in Georgia: Russians sending more troops into the region; the EU putting a rapid-reaction force in. 'You're kind of like a condensed index of alternate American history. I call your lessons American History Y.'

'Yeah, I know,' he replied. 'So then William flies the kite and Ben Franklin is saying, "*When that key's charged, touch it!*" Then William touched the key and it sparked and proved to

Franklin—' another hiccup '—that electricity comes from the sky. His son became the world's first lightning rod.'

Fox nodded and ate some hamburger. Gammaldi hiccupped, a big one this time, and then clutched his ribs in pain.

'Interesting, Al. I'm not sure if that's entirely accurate, but it's a good story.'

More room service came in from the connecting suite where Special Agents Duhamel and Brick were set up. The Feds' room was a hive of activity as waiters came and went – all staff had to clear through them and a couple of Indian cops who sat out in the hall.

'I love cricket . . .' Gammaldi said as he worked his way through a selection of curries and breads, alternating between the beer and juice, and watching the Australian cricket team getting its arse handed to it by South Africa, '. . . except when it seems we have forgotten HOW TO PLAY!' he yelled at the television, then winced again. 'You know, I'm gonna be a dad?'

'It's pretty awesome.'

'That'll make you an uncle.'

'You say so.'

'You're family. Hey . . . What do we do about Amar Singh?' he said. 'What did Thomas say when you called him?'

'He didn't sound pleased,' Fox replied, looking up from the computer. 'But he was certain his brother would show at the Golden Temple tomorrow – so I guess we have to just wait and see what Amar has to say.'

'Does Amar know we're out?'

'I doubt it,' Fox replied.

'Did Thomas believe you?'

'I think so,' Fox said, popping a can of Coke, loving every sip of the sugar. 'But he's a cagey one . . .'

'Doubting Thomas . . .' Gammaldi said. He removed a lid of a new dish. 'Oh man, hot dogs.'

'You're sick, Al.'

'I'm trying to get the taste of that prison out of me.'

'Taste?'

'Yeah, you know – it was disgusting on so many levels . . .'

'Right, the whole kind of . . . *mise en scène* of the thing.'

Gammaldi smiled through half a hot dog. The two men looked around their new accommodation. The room cost five grand a night, with either GSR or Uncle Sam footing the bill, and the walls were lined with signed photos of some of the world's rich and famous who had stayed there. Fox wished he could have added a picture of how Gammaldi looked right now – he'd hang it in between Bono and Bill Gates.

There was a knock on the interconnecting door, and Duhamel came in.

'We're going to get a couple of hours' shut-eye,' he said. 'You guys all good?'

Fox gave him the thumbs up, kept typing; Gammaldi burped. The FBI man disappeared into his room.

70

GORI, GEORGIA (EASTERN EUROPE)

Nix watched as his mortar squad tore off in their Humvees. He and his crew completed their final preparations to go in under the cover of darkness: night-vision gear, M4s locked and loaded. They were a well-oiled fighting unit, experts at infil by night, and Anna was acting as their local guide.

Another Humvee dropped them at the edge of the Blue Zone, from where they would make the journey into South Ossetia on foot. Sara, their GSR embedded reporter, was hanging back inside the Blue Zone, ready for a vehicle-supplied exfil if needed. Three small fire teams made up the assault: Nix and Top would go into the house with Anna with Mac and Kynoch providing sniper cover, and the mortar team as heavy hitters if that call had to be made.

Mac and the spotter had headed off first, just after nightfall, on foot. They were the eyes on this op – no one wanted to take out a civilian. Nix had reminded all those heading out that engaging hostile targets was a last resort. They all knew that enemy snipers operated in the area, and they were entering no-man's-land without their specialist anti-sniper weapon, the vehicle-mounted Boomerang sniper detection system.

'Why does this sort of mission keep happening to us?'

'I guess we're just lucky, Top,' Nix said.

They walked through a deserted street, using the back fences that bordered a laneway as cover. There were no street lights on, and Top led the way with night-vision goggles. Anna was behind him, Nix brought up the rear. They paused at an intersection to catch their breath, more for Anna's sake.

'Why are you doing this?' she asked them, adjusting the dark blue Kevlar vest she had borrowed from Sara.

'Getting this video?' Nix asked. 'Or being here in Georgia?'

'No, the Army,' she said, as Top re-did the straps for her on the Kevlar, far too big for her small frame. 'Fighting in Iraq, Afghanistan, all these places – why would you want to do that?'

Nix watched as Top pulled out a laminated photo of his wife and two kids from his shoulder pocket. It was just discernible under the moonlight.

'This is why. I look at this, and I know I'm missing out on so much by being away,' he said. 'I'm sacrificing everything because I want to make this world a better place for them, for my kids to grow up in.'

71

AMSTERDAM, THE NETHERLANDS

'Miss Dawson, I need to go to the bathroom,' the little girl said.

Kate Matthews wasn't sure she would ever get used to that name. Maybe she would. Harder still was trying to forget her real name, to not turn around if someone called it out.

'You can't wait for the bell?'

The little girl shook her head.

'Okay, take Milly with you.'

Kate turned her attention back to helping the rest of the kids with their English literacy work. The schools here were good, even this preschool and first-year class of four- and five-year-olds was far better than Stateside with the ratio of teachers to students. She alternated the content of her classes to keep things interesting: reading books to them, playing guitar and singing in English – thankfully the kids weren't harsh critics – and setting writing tasks. Now, they were copying down sentences from the blackboard and then reading them out. Despite the chaos that often ensued, words had never sounded so pure.

She knew her parents would be proud. Her mum had spent twenty-five years teaching in a Manhattan school not dissimilar to this, and she had always quietly encouraged her to follow this career, while her father was a professor who encouraged any career choice she'd made. It certainly had its rewards – no happiness was as contagious as the happiness of children – and it was infinitely more fulfilling, in a personal sense, than the corporate law of her past career, her past life—

Kate stopped herself before she cried, then wondered why and how long she would have to live like this. The emptiness broke into a smile as she received a hug from a little boy, full of genuine love and affection and for no special reason. The bell rang.

•

He had watched her go about her everyday work, and he had watched her at night.

She taught three mornings a week, and spent two full days working in a small legal office. She spent her spare time doing pilates, reading, watching DVDs, and she had an address book and email inbox full of local friends, none of whom – nor any file on her computer, nor any diary in her apartment – went back further than six months. She may have been fucking a guy called Johan De Groot, which made him laugh for a couple of reasons, or Jacob Van Rijn, or maybe even a Swedish woman named Cecilia. There were several pictures of her with a guy, taken on different occasions, but there was no name to the face. She lived alone, with a black cat that was overly friendly with strangers.

He had spent the night in a very nice hotel, and even picked up a decent New Zealand backpacker at a bar. It was his second time in Amsterdam and he wondered why he didn't come here more often. The question was: would he leave empty-handed? And if he chose to take Kate with him, who was best to help get her out of the country?

He walked away from the school, trudging through the snow-covered sidewalk along a canal to where he would show his credentials at the Russian Embassy and have a good discussion with the FSB station chief. He had little doubt that with money to grease some wheels, he could move any number of people around Western Europe within the shortest of timeframes.

72

SOUTH OSSETIA (EASTERN EUROPE)

Nix led the way and hoofed it double-time across the bridge. On the other side he took cover in the large doorway of an empty store.

'You're sure you can't persuade him to give this thing over?' Top asked Anna, heaving for breath.

She shook her head. 'They humiliated him, the South Ossetian militia, Russians mainly,' she said. 'They made him and all the men in our street take their clothes off and lie on the road. They kicked them, they hosed them down, they took their money and then they came in the house and took what they wanted. All our family's valuable things, modest things like silverware, they took it, stuffing it in their pockets. Then, before they left, they shot a man who yelled at them – he just yelled at them! – just to prove a point: if you stand against them, they will kill you. They come around now . . . every week or so, and they are recruiting all the young men my brother's age, into the militia. They give them guns, get them to wave them in the faces of people who voice opposition to Russia. My family, they are not that happy with Georgia as it is, but they would like a separate South Ossetia – not a South Ossetia that is a puppet of Russia, a place to station Russian troops for the next hundred years, but a free place that we can call *our* home. My brother – maybe he now thinks it's easier to join them, I don't know—'

'Shhh . . .' Nix said, pulling down his night-vision set and raising his M4. He saw four guys with guns messing around in the street about six hundred metres away.

'They're militia,' Anna whispered.

'How do you know?'

'I know the difference a mile away,' she said. 'The Russians are always drinking and smoking. The militia don't do that in public, not while on duty. They've learned the hard way.'

Top smiled at Nix. Judging by the house lights, these militia were near civilians – 'hugging', they'd termed it in Iraq, where they deliberately used crowds at schools and hospitals and churches as shields. It meant artillery and mortar fire were not an option, given the wind conditions, which could cause the round to stray significantly. There were smart artillery rounds, but not on hand here. Damn, right now Nix would take a pay cut to have that kind of firepower parked back in Gori.

'They are welcome here,' Anna explained. 'They form a kind of local police. Villagers make them food – strong sweet coffee, dips, dried and pickled foods, flat breads.'

Nix wondered what that felt like. Liberators. Keepers of the peace. It must have been like that for the GIs in Western Europe after WWII ended.

This girl who looked as if she could break any man's heart managed to break theirs back in the Blue Zone while they were prepping for this night-time run. The stories she had told them – what she'd seen, what she'd heard, her missing friends and family. She could not understand how they, as Americans, could not go out there and find them.

Nix couldn't, despite what he might want to do. He had to make sure his RSTA looked tough for the Russians, to hold his corner. There were others looking into that sort of thing, surely? There was a UNHCR group recording evidence for possible war crimes charges, and with the embedded reporters the world would hear and see what had really happened here.

Nix watched the guys with guns walking away. He looked at the girl and said, 'They'll find a political solution for your people.'

'No,' Anna replied. 'We need fresh minds for that – if fresh minds aren't brought in to find a political solution to this conflict, then this war could go on for years and years.'

'They'll work this out, things are changing.'

'Maybe in your country. Here it's always same-same. When the Russians come again, and they *will* come, you can't stop them,' she said. 'We will all be killed next time, they won't leave witnesses behind.'

'They won't try anything while we're here.' He looked into her eyes, trying to convey his sincerity, his promise. 'We won't leave you until you're safe.'

Maybe she misread his look. 'They don't care who you are. They will come again, they will kill us all. And we won't be missing, we'll be dead, and there's nothing anyone will do about it because . . . what can they do?'

It was sobering. He knew the sense of it to be true: they couldn't hang around forever – like Iraq, like Afghanistan, like Somalia, they would eventually move on. He settled into the cover of the shop's entrance, just a few streets south of Anna's home. They waited for the right time, for all the units to check in. They already had the absolute cover that darkness would provide, and dawn was a couple of hours off – the perfect time right now for this kind of op.

They waited for the right moment – a moment in time that would change everything.

73

AMRITSAR, INDIA

'Recently, I have seen a rise of human trafficking through here,' Thomas Singh said. 'Young women mainly, either being moved out of impoverished situations where they have no hope other than a nicely presented deal from some slick human salesman, or . . .'

Thomas let out a long sigh. He and Fox were parked in a Land Cruiser across from the Golden Temple, which glowed, iridescent, in the early morning light. There was traffic and a surprising number of people milling about, dozens of tourists braving the cold to visit the sacred site and take photos. Gammaldi was across the road with Duhamel; Brick and the others were scattered within the vicinity.

'It's just plain wrong,' Fox said, turning up the heating a little. 'It was one of the first stories I ever worked on – the first real big story, actually, the first thing that made me realise that this kind of job really can make a difference. It helped bring down a people-smuggling outfit in Indonesia.'

Thomas was silent for a while.

'I will find out if what you say about my brother is true . . .' Thomas trailed off. 'When I met you, I did not understand what you did.'

'How so?'

'I was educated abroad, in the UK, as a lawyer, then a journalist, but I always intended to come home to ply my trade for my people. I have always known it was the right thing to do, and I did it. You – you have done what so many in the world have done, you have elected to work abroad . . . but now I can see why.'

Fox tilted his head, trying to read Thomas's meaning.

'Lachlan, you are a warrior, a war-like one from the water, as your name's roots suggest – not dissimilar to the Sikh tradition of warrior saints,' Thomas said. 'I see this place, my nation of India, as the place where I can effect change and make a difference, and you see this too. You and I are similar, but you are a global man.'

Fox nodded slowly, gazing out the front window. 'Here comes your brother,' he said, as Amar Singh walked towards them.

74

SOUTH OSSETIA (EASTERN EUROPE)

Nix and Top walked through the back door of the house behind Anna. Nix felt his heart rate quicken with every step on the tiled floor. They were in their cams gear and bristling with war-fighting equipment, standing in the living room of a house in a hostile area . . . and there was nothing Nix could do to downplay it. Anna's mother was asleep on the couch under the light of a lamp – she awoke, looked up at them wide-eyed.

'Mum, it's okay, they're here to help,' Anna said. 'They're friends.'

The woman nodded, she seemed calm. She was a small, stout woman: Nix wondered, not for the first time, if she was an example of what happened to all beautiful Eastern Bloc girls: they started out looking like the bomb and ended up, after a life of hardship and repression, looking like Boris Yeltsin.

'Is my brother here?'

The mother shook her head: 'Out.' She looked disappointed, surveying Nix with a mixture of alarm and curiosity about what he might want with her boy; or perhaps it was a plea for him to help her son. She shuffled into the adjoining kitchen and came back with a decorated tin.

'You would like some cake?' she asked, offering pastries dusted in icing sugar.

Nix nodded, took one; Top followed suit. The woman smiled, and the two men followed Anna upstairs.

•

Mac had watched them go in, their fluorescent tags on their cams giving him a clear ID on which figures were his friends. The big thermal scope clicked in front of the fixed sight ate the distance up with ease.

His M110 was locked and loaded, the safety off. He lay there, watching and waiting, his spotter next to him. A squad of guys were two clicks to the east, and a hundred metres beyond them was a squad with an AT4 rocket launcher and a spotter to call in mortar fire from well inside the Blue Zone with the Humvees that could rock in for a rapid exfil.

•

The bedroom door was locked with a bolt and padlock. Anna retrieved a key from where her brother hid it atop the doorjamb – she could just reach it on her tiptoes – and opened the door slowly, as if afraid of what she might find.

•

Kynoch called the scene over his closed-circuit tac mic: 'This is sniper team. Be advised we have a technical approaching the house, coming south down the street – heavy military vehicle – make it a three-tonne truck, ID as Russian military type, no visible markings.'

Mac looked in the direction and trained his scope there, tracing it. He loved his 110, especially the semi-auto nature of it, making it ideal in a target-rich environment like the one that seemed likely to present itself any second, like his compatriots sometimes encountered in Iraq and Afghanistan – he could really make a big difference to a battlefield. This ability to keep shooting fixed a failing of the older M24, where the shooter had to pull off target ever so slightly while reloading. With the 110 the bolt didn't need to be touched, which halved the time it took to get rounds off, and a nice big suppressor saved sound and muzzle flash. The 110's long-range thermal optical sight worked day or night, and it doubled the magnification, attaching in front of the fitted sight. He adjusted it and watched as the truck stopped in the street outside the house next door: the cargo tray was full of guys, but only one jumped out.

He was carrying an AK.

'Armed target approaching the house,' Kynoch said into his mic.

The truck rumbled on, grinding slowly up through its gears. It turned the corner and disappeared, out of sight. The lone figure walked towards the house – the way he walked, the way he held his gun, clearly told Mac he wasn't a trained soldier, but then most of these guys weren't.

'Make him male, late teens, civilian clothes, AK that's seen better days,' Mac said without moving, then went quiet, the long barrel of the M110 trained on the target, ready for action. 'Captain, you've got company. Your boy is about to enter the front door. Make him fifteen seconds out, we have the shot.'

75

AMRITSAR, INDIA

'Remember when the Hindu train from Ayodhya—'

'Amar—'

'More than fifty were killed, and the RSS? They killed 2000 Muslims in reprisal.'

Thomas struck his brother across the face with the back of his hand.

'I am here to listen to you talk about what *you* have done,' Thomas said, his voice patient, the look behind his eyes that of a caged animal.

'In reprisal! Then they kicked 200000 out of their homes – and this was in 2002!' said Amar, his breath ragged. He was in a state, seemed delirious. Blood poured from his nose; he wiped it away impatiently. 'We have over 300 million middle class, the world's biggest democracy – we have the vote but we don't have *food*. Don't have *shoes*. Can't . . .' His voice died out in desperation. 'Some say there are two Indias, but I have not seen beyond this one . . .'

Amar had tears in his eyes. They stood outside the car, three men, talking.

'Our country spends less than one per cent on healthcare—'

'Brother—'

'Do you remember, Thomas, when our cousin died?' Amar said. He looked like a child as he leaned on the fender of the car. Thomas was silent. Amar turned to Fox. 'Lachlan, when I was fifteen, my cousin was fifteen, and he had appendicitis. Our father was a doctor, here in Amritsar, and he would perform surgery on the one day off he had each week, in the villages. He was too late for our cousin – he took out the appendix but it had burst. He took our aunt's hand, took my hand, and said to her, *"Sister, you have lost your son. Here, take mine."*'

Amar looked at his hands as his tears fell on them.

'I was left with them with what I knew at that age, with what I had at that age, and I never learned more – I got nothing new. I started as I am and am now as I am. But you, brother . . .'

Fox looked at Thomas; the older man was aware that the brother he thought he knew was now gone, but the boy he had once said goodbye to had never really left.

'Amar, how did you get out, when these men were taken?' Thomas asked softly.

'I was there and I saw what you did,' Fox said. 'Saw it with my own eyes. You took us there. You handed us over.'

Amar nodded, took a deep breath, reached into his jacket – Thomas grabbed his wrist, brought it out. Amar held a folded stack of paper.

'This is what I have done,' he said. 'Names, money, things I have done – everything I have done. Leverage. Proof.'

Amar stared at the ground. Fox took the papers from his hand.

'You can't conceive, my brother,' Amar said, 'the appalling strangeness of the mercy of God. I never wanted it to be like this – I never asked for this. Between us, there is such a gulf that I cannot see across.'

76

SOUTH OSSETIA (EASTERN EUROPE)

Anna saw the look exchanged between Top and Nix.

'What?'

Nix shook his head.

'Negative, sniper team,' Top said into his mic. He moved back to cover the door of the bedroom with his M4. 'Hold position and await orders.'

'Anna, your brother is coming—'

She made for the door but Nix caught her.

'Do you know where his camera is?' he asked.

She snapped into action, scanning the room. She opened a drawer in his desk and pulled out a cardboard box with the camera inside.

Nix flicked it on, a little Japanese digital camcorder. He checked the image . . .

•

'Copy that, Top,' Kynoch said. 'Target entering the house momentarily.'

Mac lay there, his finger through the trigger-guard. He breathed steadily, consciously keeping his heart rate slower than normal rest.

•

Nix heard the front door open downstairs. Anna stood by Top, who was peering out the open bedroom door.

The image on the fold-out viewfinder showed the city square in Gori – Anna posing in front of the statue of Stalin. He scanned through it at double-speed, then came the explosion that ripped through the air. He watched it for a moment, their reactions . . . then the screen went to black, then flickered to life again with the day Nix and his team engaged the attackers across the river.

He heard the mother talking to the son downstairs. They were speaking Georgian; he couldn't make out the words but the tone was typical of a mother and teenage son, even if the son had just come through the front door with an assault rifle. It quickly became heated – was she trying to stall him? Nix watched the screen: the brother had been filming about a hundred metres from the fighting position of the attackers, the large-calibre rounds of the heavy machine gun sounding over the tinny speaker. The view changed angles, zoomed into the treed section where Nix's team had been positioned . . . focused on the Humvee as it was torn up to shit . . . then the camera went back to the attacker's position . . . continued moving towards them . . . fifty metres, close now—

•

'Shit, they're coming back!' the spotter said.

The truck rumbled back down the street, its lights on full-beam this time, the engine louder – they were in a hurry.

'Be advised, House, technical is coming back towards your location, make it less than sixty seconds out.'

•

Nix heard the warning over his mic as he watched onscreen the tracer rounds of his squad's SAW spraying cover fire over the attacking positions. It was over in seconds, the twin cracks of Mac's M4 not audible on the video. The brother had taken cover and crawled along to the two downed targets, the video never stopping . . . Both men were sprawled on the ground, both head shots, right on the money . . . They wore Russian cams but had Georgian weapons . . . Then he saw the Kevlar vests, not Russian military – they were good spec-ops gear as worn by private military contractors . . . a small orange patch on the pocket – a small orange 'U' inside a black square. He had seen it before but didn't have time to think where right now.

'Got it,' Nix said. He ejected the memory card, undid the top of his own vest and put it in the breast pocket of his cams, then did the velcro back up.

'Sniper team, what are we looking at?'

•

'Be advised, we have six guys getting out of the truck and heading towards your location,' the spotter said. 'All are headed to your front door, all armed with AKs, forty seconds out.'

77

AMRITSAR, INDIA

'I recorded the current address of Art Kneeshaw there, too.'

'Who is that?' Thomas asked.

'An engineer we've been trying to get hold of,' Fox said. 'What's—'

'He always did free work in the northern areas and Kashmir,' Amar said. 'I told him to get out when I knew what they were doing. He never did wrong, he has spent his life working for other people, getting wells put in. For decades he did this work for people, not for money . . . Thomas, look at me . . .' He begged his brother with tears in his eyes.

Thomas looked down at his brother, who now sat slumped on the ground by the car.

He stayed silent, disappointed, trying to understand, trying to summon up empathy. 'What did you do?' Thomas asked.

Amar shook his head: 'Nothing! I did nothing . . . but this. I've become part of something . . .'

Thomas looked away. Fox looked over at Gammaldi and Duhamel across the street, then knelt down to Amar.

'But you knew what was going to happen?'

Amar let go, silent tears streaming down his face.

'We never had a chance to talk,' Amar said to his brother's back. 'We never—'

'We? We – this is *us* now? Now I don't want to talk to you,' Thomas said, facing them. 'You should have talked to me about this, Amar. I could have done something.'

Amar couldn't look at him. Fox felt the heat coming from Thomas, the white-hot rage the older brother was just managing to keep a lid on. He walked away, across the street, stood before the Golden Temple, his back to them.

Amar spoke: 'Our father taught us that when we can prevent suffering without sacrificing anything of comparable moral significance, then we ought to. But what I have done—'

'Come on, let's get out of here,' Fox said, offering a hand to help him up from the ground.

Amar clasped Fox's hand, and said: 'I'm sorry.'

'Don't be, not to me,' Fox said. He helped him up, watched him wipe the blood streaming from his nose.

'Is there an honest thief, a tender murderer?' he asked Fox, who shrugged.

'I'm not sure, Amar, but we can always work hard to make up for our mistakes.'

Amar nodded and looked back across the road to his brother. Thomas's back was still turned.

'I will dedicate my life to it,' Amar said, leaning on his car, holding the edge of his scarf against his face. 'I went off . . . I forgot so much. I will make it up, with whatever I have. I will do good for these people for however long I may live, but I know it will never be enough . . . if only I were immortal.'

Fox nodded, helped steady Amar on his feet and turned towards Gammaldi and Duhamel. He waited, watching for a break in the motorbikes and trucks and bicycles for a chance to cross the road.

To his right, he saw Brick scanning the crowd, noticed his expression change.

To his left, Fox heard a whistling, a sound he hadn't heard for a long time, a sound that a soldier who had heard it never forgot.

'RPG!' Duhamel yelled from across the street.

78

SOUTH OSSETIA (EASTERN EUROPE)

'Is there another way out?' Nix asked Anna.

'The back door, but it's through the lounge, and my brother—'

She stopped talking as they heard her brother bounding up the stairs towards them.

'Disarm him,' Nix said quietly to Top. His Sergeant nodded, drew his Beretta pistol and took position just inside the door, his M4 hanging by his side.

'No!' Anna whispered.

'We won't hurt him,' Nix said. He pulled Anna in close to him and behind the bulk of Top.

'Mortar team, get a bead on that truck and engage on my call,' Nix said quietly into his mic. As the footsteps in the hallway neared, Top tensed up and Anna dug her hands into the sides of Nix's Kevlar.

Then there was a loud noise from downstairs – a pounding on the front door.

•

At the top of the stairs they heard several men talking, then movement, then the fridge in the kitchen opening and bottles jingling. It sounded as if a party was about to get underway. Someone said something that elicited cheers, then the mother started yelling but was quieted by a slapping sound. Then crying, more laughter, more talking; the pure bravado of stupid young men mad with some kind of power in this place where they made their own laws with the guns in their hands.

'Captain, we have a clear shot of four targets in the kitchen,' the spotter said.

'Standby,' Nix whispered.

'What are they saying down there?' Nix asked quietly into Anna's ear.

She was trembling, tears in her eyes. He stooped down a bit, gently shook her shoulder, looked into her eyes.

'They are waiting for me,' she whispered. Her bottom lip quivered. 'They are waiting for me to come home and they want to . . .' She didn't finish.

Nix pulled them both back down the hall a little and whispered to his Sergeant, who nodded and led the way as they crept downstairs.

The brother saw them first. He moved towards them, his eyes wide in wonder, then rage as he computed what his sister was doing here with American soldiers.

He said something to her in Georgian. She shook her head. He took a step towards them. She spoke and motioned, put forward some kind of explanation of why two Americans would be here, but he wasn't buying.

He spoke in English: 'You brought them here to arrest me?'

Nix held up his hand for him to stop advancing, and the guys in the kitchen used it as their cue to raise their AKs.

The kitchen windows shattered, and three men fell before they could get a shot off, spraying the entire far wall with a whole new kind of wallpaper. One twitched and gurgled, and Top popped him in the head with a round from the nine mil as he and Nix backed away.

The remaining three men wore the gore of their comrades. They seemed in another world as they took in what had just gone down: an unseen force outside in the dark of night, two tooled-up Americans here in the living room of their friend.

'Put your weapons down!' Top yelled at them. Two seemed to consider it but the third, the closest and oldest-looking, didn't budge. Nix knew the look in his eyes – it was hatred, and revenge wasn't far away.

The mother started to scream and got down on the floor; she crawled over to her son on her hands and knees, started to beg and plead with him.

'Anna, tell your brother—'

He stood there facing them, his mother clawing at his legs. He slowly brought up his AK to fire at them from the hip, and let loose a few rounds.

Top took two in the vest as he moved to his right to cover Nix and Anna, returning fire and shooting the brother in the shoulder.

A whistling sound was heard as a soundtrack to the gunfire now coming their way from the three men as they backed away through the front door. Then the truck outside was hit with a 120-mm mortar round, the force shattering the front windows of the house.

Top doubled over and was blown backwards at the same time, the kinetic force of several more AK rounds having knocked the stuffing out of him. Nix reached forward but his Sergeant was up and on the offensive as he backed towards them, a protective wall, his M4 on full auto at the three guys standing in his sights.

•

'Come on, get out of there . . .' Mac willed his fellow soldiers in the house, his rifle still sighted on the large smashed-out window that revealed the kitchen and living room illuminated from the inside. He kept his eye trained on that; didn't look at the bright flaming wreck that was the truck.

•

Nix slapped another MEC-GAR magazine into his pistol and fired rounds in double-taps every second as they headed towards the back door. Two guys backed out the front door for cover; both crumpled to the ground within the same second, both head shots spraying the front door.

The mother screamed.

Nix had his left hand on Anna's back, pushing her to lead the way out the back door, his right stretched behind him with the M9 and the back collar of Top's Kevlar, pulling him backwards, guiding his sergeant out so the man could continue firing his M4.

'No!'

He heard Top yell, then felt the awful dead weight of his friend slump against him.

79

AMRITSAR, INDIA

Fox yanked Amar's coat-sleeve with him as he dived away from the noise, into the traffic.

KLAPBOOM!

Thomas's Land Cruiser exploded into flames behind them, the concussion winding Fox. He could hardly breathe . . .

Automatic gunfire tore the air around them. People screamed and shouted and wailed. Fox felt hands on his shoulders: it was Brick, dragging him free.

Amar lay on his back on the road, the side of his jacket smouldering under the intense heat of the fire.

Brick dragged Fox away, but Fox fought against him and went to Amar.

The man was almost dead. Dark blood ran from his mouth, yet he looked peaceful, like a child. Fox whispered into his ear as his eyes closed, then let himself be half-carried away by Brick as the gunfire petered out.

80

AMSTERDAM, THE NETHERLANDS

Kate took the tram home. She usually walked but it was raining and her cheap umbrella had broken. She walked into her apartment very late – she had gone to the office and then out for dinner with a friend, and then drinks, which had turned into dancing . . .

She put her bag, keys and mail on the small dining table, hung her wet coat on the back of the front door, took off her boots. She checked the time, then her phone messages – none. She shut the blinds, went to the bathroom and switched on the towel heater, then flicked on the news on the small TV in the bedroom and removed her jewellery and clothes. She walked naked into the kitchen, pulled a bottle of vodka from the freezer and poured a double measure into a glass, added a slice of lime and some soda. She sat and drank it at the dining table while flipping through her mail. Then she poured another.

A letter from Jacob: his familiar handwriting made her smile, its content made her cry. She walked into her bedroom and sat, hardly recognising the stuff she had accumulated from local stores and flea markets.

She looked at the few photos littered around the room – recent photos of her with new friends – and wondered why she had to have her life reset like this. Her thoughts drifted to her parents, then to Fox. Did Lachlan think about her in times like this? She went into the bathroom, a little uneasy on her feet, and rinsed her face with warm water. She pushed back her hair and inspected the small scar running along her hairline; then she let her hair fall back over the scar – this new hairstyle hid it well. Lighter, shorter, with more volume. She lifted her hair again, leaned in to the mirror – it didn't look too . . . it was awful. She let her hair cover it and turned away from the mirror.

She didn't miss her old job; working as a lawyer in a US government department was not what she had planned for her life, the kind of job that slowly kills you. As a college student she'd had a point when she wanted to bring down the government, and she'd been corralled into thinking she just might have a chance to do something about it, to take out what she saw was a problem with it . . . only to be played like a pawn in a bigger game. She had a quiet life here, and with that came a quantum of happiness, but it was the same or worse in ways. Memories were killing her, despite all the Eckhart Tolle she read; the pain was still there, it lived in her, a shadow that would not budge, bruises that would not heal.

Hutchinson had broken protocol when he'd relocated her – he had gone into her Washington DC apartment armed with a list of items she wanted as keepsakes of her life, and loaded them into a gym bag. Today, those few things – pictures of her family, a few letters, a couple of books, an iPod nano Fox had given her preloaded with a playlist – were usually shut away in a drawer in her dresser. She muted the TV, plugged the iPod into her Bose system and hit play: Radiohead's 'No Surprises' sounded out through the speakers. She remembered how he had left the iPod with her parents after he had brought her home from Russia, when he had saved her life . . .

She showered for five minutes, washing her hair under hot water that steamed up the little room, then dried off watching Letterman do his top ten. The iPod was on shuffle; it was still Radiohead, 'Fake Plastic Trees'. Fox was right about Radiohead, they were special – but did it seem louder since she'd switched it on? Maybe that was just her hangover arriving early.

She stepped into a robe and wrapped a towel around her hair, went out and turned it down – the volume *had* gone up . . . Must be playing up. She turned to get her cell phone from her handbag, almost slipping on the parquetry, and caught herself on the back of a chair.

There was water on the floor. She looked at her coat, thinking it must be dripping and pooling . . . Instinctively she picked up her keys from the table.

There were wet patches leading into her apartment.

Footprints.

A presence. She couldn't breathe. Her chest was tight – an arm around her throat. Something was pressed onto her face . . .

•

Kolesnik felt her go limp in his arms, and her keys clattered to the floor. He nodded at the two men in the spare room, who came out with a large wheeled bin like the laundry ones used in hotels. They slid her into it, bending her knees and folding her legs up. He put a blanket from the back of the sofa on her before closing the lid.

The drugs would keep her out for two hours, by which time he would have her loaded onto a private jet and drugged again . . . Or not, he would wait and see.

81

AMRITSAR, INDIA

The gunfire ceased. The crowd stopped screaming – open faces, watching, listening, present in that moment, participating in it. There was a beckoning silence as Fox picked up Amar's body.

Across the road he handed Amar over to his brother. Thomas looked at Fox, at his battered and now burned hands, touched the cut on his head that streamed blood down one side of his face. He finally looked like he accepted what Fox had come to achieve – not the death, but something far nobler. The body seemed weightless in his arms.

'What did you whisper to Amar as he died?' Thomas asked.

Gammaldi was pouring water over Fox's face and the back of his hands, which were red-hot but not blistered.

'I told him,' Fox said, cringing at the stinging in his eyes, 'that he was immortal.'

Thomas nodded and looked down at Amar. He had died with a content smile, one that spoke of knowledge.

'*Gurmukhi*,' Thomas said. 'Thank you, Lachlan. That he died here, in Amritsar, by our temple, it is destiny.'

It was Fox's turn to nod, humbled. A brother carried by a brother. A family resolved, in some way, with the ultimate cost.

An ambulance and a police car screeched to a halt near them. Bystanders remained hushed. Sikhs from the temple stood sentry, providing the FBI men and Thomas, Fox and Gammaldi space. Fire-trucks arrived.

'We should go,' Gammaldi said as a couple of paramedics rushed towards them with a trolley.

'My friend will take you all to the airport,' Thomas said, signalling to a Sikh man the size of a small house. '*Jo Bole So Nihaal*, Lachlan Fox, you are *Khalsa* – you are pure, you are truly one of us.'

The fire crew had their hoses out, hitting the line of blazing cars with water and foam. Thomas leaned in close to Fox and Gammaldi.

'By means of water,' he said quietly, 'we give life to everything.'

'Who said that?' Fox asked. 'One of your gurus?'

'No. It is from the Koran.'

82

FORT EUSTIS, VIRGINIA

'It's over, buddy,' Hutchinson said.

The man shackled to the chair had spent the past few hours in an aircraft, most of them drugged. After flying a circuit over the Atlantic, the government-contracted Gulfstream jet had landed, and Army personnel had shepherded him, hooded and in arm and leg braces, across a concrete tarmac, where he had been forced into a Humvee and driven over several miles of track, and then taken into a windowless concrete room and shackled to a steel eyelet fixed to the floor. The whole effect was made up to look and feel like he was now somewhere in the Middle East.

In the World of Warcraft he went by the avatar name *SwordsmanM*. In person, he had once been a hard-ass Marine and still looked pretty tough at forty, with a shaved head, and some serious scars that said he'd gone through some plate glass. He was dressed in coveralls and had a diaper on underneath.

Hutchinson stood a few paces in front of him. The guy wasn't showing any interest. The room was lit by a single recessed bulb above them, and there was a card table with some documents on it. A small camcorder in the corner took in everything.

'You're fucking sloppy,' Hutchinson said, showing him the printouts of the game's mail transcripts, intercepted by a team in the NIA's Open Source Centre. 'We tracked this back to your computer and ISP . . . sloppy. And you're selling out your country. How did *that* happen?'

Resolute. Silent.

'Been looking out for you for a while now,' Hutchinson said. 'We lifted your DNA from the house of Ira Dunn, former Deputy Director of the NSA.'

'Never heard of him.'

'Doesn't matter. He's dead now, he won't mind that you forgot him already,' Hutchinson said. 'Like I said, your DNA was found in his house, the day our lab guys went through the place. Traced the drug in Dunn's glass back to a particular strain of poison developed and used exclusively by the CIA. I take it you didn't break into their lab and take it and poison this guy at random? But that doesn't matter, not today.'

He looked up at Hutchinson, there was intrigue there. Good. Hutchinson took a file from the table, opened it.

'Prior to Iraq you were posted as an embassy guard?'

'That's what it says.'

Hutchinson nodded, pulled out a colour photograph from the file and showed it to the guy.

The guy's eyes gleamed with recognition.

It was a clear headshot of an attractive young woman.

'You had a relationship there with this woman.'

Sucker-punched. He looked at the ground, shook his head.

'Most guys would have done the same,' Hutchinson said, looking at the picture. 'Bet she was worth it, too.'

'I don't know what you're talking about.'

'She blackmailed you.'

He looked like he pitied Hutchinson on this course of questions.

'Clayton J. Lonetree, a Marine Sergeant embassy guard in Moscow, was entrapped by a female Soviet officer in 1987,' Hutchinson said to him. He leaned down, spoke into his face. 'He was then blackmailed into handing over documents when he was assigned to Vienna, becoming the first US Marine to be convicted of spying against the United States. He didn't even know what he was doing, and he got thirty years.'

No reaction.

'It's all right, it's not really my concern, just thought I'd bring it up,' Hutchinson said. He leaned forward again, holding up the photo. 'You are aware that she was a CIA agent?'

The guy laughed – then the sound petered out, his eyes clouded.

'It's called a honeytrap. Old-school espionage. She's actually Mossad, the Agency just uses her as a contractor. Mossad are better than us at this type of thing, you see. She's been very good for them and us over the years.'

Hutchinson put the picture of the woman back in the file, and pulled out the guy's Department of Defense file. All his service records were there: he had seen duty in pretty much every conflict the US had been involved in since the late eighties.

'You know what Jay Bybee and John Yoo did for us?' Hutchinson asked. 'Yeah, you know. They wrote those torture memos for Bush. Been kind of useful for us. Of course, that's just the grey-area legal stuff. We can do all sorts of shit in places like this to people like you, but you know all that already . . .'

He flicked through the ex-Marine's file. It seemed he had never done much of anything special; didn't rise quickly, didn't achieve any sort of rank to be proud of. Had some close calls, was well liked. Got some heat for some drunken shit that got out of hand in Iraq. Family: divorced while away during the first Gulf War.

'Your ex-wife and kid live in Dover – where's that, Delaware?'

'Fuck off.'

'Sorry?'

'Fuck off from my family.'

'It says here they're not your family anymore.'

'I pay support.'

'Yeah,' Hutchinson said, looking up from the file. 'What *is* your job?'

He went back to looking at the floor.

'Your daughter's on a waiting list—'

'Fuck off from my family!' His face was red, veins big and tight in his tattooed neck.

Hutchinson moved closer, right in front of him. Checked his watch. 'The information I need, I need in a hurry,' he said. 'I'm going to walk out that door in five minutes unless you start telling me what I want to hear.'

The ex-jarhead laughed.

'If the information you give me doesn't check out, if it's wrong in any way, I won't be coming back to question you again,' Hutchinson explained. 'If it checks out, you get cut loose, and you get legit work within three months – and I'll have a federal probation on your ass for the next five years.'

The guy laughed again.

'I know you don't care about the Marines I've got outside the door – guys who view you as a traitor to their kin, guys who are just hanging to say hi to you,' Hutchinson said through a smile. 'I know you don't care that you're in Jordan, either.'

The guy looked up at him. Hutchinson checked his watch.

'You've got three minutes,' Hutchinson said, watching him. 'Two minutes fifty-five. For what it's worth, we're not going to waterboard you or fuck around with broomsticks, because you're not worth the time. I want the names of your game friends – *Darkshadow* would be a good place to start. You give me that, great, we can deal. If not, when I'm gone you're going to rot here in a dark cave while we build a multi-life sentence against you – and we'll get a conviction that can't be appealed. And I'll spend my waking hours and use every power I have as a Federal Agent to make sure your family is fucked up for life.'

He struggled against his shackles, which grated through the large steel eyelet embedded in the concrete floor at his feet.

'Two minutes thirty . . .'

•

Ten minutes later Hutchinson walked out the room with what he needed to get to the next step, all recorded on the camcorder he carried.

But first, he had an apology to deliver, and a good man to bring well and truly onside. As he walked to his chopper his BlackBerry chimed.

A Quantico number, a female agent who wasn't making sense to him.

'Sorry,' Hutchinson replied to her, 'I don't see why you're calling me.'

'I'm calling from Protective Services—'

'And I haven't looked after any—' Then Hutchinson knew, and he tasted bile. He had only ever placed one person in witness protection.

'There was an abduction in an apartment on the Prinsengracht in Amsterdam,' the agent said. 'I just had the Dutch FBI Legat call me. He's at the scene now with local forensics.'

'When did this happen?'

'Within the past hour,' the agent replied. 'She hit the panic alarm on her keychain, so our guys went and checked it out. They broke the door down when there was no answer. Her alarm had a locator, which was found on her keychain in her apartment.'

'Any sign of—'

'We think she's alive,' she replied. 'A quick chem check turned up some form of TCM-type compound.'

'So she was taken out of the building unconscious?'

'Crude drug of choice, but yes.'

'Footage?'

'We're checking on that, possibly a cleaning company that wasn't scheduled to be there showed up on the lift camera; we can't say it's definitely them.'

'But you're tracking them?'

'Yes – they had a large bin, and it timed with the abduction. Three white males. We have pretty good images from a camera behind the lift's mirror. We've notified all relevant European agencies about the persons of interest.'

'Good. Get those pics into the database as soon as you get enough info on them.'

'On it,' she said. 'Would you like to get in touch direct with the Legat in Amsterdam?'

'Yeah, I'll do that now,' he replied. He stopped walking.

'Sir?'

'Yeah, I'm here,' Hutchinson said. 'Look, we have watermarks on the witness protection files, don't we? Traceable, I mean, to anyone who accesses them?'

'That's still a work in progress, but yes.'

'Run it.'

'You'll need to provide a—'

'Just run it. Now.'

Silence on the other end for a moment.

'Sir, what if it leads internal?'

'I'll worry about that if it happens,' he said.

'You won't be able to use it in court, if it comes to it.'

'Let me worry about that.'

83

HIGH OVER THE MIDDLE EAST

'Thanks,' Gammaldi said, taking a couple of painkillers and a drink from Brick.

Fox shifted in his seat, trying to get comfortable enough to sleep, but his mind was racing. He felt a dangerous kind of tired, the sort that lured you in and from which you never really woke up.

'This better all be worth it,' Gammaldi said, flinching under the pain of his broken ribs.

Fox's right hand and forearm were bandaged, and he had burn cream on the backs of his hands. Numb all over – tired, weary, fed up. He looked out his window. Gammaldi was right. How much more blood would be on his hands before this was over?

'Lach, are you asleep?'

'Yeah, Al.'

'Do you think India and Pakistan would ever go nuclear against one another?'

Fox looked at him, too weary to really think about it.

'I mean – they've got a – they're . . .'

'Al,' Fox said, 'if it gets worse than it is – if we can't put a kink in Umbra's plans and they spend the next fifty years pumping India's underground water table dry – yeah, maybe.'

'But nuclear?'

Fox looked around the cabin. Duhamel was on a phone back to Hutchinson prepping the next leg, Luigi and Ivan were alternating between sleep and playing chess. He felt a lead weight in his gut about finding Art Kneeshaw, knowing so much would depend on what Duhamel and Hutchinson could get mobilised on the ground in Italy.

'Look, Al: in seventy-four, India set off a "peaceful" nuclear explosion. Indira Gandhi herself said they had no intention of building a bomb, they just wanted to know they *could*. Twenty years later they set off five nuclear explosions. Who gets nervous? Pakistan. And when Pakistan gets nervous, everybody gets nervous. You know why? Because we're all going to die.'

'We're all going to die?' Gammaldi said, loudly enough to be heard by everyone.

'They've got, like, a one-minute warning or something,' Fox said. 'There's no lag like the US and Russia used to have, no time to get more information – they're fucking next door to one another. So do I think they'd go nuclear? Let's just not think about that, okay?'

84

WASHINGTON DC

'Sorry, I thought—'

'You *thought*!' McCorkell flushed, then calmed himself down quickly. He had stared down foreign heads of state as they threatened to kill American troops and those of her allies, he had woken three Presidents countless times with bad news, and he had . . . But this was personal. 'You thought I was leaking intel? You thought I was – *fuck*!'

Hutchinson didn't fight, didn't respond, just sat on his barstool, drank his beer and took it like a man. They sat in the Off the Record bar at the Hay-Adams Hotel, a few minutes' walk from the EEOB, across Pennsylvania Avenue and through Lafayette Park.

'I mean, seriously?'

'Bill, I had to be careful,' Hutchinson explained. 'I had to check everywhere, everyone.'

'Do you know how far I go back with Tas Wallace at GSR?' McCorkell said to him. 'We were the original homies – we started that closed-fist high-five thing at college in the seventies.'

'Did you invent electricity too? Maybe the wheel?'

'And all this from a man young enough to be my son.'

'Look, Bill,' said Hutchinson sincerely, 'I'm sorry. I was wrong.'

'Clearly.'

'And for the record,' Hutchinson said, 'I never actually *believed* you would do anything like this, I just had to check it out.'

'Yeah, you said. What a fascinating story . . .' McCorkell said, draining his beer. 'So entertaining and full of useful information.'

Hutchinson felt like a chastised child. McCorkell looked around, sighed, let it wash over him.

'Anyway, forget it,' McCorkell said before ordering another beer and a single-malt Scotch. 'What have you got? Seriously, give me everything. Lay it all out, right now.'

As Hutchinson updated him, McCorkell listened, asked a few questions and ate his way through an entire dish of cocktail nuts, which was cheerfully refilled by the bartender. After a few drinks McCorkell felt comfortable enough to forgive Hutchinson – he was a pro doing his job. He wouldn't have done much different himself.

'The leak at CIA goes back to Merlin too.'

'Oh?' McCorkell said. He remembered Merlin too well. A covert operation under the Clinton Administration, Merlin aimed to delay Iran's nuclear program by providing – via a defected Russian nuclear scientist – flawed blueprints for a nuclear warhead. The plan backfired, however, when the nervous Russian noticed the flaws and pointed them out to the Iranians, hoping to enhance his credibility while still advancing what he thought was the CIA's plan to use him as a double-agent inside Iran. Merlin ended up unwittingly accelerating Iran's nuclear program by providing useful information, once the flaws were identified and the plans compared with other sources, such as those provided to the Iranians by Abdul Khan, the founder of Pakistan's nuclear program. The ugly fact was, while there was serious money to be made selling secrets, be it military technology or a simple phrase that gets agents killed, men like Hutchinson would be in high demand to play defence.

'It's the same guy inside the Agency who tipped the Iranians off in the first place,' Hutchinson said.

'And he's your man,' McCorkell said, 'who intercepted and replaced my email to GSR about clearance to land in Spain, and then sold out Kate?'

'Yep.'

'So how did you get him?'

Hutchinson explained about the work done by the Open Source Centre team, how they'd played the computer game and tracked these guys, watched server traffic and tracked ISPs, all for not much until they narrowed in on the ex-Marine with some kind of remote access Trojan that the NSA helped plant.

'Like what was being employed at the hotbed of al-Qaeda internet cafés on the Pakistan–Afghanistan border?'

'Exactly,' Hutchinson replied. 'I used an OSC team to catch a US-based traitor and murderer.'

'Murderer?'

'I'll go into it later.'

'Right. So, you're going to send Lachlan Fox in to face off with Roman Babich, without telling him Babich has Kate – his world is going to explode! You don't know Fox like I do, Andy.'

'We'll keep him on a leash, and he's well protected.'

'Maybe,' McCorkell said. '*And* you tell me that Babich has someone in the CIA helping him out—'

'We know who, and we're taking him down next.'

'And – really?' McCorkell savoured the weight of this. 'Okay . . . When is this going to happen?'

'Soon,' Hutchinson said, checking his watch. He stood, picking his coat off the back of the barstool. 'I'm headed to Italy in a few hours to coordinate the arrest of Babich, taking my full team over there. We've got local support setting up shop in Italy as we speak.'

'So Fox is scheduled to meet with Babich?'

'He will be. This is it, Bill,' Hutchinson said, peeling off a few bills and leaving them on the bar. 'This fucker's been flaunting it since the end of the Cold War, and we're finally bringing him down.'

'Yeah, but Andy?' McCorkell said. 'The Agency guy, when are you bringing him in?'

'I'm not bringing him in,' Hutchinson said, pulling on his jacket and pocketing his BlackBerry. He shook McCorkell's hand. 'You are.'

PART THREE

85

ROME, ITALY

Fox scanned the crowd until his eyes came to rest on Art Kneeshaw's friendly face. The old guy looked like he was in heaven sitting there, watching the crowd, enjoying life around him.

Kneeshaw saw them approach the café; saw Gammaldi throw a few coins into the Trevi Fountain and heard him whistling 'Three Coins in the Fountain'. He appeared alarmed, but not surprised.

'We're friends, Mr Kneeshaw,' Fox said after introductions.

'Ah, Australians,' he replied. 'A beautiful country – not without its own water problems.'

'May we join you for a moment?' Fox said. The man nodded and they sat at his table, under an umbrella set up outside on the cobbled street. His gaze seemed to take Fox in, and there was realisation there that showed he must have seen Fox on television.

'How did you find me?' he asked.

'Facial recognition at the airport.'

'Ah.'

'Your passport didn't flag the Italian authorities, though.'

'I have an old friend in the Canadian Foreign Office,' he

said with a cheeky grin. 'He'd warned me to stay low, organised me a clean passport . . . I'm glad to hear there are still smart people there.'

Fox smiled.

'But here – how did—' Kneeshaw stopped, saw the FBI men across the street. 'Someone from the US embassy followed me to this café, I suppose?'

Fox nodded.

'And you're not a spy?'

'No,' said Fox. 'I'm a reporter, and Al here is my shadow. Those guys over there—' Fox motioned with a tilt of his head '—as well as a couple you can't see, are with us. They're FBI, mainly.'

'All this for me?'

'There's a contract out to kill you, Mr Kneeshaw,' Fox said. 'The men who financed the big water project in Kashmir are cleaning out those involved.'

He nodded.

'You know? Your friend in the Canadian government warned you of that?'

He looked at Fox with mischievous eyes.

'Amar Singh warned me, too,' he said. 'He didn't mention who was behind it, although he didn't have to.'

Fox sensed this guy wasn't one to budge.

'Mr Kneeshaw, Amar is dead.'

The mischief dimmed in his eyes, was replaced by sadness.

'We can protect you—'

'If they find me here, so be it,' he said, looking out at the Trevi Fountain. He let out a long breath. 'This is where it all started.'

Fox looked at him, unsure what to read into it.

'You see that? The passage of the water in that fountain, an aqueduct running for more than twenty kilometres, is over two thousand years old. Two thousand years!' said Kneeshaw. 'Romans have been using water from that source since 19 BC, when Marcus Vipsanius Agrippa built it . . . a remarkable man, Agrippa.' Kneeshaw sat back and smiled benignly towards the fountain, watching the hordes of tourists clamouring for a picture in front of it despite the biting cold.

'These people come to see the fountain because they have read about it and have seen movies – maybe even for some luck – but do you think they *really* appreciate its perfection? Do you think they realise that fresh water is life?'

He smiled at Fox, suddenly looking a little closer to his eighty years.

'If it is my destiny to be found here, Mr Fox, so be it. I feel that I have lived in balance, and that the right thing will happen. It will be just.'

Fox looked at Kneeshaw with interest. He was hard to read, but intriguing.

'It's going to rain in a few minutes,' Kneeshaw said.

It was overcast, with not a patch of sky to be seen. The air felt heavy.

'Can you tell me about your work in Kashmir?'

'I have such clear memories of my first time in India,' Kneeshaw said, smiling. 'I remember rain like I had never seen. From my window I'd watch it, listen to it, for hours, watching as the river swelled and the parched red land turned green. At night I'd lie on my bed listening to the fat drops drum on the roof, a sound like the galloping of horses—'

'Mr Kneeshaw,' said Fox, leaning forward. 'How did you come to work on this water project? What did you mean when you said it all started here?'

'I worked on an aqueduct repair here in Rome, over ten years ago now, and Umbra was a major donator to the restoration project – Babich buying up favours with the political elite, I see in hindsight.'

'Hindsight?' Fox said.

'I met him when I worked on the repair, and he asked me to consult on a couple of engineering projects. I mentioned to him I'd once worked on a Kashmir pipeline project – I was an infrastructure engineer with Canadian Rail, and we worked on the sub-continent, then I returned later and helped plan that pipeline that ran under the road . . . I liked that area, liked that work. We spent time getting wells put in – artesian wells – in remote areas on both sides.'

'And what was his interest in it?' Fox asked, pulling from his jacket pocket a pen and his map of that area.

'I guess money. Here was a half-completed thing; he was already in the process of developing the gas pipeline—' Kneeshaw took Fox's pen, put on his glasses and drew a shaky line that fed gas across the country. 'I had been in the region for a long time, knew the terrain and work crew as well as anyone.'

'And consulted on the new project there – this Iran–Pakistan–India gas pipeline that would deliver natural gas from Iran to Pakistan and India?'

'It may one day end up going into China,' Kneeshaw said. 'The project will greatly benefit India and Pakistan, because they simply do not have sufficient natural gas to meet their rising demand for energy.'

'I remember the trilateral talks about the project,' said Fox.

Kneeshaw nodded, looked absently at the map of the places he obviously knew so well.

'So,' Gammaldi said, 'Babich just saw this as a way of doing more with the resources he already had there working on the gas pipeline?'

Kneeshaw nodded again.

'The water pipeline runs under the highway south, as you have marked on here already,' Kneeshaw said. He adjusted his glasses, and marked in a new line, a continuation of what Fox and Omar Hasif had put there two days ago. 'Then it links up with the gas pipeline and follows that, all the way west.'

'You've drawn too far,' Fox said. He tapped the map, figuring that Kneeshaw's sight wasn't good despite his thick reading glasses. 'Pakistan's western border is there.'

'I know.' .

'Your line goes into Iran,' Fox said. 'We're talking about the water pipeline, not the natural gas line.'

'I know,' Kneeshaw said. He put the pen down and sipped his coffee. 'The water pipeline goes there. Into Iran.'

86

GORI, GEORGIA (EASTERN EUROPE)

Top was gone. The Blue Zone looked the same, but everything was different. A few of the senior US officers who knew of the overnight mission had been in meetings all morning. That mission had changed everything. Nix knew what he had to do.

The camcorder footage was with Sara, the GSR reporter, downloaded to her computer, on which Nix had watched it in full high-res definition. On that same memory card, before the footage of the snipers that Mac took out that day, was the scene of Anna posing outside the Town Hall the day of the bombing.

'Make a copy of this and get it to your people,' he'd said to her. He'd kept it quiet, away from the eyes of the Army's media liaison detachment. 'I want this to get out there.'

His Colonel wasn't happy – he was getting chewed out by the French commander about the way the mission ended. Nix knew he'd be next, didn't give a damn. If this was the end of his career, so be it. He would defend Top's fine work with his own dying breath. The Western world held understandable anxiety about South Ossetia, and Russia's role in the South Caucasus. The oil and gas pipelines running from Azerbaijan through Georgia and into Turkey impacted Russia's support for South Ossetia's independence, especially heated since Georgia's attempts to move closer to the West and join NATO. Russia also viewed quite unfavourably the West's recent recognition of Kosovo's independence, and wanted to give the West a taste of its own medicine.

And it was medicine that was hard for Nix to swallow. He would probably be stuck here another few weeks searching for unexploded ordinance from the war, after a UN observation team found a cache of unexploded phosphorous rockets in a local potato field.

The war had changed everything. The press room at the Blue Zone headquarters was filled with photos of the terrified townspeople as they'd begun to shut up their houses and bury their valuables, and the next phase that showed the refugees who flooded through the streets with hastily wrapped bundles of possessions on their backs. Nothing could equate to the terror of war, no act of witness or truth-telling. A severed head. The blackened stump of a tree. Charred fields. A crow, picking at the body of a child.

Top was in the base morgue, wrapped in a body bag. Blue helmets were everywhere. The people of Gori were moving back to their shattered homes, rebuilding, cleaning up, replanting crops, mending broken lives. They were resilient, formed by an idea of who they were rather than the sum of what had happened to them. There was much beauty to this place, and war could not tarnish that – it was in the faces of the Georgian children, and their eyes spoke a truth that the world needed to hear. American guns were lying low – no one wanted to escalate the situation.

The images on the memory card showed the man who set off that bomb, and Nix was sure it would get out there; something would be done, so this place could heal. The Anna's of this place would be heard and a calmer generation would prevail. When he got home, it would be time to hang up his uniform at the back of his closet. He had learned so much the hard way, from an innocent young woman and a hardened soldier he'd known as family.

All wars are crimes.

87

ROME, ITALY

'Iran?' Fox said, watching Gammaldi's fingers dart over the keyboard of his BlackBerry as he emailed an update through to Hutchinson, McCorkell and Wallace. 'Indian–Pakistani water is going into Iran?'

'That's where one of the main pipelines goes; it piggybacks on the Iran–Pakistan–India gas pipeline,' Kneeshaw replied. 'There are a few splits along the way, to supply the Pakistani cities to the south.'

'Iran is taking India's water . . .'

'Depends on how you look at it,' Kneeshaw said. 'The water goes from the shared Indian–Pakistani region, flows through Pakistan, and some goes to Iran. As to ownership, that's for someone else to decide.'

'Was this what you started decades ago?'

'Partly – it wasn't a new concept, that's for sure,' Kneeshaw said. 'The Iranians asked me about the possibility of it thirty-odd years ago when I was in the country drilling wells – it was all very hush-hush top-secret at the time, which I found amusing . . . Then they told me they wanted a way of getting Iranian oil out to Pakistan after the revolution in seventy-nine, which I found out much later was to be in exchange for weapons and munitions – and maybe even more. I attended some meetings then, nothing more.'

Maybe even more? Fox's head was spinning. That much water . . . for a country with gas and oil to burn on desalination plants. Why did they need all that extra water? 'What do you mean by exchanging for weapons and more – heavy water?'

Kneeshaw shrugged.

'Nuclear weapons?' Gammaldi said, his thumbs paused on the keys of his BlackBerry.

'That, I don't know,' Kneeshaw replied. 'But I have no doubt about nuclear technology changing hands between the two countries, especially after it came out about Abdul Khan.'

Fox tried to compute everything he was hearing. Abdul Khan was the founder of Pakistan's nuclear program. Caught out recently, Khan confessed to having been involved in a clandestine international network of nuclear-weapons technology proliferation from Pakistan to Libya, Iran and North Korea. All, Khan said, for the national interest of his country – a nation that promised him complete freedom, which he still enjoyed today.

'Khan did his best to extend the reach of nuclear weapons across the globe, and *I'm* the hunted one?' continued Kneeshaw.

'I feel for you, Mr Kneeshaw,' Gammaldi said through a mouthful of chocolate cannoli. 'And if it makes you feel any better, we're on the list as well.'

'It's just so unbelievable – I mean, I was proud to be part of the project in Kashmir,' he said. 'It was so many years in the making; abandoned, disputed . . . I don't think it will be nearly as damaging to the Indian water supply as some make out in the media. This water will provide so much . . .'

'Where does that water go in Iran?' asked Fox.

'Show me the map again,' Kneeshaw said, putting his reading glasses on. He looked at Fox with a smile. 'You know, water never disappears. It's transferred, goes from one spot to another, is used and converted to something else, evaporates and falls and is used over and over again. As I said, Mr Fox, water is life.'

The old man stood, tapped a spot on the map on the table. Just inside Iran. Not far from where his pen line crossed with the gas pipeline.

'This town,' he said, 'Look there. Zahedan, formerly known as Dozz-app. It comes from the Persian Dozd-aab, which means . . . water thief.'

'I don't even know if that's ironic or not,' Fox said.

'They'd probably say it was destiny.'

So this had started in Iran so long ago – they'd gone in search of water and finally found it in the willing grace of Umbra Corp. That water belonged where it was. The water went west . . . Nothing ever really ended.

88

GREENBRIER RESORT, WEST VIRGINIA

McCorkell rode in a golf cart driven by a resort staff member. He thought he could still hear his Bell chopper on the helipad to the other side of the resort's main building, then realised it was the noise of his back-up guys, a team from the FBI's active Hostage Rescue Team. They had just landed on the seventh hole, their chopper black and ominous.

The day was cold but sunny and clear, the frost on the grass slippery under his leather-soled shoes. He sure wasn't going to go chasing this guy if he ran, but then, he had six heavily armed Special Agents for that. Spring wasn't far off, as heralded by some early tulips blooming; it was the type of weather that only the truly committed or insane players braved. Through the Cold War until 1992 this expansive estate had been the location of the bunker that would house the legislative branch of government in the advent of nuclear war. The *Washington Post* had broken the story, and as the secrecy was lifted and the location became a target – even with the changing geopolitical climate, it was still to this day a target – it had closed its secret function. It was now, as it had been for a hundred and fifty years, an elegant resort.

The cart stopped on his signal, and he tipped the driver, who took off back to base.

McCorkell stood watching the two CIA agents. Ryan Kavanaugh teed off, a big three-hundred metre thing that sounded good off the club. All three men watched its flight. James Riley moved to set up his shot, saw McCorkell, recognised him.

Riley stood back from his ball, leaned on his club. McCorkell walked towards them, stopping a few metres short.

He stared intently at Kavanaugh.

McCorkell wasn't a tall man – someone had once told him he was closer in looks and stature to Napoleon Bonaparte than Arnold Schwarzenegger – but over twenty years of government service, much of it in top jobs in the Executive Branch, had given him the learned swagger and presence, imposing in a Lyndon-Johnson-visits-Congress sort of way.

Kavanaugh looked at Riley – his face said it all.

There were other players about but all out of earshot, many of them intel workers on a three-day conference.

McCorkell tossed onto their golf cart a transcript of the WoW mail contents, a list of their guild players, and avatar names – two of which had actual names written beside them. Kavanaugh glanced down at the papers as they flapped in the breeze, and then up at McCorkell.

'What's this?' Kavanaugh asked.

'We really don't mind that you log onto game websites in work hours,' McCorkell said. 'We just mind what you do while you're on there.'

Kavanaugh took half a beat to catch himself, looked down the golf range: 'Bill, what are you talking about?'

McCorkell looked around, could just make out two of the HRT members in their olive drab coveralls and black tactical gear, watching, action-ready.

'Ryan,' McCorkell said. 'We got a confession from your guy. We've got evidence up to *here*. All on tape – it makes good viewing.'

Silence. Kavanaugh looked at both men, then picked up the thick printout, flicked though a couple of pages, set it down. 'Drink?'

McCorkell shook his head.

'Okay . . .' He reached into the cooler at the back of the cart, took out a beer, leaned on the seat and popped the can.

'Ryan,' Riley said. 'What's this about?'

'Seriously?'

He nodded.

Kavanaugh casually looked around, scanning the area after something caught his eye, then leaned forward on his seat, his hands behind the cooler, and looked up at the two men. A moment of truth in his heavy eyes.

'I was part of the downsizing, you know,' he said. 'After the Cold War. I'd worked hard in Europe, specialised in Russian intel – all those contacts I'd worked so damn hard to cultivate, then the Company downsized, the Cold War ended . . .'

Riley and McCorkell looked at each other, then back to Kavanaugh, who was staring out over the fairway.

'I made a name for myself in private contracting, was brought back in after 9/11—'

'Yeah, I know, Ryan,' McCorkell said.

'Do you?' He shook his head. 'DC cops make more than we do. I came back because I believed, I mean truly believed, that what we were doing was right. I was part of the winning team!'

'What the fuck is going on here?' Riley asked.

'What fucking acknowledgment do we ever get?' Kavanaugh snapped. 'We get told when we fuck up, and that's it!'

'Gratitude is the prerogative of the people,' McCorkell said. 'Not part of what we do. This is over now, Ryan.'

'Your ignorance is encyclopaedic,' Kavanaugh said, leaning a little further towards the cooler, then showed them a compact automatic pistol resting in his hand.

McCorkell didn't flinch. Shook his head at the man.

'Check your chest,' McCorkell said. His eyes went from the cooler and the pistol to Kavanaugh's sternum – a red dot appeared.

The CIA Section Chief looked down, saw the laser pointer aimed over his heart.

'They're listening in and will take the shot if they need to,' McCorkell said. 'Don't go out like this. Tell us what's going on.'

Kavanaugh's shoulders dropped a little, his eyes transfixed on the dot.

'Undo some of this before it gets any worse.'

He shook his head slowly, might even have shed a tear as his arms went slack and he stared at the gun in his hands.

'It was all about money,' he confessed, without looking up.

'We know.'

'I – people have died so that I could get money . . .'

'Help us end this,' McCorkell said. He walked around the cart, careful to steer clear of the shot that could pass through the condemned man. He took the pistol and cleared the rounds into his palm. The laser designator remained, the two FBI sniper teams in place at hair-trigger. Two agents in the tree-line of the rough approached, heavy hitters who still had their sights on their target.

Riley looked at his mentor with what could be sadness, or maybe just disappointment.

Kavanaugh looked at him – then away. He almost seemed pleased as the HRT men forced him to the ground and flexi-cuffed his hands behind his back.

'Leave James out of this, he knew nothing.' Kavanaugh's eyes showed admiration for the man he had groomed over the years, working day and night side-by-side in a small office, sleeves rolled up trying to shape the part of the world in their sphere of influence.

'Did you know what they were doing?' Riley asked him. 'Killing people so you could make money?'

Kavanaugh was silent, rested his head on the grass as he was patted down.

'Jesus, Ryan, there might be an Iranian bomb out of this,' McCorkell said.

His eyes didn't seem to register. He was gone. McCorkell watched as the FBI hauled him away, knew too that Riley's world as he'd known it had just crashed down around him.

McCorkell picked up Kavanaugh's BlackBerry from behind the cooler.

'Son of a bitch wouldn't even—' Riley said. 'I mean, after everything—'

'James,' he said, looking at the younger agent, who was still too shell-shocked to be angry at his former mentor. 'Know this: we remember not the words of our enemies, but the silence of our friends.'

89

ATHENS, GREECE

Text flashed on the screen of Sirko's phone.

It was the message he had been waiting on for years . . . It was go time. Resolution. Retribution. This was it.

His dog – the stray he had taken in a couple of years ago – was still with his neighbours, and he left them a note in an envelope with a few hundred euros. They would take care of him.

He had been taken care of, once. The Hypatian Monastery; he was there in his mind as he walked out of his apartment complex and hailed a cab in the street. As he rode to the airport he remembered playing with the other kids, behaving most of the time. It was a cold place to live, and he had disliked the cold ever since. His best and worst memories were of that place and time.

He remembered Roman Babich visiting him, taking him on holidays, treating him like a son over summer holidays – and then sending him off to boarding school at thirteen. While Kolesnik, his true son, lived in luxury. No corrupt men in dark shadows loomed over his childhood. The vast halls of monastery buildings dating from the sixteenth and seventeenth centuries: towering ceilings and bleak rooms inhabited by hungry boys. The Trinity

Cathedral had an incredibly elaborate painted interior, his place of solace, and he could see it in his mind as clear as day.

Sirko had done his time in the Army; a few years in Chechnya, and then in the breakaway States training government and militia soldiers. He didn't care that he might die. He had been decorated as a hero on several occasions, but he wasn't heroic – he wasn't there to fight for his country or cause, he simply didn't care about the consequences. Death was constantly around him, death became his family, death was where he belonged.

But now, here was his moment: first he would take out Babich, then he would take care of his little brother. Little Nashi bitch.

•

Sirko had met the CIA man during the first Chechen war. They had become friends – then enemies when, one night drinking, this guy, posing as a reporter, presented him with information that he couldn't accept as true; information on Babich, a man he had once looked to as a father.

He killed your father. That's what the American had said as he handed over the file and walked out of the makeshift bar. Sirko had tracked him down four days later, after he had expelled most of his hatred, after he had checked and checked again with every source he could to verify what he had been told and given. Turned out it was true.

He wanted revenge and wanted help doing it – he knew then that the American was not a reporter, and he had been good enough to admit it. He was part of a new taskforce set up to bring down Babich and men like him . . . But it was not what Sirko lusted after; it would be a slow burn, a methodical documentation of the Umbra network of ex-KGB and FSB men, infiltrating their organisation through men like Sirko had been the aim at the time. He had been convinced by his American friend there that night, and so many times since, that this was the right way to go about retribution. A slow death of a thousand cuts.

One day, he would get the chance to exact the revenge he craved. He would be told in a simple message, a message he had memorised all those years ago – the message that had just come in. It was destiny – he was here, so close, and he was ready. He had the gear he needed stashed in a hotel there; it had been there for years, waiting for this moment. He looked at the text on the screen, knew what it meant, and hoped his American friend, Ryan Kavanaugh, would be okay.

90

BELLAGIO, LAKE COMO, ITALY

Babich hung up the phone; he would meet young Sirko in Guzzi's Café in the morning. He hadn't seen him in so long – perhaps Babich would bring Kolesnik too; they could start patching things up now that this affair was almost behind them. He sat by an open window of his Villa La Cassinella and thought about his boys and how they had become men.

He looked out across the lake towards Bellagio. He loved it here this time of year. The heavy clouds parted and the water sparkled like diamonds. Grand villas were strung out along the shores, the old ghosts of European aristocrats, haunting with their legacy of creating beauty in a place already so naturally beautiful. He had been one of the first of his countrymen to buy here, and now its days were numbered. Back then, the only sounds heard here on weekends were sails flapping on the lake, champagne corks popping, tennis balls on clay courts, and evening laughter. Now it was speedboats and super-cars; new Hollywood was here, new European money – the flashy kind, the kind Babich detested.

His press secretary came in, pointed to the phone with the light blinking on his desk: 'I have him on the line.'

Babich took the handset, waited for her to leave and shut the door.

'Finally, we speak.'

'Finally,' Lachlan Fox replied. 'You got my message?'

'Yes.'

'I'm filing a syndicated story all around the world and I want your comments,' Fox said. 'I have spoken to Art Kneeshaw, as well as Amar Singh. It seems you have been quite busy, in Zahedan, Iran, just across the border from Pakistan. I'm sure you know it?'

Babich's jaw clenched. 'Meet me in Bellagio, ten o'clock tomorrow morning,' he said. An hour before his catch-up with Sirko.

'Where in Bellagio?'

'I will inform you in the morning, at five minutes to ten.'

'That's not going to happen,' Fox said. 'You tell me now or I'll set the place and time myself.'

Babich smiled. This guy wasn't stupid. 'Okay, Guzzi's Café. It's on the lake.'

'I'll see you there.'

The line clicked out.

He would make that meeting tomorrow; he would show Fox the woman, give him an ultimatum. Then, only then – when Fox and his precious girl were in each other's arms, after Fox had given up the location of where Art and any others are – would he take care of this.

His boys had failed him on this. All is not gold that glitters, he reminded himself. His faith in others had been put in check, and when this was over he'd need to reassess those he trusted with such work.

He dialled Kolesnik on his cell. 'Where are you?'

'Just landed in Milan.'

'Bring our guest to my villa,' Babich said. 'The room beneath the garage. I will see you here soon.'

'I'm on my way.'

He would accept no more excuses from Kolesnik after this. Where something is thin, it tears, and Kolesnik's mistakes were costing Babich. He could not afford them anymore. It is a bad workman who has a blunt saw, his father used to say, and unless Kolesnik picked up his game, he was out on his own. Babich had given him so much and asked for little in return. Tomorrow, he would bring Sirko into the family; for too long he had been on the outer, and for what, pride? To waste away his talents?

The clouds came together, the water darkened and he pictured Lachlan Fox. He was reminded of another line his father used to say: 'Beware of a quiet dog and still water.' The reporter had been asking him for a face-to-face meeting for weeks. Now it was time to see how far he was willing to go, if he would risk rolling the dice with the ultimate kind of leverage. One thing Babich had learned was that every man had his price.

91

LINATE AIRPORT, MILAN, ITALY

'Where are you taking me?'

Kate was dragged down the stairs of a private aircraft, just managing to keep her feet – it was hard to walk, she felt drunk. Each time she had questioned this man, the only person she had seen in the plane's cabin, he had slapped her across the face. Her left eye felt as if it was going to burst; she tasted blood on her swollen lip.

'Get in,' the man said, pulling her roughly towards the BMW 5-series sedan, the boot opening as she neared. She shuffled towards it, looked in, then back around. The corrugated steel hangar was barely big enough to house the plane, and had only one bank of dim fluorescent lights. It was cold and dark and there was no one around – not even the pilots.

He pushed her roughly, head first, into the boot. She felt her legs being lifted in and folded uncomfortably. Then it was dark and quiet and they were moving.

92

FBI WASHINGTON FIELD OFFICE, WASHINGTON DC

Kavanaugh's hands were cuffed in front of him and he wore orange overalls. He sat in a holding cell that contained a thin foam mattress on a single bed and a stainless steel bowl that served as both toilet and water spout. He was supposed to be staying in a resort.

He had a wife and kids, he had been successful, and earned good money by selling secrets – had almost three million in a separate account, but whether or not he ever got to spend it would depend on the outcome of the next twenty-four hours.

He had two long-standing draft emails, both of which he had sent via his Blackberry within seconds as he stood listening to McCorkell, and then he had shown them the pistol to buy some time. Actions were in motion, and he was not done yet.

That the FBI had cracked the dead-drop site he'd set up in World of Warcraft surprised him, but in hindsight Hutchinson was an SOB who surpassed most others. The benefit was, like traditional dead drops, that it was a true cut-out device: none of the operatives who used it to communicate and exchange information knew one another or saw one another – perfect for preventing an entire espionage network from being compromised.

Sure, he'd been made, as had his point man, but that was it – Sirko was in the clear, no one knew who he was outside the game.

They might be at his computer now, using his avatar, the counter-espionage agents setting up another dead drop that was ready for pick-up – in person perhaps? Beyond Sirko, he didn't care. The others didn't know him, the Umbra guys who paid him for intel only knew that he was highly placed, reliable; and of course they knew his account number.

His lawyers would be here soon, and through them he knew he could make a deal – if it even came to that. He had made good money but spent none of it; it could easily be handed over – *mea culpa*. If his Plan B worked in the morning – if both his directives were carried out – there was every chance he would walk away from this.

He didn't get this far in intelligence to go down without swinging. His back-up plan would never be traced back to him, and at worst he would come out of this with a few years' easy time and a fine. Best case, he'd get home detention, maybe even be able to work at a private firm in DC. Or maybe get the fuck out of DC, move to SoCal maybe, write a book.

A man like Hutchinson would never understand, McCorkell either. Well, it *had* been complicated, but he had always planned to clean things up himself.

He had gone to Grozny to meet Sirko, a target designated as being an easy way into Umbra's highest echelons of power. They'd been young, the Cold War had ended, and in the spirit of the new relations they had got along well. Digging around on his own, Kavanaugh had discovered the details of Sirko's father's death at the hands of Babich. He had shown his friend, shown him the KGB files that had come through a much earlier defection. Sirko had been disbelieving, refused to accept the truth about his own agency-sanctioned double-murder. Kavanaugh had pulled in a source who had confirmed it, and when Sirko still wouldn't believe, he had helped Sirko pick up Babich's long-time heavy man and made him talk over four days in a rendition camp. Oh, how that scum had talked.

Then and there, he had restrained Sirko from going out and killing Babich. Then and there, they had formed a plan that was now finally coming to a head. They'd become genuine friends who looked at the world in the same way. He had supported Sirko, treated him like the brother he'd never had, kept him busy and informed, showed him there were better ways to exact revenge.

Over the years they had been building up to this moment, chipping away at Babich and his organisation: Kavanaugh on the legit, driving a desk at Langley; Sirko retaining his FSB credentials and working on Babich's side – for Umbra and its collection of ex-spies, as well as the FSB. And the FSB *was* Russia – they had the run of the place and would continue to as long as men like Putin and Babich were around . . .

Babich would soon meet his deserved fate and Sirko would serve his revenge cold – or rather at the temperature that plastic bonded explosives ignited. Things would be cleaner and leave fewer loose ends; and then Kavanaugh's second, final directive, would cause some FBI collateral damage.

Kavanaugh smiled, thinking of Sirko, the release he would feel when he finally settled his score with the man who had orphaned him. He would be free to start a new direction in life without the weight of this burden hanging around his neck.

Kavanaugh had made the mistake of getting caught, but victory... that went to the player who made the next-to-last mistake.

93

MALPENSA AIRPORT, MILAN, ITALY

Emma Gibbs and Al Gammaldi embraced as if they had been separated for years.

'You good?' he asked her, his hand on her belly.

'Yeah. Here,' she said, smiling as she handed over a paper bag containing a pound of loot from Rivington Street's Economy Candy.

'Oh, man,' he said, wolfing a handful down.

'Fructose coma is headed your way, Al,' Fox said, coming into their space. 'Any day now.'

'Pure, over the top New York candy,' Gammaldi said, chomping on a caramel chew. 'This would have Willy Wonka weeping into his cocoa.'

Fox pinched a few Gummi Bears.

'And they told me there that trick-or-treaters get complimentary goodies on Halloween,' Gibbs said. 'The only catch: you have to be a kid.'

'Listen, Lach . . .' Gammaldi said, putting an arm around his future wife. 'I was thinking, since it's probably going to be a light day tomorrow, maybe I'll blow off work, go shopping or something?'

'Yeah, Al, take Emma and go blow some money,' Fox said, working collateral Gummi Bears from his teeth. 'Maybe squeeze in a little afternoon delight.'

'I was kidding,' said Gammaldi. Emma rolled her eyes and walked towards Duhamel, Brick and the other FBI men. 'Although now you said that, this *is* Italy . . .'

'I forgot for a second that you're hilarious,' Fox replied. 'Your call, Al, but you should know, your better half will be there looking through a scope expecting to protect your sorry ass tomorrow.'

'Did you forget that I'm going to be a dad?'

'I'm kidding – I'm cool if you guys stay behind, I've got all I need out there,' Fox said, with a hand gesture to the FBI guys loading up a couple of vans. 'Seriously, there'll be so many cops around it'll be like an inauguration parade.'

'I'm not sure what to say to her,' Gammaldi said, watching Emma talking shop with Brick. 'She doesn't want me in the firing line.'

'Well, put on a helmet and pads and get in there,' Fox said.

'Okay, people,' Duhamel said, hanging up his phone. 'We've got to roll now – got to set up with the local cops.'

'They might be compromised,' Brick said.

'I don't doubt it,' Duhamel said.

'But Italy has very strict anti-mafia laws, so Babich can't be moving large sums of cash money around without judicial . . . what's the opposite of oversight?'

'So . . .' Fox trailed off, waiting to be convinced.

'So, I've got Luigi and Ivan with me, and SAC Hutchinson has a detachment of EGF cops on this; they're as good as it gets around here and they're really fucking happy to be able to get some headway against the fucking Russians who are moving in and taking over their sleepy holiday spots.'

'Maybe you should work for their anti-tourist bureau when all this blows over,' Fox said.

'Besides,' Duhamel said, 'no one local knows who our target is yet, and it'll stay that way until as late as possible. Right now, they're prepping a place on Lake Como for us to set up all our comms gear. Hutchinson will meet us on the ground there ASAP.'

'Define ASAP,' Fox asked, climbing into the back of a passenger van.

'Hours; momentarily; very fucking soon,' Duhamel said. 'Hell, he'll be there about the same time as us at this rate, and we'll be ready to rock for the morning's meeting.'

'Yeah, seriously,' Gammldi said to Fox out the side of his mouth, 'these guys have this covered. You'll be fine; it's just a meeting. I'll sit in a café and read a newspaper and watch from afar . . . '

94

EEOB, WASHINGTON DC

'You seen the Georgian thing on the news?' Wallace asked.

'Yeah,' McCorkell said. 'This will make my life *so* much easier . . .'

'Save your sarcasm, buddy,' Wallace said, handing over a DVD to his old college friend. 'That, there, is the full footage of what went down in Georgia; save you waiting around for the Department of Defense to get it to you.'

'Thanks,' McCorkell replied, putting the disk by his PC.

'Are you convinced Hutchinson can pull this off and get out with my men in working order?'

'He's got the best out there with him,' McCorkell replied. 'It's all happening in Italy tomorrow morning their time.'

'Pray they get enough to bring the bastard in.'

'They will. They already have enough for some action against his water company,' Hutchinson said. 'Half the water is running into Iran.'

'Jesus. They've got their own water problems, but they've got de-sal plants and oil to burn,' said Wallace.

'Exactly – it doesn't take much imagination to figure out why they'd need this kind of volume of water running into a middle-of-nowhere town.'

'Have you got proof?'

'I've got a team working satellite images as we speak.'

'It almost makes me wish we still had forty-three in the House so our boys could go out there and just bring Babich in, no questions asked,' said Wallace.

McCorkell laughed. 'It does sound more like a Cheney or Rumsfeld thing, I'll give you that.'

'It's not fair what people say about Bush junior, though,' Wallace added. 'Sure, he was a good-time Charlie, but he had to deal with a lot of shit in his time, more than most cats had to.'

'That's true.'

'It's just that he's used his whole life to front questionable business endeavours, and in a way that's what his presidency was,' Wallace said. 'He didn't quite have Cheney's cartoonish need for power and greed.'

'Whoever said political satire became obsolete when Henry Kissinger was awarded the Nobel Prize?'

They were both laughing hard.

'You can hang around here while it plays out; come back in?'

'All right, call me in my hotel when you're ready.'

95

BELLAGIO, LAKE COMO, ITALY

Sirko arrived at his hotel, backpack over his shoulder, bag of shopping from the local providore in his hand.

He had a haircut scheduled via the concierge, during which he would ask the hairdresser for a 'fresh look'. There were many Russian eyes around this town, and they were all, by his reckoning, loyal to Roman Babich, a figure so much a part of the economic prosperity they enjoyed. When things went down, there would be plenty of heat around, and while it wasn't the local cops he worried about, having a different appearance wouldn't hurt.

He made himself a meal from prosciutto, tomato and bocconcini on a panini, and popped a Chinotto. He sat by the open balcony doors that overlooked the street, just two blocks from the Lake – not quite *la camera con la vista*, but it had the right view for what he needed.

Tomorrow would be a new chapter in his life; justice at last. First thing in the morning he would go to Guzzi's Café and plant the device: a US-military M112, 1.25 pounds of C4 wrapped in dark green Mylar plastic; he had readied the small detonator and secured the copper wire that would act as an aerial for the receiver, which was a simple garage door opener. He knew the exact place to secure it: near the seat he knew Babich always booked when he went there. It was enough explosive to take down the front half of the café – maybe even the whole building. He would leave a jamming system there, too, to allow his detonator to be the only frequency available. And he would tip the waiter to do a little job for him.

It was all simple enough, a system that evened the odds against well-equipped adversaries: basic asymmetric warfare that involved a big bang.

Tonight he would prepare his rifle. He would wait until the right moment tomorrow to make the decision: shoot Babich in the face, or take him out with the C4. He had imagined the look on Babich's face for so long and to not see it might be to deny himself the gratification. A bullet or a bomb. Either way, he would think of his parents when he killed him, think of Babich lying to him, smiling at him, taking the place of his father. The collateral damage would be regrettable; the staff and clientele of the café could not survive if Sirko chose the louder option, but his focus had to be on one man, not the welfare of bystanders.

Sirko knew more about war than about peace. But after tomorrow, and his last act of violence, he would spend a lifetime exploring the latter.

96

BELLAGIO, LAKE COMO, ITALY

'I want an iron curtain around this place,' Hutchinson said. 'If I give the order, nothing gets out, no one. I don't want him slipping through, because he may just disappear for good.'

They were in the suite at the Hotel Du Lac where they had all spent the night. Sunrise was just around the corner, and final plans were made and triple-checked. Everyone knew what they had to do.

'Why are you smiling?' Gibbs asked.

'Happiness is my default position,' Fox replied.

She shook her head, incredulous.

'Yeah, well give it time,' Gammaldi said to her. 'You live lives like ours, saving the planet every few months, and without humour you'd go nuts.'

'It's true,' Fox said.

She smiled, punched Gammaldi in the arm.

Hutchinson looked over at Fox, concerned.

•

She woke after a few hours, shook her dream from her mind. Her face throbbed. When she raised her head from the pillow it was coated in clear fluid and blood that had leaked from her nose through the night. She still felt groggy, and was overwhelmed by a sense of vertigo as she tried to stand. The door was locked from the outside and the walls were solid; there were no windows to climb out of. Her breath quickened and her heart rate rose as she looked around the room, desperate. She forced herself to sit on the edge of the bed and look at the ground while she concentrated on her breaths, counting them until they slowed to something closer to normal.

This was why she had been moved around by the FBI. *This* was why they had told her to be so careful – and she had been, but part of her had always been sceptical, had always resented it.

Every now and then she heard Russian voices outside the room. The man who'd hit her had a Russian accent, too – but it didn't feel like Russia, if that were possible.

Of all the people to think about now, she thought about Lachlan Fox. Not her family, not her new friends or her old friends nor any of thousands of other memories. She had dreamed about him like she had done so often, and she felt guilty because of it.

•

Something was up with Hutchinson – he wasn't quite himself. Fox couldn't figure it out. Maybe he was nervous about what was about to go down.

Fox took Gammaldi aside, along with the two GSR security staff, Emma Gibbs and Richard Sefreid.

'Al, I want you to get a boat and keep in out of sight of the café,' Fox said, 'but as close to the waterside area of the café as you can get.'

'Where am I going to get a boat?'

'Surprise me,' Fox said. 'The Feds are organising a police boat on the other side of the lake, but I want an escape option close by in case I have no other choice, okay?'

Gammaldi nodded.

'And look sharp,' Fox said to him. 'I need your A-game, Al. Even if you see Maria Rosaria Carfagna, I need you to concentrate.'

'Got it,' Gammaldi replied, taking a bite out of an egg-and-bacon baguette.

'How about us?' Sefreid said. 'We don't want to be holed up here at the hotel waiting to hear word that you're okay.'

'No way is my man going out there with you again without me watching out for him,' Gibbs said.

Fox smiled and pulled out a tourist map so they could trace sight-lines.

97

THE WHITE HOUSE, WASHINGTON DC

McCorkell was in one of the smaller rooms of the Situation Room complex, watching the big screens as they flicked through satellite images. If he found what he expected, there would be a B2 Stealth bomber in the air with JDAMs ready to rain down.

'That piping there – is that the gas pipeline?'

The Air Force Major checked the notes that corresponded with the files.

'Yes, the Iran–Pakistan–India gas pipeline, about 2800 kilometres of it. This is the border with Pakistan right . . . there.'

The image paused and he drew a line with a laser pointer.

'It takes gas from the South Pars/North Dome gas condensate field located in the Gulf,' the other guy in the room said. He was a CIA analyst with glasses so thick he could watch a ball game from the parking lot. 'It's the world's largest gas field, shared between Iran and Qatar.'

'We've got a lot of eyes in the area, mainly tasked with looking at Taftan,' the Air Force Major said. 'Town located in Chagai District, Balochistan, Pakistan, their only legal official border crossing into Iran. This is the most up to date sat image of where the gas pipeline heads into Iran. It was taken by a War-fighter 3, eight hours ago.'

Satellite images of the town cycled through.

'What's this place?'

'That's Zahedan, the capital of the province of Sistan and Baluchistan in Iran,' CIA explained.

'We have a UAV overflight scheduled for tonight for an infrared sweep,' Air Force said.

'Why infrared?'

'They've been busy at night,' Air Force said, evidently impressed with himself, clicking through more images.

'Zahedan has a population of almost 600 000,' CIA man said. 'The place is dry as shit and as picturesque as Satan's asshole. It's a sandy land formation that swallows up any water that falls on it, be it rain or irrigation water.'

McCorkell nodded. 'Do you think Pakistan is complicit in this – giving so much water to Iran?'

'Given the current political situation?' CIA man replied. 'Unlikely.'

'You're the pro in this area.'

'Yeah, I am, spent most my working life in Iran,' CIA replied. 'Look, the relationship these countries share goes back a long way. In '47 Iran was the first country to recognise the newly created state of Pakistan, a relationship further strengthened in the '70s to suppress a rebel movement in Baluchistan, a tri-state conflict across provinces of Iran, Pakistan, and Afghanistan. The Shah offered considerable development aid to Pakistan including oil and gas on preferential terms . . . even assisted Pakistan financially in its development of a nuclear program after India's surprise test detonation – Smiling Buddha in '74. Both countries opposed the Soviet occupation in Afghanistan, because they were providing covert support for the Afghani mujahideen.'

'And we were with them on that, too.'

'Bill, here's what we found,' Air Force said.

On the screen was an image of a massive structure, like a covered velodrome, Madison-Square-Garden big.

'This – what's this?'

'That's a high-security fence, enclosing a couple of acres, with a gravel road that's run by perimeter security vehicles,' Air Force said. 'If there's a heavy-water plant in this city, this is it.'

McCorkell leaned forward for a closer look at the image.

'Does the main building look new to you?'

'Yes.'

'The serious rail upgrades are new, definitely in the last few years,' CIA said. 'Is that airstrip sealed?'

'Yes. Two hangars, each big enough for a C130. I'd call those buildings there—' he pointed with a laser pointer, 'barracks.'

'How tall is it?'

'Triple storey.'

'Go back a few months – maybe we can find it in construction, some kind of before and after—'

'Already did that,' Air Force replied, and clicked to an image of bare land.

'When was this?'

'Eighteen months ago . . . Here's one—'

'That's it,' McCorkell said, standing up and looking closely at the big LCD screen. The warehouse was nothing more than a maze of foundation piles.

'We had daily passes for a while there, looking at a terrorist training camp on the Pakistani side; we got six weeks' worth of dailies.'

'Can you slideshow it?'

'Yes – starting with day one.' Air Force brought up the image: day one showed a bare area where the warehouse was yet to be built. Same for the next ten shots, then earth-moving equipment started showing up, serious trainloads.

'Angles change slightly each day,' CIA said.

The hole in the ground grew bigger each day, and wear tracks in the gravel and dirt were clearly visible, but none of the machinery seemed to have moved.

'These – what are they, lights?'

'Yes, lights on generator stands.'

They had a couple of dozen big portable lamps set up. These guys were working only by night.

'Do you have any night shots?'

'Sorry.'

By the end of the series of images, a massive concrete basement had been poured – easily six times the size of the warehouse that now stood, meaning there was underground space.

'They didn't want us watching them work,' McCorkell said. 'They didn't want to call attention to it.'

'They did that at Chalus too,' CIA said. 'Northern Iran, on the Caspian?'

'That was the underground nuclear weapons development facility built in the Alborz mountains,' McCorkell said, recalling a long-ago Pentagon briefing.

'So they've got the know-how . . .'

'Okay, keep working through all the images you've got – everything – and focus on what comes and goes from this point in time. Page me when you're done.'

'Sure thing,' Air Force said.

McCorkell moved to the door.

'Bill?'

He turned.

'Do you really think it's a new Iranian nuke thing?'

'Well, look at that,' McCorkell said, pointing to one of the smaller monitors, which showed a static overhead image of IR-40, Iran's forty-megawatt heavy-water reactor located in Arak. 'They built that, and it'll produce twenty kilos of plutonium a year from spent nuclear fuel,' McCorkell said. 'That's enough for two nuclear weapons a year. And what you've just shown me—' he pointed to the image on the big screen, 'that's easily four times the capacity. We know they're seeking bids for two additional nuclear reactors to be located near Bushehr. We know in 2008 a fourth Russian shipment of nuclear fuel arrived in Iran destined for the Bushehr plant. So do I think this is a new nuke thing? Let me just say, there's plenty of countries out there that hope it's not. But if we confirm it is, we'll have to do what's responsible. It shows sanctions aren't working, and at the end of the day, we're still the big stick in the—'

Tony Niemann stood in the doorway, slightly out of breath.

'Guys, can you give Bill and I the room?' he said.

They packed up their notes and left. The senior intelligence man took a seat opposite McCorkell, waited for the door to close.

'Bill,' Niemann began. 'We know about this, in Iran.'

McCorkell tilted his head to the side, expectant.

'It's complicated,' Niemann went on. 'We're not going to act on it.'

98

BELLAGIO, LAKE COMO, ITALY

'I'm not afraid. I'm going to do this; someone has to,' Fox said.

Hutchinson nodded. He looked back across the water at the mountains surrounding the lake under the sun's first rays.

'You really want to get him?'

'Of course I do,' Hutchinson said. 'You know that.'

'What are you prepared to do?' Fox asked him. They stood alone in a corner of the suite; the rest of the team had headed to their base of operations and positions.

'Everything within the law,' Hutchinson replied. 'But what are you saying?'

Fox looked at the few boats out on the water already. He thought about Amar, the look on his face as he died. 'With these people, you've got to be prepared to go all the way,' Fox said. 'Because Babich won't give up this fight until either he's dead – or I am.'

'We can do this other ways, Lach. We just need him to start to talk. You need to bait him with this Iran stuff—'

Fox looked Hutchinson in the eyes. 'He's been a step ahead of you and me the whole time. What makes you think he's going into this meeting blind?'

'You're thinking this and you still want to go in?'

'I do, and, like you said before I left New York, I'm not going to trust anyone, especially him,' Fox said. 'He doesn't want to talk to me. He's certainly not going to help us. *You* swore to uphold the law, not me, and certainly not him.'

'Come on, Fox, what are you saying?'

'I'm saying one way or another, this ends this morning,' Fox said.

Hutchinson looked pained. 'Look, Lach, you've got to do what you've got to do,' he said. 'But know this: we've got your back. And no matter what happens in there, no matter what Babich says or how he tries to get to you, all you have to do is get him to admit some guilt and we've got the leverage we need. Just don't . . . Just try and keep your head, okay?'

•

Gammaldi was getting tired of haggling with the guy – he only wanted the boat for a couple of hours, and the owner was being testy about not being able to get work done without it. He could have bought it outright for what the guy was suggesting he pay in a hire fee.

'Look,' Gammaldi said, pulling the stack of euros out of his wallet and flicking through it. 'I've only got . . . 820—'

'That will do,' the man said, snatching the cash from Gammaldi's hand.

•

Fox walked to the café, alone. He knew there would be protection, knew what he wanted, but the butterflies were still there in his stomach. His hand throbbed; he hadn't taken painkillers this morning, he wanted to be as sharp as possible. The streets were busy, mainly locals by the look of them, and he pulled the collar of his coat up against the wind.

He passed a couple of brawny-looking guys waiting outside the café. They watched him intently, jackets open, faces passive.

Inside, the café was warm and smelled of good coffee and freshly baked bread. There were a few people scattered around the tables, and he saw Babich sitting at a long table that fronted the large window facing the lake. On the way over he was stopped by two men, both of much the same appearance as the two outside. One ushered him to the men's room where he was searched for bugs – shoes, hair, in and around his ears.

'I feel like I have to buy you dinner now,' Fox said as they walked him out.

Fox sat next to Babich, waited silently for a full minute until the Russian rested his coffee on the table and closed his newspaper. Through the window the morning sun twinkled on the water. Boats putt-putted; it was too early or too cold for the rich to frolic in their playground.

Lachlan Fox looked Babich in the eyes and saw three things: a K, a G and a B. He may now be a businessman, thought Fox, even a world leader, but once a KGB officer, always a KGB officer.

•

Brick sat in a black Mercedes van parked at the back of the restaurant next door to Guzzi's.

He crouched in the back with Ivan; Luigi was up front in the driver's seat. The three men wore black tactical assault gear and Kevlar vests, and had their full complement of weaponry ready to roll.

99

THE WHITE HOUSE, WASHINGTON DC

'I don't follow,' McCorkell said.

'You don't have to,' Niemann replied. 'Look, I'm sorry, but this decision has been made.'

McCorkell stood, paced down to the end of the conference table and back.

'You son of a bitch,' McCorkell said. 'What, I won't be around for much longer so you leave me out of this? I've been cleaning shit up in Iran ever since your agency . . . Nearly sixty years you've been fucking with that country.'

'As directed by decisions made in this building,' Niemann said. 'And now we're handling this delicately. Or, what, you want to take designated targets to the president like you did with the North Korea thing in '04?'

McCorkell felt anger clench his jaw; he breathed through it. He'd once been part of the decision-making process that green-lit a Tomahawk strike that had taken out a key component of North Korea's nuclear program being shipped in from China. Unconfirmed collateral damage in the town of Ryongchon was the unfortunate byproduct of a successful operation that set their nuclear program back four years. Action like that needed to be taken here, now, at this Iran site.

'Bill, please, take a seat so we can talk this through.'

100

BELLAGIO, LAKE COMO, ITALY

Lachlan Fox had come for answers; Roman Babich wanted the questions to end. Both were in the military once, a life never truly left: there was no such thing as an *ex*-Special Forces soldier.

There was a dangerous tension in the air. Fox was at ease but on alert. Babich had not a care in the world.

'Have you ever been face to face with an animal that could kill you graveyard dead, Mr Fox?'

Fox remained deadpan, expressionless.

•

They called it the Hub: FBI agents crammed into a pre-war apartment two blocks south of the café. The windows sweated between the drawn curtains. Shirtsleeves rolled up, it was go time. Coffee was perpetually on the boil; the chatter was constant and hushed.

It was a secure, anonymous apartment block in the city. The living room and bedroom were littered with gear and cables, the tech crew having covertly tapped into the power mains via the roof. Modernity met a renaissance colour palette, the paint on the walls thicker than it was bright. On screens and over speakers the agents saw and heard from several vantage points in and around the café on the lake: Lachlan Fox in colour and black and white, blurry from a long-lens camera operating from a boat docked out on the other side. His voice and Babich's were recorded by a digital mic inside the café, but the real-time radio feed was having issues coming through. The six agents were all far more nervous than they let on.

Hutchinson hovered, watching, plotting, directing, palms sweating despite his experience. There were too many guns out there near Fox that didn't belong to his men. Too many unknowns. He looked at the image of Fox onscreen: the reporter looked his thirty-two years and then some. Not old exactly, more like a guy who'd seen a lot of darkness . . . Hutchinson knew something was very wrong, knew he was gambling, knew he had the manpower to stop the worst from happening. No doubt, when it was over, whatever happened, however it went down, Fox wouldn't forgive him. No doubt.

•

Sirko waited in his hotel room, could see the café through gaps between buildings and the topiary trees the locals were so fond of. He drank from the water bottle beside him and waited a moment, calmed his breathing and heart rate. He ran a hand through his short dark hair, adjusted his foam earplugs. He had seen Babich go in. He had watched Fox go in. Both men he wanted dead, one especially. They had minutes to live.

He lay prone by the window, behind the lace curtains. He sighted his rifle, adjusted his position, the gun steady on its tripod, the garage-door radio detonator ready by his left hand.

•

Alongside the agents in the Hub were the FBI legal attaché from the Rome embassy, the local police liaison, and a Russian cop from Interpol; silent sentinels, taking a back seat to Hutchinson. One of his junior agents did the rounds with coffee, which was much better here than back home. Hutchinson was five cups in and sweating bullets.

Three techs, two FBI agents and a specialist from the NSA worked laptops, tweaking sight and sound. Another two were handling communications with agents out in the field, guiding their charges in real-time like pro coaches watching the plays from afar. Lachlan Fox's voice wasn't coming through, but the conversation was being recorded. An image of his back – streaming from a small camera on their man inside the café – was on the main screen, a thirty-two inch LCD in the centre of the trestle tables. Over Fox's shoulder in the centre of the frame was the face of Roman Babich.

Hutchinson put his hand over the foam cover of his tactical mic headset, spoke to his comms specialist: 'Have we got communication up with the agent in the café yet?'

'Radio's still down.'

'Why?'

'Interference from something, localised to the café; could be some electrical equipment the café uses.'

'Not a jamming device?'

'Could be, but the one-way bug near Fox is on and recording fine. It's definitely some kind of broadcast interference from something inside the café.'

'Are you telling me their fifty-year-old espresso machine is blacking out our million-dollar comms gear?'

'All I know is that it worked when we planted the bugs in there last night, and our agent's gear worked until he got into the building this morning.'

Something wasn't right. Hutchinson didn't like unknowns, didn't like mistakes, especially avoidable ones like comms-gear failure.

'Cell network is fine though?'

The tech grunted *yes*, checking the frequencies with an ear glued to a headphone.

'Call our man in there,' Hutchinson ordered. 'I need to hear a voice. Find an open radio channel that you can secure, and send him the new frequency via SMS.'

The techs shared a look and then dialled the cell. Prearranged protocol was being broken.

'Jake, what have you got?' Hutchinson said into the headset's mic. 'What do you see? What do you hear?'

•

The FBI agent in the café was reading a newspaper at a table littered with a couple of empty coffee cups and a plate of hardly touched pastries. Special Agent Jake Duhamel knew that if it came to it he would have enough time to get the drop on the two guys in the room he knew to be threats. They were without doubt Babich's guys, thick-necked goons sitting facing the door. He had an H&K USP Compact Tactical pistol locked and loaded in a quick-release hip holster under his jacket; he had brought a couple of spare mags of .45 rounds, but he was unlikely to need them: he was an Olympic-grade marksman with a pistol, and had a silver from Sydney to prove it. Outside in the nondescript, idling Mercedes van, he had three men ready to rock with an arsenal of heavy firepower.

'They're talking, nothing happening,' Duhamel said, turning pages of the *International Herald Tribune*. He looked around. 'What's with the comms being down?'

•

'We're working on it,' Hutchinson said into his mic, looking over the tech's shoulder at a thermal image of the café on the laptop: it showed the staff milling about, the dozen or so customers, the heat flare of the espresso machine. Another screen showed a noise-frequency graph, which indicated that the demodulating sound pointer being aimed at the glass pane in front of Fox was picking up too much background noise to get a clear vocal feed. 'The guy to your immediate right,' Hutchinson said into his mic. 'Who is he? Is he anything to be worried about?'

•

'Well, I have been before such animals, Mr Fox,' Babich said, sipping his coffee, looking out to the lake. 'Almost twenty years in the KGB and FSB; I have even seen it in the eyes of men.'

He turned to Fox with a hard, measuring gaze, and lit a cigarette. Babich's left eyelid drooped, so that it looked half-closed; the slight scarring could have been from a burn or a bomb blast. His hands were gloved.

'Killers, assassins, murderers . . .' Babich said, his accent well Westernised, without the usual heaviness, the kind of practised elocution no doubt honed for media appearances. He licked at his top lip, picked off a speck of tobacco as he blew out smoke.

Saliva glistened in the corner of his mouth, which he occasionally patted away with the thumb of his cigarette hand. 'Some were on my team. Some weren't. They weren't so lucky, but then those kinds of men never really are. Not when it comes to being so close to death. It's just a matter of time, do you see?'

Fox watched and waited, conscious that he still didn't have a measure of this guy. He knew his bio, knew his life – everything the media and intelligence agencies of the US and her allies knew about him – but he didn't know where this meeting would go. Babich was unpredictable.

'It's something that I see now, in your eyes,' he said with a small smile, thumbing away more saliva. 'You have killed before . . . more than once.'

He leaned back a little, gave Fox a look that said he knew everything he needed to know about him. 'You know what it means to take lives, Mr Fox. To live by the gun. To serve your country. One would think you have been doing this all your life.'

Fox drained his coffee and motioned to the passing waiter for another. He gave Babich a tired look. 'What makes you think I haven't?' Fox spoke for the first time.

Babich focused his gaze out the window in front of them. The left side of his face had a slight tic. He tapped a fresh pack of Stuyvesants against the timber table.

'You are ex-military,' he said. He stirred his coffee, stubbed out his half-burned cigarette. 'And you know pain. Pain of many kinds; the kind of hurt that only the sentimental suffer. That is a weakness, Mr Fox. I know that much about you. In fact, I think you would be surprised by how much I know about you.'

Babich paused for effect, squinted out across the lake. 'That's why we are here.'

•

'He's local,' Duhamel said quietly.

His cell-phone speaker carried the reply: 'You're sure he's not a threat?'

The Special Agent knocked a spoon off his table, sending it clattering loudly to the tiled floor. No one bothered to look towards the commotion. Duhamel took his time picking it up, getting a good eyeball of the guy to his right: early thirties, black hair, Roman nose, short but stocky – any more local and he would have roots growing into the ground.

'Negative,' Duhamel said. 'Definitely local.' Only a threat to the mountain of spaghetti in front of him, he thought to himself.

•

'Tell me,' Babich said, rubbing his gloved hands together. 'Why would a reporter still have that look?'

Fox looked out over the lake, his patience waning. He managed a half smile.

'Perhaps you are working for the FBI . . . Counter-terrorism or espionage division maybe . . . Some kind of economic outfit?' Babich sucked at his teeth. 'You think I'm the problem here? That what I do is evil? I am a businessman; I see opportunities and sell whatever can be sold, to whoever is willing to pay.'

Babich looked at Fox, long and hard. He spoke quietly. 'Do you think I am any more corrupt than an American company? A British one? An Australian one? Hmm? Corporate greed, gross negligence that led to a global credit crisis? That had nothing to do with *my* country, *my* people. It took America two hundred years to get to where the West wants us to be in just a few years – Putin came in when the country was in chaos, our people were starving, and men like him, men like me, have created something from that chaos, you see? While I shape history, men like you stand in its way, trying to cling to something, to have your fifteen minutes of fame.'

Babich sat back in his chair, eyes still on Fox: 'I will be remembered by my country as a maker of better lives – that is important to me. Who will remember you? A few literate liberals, members of some small elite club who read the foreign affairs crap you write and talk about? Certainly not your Young Republicans – they know the truth as they see it, and it's not what reporters like you try to ram down their throats; they're smart, patriotic, like our own Nashi.'

Fox sipped his espresso, signalled to the waiter for pastry.

'This is some anti-American thing?' Fox said. 'You know, they don't look at your country that way. They've moved on. And you want to know how? Because their problem wasn't with your people, it was with a political system that was forced onto innocent people who had no choice but to accept it or be purged.'

Babich shook his head. 'Perhaps you should accept that you won't be remembered – not your work, nothing. Maybe you will get lucky one day, and have a woman around long enough to care, hmm?'

Babich let it hang in the air. Fox, a little unsure, smiled it off.

'For the record, I have nothing against your people or your country,' Fox said. 'Just its leaders. Just people like you. You're the same the world over, whatever the nationality – driven by nothing but greed.'

Babich laughed. 'Greed?'

'How much are you getting for selling one country's water to another?' Fox asked. 'Where does that money go? Was it worth killing all those people to silence this story? The hundreds who worked on the water-diversion plant? I worked with some of those people; they were good, innocent people who did nothing but their jobs. How many lives is this cover-up worth? What was the dollar amount for all those lives? For trying to kill me and my friends? How much did it cost to take so much water, the lifeblood of a nation, from hundreds of millions of Indians?'

Babich looked around the café, spoke a little more quietly: 'I had expected you to talk more, to ask more questions,' Babich said. 'Now that you have your audience with me, you say *this*? You accuse me of killing all these people? Do you think I am some kind of terrorist?'

'You're not a terrorist, Roman,' said Fox. 'You're a *tourist*.'

'Okay, okay,' Babich seethed. 'This water-utility project? Pakistan will prosper, that is undeniable – where are my accolades for that? You say India will lose out? Maybe they should have done this first, instead of making nuclear weapons. Instead of spending billions on arms, they could have taken a billion people from poverty. These deaths, these Indians you say will miss out – Mr Fox, surely you realise that these are the kind of externalities that corporations contend with every minute of every day. Someone, or something, always loses out – that is *your* economic system. I am just better at it than most of your guys. Can you not see that?'

Fox squinted to look at the far-off boats on the lake: such a perfect-looking, temperate place to be.

'Can you?' Babich said, leaning towards Fox. 'Or are you unable to accept that?'

Fox exhaled deeply, concentrating on slowing his heart rate. He was tempted to end this conversation right now; career- and perhaps life-ending violence would be so easy, like driving the coffee glass into Babich's face and grinding it in while thinking of all the pain and death this man had dealt out to ordinary people. Maybe the Feds would intervene in time to stop Babich's bodyguards blasting him away – but probably not. Either way, he would think of those people while he killed this man; either way, both their lives would be over.

He took a breath and spoke to Babich. 'Look, Roman, you know that I know what you're doing with all this water running through Pakistan.' Fox watched Babich for a reaction, and was satisfied to see the facial tic resume. 'Why don't you tell me what you've got to offer?'

Babich smiled. Fox felt that this was it: an admission of guilt. On tape. Enough to get this guy into court.

'Tell me what you're after,' Babich said, brushing an invisible speck from his jacket sleeve. 'This is not your fight. This story you are chasing, it does not concern you . . . well, it didn't. So, tell me, what will make you go away, this whole story go away? Maybe if you left this alone, I could get on with things – back to business.'

'If.'

•

Through the scope of his rifle Sirko watched the door of the café. Every now and then he checked over the optical sight to get a bead on activity occurring around the building and in the street. His watch beeped a warning. He had tipped a waiter fifty euros to deliver a very particular plate of food to Babich at an agreed time: in five minutes that food would arrive, and it would carry such meaning it would haunt him in the afterlife.

Sirko picked up the detonator while still supporting the rifle on its tripod. Babich would be served his last supper, and then, as he walked out of the café, Sirko would either press the button or pull the trigger. He would either blow him up or shoot him through the heart; Fox too – either way, they would both be dead.

•

'Just the truth would be good,' Fox said. 'And the justice it will bring.'

'Ah, the truth,' Babich said with barely concealed contempt. 'Mr Fox, do you *really* believe the truth will set you free? Are you *really* that foolish?'

'Justice comes to all of us, Babich, no matter how much money or power we have,' Fox said, watching the tic jump in the older man's angry face. Fox stirred his coffee, his arms tense. The thought of breaking this guy's face was more tempting with every second, but he needed to stay in control a little longer.

'Why don't you tell me why we're really here?' he said, palms open to receive. 'Finally, you and me, face to face. Now.'

'Okay, killer,' Babich said, looking out the window. He smiled and leaned forward, his arms crossed on the timber bench. 'We are here because I want to make you an offer. You want to know about water going into Iran? Sure, it goes there.'

Gotcha, thought Fox. 'Why?'

'Money. You think that water was used for something specific – who knows, hey?'

'You know.'

Babich smiled. Yeah, he knew.

'I am here because I have an offer for *you*,' Babich said. 'An offer you can't refuse. And remember, you are the one who wanted a stake in this. You rolled the dice . . .'

•

'Hub, this is Water One, we've got a boat coming in hard and fast southbound towards the target's location,' the agent said from aboard a nondescript white speedboat, just another speck on Lake Como. He tracked the craft with his hand-held high definition camcorder, zoomed in while his partner kept the long-lens pointed at the café.

•

Hutchinson watched the real-time footage of the speedboat flash by the agents.

A guy was at the wheel, two were in the back, and someone smaller was in the passenger seat.

'Can you zoom in closer?'

'That's as good as it gets, unless you want the café lens—'

'No, keep it on the café.'

'Copy that, Hub,' replied the agent on the boat. 'Shall we pursue?'

'Negative, keep your cover and stay put,' Hutchinson said. He turned to the room and pointed at the ops agent. 'Get one of your snipers to get a bead on that boat ASAP.'

•

Fox watched as Babich placed a small pair of binoculars on the table in front of them.

'Are you telling me to go to the opera?' Fox quipped.

A crooked smile. 'Take a look out there,' Babich said. His stubby finger pointed out over the lake. 'Look out there and tell me: why would you want to save another country's water supply when the stakes are rising for you so fast?'

•

'Keep on Babich,' Hutchinson said into his mic. 'Why don't we have sound from the café yet?'

'Still working on it.'

'Damn it!' Hutchinson turned to the op leader. 'Get another agent in there with—'

'Look,' replied the agent firmly. 'I've got vision set up; I've cut into existing CCTV feeds at four locations; I've installed a high-res camera clocking both exits of the target building, and another on a boat in the lake with a long-lens to watch Fox and Babich. I've got a helicopter on standby. Sending in another agent will only—'

'I've got something!' interrupted a tech.

'What?' Hutchinson said.

'Intel from the FBI database search . . . Coming through now – a hit on the guy who did the Gori bombing. Sirko – Petro

Sirko. He visited the café this morning, about an hour before our guy went in. Facial rec just ID'd him.'

'We've got a known bomber who just took out a bunch of delegates – in the area?' said Hutchinson. Fuck. 'Get everything you can on him—'

'We're getting Agency and MI5 files through now,' the tech said, bringing up files onscreen. 'He's a known associate of . . . Vladimir Kolesnik.'

'And?'

'Kolesnik is Babich's son,' the Russian cop answered. 'Took his mother's family name to stay under the radar. And this Sirko – he was raised like a son by Babich.'

Hutchinson turned to the Russian, his eyes wide and angry: 'And you didn't tell us any of this before now because . . . ?'

'It's all in the files,' the Russian said. 'Kolesnik runs clubs, maybe he was set up by his father, but he's never done anything of interest to us. Sirko, on the other hand, served in Chechnya – fighting for both sides before being kicked out of the Army. We want him.'

Hutchinson's mind raced.

'Yeah, well, if he's responsible for killing the US and EU delegation in the Gori bombing, you'll have to step in line,' Hutchinson said. 'We've got to find him, we've got to keep eyes on him; we take him down as soon as we get Babich.'

The tech brought up the footage that had just been sent through: in the background, Petro Sirko, dressed in a local police uniform, walking though the square . . . past the statue of Stalin . . . past a young girl signalling to the cameraman to give her a moment to compose herself by the base of the statue . . .

The camera followed Sirko . . . his hand came out of his pocket, holding a small object.

Hutchinson knew immediately what it was: 'That's a remote—'

Over the speakers came the tinny sound of the blast. The cameraman was almost blown over but steadied himself. The image panned back around – the Town Hall was all fire and debris and smoke and dust.

The camera snapped back to Sirko, remote detonator still in his hand. He turned and looked directly down the lens. The image froze on his face as he smiled.

'Okay, I want to find him.' Hutchinson ordered. 'Get this image out. He's likely to remote detonate—'

'That's got to be the frequency interfering with our audio!'

The technician was right. Fuck.

'Do we get Fox out?'

•

Sirko rubbed his thumb over the detonate button, savouring the feel of it.

He stopped himself and squinted down his scope. A van pulled up violently not far from the café.

•

'I found an open frequency, spectrum range three-fifteen MHz,' the tech guy said. 'Our gear's all running around three-eighty to four hundred—'

'And?' replied Hutchinson.

'It means everything else is being jammed,' he replied. 'Three-fifteen is all that's open? That's the standard channel for garage-door openers—'

'That's our IED trigger-type frequency – jam it!'

'Sir,' a female agent held up her hand to get attention. 'I have a spike in NSA real-time Echelon chatter, local, getting loud—'

'Hub, Sniper Two, we've got company!' crackled the main comms-channel speaker. 'Coming in via the road to the north.'

The room went silent.

'Company, what kind of company?' asked Hutchinson.

'Make it a blacked-out Transit van with two chase sedans, approaching the café double-time.'

•

Sirko saw a couple of cars pull up too. A few guys got out – had to be Americans. He looked over his scope, took in the scene. They were headed straight towards the café. The lace curtains blew apart in the breeze through the open balcony doors, and he tensed until they settled again, concealing him.

•

Hutchinson looked wide-eyed at the screens: 'Range on that kind of transmitter?'

'With a boosted receiver, up to five hundred metres.'

'So he's in the neighbourhood. Find him. Take him down. Do whatever it takes.'

•

Sirko had counted six of Babich's bodyguards out in the open – this should get interesting. He waited a moment; no rush now.

He had two good options to finish what he came to do, and he had waited many years for this moment of retribution.

•

'You killed people involved in this water project,' Fox said. He wasn't going to play Babich's game until he got something more from him.

'No,' Babich said. 'I had problems solved for me. That's how I operate, and I'm sure many Americans wish they could do the same.'

'And Iran?'

Babich leaned in close, pushed the binoculars closer to Fox. 'How long do you think America will stay in Afghanistan?' Babich asked through cigarette smoke. 'When they leave, that state will fail. Pakistan will fail. That whole region will need someone to go in and fix it.'

Fox couldn't tell if by 'someone' he meant Iran, or Umbra. Maybe both. He knew this man before him spoke like he had all the aces. Whatever was to be seen through those binoculars wouldn't make things any clearer.

•

'We've got visual,' the tech agent said.

The image showed the van screech to a halt with the two sedans. Six men got out: buzz-cuts, slacks and open jackets, a couple of holstered side-arms visible. One guy carried what looked like a black cloth sack.

'Holy shit! Hub, you getting this lake feed?'

'What?' Hutchinson said, looking from the monitor of the van to the main screen, which showed a boat.

'Is that Babich's son . . . That's a confirm, it's Kolesnik!' an agent in the room said. 'Kolesnik is on that boat with two armed men and a female. The female has been worked over, she's a possible hostage.'

'The van, they're Babich's guys? Who are they?' Hutchinson asked. Then he moved closer to the main screen showing the boat, looked at the grainy image of the woman's face. 'The van, guys – I need an ID!'

'They're going to take Fox?'

'Do we get him out of there?'

Hutchinson saw his team looking up to him as they chorused their questions but he could not focus on them – this was all happening fast, now. Time to shut it down.

'Get the café agents on their cell phones now!'

'The van – they're CIA!' the FBI Legat said, getting a good close-up of the guy who had stayed behind the wheel of the van. 'They're local spec ops from NCS!'

Hutchinson paused, but only briefly. Operatives from CIA's National Clandestine Service would only deploy for—

'Oh shit!' he said. 'It's a rendition team – get Fox and Babich out of there *now*!'

'Our guys moved out.'

'*What?*'

'Our back-up in the van outside – they're gone!'

●

Luigi dropped Brick and Ivan at the apartment.

All comms were down and he was leaving his post. He was breaking just about every rule, and he was sweaty as hell, but what choice did he have? None.

'Go back now!' Brick ordered Luigi, who took off in the van towards their station: guarding the rear of Guzzi's.

Brick and Ivan approached their target building from the side, hugging the wall of the neighbouring building, Gatecrasher in hand. They had seen a shooter, and he wasn't one of theirs. They ran up the stairs; Brick swore as they kicked down the door to an apartment and rushed for the wall.

•

Fox looked through the binoculars. It took him a few seconds to find the target: a small speedboat bobbing in the water, doing slow circles two hundred metres out.

He saw the burly driver and the guy next to him, could make out two occupants in the back – a man and a woman. But he didn't have a good view of either.

'I want you to leave this alone,' Babich said quietly. 'This story, this investigation of yours, I want it to end. If you do, she lives.'

'Your water operation in Pakistan, I need to—'

Fox stopped talking. Looked over the binoculars to the speedboat. Looked through them again, focused. Searched the faces, found her.

'You leave this alone, you make sure it's left alone – and she lives,' Babich said. 'You tell me who your sources are, you tell me where they are, you give me everything – and you will get to live, too.'

Fox's world was on the head of a pin. Time was frozen.

'This is it,' Babich went on. 'The time has come. One way or another, you will stop your investigation. This is the end of the story.'

That face – that face had haunted his dreams for months . . . And she was hurting, she had taken a beating.

'So, Mr Fox. What are you prepared to do?'

•

Sirko checked his watch – time for his delivery. He would give it ten seconds. He would count up slowly, calmly – then detonate, and stay ready to fire high-calibre rounds if anyone managed to emerge alive. He settled in behind his sight, his thumb on the detonator, a smile on his face.

•

A bowl of chocolate gelato was placed on the table in front of Babich. He looked up at the waiter with a smile: 'What is this?'

'Your friend,' said the waiter. 'He ordered it for you earlier this morning.'

Babich smiled, looked down, unsure . . . Chocolate gelato. His friend. Who – who would have – this was the meal that . . . No. *But it was.* Little Petro's mother had served them chocolate ice-cream for dessert . . . The mother and son weren't supposed to be there on the father's government trip – the little baby boy, his parents . . .

He looked up at Fox wide-eyed: it seemed that none of this mattered now anyway.

•

As he reached nine seconds he saw the men from the van rush towards the café's doors. Babich's guys drew guns, a shot rang out.

The small plastic garage-door opener was steady in his left hand, pressed tight against the forward grip of his rifle. His thumb was light on the detonate button.

Ten.

He pressed the button. The explosion was immense, knocking the air from his lungs, even from up here.

101

THE WHITE HOUSE, WASHINGTON DC

He'd listened and heard enough. *A rising Persian state* . . . Jesus.

Sure, there was a new administration here at the helm, but this was an opposite course of action to anything he could have imagined just a year ago.

'You know, if Iran does absorb Afghanistan and Pakistan?' McCorkell said. 'You'll be creating a monster.'

'Better the devil you know.'

'When they can, they'll be after Mecca. They'll go on to all the oil states and we'll have a resurgent Persian Empire with more than just the bomb to contend with.'

Niemann stood, extended a hand to McCorkell. He took a moment to take stock, shook the intelligence man's hand, watched him leave the room, and he remained behind, alone.

Times were a changin'. His country had set many a precedent for preemptive action and now none was to be taken. Wars had been fought over oil and water and land and religion and a million other reasons and that would likely always be the case. Fact is, you can't win them all.

102

BELLAGIO, LAKE COMO, ITALY

Brick was through the hole in the wall that the Gatecrasher had blasted. He rushed the room, dust coating his goggles, scanning with his H&K UMP submachine gun.

He pushed his gun onto Sirko's head, heard it smack down on the tiles.

Sirko was covered in dust, the blast debris all around him. Before he could register what had happened there were strong hands pinning him down, flexi-cuffing his hands behind his back.

Brick patted him down, hauled him to his feet – and in that moment, Sirko saw that the café was still there.

Brick spoke right in his face: 'We know how to jam frequencies, too.'

•

On the lake the bomb blast echoed out, carried on the wind.

Kolesnik swivelled towards the café – it was fine. He scanned the streetscape, couldn't see anything from here. Then gunfire started up, sporadic, then violent. On the shore men were running . . . Now it was automatic gunfire from several weapons; it sounded like a war zone.

He heard a siren bleep and turned. An Italian police boat was coming in fast, a few hundred metres out, headed straight for him. He looked at Kate, her eyes no longer so frightened. In that split second he knew what to do.

He punched Kate in the side of her head, sending her overboard, unconscious, her limp body bobbing in the water face down. Then he powered off at full throttle.

●

As the shots rang out, Babich's men inside the café moved towards their principal target.

Within seconds Fox had Babich on his feet, a butter knife to his throat and his arm twisted behind him in a pain-compliance hold. He held Babich as a human shield between himself and the two bodyguards. As he dragged him through the café, both Russians drew their side-arms.

In one fluid motion Duhamel stood, drew down and fired: double-tap, both targets down – blown back hard off their feet as blood splatter-painted the wall behind them. He scanned the crowd: no other threats, everyone frozen mid-movement.

He stayed in tight next to Fox as they backed Babich out of the kitchen door, just as shots resumed outside in a full-scale firefight, and a squad of Babich's guys burst through the front door.

Fox was through the rear door of the café, and almost collided with Luigi, who was on his way in.

'You'll burn in hell for your sins,' Fox whispered into Babich's ear, roughly palming him off to Duhamel. He sprinted towards the water.

•

Gammaldi had the timber speedboat ambling in a circle. He stood behind the wheel, watched Fox running from the café, caught glimpses of him through trees and between tourists. He lost him in the fracas of the gun battle in the car park, came closer to shore and saw him emerge over the bonnet of a car and point towards a jetty several hundred metres along the foreshore.

•

Fox ran flat out, saw Gammaldi would get there first. He heard the sound of a scooter on the road behind him; in a second he had pulled the tourist off and had climbed on, hammering the little Vespa's engine flat-out toward the stone pier, people scattering out of his way. He headed straight for the edge, continually measuring the distance to Gammaldi.

He flew off the edge of the pier, landing twenty metres out in the lake, well ahead of the little Vespa. He swam a few strokes towards the boat before Gammaldi swept by, arm out, and hauled him in.

Gammaldi was already on the throttle as Fox got his feet and scanned the water – Kate was floating, the police boat was pulling up next to her.

'There! The police boat!'

Gammaldi steered for the boat. In the distance a helicopter came thundering down the lake.

•

Kolesnik pushed the throttle but it was already fully engaged. Behind him the police boat was occupied with the woman.

The chopper wasn't friendly – Italian cops, coming in at him low and purposeful. It buzzed overhead and let rip with a machine gun, water spraying him under the fire. As he yanked the wheel hard to port, one of his two guys slipped overboard; he completed his one-eighty degree turn, saw Lachlan Fox rushing to rescue his woman, and headed straight for him.

•

Gammaldi pulled up next to the police boat and yelled to them in Italian to pursue the other craft. The cops passed Kate's limp body over to the timber speedboat and headed off towards the threat.

Fox hunched over Kate, checking vitals, while Gammaldi watched, wide-eyed.

•

Kolesnik noticed the bow of the police boat lifted into the air as it raced towards him. They were headed on a collision course, both powering flat out, both with armed men waiting to get inside kill-range.

•

Kate's lips were blue and water trickled from her mouth. Her chest was still.

Fox rolled her on her side, emptying her mouth and throat. She was cold and inert. He pinched her nose closed, locked his lips over hers and started mouth to mouth. He did this three times, then pumped rhythmically on her chest with his hands, hard, and counted to ten under his breath. He repeated the process.

'Kate, come on! Kate!'

•

Kolesnik's man sprayed the police boat with an MP5 on full auto, forcing them to turn and head out of immediate range. Dark smoke billowed in their wake.

The sound of the chopper's machine gun tore the air in another strafing run. Kolesnik continued at full throttle towards Fox's timber speedboat just a couple of hundred metres ahead, the distance closing as the water-cutting machine-gun fire arced its way towards him.

'Shoot them!' he yelled to his gunman, who retrained his submachine gun from the chopper to the timber speedboat.

•

'Fire,' Sefreid said.

Emma Gibbs was in a squat position, her Accuracy International AW sniper rifle sighted, super-magnum round loaded, her finger's weight on the trigger.

Pop.

The gunman on the boat was hit in the chest, blown overboard.

'Target,' Sefreid said. 'Pull right.'

Gibbs reloaded. Fired.

'Missed. Lower.'

The driver had taken cover. Gibbs hit the side of the boat, and again, and again – *click*, out of ammo. The boat was fifty metres out from Gammaldi and Fox.

•

'Lachlan, we got incoming!' Gammaldi said.

Fox stared down into Kate's half-open, motionless eyes. Pressed down on her chest five more times, a couple more breaths of air into her lungs – he felt her lips move slightly under his, or did he imagine it? He repeated the process, pressing, breathing, his lips over hers, frantic, the kiss of life.

'Kate, come on. Do it for me—'

She convulsed. Her eyes opened wide. She coughed, spurted water and heaved in lungfuls of air, rolling onto her side and clutching the floor of the boat, alive but groggy.

'Hang on!' Gammaldi yelled. He had their boat hitting full speed and the wheel turned at full lock, but it was no match for the speedboat heading towards them like a homing torpedo.

'Jump!' Fox yelled as he picked up Kate and launched them aft. Gammaldi flung himself over the port side.

•

Kolesnik's boat sliced the timber craft in two.

He jumped out as his boat became airborne, hit the water hard. As the chopper strafed it broadside, his boat caught fire, then blew, the explosion concussive as he stayed underwater. When the rotor-wash faded he surfaced, scanned, found his targets.

•

Gammaldi swam over to help Fox with Kate, who was becoming more lucid with every moment.

'Kate, stay with Al, okay?'

She nodded and Gammaldi took her, neither of them comprehending until Fox turned and swam hard towards the fast splashing form headed for them.

Kolesnik elbowed Fox in the back of the head, dazed him, and seconds later set on Gammaldi. His punch glanced off Gammaldi's face; he grappled Gammaldi and Kate underwater.

•

Fox's head was ringing, but he knew what he had to do. He pushed through the pain and swam towards the struggling trio. He took a long, deep breath before pulling Kolesnik off and dragging him under by his hair.

Ten metres down it was dark. Kolesnik fought, but Fox had control. He stopped swimming down, then let go of Kolesnik but caught him again as he tried to kick for the surface. Fox held him at arm's length by a handful of his jacket and shirt. Kolesnik attacked Fox's outstretched arm, punching and clawing, but Fox kept still, kept a slight downwards motion to his movements. It took almost a minute for Kolesnik to go completely limp; Fox held him for another thirty seconds before letting go and heading for the surface.

•

Hutchinson stood in the street outside Guzzi's Café. The lights of two ambulances flashed: two CIA rendition men were dead, as were five of Babich's bodyguards. Duhamel and Brick had Babich and Sirko secured in the back of their van. Italian cops were everywhere, as well as Hutchinson's own men, all of whom had left the Hub and were surveying the scene.

He walked into the café and looked out at the figures in the lake – they all seemed okay, alive at least. He retrieved the hidden digital voice recorder, pressed stop, backtracked, played it – a loud and clear recording of Fox and Babich talking. They had got their man.

•

Fox and Kate trod water and held on to each other.

The helicopter dropped a life preserver, which Gammaldi grabbed on to. The police boat was almost to them.

There was a bigger world around them, but in that moment it was just the two of them.

Fox looked into Kate's eyes: this is real.

All that had been, all that was, would never be the same. She looked at him, smiled and rested her head on his shoulder. As they floated there, the sunlight warming them, he kissed the top of her head, whispered, 'It's over.'

Epilogue

HIGH OVER EUROPE

Captain Garth Nix sat in the noisy cargo hold of a C17 cargo plane, flying his boy home. A group of soldiers rotating back home sat silently around the flag-draped casket.

These would be the last hours he would spend with his best friend, the closest thing to a brother he had ever known. He was reading to him – Garry Trudeau's *The War Within,* a collection of Doonesbury cartoons he knew the Sergeant loved. Nix laughed as he read, imagined his mate laughing too, hoped that voice in his head would never truly go away.

WASHINGTON DC

Bill McCorkell sat back in his chair as he watched the news report: the wash-up of the shoot-out in Bellagio. Italian press were reporting it as a botched US rendition, while the CNN reporter on the scene called it pretty close to the truth. A Russian official came on and McCorkell switched channels. The BBC had a couple of well-dressed anchors commenting on the UN's progress with a new trans-boundary water treaty.

McCorkell switched off the screen as his secretary entered with a pile of manila folders for his in-tray. Under the official White House symbol, the top file was labelled: India–Pakistan Water Negotiations. The two countries were at the peace table, working out a new water treaty under the guidance of the UN. Kashmir was still an issue, would be for a long time, but at the very least the water was to be shared, and that was a step in the right direction towards some greater measure of peace and reconciliation. Iran – well, that was a potential problem for the future.

McCorkell packed his case and headed home; the files could wait until the morning. He decided that he would take that UN job. He liked the idea of brokering peace for times ahead, rather than dealing with security problems as they arose.

He walked out of the foyer and into the cold Washington night as his internal page beeped. McCorkell dialled and indentified himself.

'Sir, this is the Situation Room. Russia and Georgia is happening—'

He looked back over his shoulder at the White House all lit up, then looked away again.

'Can't the National Security Advisor handle it?' he asked.

'Yes, sir – I – I just thought you'd like to know . . .' the White House military aide replied.

He smiled. Still a figure to be trusted and relied on. 'I'll catch up to speed in the morning.'

The Russian Ambassador would be called into the Oval Office first thing. He would ask for the release of their national,

Roman Babich. The story was opening up; Babich's take-down was big news. He had been identified with Americans in Italy's Lake Como via shaky footage of tourists' digital cameras and cell phones; something like a low-budget Paul Greengrass film. The ambassador would have a list of demands; the President's team would be resolute.

The UN would be another interesting chapter to an already full life. A final snow was meant to dump overnight, and tomorrow would look very different.

SOUTH KENT, CONNECTICUT

In the main house of Tas Wallace's sprawling farm in Litchfield County, Fox sat at his new MacBook, finishing an editorial for gsrnews.com.

> *. . . India and Pakistan have entered peace talks and are implementing a new water treaty that the UN is setting up as a model for other nations.*
>
> *This story isn't going away, it's developing. Thankfully, in the right direction – towards peace.*

As he emailed it through to the sub-editors at the Seagram Building, Faith Williams stood behind him, reading over his shoulder.

'You're like Carrie Bradshaw with a gun.'

Fox turned, looked up at her, realised he had been speaking aloud as he typed. Faith put her hand on his shoulder and he held it for a bit.

Tas Wallace came in, fresh from Washington. 'You did good, again,' he said, smiling. 'And you're relatively unscathed this time.'

Fox smiled. He felt the pain in his crushed hand, but that wasn't what bothered him; there was pain of a different kind. 'I find that the harder I work,' Fox said, 'the more luck I seem to have.'

'That's a fact,' Wallace said, clapping him on the back. 'You did real good, Lachlan, real good.'

'There are no facts, only interpretations,' Fox said, closing his computer and packing it away in his backpack. 'But as long as good people don't need laws to tell them to act responsibly, and bad people continue to find ways around the laws, I'll keep interpreting for you.'

•

Outside, the fog had lifted. Fox put on his jacket, looked around. The FBI presence was heavy and visible: six vehicles, both gates covered, agents in tactical gear around the perimeter. A few GSR security people were about, too; a last line of defence if needed. A helicopter was parked on the north lawn, rotors still slowing to a stop from Wallace's arrival.

Fox joined Hutchinson on the lawn, from where they had a view of the glass sitting room that jutted off the converted barn. Inside at a table sat Kate Matthews, her parents at either side of her, listening, talking.

'Their world has changed, again,' Hutchinson said. He sighed and looked sideways at Fox. 'Umbra – or what's left of it – wants Babich back. They probably won't stop until you're dead, one way or the other.'

Fox smiled, looked at the lawman. 'He'd be enormously improved by death, himself.'

'Unfortunately, Lach, it ain't that simple.'

'Of course not,' Fox replied, looking back at Kate. She may have been looking at him but it was hard to tell.

The Feds had picked her parents up and driven them here two hours ago. The family had been together ever since; an FBI shrink and medical team were also around someplace. Kate's parents seemed to grow younger with each minute they sat with her. What a feeling – he felt that way, too.

'Where's Al?' Hutchinson asked.

Fox almost laughed. 'Purgatory,' he replied. 'Shopping with the missus for wedding stuff.'

'Serves him right,' Hutchinson said. 'Tas and Faith are there in the main house?'

'Business as usual,' Fox replied, picturing the pair of them working the phones, putting out fires.

The two men were quiet for a few minutes.

'Look, Lach—'

'Save it, Andy,' Fox said, zipping up his leather jacket. 'Seriously. Kate and I had something. A lot of shit happened. She left – you fucking hid her.'

'I did what I had—'

'You didn't tell me, even after all I was doing for you!' Fox was up close in the agent's face with a tight fistful of the lapel of Hutchinson's coat. 'I trusted you and you left me out. I could have helped protect her; this might never have happened like this—'

Kate came out of the guesthouse door and started across the wet grass lawn, her arms wrapped around herself for warmth.

'Yeah, and maybe you would have been the one taken captive,' Hutchinson said, freeing himself from Fox's grasp and taking a step back. 'Maybe they would have just popped you or her off somewhere, somewhere we never would have found you.' He paused. 'Look, I know this is all a shock to you.'

A look from Fox said it all.

'I know you're not one to back down from a fight,' Hutchinson said. 'And this *is* the good fight, Lach. Keep doing this, and not just for Kate's sake – do it for everyone. Babich's trial is going to be the biggest since Saddam's – and you made that happen.'

Fox watched Kate approach, silent.

'Babich is rolling, giving us some of what we need to go further, but the old boys at Umbra won't like it. They'll want you to drop the story.'

'Fine, I'll drop it. Done.'

'Or . . . you can join my team. It's growing – come check it out at least, you'll like it. Or you could get on a plane and bug out, no hard feelings. But we've got one shot at this,' Hutchinson said, his tone quiet and final. 'One chance to deal out the biggest piece of real justice against these guys since the Wall came down. This is a defining moment in history. This is just what we need to do post 9/11 and Iraq.'

'And what do I need? What does Kate need?' Fox looked at Hutchinson, angry. He spoke quietly as she came within earshot. 'It hasn't been easy for her. There's a defining moment in history occurring for the people right here today. It wasn't easy at her funeral.'

'Lach . . .' Hutchinson said. 'We were on a boat out on the Hudson, Kate and me, watching – watching her own funeral.'

Kate reached them, stood in close to Hutchinson. The lawman put an arm around her shoulders. 'It was the closest goodbye to her family she could get,' he said, 'wasn't it, Kate?' She gave the briefest of nods, distraught. 'Do you think it was easy for her to move on? Do you think she *wanted* to? I mean, fuck, the people in witness protection lose everything – no more family, no old life. They have to make a new life, fast, or they go nuts. This doesn't end for her, Lach. She has to go back under. It will be like dying again.'

'Is that what you want to do, Kate?' Fox searched her eyes, red from crying. She shrugged, looked at Hutchinson.

'Part of me wants to stop hiding now,' Kate said. 'I'm sick of fighting and hanging on. Yeah, Lachlan, for you this is a big story, and we're both part of it now, but it feels almost too late to do anything except stand in the dark and let them come.'

Fox gritted his teeth.

'You know you can't be lucky all the time, Lach,' Hutchinson said. 'This isn't over. Stay here where we can protect you. They're out there and they're probably closer than we know.'

Fox thought back to the moments he had shared with Kate earlier that morning. They had walked along the creek, watched the Connecticut sunrise through broken clouds.

'This will get messy,' he'd said. 'But it's all right; I'll be with you every step of the way.'

Kate had looked off to the distance, at the FBI agents on perimeter duty. 'I'm so sorry,' she had said.

Fox had looked at her, nodded.

'You're really there for me, after everything?'

Fox had smiled, touched her shoulder, let his hand rest on

her face and neck. She had looked so happy. In that moment she should have been sad . . .

'I'll be in touch, Andy,' Fox said, back in the moment. He walked over to his motorbike. Kate followed him.

The FBI man gave the pair some space. Rain fell.

'Lachlan, please, stay here with me until we know more,' Kate asked. 'Please?'

Fox began to put his helmet on but she stopped him, holding his face in her hands. He turned in to her, close, gently pushed her wet hair out of her eyes.

'Why go now?'

'It's complicated,' he replied.

'Complicated? Stay. Stay for me.'

Fox shook his head, looked across at the long gravel driveway. They were out there, coming for him, coming for her. Either way, he'd find them or they'd find her. It was only a matter of time.

'Please don't leave me again.'

Fox smiled, looked into those eyes he'd dreamed about for so many sleepless nights. He kissed her, held her . . . Such a familiar embrace.

'Kate, look at me.' Her eyes met his. 'I never left you.'

She bit her lip, took a step back. Maybe she understood. Time would tell.

Fox started the bike up and thundered down the driveway. He knew what lay ahead wasn't much different from what he'd already been through. He knew he could either watch it unfold or deal with it as it happened.

He turned onto the highway and hit a hundred in three seconds. He buzzed around a few cars, wound out third gear to nine thousand rpm, then fourth, fifth. Two hundred clicks per hour and the bike had plenty more to give.

He knew his life, like Kate's, was changed forever, again. Nothing that had happened could be undone, nothing could be redeemed.

Another turn. Another gear. Whether his future lay ahead or behind him he was unsure. Either way, it was a new place and a new life that was going to get more dangerous before it got easier. He wished he could head west, follow the sun – but they were out there, somewhere, close. He headed south.

It's never over.

Acknowledgements

Big thanks to the talented crew at Hachette Australia. Vanessa Radnidge, Claire de Medici, Roberta Ivers, Joan Beal, Louise Sherwin-Stark, Fiona Hazard, Luke Causby and many more not only have helped shape this novel and get it out there but have been guiding me along for four years and four books now. It's a nice family to be in.

As usual I am indebted to all my family and friends. Special thanks go to my early readers, Tony Wallace, Malcolm Beasley, Emily McDonald and Tony Niemann.

Thanks to my agent Pippa Masson and the team at Curtis Brown for another year of dedicated representation and many more books contracted . . . Busy times ahead.

Nicole Wallace, thanks for giving me a reason to put my pen down at the end of the day.